Books by Tim Powers

The Skies Discrowned
An Epitaph in Rust
The Drawing of the Dark
The Anubis Gates
Dinner at Deviant's Palace
On Stranger Tides
The Stress of Her Regard

Fault Lines series
Last Call
Expiration Date
Earthquake Weather

Declare
Three Days to Never
Hide Me Among the Graves
Medusa's Web
Alternate Routes

Short story collections
Night Moves and Other Stories • Strange Itineraries
The Bible Repairman and Other Stories
Down and Out in Purgatory: The Collected Stories of Tim Powers

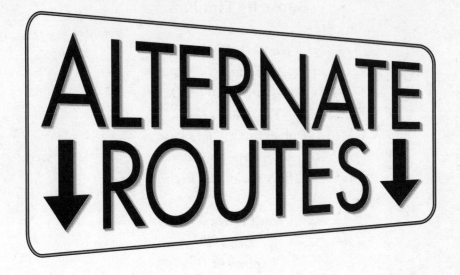

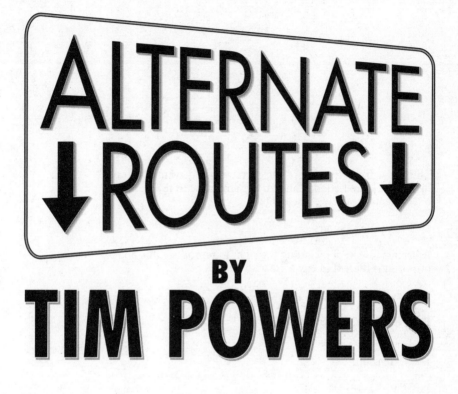

ALTERNATE ROUTES

BY
TIM POWERS

BAEN

A Baen Books Original

Baen Publishing Enterprises
P.O. Box 1403
Riverdale, NY 10471
www.baen.com

ISBN: 978-1-4814-8340-7

Cover art by Todd Lockwood

First Baen printing August 2018

A signed limited edition of this book has been privately printed by Charnel House. www.charnelhouse.com

Distributed by Simon & Schuster
1230 Avenue of the Americas
New York, NY 10020

Library of Congress Cataloging-in-Publication Data

Names: Powers, Tim, 1952- author.
Title: Alternate routes / by Tim Powers.
Description: Riverdale, NY : Baen Books, [2018]
Identifiers: LCCN 2018015167 | ISBN 9781481483407 (hardcover)
Subjects: | BISAC: FICTION / Fantasy / Contemporary. | FICTION / Fantasy / Paranormal. | GSAFD: Fantasy fiction. | Adventure fiction.
Classification: LCC PS3566.O95 A79 2018 | DDC 813/.54--dc23
LC record available at https://lccn.loc.gov/2018015167

Printed in the United States of America

10 9 8 7 6 5 4 3 2 1

To Russell Galen

—and with thanks to Jennifer Brehl,
Rebecca Erickson, Ken Estes, Steve Malk, Serena Powers,
Mike Rottiers, and Michael and Laura Yanovich

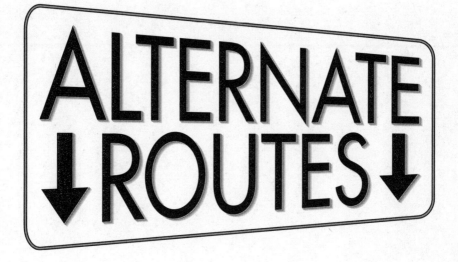

. . . and on that day
When highways curve both east and west at once,
And fugitives must blindly find their way
Between two worlds . . .

                —Guillaume Cendre-Benir

↓ CHAPTER ONE ↓

When a car slows down on a freeway, a spreading wave of brake lights flickers on behind it; cars further back slow in response, and then cars behind them, and even when the original car has sped up again, the wave of deceleration continues to move backward. Sometimes the wave seems to take on a life of its own, and moves backward for miles.

Even on this Sunday afternoon, traffic on the 405 freeway curling down the California coast past Los Angeles International Airport was stop-and-go, and inland the northwest slant of the 5 had sluggish patches through Downey and Commerce; on "Old Man 10," as the freeway-side gypsies called the Santa Monica Freeway, traffic had just resumed its normal sixty-mile-an-hour, twenty-five-cars-per-minute pace after one of the retro-waves had moved away down the lanes to the east, where it might reach Alameda or even cross the LA River before it would disperse.

The freeway-side oleander bushes on the shoulder shook now in the intermittent wind from fast-passing trucks, and a plastic water bottle flew away from the jaws of the hand-held pickup tool wielded by one of three men in white hard-hats and orange vinyl vests. Through protective dark glasses he squinted after the bottle as it skittered away along the dirt shoulder until it bounced off the post supporting a sign that read ADOPT A HIGHWAY—THIS MILE MAINTAINED BY LADY GALVAN TACO WAGONS and was swept away in the once again rushing traffic.

The man sighed, hefted his white plastic bag and stepped back into the shade under the boughs of a pine tree, and took off his gloves and hard-hat. Three nylon-web beach chairs had been set up in a little clearing at the top of the embankment away from the freeway, and he sat down and used the pickup tool to grab a can of Coors beer from the ice chest in the center of the clearing; the jaws slid off the wet can, so he dropped the tool and leaned out of the chair to fish up the beer with his hand.

At the east side of the clearing, in the center of a ring of glass jars, a two-foot tall wooden metronome pole rocked rapidly back and forth on its wide metal base. A crudely whittled wooden head had been stuck onto the top of the metronome's pendulum, and its glass-chip eyes glittered as it moved.

He looked past the thing, out over the receding rooftops and towers of central Los Angeles, and popped open the beer can. An intermittent breeze from below pushed the scent of citrus blossoms against the exhaust reek of the freeway behind him.

A man followed him into the clearing and dropped into another chair. He shed his gloves, took off his dark glasses and hard-hat and pushed back locks of damp white hair, then peered with raised eyebrows at the first man. "Gonna drive with beer on your breath?" he asked.

"You think she'll have us driving today? We also serve who only pick up trash."

The other man nodded past him at the wooden head on the jerking pendulum.

"That's a heavy current, Vick. Any driving she wants done is gonna have to be by experts."

"Spectral warming," Vickery agreed reluctantly. He frowned toward the swinging metronome and then set the beer down in the dirt beside his chair. He reached under his orange vest and pulled out a cell phone and squinted at it. "Nothing yet," he said; then sighed and waved behind him, toward the muted roar of the freeway lanes. "But yeah, Ramon, tell 'Turo we might as well clear out. Let's sign off the log for the day and pack up the metronome and the trash bags—we'll all probably be chauffeuring—"

The oleander branches on the west side of the clearing thrashed, and then a black-haired boy in jeans and a white T-shirt emerged from the greenery and stepped up beside Vickery's chair. He was panting, and the leather bands he wore on his wrists were dark with sweat.

Vickery knew him—the boy's name was Santiago, and he was rumored to be a freelance watcher and courier.

The boy nodded down the slope. "Woman looking for you," he said cheerfully, "gave me ten dollars to find you. Dressed nice, *business* woman, and she got a gun under her coat in the back, I can tell." He brushed long green leaves out of his hair. "*You* give me ten dollars and I'll tell her you're nowhere around."

Vickery's fingertips were tingling as he quickly took off the dark glasses. "Is she a, a cop?" he asked, afraid that she might not be. "Did she know my name?"

"Cop or close enough, I think. No, she just say the guy who drove up in the taco wagon. She—ah, she comes up now, even with good shoes!"

Vickery stood up and tucked the glasses in his shirt pocket. He could hear someone scuffling up the embankment west of the clearing, behind the boy. "Is she alone?"

"I guess. Got out of a Chevy Caprice down on 20th."

Ramon had got up too. He nodded toward Vickery and muttered, "This sounds personal. I'll be out with 'Turo in the current." Snatching up his hard-hat and gloves, he turned and hurried back out to the freeway shoulder in the daylight. Vickery heard him call to the other man, "Down the east side here—*andele!*"

"Loop around above," Vickery told the boy quietly, "where you can see her, and whistle if she drops the gun. Ten bucks for you." The boy nodded and followed Ramon out of the clearing, and Vickery turned toward the slope and called, "You're covered from two directions, lady—take out the gun and drop it."

The sound of clumsy shuffling in the dirt stopped, but there was no other sound.

"Counting down," Vickery called harshly.

Three seconds later Vickery heard the boy's whistle and then a muttered curse from the shrubbery ahead.

"Okay," Vickery went on, "come forward."

His eyes narrowed and his face was suddenly cold when the woman pushed her way through the oleander branches into the clearing—she was paler now than when he had last seen her four years ago, and there were new lines in her cheeks; it occurred to him that she must be at least thirty by now. She wore a navy blue jacket and gray trousers and low-heeled gray pumps, and her short auburn hair was in disarray from her passage through the freeway-side bushes.

Vickery was tense, and ready to jump in any direction, but he nodded. "Miss . . . Castine," he said, remembering.

"Mr. Woods," she replied, a bit breathlessly. Her forehead was misted with sweat. "I don't think you really had me covered."

"Santiago, fetch the gun," Vickery called; then said to her, "I will in a moment." It was an effort to keep his voice level. "Do you have back-up, are you . . . arresting me?"

"You idiot." She shook her head and went on, clearly angry, "They may very well arrest *me*. Early this morning we got a—" She paused for a moment, pursing her lips—and, Vickery thought, blushing—then went on, "—a sort of *lead* on you, and they checked it out, and a couple of hours ago they found your fingerprints in that apartment on Carson in Culver City. I had to find you and stop you from going back there."

"Four years ago you helped arrest me."

She inhaled impatiently through clenched teeth. "Oh, it's different now. Or I know more now. This isn't a safe place either—you need to get out of here."

But Vickery stepped to the north end of the clearing and glanced down the embankment to the service road that ran behind the back walls of a closed bowling alley and a thrift store. From this elevation he could see most of the cars parked on the two nearest north-south streets, and he didn't see any obvious signs of occupants or idling engines. If this is a trap, he thought, it's needlessly elaborate.

He turned back to her; she was standing right behind him now, peering down past his shoulder at the streets as he had been doing. "How did *you* find me?" he asked.

She stepped back, throwing a quick glance at the glass jars and the rocking metronome. "Are you *hearing* me? You've got to get *out* of here. *I've* got to get out of here, I was sitting in my car down there for too long, working up nerve to climb up here and do this—will you tell your, your *Santiago* to give me back my gun? They're looking for you at the Carson Street apartment, but our chief routinely has two-man teams checking out these . . . freeway nests, looking for spots with particularly good depth of field."

She took a step back toward the shrubbery, then stopped; he hadn't followed her. She stamped her foot. "What does it—oh hell, what it was, I remembered you said you went to Latin mass on Sundays, and I figured maybe you still do. I Googled it after they all drove off toward Culver City, and Archangel Gabriel Chapel is the Latin-mass-type Catholic church closest to your apartment, so I went there and saw you. I followed you to that kitchen place on Western, and then when you got in your truck I followed you here."

"What would you have done if I'd headed straight back from church to the apartment?"

"I don't know. Honked. Collided with you. You're lucky—*I'm* not lucky, but you are—that I even recognized you—your hair's longer now, and you're a lot darker." In spite of her evident anxiety, she almost smiled. "And you used to be kind of chubby for a Secret Service agent."

"I had a better appetite then." He took a deep breath and let it out. "You go ahead, scoot. Thanks. I have to check out the local weather."

"I need my gun."

"Give me ten seconds."

He crossed to the ring of glass jars around the rocking metronome and crouched beside the one farthest from the freeway. It was half filled with water, and a popsicle stick with a string tied around its middle had been laid across the top of the jar; the string, visibly wet, hung down to within an inch of the water's surface.

Over his shoulder he told her, "Look at this."

"For God's suffering sake!" Castine whispered, but she hurried over and crouched beside him. "*What?*"

"Watch the water."

After a few seconds a bump appeared on the surface of the water, and then it formed a drop that fell upward and soaked into the string.

Castine gave a huff of surprise.

"It's arcing," explained Vickery. "Amplified possibility field. Stuff rides on that. I'd rather not drive on the freeways right now if I'm not getting paid for it."

"I," she whispered, "*hate* all this shit."

They both stood up and crossed quickly to the other side of the clearing, and Vickery lifted a leafy branch out of her way. "Santiago," he called, "bring the gun down here."

Castine stumbled ahead of him down the narrow winding path through the overgrown bushes, stepping over old beer cans and diapers. "I left my phone and my pager at the office," she said, "I've got to get back there and hope they don't look at the GPS record on my car. They don't know about your taco wagon connection—get into it and disappear." She paused to look back at Vickery, brushing damp hair back from her forehead. "Where's that Santiago?"

Vickery lifted his head. "Santiago! Ten more bucks!" After a few seconds he shrugged and waved ahead. "Gun's worth more than ten bucks, I'm afraid."

Castine rolled her eyes, and Vickery thought she was near tears. "Damn you people! I've got three hundred, but if things go wrong I can't get much more, even if I can get to a Versatel."

"Your call."

"Santiago!" she yelled at the clustered greenery uphill. "Three hundred, right now, cash—or I report it stolen! And it's government issue!"

"Keep moving," said Vickery. "He'll be down there on the service road, or not."

Castine exhaled and resumed edging down the path. "Have *you* got a gun?"

"Haven't touched one in four years."

Below the tangled plantings on the freeway-side crest, the embankment was just littered dirt, and Santiago rode a bicycle down the slope to their left, kicking up dust in the sunlight.

Vickery and Castine made their way down the last few yards at a clopping run, their arms out to the sides, and Santiago, on the cracked service road pavement now, swerved his bike in a half-circle to meet them. The boxy brown-and-gold food truck stood a dozen yards away, by the thrift store loading dock, and its perpetual aroma of spicy *carne asada* contended with the rotten-strawberries reek of a nearby Dumpster.

"Lady wanna buy a pencil sharpener?" Santiago asked merrily.

Castine didn't answer, but pulled a leather billfold from an inside jacket pocket and quickly passed the boy a sheaf of bills. He counted them, then lifted his T-shirt and pulled a stainless steel semi-automatic handgun from the waistband of his jeans and held it out. Vickery recognized it as a SIG-Sauer P229, probably .40 caliber.

She tucked the billfold away, then took the gun and reached around with both hands to hike up the back of her jacket—but a moment later she was staring past Vickery, and her eyes widened and she quickly swung both hands to the front, holding the gun pointed at him.

"Play along and say nothing!" she snapped.

Vickery's chest felt suddenly hollow, and after a moment he slowly raised his hands. Santiago was just sitting on his bicycle, his brown eyes darting back and forth. Vickery heard a car door slam, and then footsteps knocking on the concrete behind him.

The muzzle of Castine's gun was shaking, and she was whispering, "Fuck fuck fuck . . ."

A man stepped into Vickery's view on the left; he was wearing a long-sleeve white shirt and a dark tie, and he was holding a gun like Castine's. He stepped back and aimed it at Vickery's stomach.

"What have we got, Castine?" he asked, then squinted closely at Vickery. "Damn, it's . . . Woods, isn't it?" he said wonderingly as another man appeared on Vickery's right, also in a white shirt and tie and also now aiming a SIG-Sauer at him. "How the hell?"

"That's Woods?" said the second man. "Here? He sure looks like shit these days. Probably been living in the shrubbery, not that apartment." He freed one hand from the grip of his pistol and unclipped a cell phone from his belt. He tapped the screen and said into it, "We've got Woods!—out by one of the nests along the 10. We're right by the car."

"It's my arrest, Mike," said Castine unsteadily as the man reclipped the phone to his belt. "I'll take him in."

"Stand down, Castine," Mike told her. "Terry and I have got this. You and the kid get out of here right now."

"I'm taking it," she insisted, and Mike turned his head to say something to her. The other man darted a quick glance at them.

Four years ago Vickery had memorably been in a situation very like this one, and now the remembered actions took over.

He spun on the ball of his left foot, crouching as his right leg shot out and his sneakered foot struck the gun and clenched hands of the man on his left, Terry. The gun was kicked upward and went off with an earsplitting *pop*, and Vickery was instantly following through with a lunge, grabbing the gun barrel and tumbling against the man; he hooked a leg behind Terry's knee to pitch him over backward, and the man's hands were still loosely gripping the gun in front of him when the back of his head struck the pavement with a solid knock.

Vickery fell on top of him, and had just pried the gun out of Terry's limp hands when a patch of concrete beside his head exploded in the same instant that another gunshot shook the air.

He lost the remembered sequence and just froze, his ears ringing and the breath stopped in his throat, and then a foot in a polished wing-tip shoe kicked the gun away.

"No!" came an anguished shout from Castine, and Vickery lifted his head to see Santiago pedaling his bicycle away very fast, and Mike leveling his gun in that direction. His finger was inside the trigger guard.

And this time it was this woman, Castine, who now fired her gun twice, and as the echoes batted away between the freeway embankment and the thrift store wall, Mike took two quick steps back and then abruptly sat down on the pavement and fell over onto his right side. Vickery saw blood on the back of the man's neck and his white shirt collar, and he looked away.

Santiago kept pedaling his bicycle, and within seconds had disappeared around the corner of the bowling alley.

For a long moment Vickery stared at Terry's gun gleaming in the sunlight a few feet away on the pavement, and he knew he had no choice now but to take it; and even before he reached out and slid his fingers around the grip, his hand knew the feel and the weight of it.

Then Castine had kicked him in the shoulder. "Get up, get up!" He rolled to his feet, and immediately she had caught his elbow and turned him around. A new Chevrolet Caprice, empty, was parked behind the Galvan food truck.

"Out of here in your taco wagon," she gasped. "GPS tracking on all their cars."

"Right."

The two of them hurried back to the gaudy vehicle, but while Castine clambered in on the passenger side, Vickery tossed Terry's gun onto the driver's seat, then stepped to the wide left-side face of the truck, squinting up at the top edge, where a long steel cylinder extended from just behind the driver's side window to the vertical back rail.

"Come *on!*" called Castine shrilly.

Vickery jumped and caught hold of two handles that dangled from the rooftop cylinder, and he pulled down a wide brown canvas sheet that concealed the vivid painting and lettering on the side of the truck. He fitted the handles around hooks at the bottom edge, then hurried around and did the same thing on the other side.

"Concealment," he panted when he had climbed into the driver's seat. He pushed the gun up under the dashboard, and when he withdrew his hand the gun stayed there. "Can't have anybody noting a Galvan truck leaving here." It bothered him to see that his hands were shaking.

The engine started at the first twist of the ignition key, and a few seconds later the truck had rocked down the service road and around a curve and made a left turn onto Washington Avenue. Vickery's cheek stung, and when he touched it he saw blood on his fingers. That shot that struck the pavement right next to my head, he thought. Lucky a cement fragment didn't hit my eye.

"You were supposed to cover Mike," he said, "when I took Terry."

A tiny metronome was glued to the truck's dashboard, and as the truck rocked over uneven pavement its pendulum occasionally clicked back and forth.

Castine just exhaled and shook her head. "Is Terry dead too?"

"I don't know." After a pause, he said, "You didn't take the other guy's gun?"

"Of course not. You were crazy to take Terry's. Think."

"I had to." To keep moving, now, he thought.

The breeze through the open window was sharp with diesel fumes. Midday sun glittered on close bumpers and back windows, and he steered into the right lane and idled along at thirty miles per hour, passing Mexican restaurants and Korean auto body shops and heavily bearded palm trees swaying over cracked sidewalks.

Castine was flexing her right hand in front of her face. "What did I just *do?*" she said softly. "Why? Oh, God, I *wish* it was ten minutes ago!"

Vickery took a quick glance at her. "Where's your car?"

"Oh—I don't think I dare go near it now."

"You want me to drop you someplace?"

For several seconds she didn't speak. Finally, staring straight out through the windshield, she said, "I tracked you down at that church this morning, and then I sat for half an hour—I shouldn't have, as it turns out, but I sat for *half an hour* in my car back there before I could make myself climb that hill—I was deciding whether I should break the law and probably commit *treason,* to save you. And then I, *I did.* And—*killed* Mike Abbott! And now they'll probably—" Her voice had grown hoarse, and she just waved toward the traffic ahead.

"Why *did* you save me?"

"It was *insane,* I should not have." She took a deep breath. "But when I helped them arrest you four years ago, in that Presidential motorcade on Wilshire, I didn't know that they meant to simply *execute* you. You killed those two agents afterward in self-defense, didn't you?"

Vickery squinted against the memory that this recent action had forcefully roused. "Yes," he said.

She went on, "Just like I, God help me, killed Mike to save that . . . worthless boy. And whatever you are now, four years ago when you were standing post at that motorcade on Wilshire, you were a . . . clean, straight, dedicated Secret Service agent. You didn't deserve what happened to you, just because you . . ."

"Talked to a dead guy, on the radio of the Countermeasures Suburban, in that motorcade."

"Yes. That's what you did. And they didn't want, they don't want, you to have heard whatever it was that the dead guy said."

Vickery exhaled one syllable of a laugh. "I don't even remember what it said. A quote from a poem, I think, or maybe the Bible."

"And there was noise in the background," she said dully. "Like pulsing, booming."

He raised his eyebrows. "I'd forgotten that. But yes, there was."

She shifted on the vinyl seat to look squarely at him. "Mr. Woods," she began, in a voice that was shaky but resolute.

"It's Vickery now. Sebastian Vickery."

"I'd rather talk to Mr. Woods. I remember him. They were all sent out to kill you today, and I saved your life—twice! I stopped you from going back to your apartment, and I stopped them from taking you a couple of minutes ago. And now I'm in big trouble—they'll at least be able to see I was there, my car . . ."

Her voice had gone hoarse again, and she looked down at her clenched hands. After a while she sighed deeply and said, "There's a, an attorney, who'll help me. He's my fiancé. He might, he'll probably help you too. If I ask him to."

The traffic light ahead was green, but the food truck was behind a bus that had stopped at the curb. Vickery waited patiently for the bus to move forward. "I'm past the point of attorneys," he said. "But you can use my phone."

She nodded, then shook her head. "No—damn it!—even from a prepaid *throwaway* I don't dare call him. Terracotta, that's my boss, he'll be . . . looking at my fiancé's phone records now, *scrutinizing* every call he gets, starting with ten minutes ago, and he'll certainly track every call that originates in the LA area. A call from a burner phone would rouse his suspicions—and a call from your phone would lead him to *you*."

Vickery started to speak, but she waved him to silence.

"My guy's in Baltimore," she went on, "he couldn't do anything today anyway. And right now I can't check into a hotel, or use a credit card anywhere, or even show up on the security cameras at 7-Elevens." She inhaled sharply at a sudden thought, then swung the visor to the side and flipped it down, and sat up straighter. "Or at traffic intersections!"

The bus moved forward, and Vickery lifted his foot from the brake. "What do you—"

"You've lived off their radar for four years, here." She was glaring at him now. "You know how to. I don't. But they're after you, and I know how they work." She shivered visibly. "I need to hide, and get out of Los Angeles as quick as possible, and I need help to do it. Will you help me?"

Vickery kept his face impassive as he steered north on Western, heading back to the commissary where the Galvan trucks parked. Castine had said that her people didn't know about his connection with Galvan, and that seemed likely—he rented the apartment under a different identity, claiming a fictitious job, and Galvan didn't fingerprint her employees, and the two men who had tried to arrest him a few minutes ago had clearly not been looking for him.

"Will you help me?" she repeated.

So she has to leave LA now, he thought. *I* don't; and I *might* have to, or worse, if I get involved in her problems. And it would be hard to go dark in a new city. I've known the secret terrain of LA for decades— as a cop, as a field office Secret Service agent, and lately as a spectral-evasion driver. Can I really afford to take this woman under my wing, even briefly? My compromised, melting-wax wing?

She did save my life. Does that sort of thing even still count with me?

For another several seconds he just squinted at the cars and trucks in the lanes ahead.

At last he sighed. "All right."

↓ CHAPTER TWO ↓

The Transportation Utility Agency maintained a suite of offices in the Hsaio Tower on Lindbrook Drive in Westwood, three blocks from the UCLA campus, but the Operations Extension was a converted warehouse eighteen miles east in the Vernon district, on Bandini Boulevard just west of the 710 Freeway.

The Extension stood less than two hundred yards from the freeway, and, separated only by a tall fence and a row of pepper trees, half that distance from the circular Bandini onramp. On the other side, facing a windowless white wall that bore the TUA logo in modest yard-tall sans-serif letters, four gray Chevrolet sedans sat in a parking lot that could accommodate eight. The whole property was surrounded by high chain-link fencing topped with coils of concertina wire.

The interior of the onetime warehouse was still mostly open space, lit by the glow of sunlight on two rows of dusty skylights in the high, corrugated roof, but the expanses of wall were now paneled in a checkerboard of blue and white wedge-foam acoustic tiles, and a layer of textured blue vinyl covered the original cement floor. An old truck tire, which had proved to be too high to reach, still hung from the roof above the tall, broad doors on the east side; personnel used a pair of conventional doors opening onto the parking lot, and the old doors hadn't been slid open in anyone's memory. The renovation smells of paint and putty had long since given way to faint scents of coffee and microwaved Lean Cuisine chicken and fish dinners.

The boxy 20th century fans and air-conditioners had all been replaced by a 20-ton Trane unit, and in the row of interior offices along the north wall of the warehouse, personnel generally wore sweaters or jackets even when the summer sun was baking the streets and onramp outside.

But in one office three young men in shirtsleeves and loosened ties now sat around a radio under high-set fluorescent lights, each holding a script and a wireless keyboard in his lap, and sweat gleamed on their faces.

"Amanda," read one of them in a flat voice, immediately followed by the man next to him reading, "Woods," and the third man reading, "where."

Continuing in sequence, they rapidly proceeded to read aloud from the scripts the words, "is"—"your"—"husband"—"now."

A faint but shrill voice vibrated out of the speaker. "A panda doesn't need to be baptized," it said, "I do. Where's my mom?"

One of the three seated men tapped rapidly at his keyboard, and the words *that's not her either* appeared on a monitor beside the radio. The other two men rolled their eyes and nodded. One of them hit three keys, and the previous observation was now followed by *duh*.

They repeated their one-word-at-a-time relayed question, and this time there was no reply at all, only the hiss of the vacant frequency.

Standing in the doorway to the next office, a tall, gaunt man in a Princeton sweatshirt, with gray hair tumbling down to his shoulders, shook his head and stepped back, closing the door on the trio huddled around the radio. In this office were two men in business suits, one seated in front of a metal desk and holding a cell phone, the other standing and looking out the window at the warehouse floor, and they both turned to him.

"No luck," he told them, "they're still getting everybody but. His wife has apparently withdrawn back into the ether."

The seated man said into his phone, "I gotta go."

"Jeez, Terracotta," said the man by the window, "let them take a break. Abbott and Vendler have *found* him."

"And they've broken off communication," said Terracotta. "Until we get confirmation from them, the scanners can keep trying to raise his wife again."

"Deleted persons are all crazy anyway."

"She was right this morning," said the man at the desk, tucking his phone into a pocket, "about his apartment in Culver City." He tapped his pocket. "Westwood still hasn't heard anything more from Abbott and Vendler, and listen, *Castine's* car is there, within a block of where they are, though her phone's still at the Westwood office."

"Why would *she* be there?" Terracotta stepped away from the closed door into the middle of the room; he frowned for a moment, then added, "I wish she were here, though. When she's part of the triangle, ghosts nearly always reply." He smiled faintly at the man standing by the window. "Sorry, Brett—*'deleted persons.'*"

"Words have connotations," Brett muttered, and added, derisively, *"Ghosts."*

"Ollie," said Terracotta, "where's the backup?"

Pulling out his phone again, Ollie tapped the screen. "Where are you guys?" he said; and a moment later he lowered the phone. "They're only a block or two away from where the cars are. They'll—huh." He raised the phone to his ear again and after a couple of seconds said, "Okay." Then to Terracotta he said, "Westwood says LAPD is responding to a shots-fired on that block. I'll—"

The door behind Terracotta slammed open, and one of the trio from the next office leaned in and said, breathlessly, "We got *Mike Abbott.* On the fucking *ghost band.*"

Ollie swatted his phone and bared his teeth impatiently, then barked into it, "Police responding to shots fired at your destination. We have at least one man down, there. Maximum caution."

Terracotta's eyes were wide as he led Ollie and Brett back into the radio room, and he held up his hand for silence; then said, "Abbott," and waved toward Ollie.

"Uh, *what,*" said Ollie nervously. His face was pale under his close-cropped red hair, and his freckles stood out like drops of spattered coffee. The three men who had been manning the radio stood now against the outer wall.

"Happened," said Brett.

"We had the goods, we had Woods," came a sing-song voice from the radio speaker. "Get me back, Jack, this place . . . who *is* that man with the wings? That factory way out there in the desert, does it *move?* What number were you trying to reach, shithead? You think you're so—"

"Castine," interrupted Terracotta.

"Was," said Ollie.

"There?" finished Brett, on a rising note.

"Castine," said the tinny voice, "shot me. Get paramedics, dammit! I'm all fucked up—"

The voice failed to answer further three-voice questions, subsiding instead into misremembered nursery rhymes; and then other voices replaced Abbott's, all just babbling nonsense sentence fragments. After another full minute of uselessly trying to elicit anything coherent, Terracotta, Ollie and Brett returned to the other office and Terracotta closed the connecting door.

Ollie slumped back into his chair. "I hate to hear Abbott like that. You think paramedics might . . .?"

Neither of the other two answered; the fact of Abbott coming through on that band spoke for itself. Terracotta found an elastic loop on the desk and carefully pulled his long gray hair back in a ponytail. "I find I'm wondering what Terry Vendler's situation is," he observed.

Brett had sat down on the corner of the desk, and he exhaled loudly and shook his head. "You think *Castine* really *shot* him? Killed him?"

Ollie jumped, then muttered, "Shit," and fished out his phone again. *"Yes?"* After a few seconds he put it away and said, "Cops are there, sirens coming, Vendler and Abbott are lying on the pavement, nobody else visible. Our backup guys drove on by."

"What a mess," said Brett.

Ollie wiped his forehead on his shirt-cuff. "We'll have to establish jurisdiction—"

"Westwood will be working that out now," said Terracotta.

"What a . . . *major* mess," Brett elaborated.

"Okay," said Terracotta. "Abbott may be confused about who killed him. But Castine was pretty clearly *there,* and if I were to lizard a guess, it would probably be that she at least interfered with the unplanned arrest. She works under the delusion that she has a conscience. There's a chance that she's with Woods now, and that's not good." He thought about what he had said, then added, "I mean *hazard* a guess."

He smiled at the other two; Ollie flinched perceptibly. "This morning," Terracotta went on, "Amanda Woods said Herbert Woods was dreaming about her, which is probably why she was accessible here—he restored some definition to her. When was it she killed herself?"

"2012," said Brett. He shrugged. "Alcoholic, depressive. Left a note and then parked on a freeway shoulder and shot her head off with a .357 magnum."

"That's right—she probably didn't like being a Secret Service agent's wife. Understandable, I suppose, if one could understand things. Well, she's been dead a while, but obviously she's coalesced, and she can sense him—we must keep trying to get her up. Have somebody find details about their marriage—vacations, dogs, what movies they liked—so we can have personal stuff to hold her attention."

Brett stood up and stretched. "It's not a good idea to get deleted persons too waked up. They can develop *motivations*."

"What can she do?" said Terracotta. "She's our main lead on Woods, and we've got to get him out of the picture." He sighed. "And we've got to get Castine back here. She really is the best at coaxing deleted persons into talking."

"What if she did kill Abbott?" protested Ollie.

Terracotta pursed his lips judiciously. "We've wanted to get an agent over there *on the other side,* one we could call back and debrief. Why do they so often mention a desert highway, a flying man, a distant factory? We hoped for a volunteer, of course, but—now we do have a man in place."

"Not really at his best, though," noted Brett.

"But will he talk to *Castine?*" said Ollie.

"He's responded to discipline before," said Terracotta. "Like us all."

Ollie shifted uneasily in his chair, then blurted out, "And of course ghosts have no civil rights to worry about violating."

"Deleted persons," said Terracotta. He tapped his chest. "They're not this anymore." Stepping to the door that led out onto the factory floor, he added, "I believe I'm about to do my *yoga* routines," he said, sounding slightly surprised. "Keep people working on Abbott, too, in two-hour shifts. Non-stop till we get something useful out of him."

"That's kind of hard on him," said Ollie.

"Can't be helped," said Terracotta. "*Requiescat in agitatio.*"

When Vickery switched on the overhead fluorescent lights at the Galvan commissary kitchen, brushed stainless steel surfaces gleamed everywhere—ranks of stoves and holding cabinets and steam tables and deep fryers, and a big range hood that ran under the ceiling from one end of the room to the other.

There had been no other trucks in the lot when Vickery parked. He had fetched Terry's gun from under the dashboard, locked the truck and released the canvas sheets from the hooks at the bottom edges of the truck sides, and when he had closed the commissary door against the sunlight, he and Castine were alone. The air conditioner came on with the lights, and the long room smelled only of bleach.

Castine was blinking around at the vast kitchen. She opened her mouth to say something, but just then a door in the far wall opened and an old man in khaki shorts and a white undershirt leaned out of an office. His name was Primo, and Vickery recalled that he was an uncle of Galvan's.

"What the hell, Vick?" Primo called. "It's not even two o'clock yet!"

"Emergency," Vickery said. "Any unscheduled rides booked for today?"

"One in an hour and another at four. Ortiz says he can take them, but he'd rather not. You want 'em?"

"I can't, I'm clocking out. I had to ditch 'Turo and Ramon. When they get back here tell 'em I owe them. I gotta be taking off here pretty quick."

"You were just doing standby shoulder clean-up work today?" the old man asked. When Vickery nodded, he went on, "Okay. You're scheduled to drive an Unterbird tomorrow morning, aren't you?"

"I'll be at the lot on time, don't worry."

The old man nodded and stepped back into the office and closed the door.

"He didn't want to know who I am?" said Castine quietly.

"No," agreed Vickery, "he did not. And," he said, hefting Terry's gun, "he didn't want to know what the emergency was. Ramon and 'Turo won't want to know either—when they heard the gunshots, they'll have moved east along the shoulder and come down in a different street, and started walking back here. They'll just be glad to see the truck parked outside. The metronome will probably be okay on the shoulder there overnight."

He sat down cross-legged on the waxed brown linoleum, set Terry's gun on the floor beside him, and rubbed both hands over his face. "There won't be anybody in here till the trucks start coming back at five-thirty to put away all the frijoles and enchiladas." He sighed and looked up at her. "You should see this place at 5 AM—twenty people chopping onions and banging pans around."

"That's what you're thinking about right now? Cooking?"

"No. I'm thinking about . . . what happened back there, in that alley behind the thrift store. I'm *trying* to think of something else."

"Oh. Yeah. Me too, me too." She shivered. "And what do I do now. Kill myself, maybe."

"You think that would take you out of the picture?"

"Oh," she said quietly, "shut up."

Castine walked a few steps down an aisle between big double-door refrigerators. On a wheeled worktable stood half a dozen six-inch-tall metronomes with wooden or bone beads at the tops of the inverted pendulums; she reached out and touched one, and it clicked back and forth twice and then fell silent.

She turned to Vickery with her eyebrows raised.

"All Galvan trucks carry them," he said. "Most of the workers think they're just reminders to stay busy—like, 'time is fleeting'—but some of the cooks leave M&Ms and cigarettes for them here, at night."

"I'd like to hide in one. Live here forever on M&Ms and cigarettes."

He nodded toward the metronomes. "Some do."

Castine sat down against a nearby refrigerator with her legs stretched out, shifting for a moment to get the holstered gun at her back into a comfortable position, then yawned so widely that tears ran down her cheeks. "So why were you up the hill by the freeway if you were driving a food truck around?"

He patted his orange vinyl vest. "Freeway shoulder clean-up—Galvan public relations, civic virtue. And . . . to be on call to do other sorts of jobs for her. She's in more businesses than just taco trucks." Pausing to take a deep breath, he said, "What was the lead your people got on me this morning?"

"Oh. You—you won't like it."

He almost laughed. "Well no, I don't imagine I will."

She sighed and looked at the ceiling. "You used to have a Top Secret security clearance. I'm with TUA, the Transportation Utility Agency—"

"I thought you were some variety of the Secret Service."

"No. Well, sort of. Until half an hour ago, anyway!" She squeezed her eyes shut for a moment, then took a deep breath and went on, "The TUA got created in the divvying-out when the Secret Service was shifted from the Treasury Department to Homeland Security in 2003. At first we worked pretty closely with the Secret Service—"

"This is answering my question?" When she nodded, he said, heavily, "So it was this *TUA* crowd, manning that Countermeasures Suburban in that motorcade four years ago."

"Yes. And another of them would have arrested you, if I hadn't! Regular Secret Service *was* forbidden to go near the vehicle! And I didn't know . . ." She glanced at him quickly, then returned her gaze to the ceiling. "It was all about reactive armor, at first. Ordinary reactive armor on a vehicle explodes outward when a projectile strikes it—"

"I know. So the projectile in effect winds up with a lot more distance between itself and the target than it counted on."

"Right, it increases the distance in *space*. Well, the TUA reactive armor increases the distance in *time*—between the awareness of an attack on the Presidential limousine and its actual occurrence."

He nodded, and she paused and gave him a sideways glance. "You don't find this crazy," she said.

"It's been an educational four years since I stepped into that Suburban."

"I suppose it must have been, at that. They—"

A sudden rapid clicking made her sit up, quickly reaching behind her back, and her glance darted from the parking lot door to the office door before fixing on the little metronomes on the work table. The bead-capped pendulums had all begun furiously rocking back and forth, and after a few seconds they all stopped. "Sorry," she whispered as she relaxed and let her hands fall in her lap. "I thought someone was coming."

Vickery was looking at the metronomes too, and he was frowning. "Somebody did," he said. "In a way. That was a big surge, we're two miles from the nearest freeway." He looked back at her. "Have you ever seen a ghost?"

"I've helped talk to deleted persons. But they have no physical substance, you can't *see* them."

"Some people can." She started to object, but he shook his head impatiently. "You were saying, about reactive armor."

"Okay. Yes. They—well, it was Emilio Terracotta, he's actually a civilian, a physicist, but they've given him a lot of power, he's in charge of their whole research division—he's written books of philosophy, too—he discovered that each of the *stationary* people in a crowd that's being passed by a motorcade carries something like an electric charge—something analogous to that—and it induces a current in the *moving* charges, that's the agents in the Suburban. And in the field of that current, with the right hardware, the agents can actually see a little way into the past and the future. Enough to evade attacks."

"Sure," said Vickery impatiently, "various pasts and futures, anyway, not always the *one*. The LA freeway gypsies have known about that since the Pasadena Freeway opened in 1940, but they work it better—they just set up a stationary nest on a freeway shoulder, and let the freeway provide the moving charges. There's probably a hundred fortune-tellers out there right now plugged into the current, and their 'hardware' is just dead people's eyeglasses and boombox speakers."

"Well, we figured that out too," she said defensively. "Our Operations Extension is a stone's throw from the 710 now, and we use the current from the moving charges in the lanes. And motorcades too, still. How far ahead can your freeway gypsies see? The TUA scouts can't get more than a few seconds ahead of themselves."

Vickery shrugged. "Maybe a few minutes. They're frauds when they claim they can see stuff like marriages and deaths years ahead. What was the lead your people got on me this morning?"

"Oh God. It was . . . the result of a related effect they're pursuing. They discovered that—well, you *know*, don't you?"

"They discovered that they could also talk to dead people, in the induced field—at least, people who died on or near a freeway. In the current. Sure, I talked to a dead guy four years ago, on the radio in that Suburban, didn't I? He recited poetry or something to me." He stood up and crossed to the worktable with the half-dozen metronomes on it, and picked one of them up, turning it in his hands. "The freeway gypsies have known *that* for twenty years, at least. It's Galvan's main business." His heart was thudding in his chest, and the look he turned on Castine made her right hand momentarily twitch again. "Your answer involves that effect," he said flatly.

She opened her mouth, then just nodded and looked away. "I'm sorry."

"I was dreaming about her last night. I suppose that brought her within your range. Whatever's left of her. Enough to identify where I was, anyway."

Castine was looking at the floor. "Yes," she said quietly. "Cruising Culver City via Google Earth on a laptop till . . . she . . . said, 'Yes, that's the place, he lives there.'" She looked up. "You're lucky you were out of your apartment when the TUA squad got there," she reminded him.

Vickery glanced at the wedding ring he still wore. "I was sorry to wake up from that dream."

The little metronome began twitching in his hands, and he hastily dropped it. All the metronomes were clicking again. Castine watched them in evident alarm.

Vickery said, speaking more loudly over the racket, "Your crowd monitors this stuff? Ghost chatter?"

Castine waited to answer until the metronomes fell quiet again. "It's difficult," she said, "but yes, we do. Solicit it, instigate it."

"I suppose Amanda . . . my wife, could track me down again." He glanced at Castine. "You think the guy you shot today could track *you*, for them, the same way?"

"Oh God, thanks for that thought. I don't know—no, well not—oh, *maybe*. It did happen fairly close to the freeway there."

"Definitely in the current," said Vickery, nodding.

"But it takes a while, even when there's no snags, narrowing it down with Google Earth on street-view, and *I'm* the best one at getting the things to talk."

Vickery stared at her with no expression. "Are you the one who interrogated Amanda?"

She looked up at him. "Yes," she said, "I was one of the three who questioned her. We didn't have to use any coercion, no feedback or anything like that." She shook her head. "I mean we didn't hurt her. But blame *me*, not her—deleted persons don't know what they're doing."

Vickery waved it aside. "I wasn't blaming her. I'll think about blaming you."

He exhaled and ran his fingers through his hair. "We have to get both of us out of here, I don't want them finding this place." He crouched and picked up Terry's gun. "We've got to assume my landlord gave your guys a description and the license number of my car—that's all the landlord knows about me. I've got dealer plates in the spare tire well that I can put on it, and we can take it to a storage unit I keep under a dead friend's ID."

She stood up and followed him toward the exterior door. "Leave the car there?"

"Right. There's a motorcycle there, part of my all-around emergency kit, but—well, this is an emergency. And it's a dirt bike, which is good, because there's a guy I'm afraid we both ought to go see, and as it happens you can't get to his place on pavement. It'll save us a hike."

"He's not dead, is he?"

Vickery laughed briefly in spite of himself. "Not yet, as far as I know. There's still lots of living people in LA."

She nodded, her eyes empty. "Dozens, I bet."

Vickery took hold of the door lever, then paused and looked back at her. "I want you to know," he said, "you and I are allies for a few hours, I do owe you that—we're not friends."

"Belabor the obvious. You want me to switch off the lights here?"

Vickery worked the key into the recessed padlock on the segmented metal door, and when the bar finally snapped back he took hold of the tethered rope end and stood up, noisily hauling the door up on its track.

Behind him his Chevy Blazer idled on the narrow paved alley between two rows of identical red and white storage units. The door in front of them was the only one that was raised.

In the dimness of the ten-by-ten space, a few boxes were visible stacked around a long, angular shape under a tarpaulin. Castine stepped into the shadowed cubicle and lifted the flap of a box with the Marlboro logo on it; the box was packed with cartons of Marlboro cigarettes.

"You smoke a lot?" she ventured.

"That's currency," said Vickery as he shuffled in, picked up a box and set it down by the wall. "If civilization collapses, money or even gold won't be worth anything."

Castine followed his example and pushed the box to the wall. "But people will still need to smoke."

"Sure. Those other boxes are jars of instant coffee and pints of Jack Daniel's." He shrugged out of the vinyl vest and tossed it aside, then lifted a dusty leather flight jacket out of a box and slid his arms through the stiff sleeves.

"Right now, though," he added, pulling open another box, "we need *contemporary* currency." He dug out a thick envelope and opened it; inside was a bundle of twenty-dollar bills. He counted out fifteen of them and handed them to Castine.

"Here," he said. "It was my fault you had to pay to get your own gun back."

After a moment's hesitation, she said, "That's fair," and pocketed the bills.

He separated a third of the remainder and stuffed them into the pocket of his jeans, then closed the envelope and tucked it into an inner pocket of the jacket. "There's another leather jacket in that other box. I think it'll fit you."

Castine tugged the unwieldy garment out of the box and brushed it off before struggling into it. She had to push the sleeves back to have her hands free.

"Good enough," said Vickery. "Help me get the rest of these boxes stacked by the walls."

When they had moved all the boxes, he lifted the tarpaulin aside, revealing a light Husqvarna motorcycle with high fenders and a black exhaust pipe that curled up nearly to the seat. The fenders were white and the gas tank was bright red with a silver panel. "I come out here every couple of weeks to charge the battery and check the tires," he said, "and the gas tank's full."

"Festive little thing," Castine said, a bit shakily. " Will I fit?"

"If you hang on to me and keep your feet on the pegs." He folded the tarpaulin and laid it aside, then wheeled the motorcycle out into the sunlight and away from the open door and leaned it on its kickstand.

He got into the Blazer and carefully backed it into the cleared space in the storage cubicle. After climbing out, he opened a box in the corner.

"This is for you," he said.

Castine sidled in beside the Blazer, and he handed her a gray open-face helmet. "There's goggles in it," he told her. He crouched over to another box and found a black soup-bowl style half-helmet and another pair of goggles. "And I can wear this. We don't want to be pulled over for not wearing any."

She paused, then tilted her wrist to peer at her watch. "Damn, it's after five in Baltimore—too late now to call the *flower shop*." She looked up at him. "I need to get a burner phone."

"You . . . want to order flowers for your fiancé." He took the dark glasses from his shirt pocket and put them on.

She shook her head impatiently. "Terracotta will be watching Eliot's—my fiancé's incoming phone calls, yes. But there's a flower shop on the ground floor of his office building, and I can ask the girl there to go up and tell him that Ingrid Castine wants him to call the number of my burner phone. I can tell her that he'll give her a hundred dollars for doing this for me, and he will."

"We'll get you one right after we see this guy."

They shuffled out of the dim cubicle and Vickery pulled the segmented door down and fastened the padlock. He swung onto the motorcycle seat and pulled his helmet on and cinched the strap.

Castine walked up beside him, hefting her helmet and pulling a pair of goggles free of the straps.

"No Bibles?" she said, fitting the goggles strap on over her short dark hair.

Vickery flipped up the kickstand and gave her a blank look, and she nodded back toward the locked door. "Cigarettes, liquor, coffee. You do still go to church."

He tromped on the kickstarter, and the engine roared to life. "Hop on," he said, and when she had climbed on behind him, he looked back and said, "No, no Bibles. And I still go to Mass, but I haven't taken Communion since that motorcade four years ago."

He tapped the gear-shift and let out the clutch lever, and they sped away toward the storage yard entrance.

↓CHAPTER THREE↓

Vickery rode the sputtering bike west to Cahuenga Boulevard, then up through Hollywood to the foothills below the Hollywood Bowl, where the Pilgrimage Bridge crossed over the 101 freeway. Cahuenga ran close alongside the freeway for several miles here, and in that stretch he cranked the throttle and leaned fast around the curves to get quickly past any ghostly attention that might be radiating from the freeway lanes; though in fact traffic in the lanes was jammed and nearly motionless in both directions, glittering and inert in the afternoon sun. The only field being generated would be the one around himself and Castine, as they moved rapidly past the stationary charges on the Freeway to the right, and Vickery was confident that it would be too small and fleeting to have any effects.

Flocks of pigeons all flying together made shapes that twisted and stretched and compressed over the freeway lanes, the fluid masses of birds flaring white when a hundred of them all tilted at once, then becoming nearly invisible in the moments when they were flying directly away. The freeway gypsies said the pigeons liked to ride the edges of the amplified possibility fields around the freeways, and Vickery was relieved to see that the birds were not straying far from the lanes here.

Passing the trundling cars on northbound Cahuenga, he was as aware of the gun in his belt as he was of the woman perched behind him. The gun felt wrong there, and he kept having to resist the impulse to shift a nonexistent holster over to the right side, where he had always worn one when he had been a Los Angeles police officer.

Now he was carrying a stolen gun, tucked into his pants.

As a low scrub-brush slope flashed past on his left and hills studded with red-roofed houses swung into view on the far side of the freeway, he thought about the fact that he was thirty-six years old and on the run again.

During most of his time with the LAPD he had worked in the Financial Crimes Section of Bunco Forgery, dealing with everything from ATM fraud and gas-pump credit card skimmers to money laundering schemes in casinos and the fashion district. And that experience had stood him in good stead when he applied to the Secret Service. After six months of paperwork and medical exams and an eight-hour polygraph test, and then nine weeks at the Federal Law Enforcement Training Center in Georgia and eleven weeks at the Secret Service Agent Training Course in Maryland, he was assigned to the Los Angeles field office. He was at a GS-6 pay scale that was less than what he'd made as a policeman, and he was investigating counterfeiting and, once again, ATM fraud.

And then, in October of 2013, President Obama made a fundraising visit to Los Angeles, and rookie agent Herbert Woods was picked to stand post on Pico Boulevard as the presidential motorcade drove past. And President Obama decided to stop the motorcade at a Roscoe's Chicken and Waffles restaurant. That had been in the late afternoon; by midnight Agent Woods was wounded and in hiding under a false name in the back room of a veterinary clinic in Simi Valley, a fugitive who had killed two other government agents.

Just past another bridge over the freeway he slowed the motorcycle and made a left turn onto a broad area of cracked concrete, and continued the left turn uphill onto Mulholland Drive. Then he and Castine were riding along the two-lane road that wound between wooded slopes, Vickery leaning the bike around curves as the road zigzagged through the hills.

White gables and sun decks were occasionally visible above the ascending green branches on their right, and scatterings of tile roofs and turquoise pools spread away into the southern distance to their left, but after riding a few miles, in which the road had looped through every point of the compass, they had for the moment left all visible houses behind, and soon Vickery downshifted and swerved into an unmarked drive that descended to the left. The driveway curled away below

Mulholland, and, out of sight of the cars passing above, widened out in a clearing with a weathered aluminum mailbox on a post at the south end. The breeze was from that direction, and smelled of mesquite.

Vickery halted the bike by the mailbox, clicked the gear shift pedal into neutral and let out the clutch lever. "I'll go slow in first gear now," he told Castine, "but hang on. The next bit is bumpy."

But Castine hopped off the back of the bike, and when he looked over his shoulder at her, he saw that she had taken several steps back across the dirt and was holding her gun halfway raised.

The motorcycle engine puttered quietly.

Vickery couldn't see her eyes behind the goggles. "What," he said.

"Get off the bike and spread out on the ground."

Vickery tensed, and he mentally rehearsed clicking the bike into gear and twisting the throttle; the bike would jump forward into the brush, and he might be able to yank it from side to side and evade her shots as he rode it fast down the wooded slope, right on past Jack Hipple's house all the way to the Franklin Canyon reservoir. He knew her gun still had eight or nine rounds in it.

He didn't like the prospect. "Why?"

"This is too perfect a place to kill somebody and hide a body!" she called. "Maybe you've buried other people out here. You might be thinking I plan to reinstate myself with the TUA by telling them where you are and saying it was you who shot Abbott—or you might just want to kill me for calling up your wife and interrogating her."

Vickery exhaled in relief—apparently she did not primarily intend to kill him, just prevent him from killing *her*.

Still looking at her over his shoulder, he said, "You can see that both my hands are on the handlebar grips. I'm going to put the bike into gear and steer it wide around you, very wide, and ride back up the path and take off on Mulholland. You can walk back up there, I'll be long gone, and I don't imagine you'll have much trouble hitching a ride, if you put the gun away. I'll come back and see this guy later."

He looked down and watched the green neutral light go out as he squeezed the clutch and tapped the bike into first gear, and then he slowly let the clutch out and swung the front wheel sharply to the left; he walked the bike around in a half circle so that it was now facing back up the road.

"Wait!" called Castine. "I may have made a mistake!"

"We don't agree on the definition of 'allies,'" he said, and then he rocked his right hand back on the throttle and rode fast across the clearing and around the ascending curve back up to the crest, where the lanes of Mulholland curled away to west and east.

His shoulders had been hunched in half-anticipation of a shot, and now he halted the motorcycle and relaxed and looked back. He couldn't see her or the clearing from up here. A couple of cars hissed past the turnout, heading east.

He clicked the engine into neutral and took several deep breaths as the breeze cooled the sweat on his face.

All she actually knows for sure about me, he reflected, is that I killed two of her fellow agents four years ago. Maybe I wouldn't trust me either. And I did say I'd help her.

And in this new situation, I could use an informed ally.

What the hell.

He turned the bike around and rode back down the semi-circular track with the engine roaring in first gear, and halfway down he met her trudging up. She was still wearing the helmet and goggles.

She stopped, and he braked to a halt beside her. "'Allies,'" he explained, "means we agree not to kill each other."

"I knew that," she said. "It just slipped my mind for a second."

"Hop back on?"

"Thanks."

She swung a leg over the back of the seat and linked her arms around his waist, and again he rode down to the southern end of the clearing and halted at the edge of the downhill slope. Leafy carob and acacia branches waved below them.

"Bumpy now," he said, and he felt her nod behind him.

He let out the clutch and leaned back against Castine as the bike tilted down. The front wheel bounced and twisted against his grip on the handlebars, and as they slewed between two trees he heard her gasp at the sight of a black-robed figure now visible in the dappled shade ahead; its face was just an oval of mirror.

"It's a dummy, a distraction," he said as he swerved around it. "He got the idea from some art movie."

"*Meshes of the Afternoon*," said Castine in his ear. "Maya Deren, in the '40s." Her helmet bumped his as she looked around. "Half these trees are artificial Christmas trees!"

"Lots of artificial flowers too," he said. "Contradiction." At a narrow stream implausibly flowing in a trench from left to right across the face of the slope, he squeezed the clutch and paused, looking for the clearest path to cross it; he angled the bike to the left a few yards and then gunned the machine across. Castine yelped as sudden steam from the bottom curve of the exhaust pipe whipped past her ankle.

"One more stream," said Vickery, "then we're nearly there."

The next stream confirmed that both watercourses were artificially maintained, for it flowed from right to left. A short green metal statue of a man stood in the brush on the far side; its arms were outstretched, and instead of hands it had spinning pinwheels, apparently made from pieces of DVDs, that flicked rainbow glitters on the surrounding green leaves.

Off to the left, a bearded man and a girl, both in denim overalls, were scrambling hastily uphill. The girl paused to wave, and Vickery felt Castine shift on the bike seat as she apparently returned the wave. There had been no vehicles in the uphill clearing, and Vickery wondered if the couple had hitchhiked here, or walked.

At last a one-story clapboard house appeared among the trees, with shingled eaves extending well out past the visible wall, which was peppered with dozens of tiny windows. The roof bristled with old-fashioned TV antennas from which dolls and sets of false teeth dangled on strings, like wind-chimes. Vickery slanted across the dirt slope to a level stretch of Astroturf in front of wooden steps that led up to a screen door.

He braked to a stop, and reached under the gas tank and switched off the engine. In the ensuing silence he could hear faint music over the rustling of branches.

Castine slid off the motorcycle seat and pulled off her helmet and goggles.

"If it weren't for you and your affairs," she said, blinking around, "I'd be at the office in the Hsaio Tower right now, just back from lunch at Ike's. Instead I'm a, a *fugitive*, in . . . low-rent Oz." She stared at the peculiar house, then turned and scowled at him. "This is *necessary?*"

Vickery flipped down the kickstand and swung a leg over the gas tank, and as he stood up and pulled off his helmet he glared back at her. "If you hadn't decided to interfere with my wife . . . my dead wife . . . I could be driving somebody around in an air-conditioned car and getting paid for it, and I'd have a place to sleep tonight." He resisted an impulse to spit. "Yes, lady, you have unfortunately made this necessary."

He hung his helmet on the clutch grip and stepped up to the screen door and knocked on it. Through the fine wire mesh he could dimly see the shapes of furniture. The music stopped.

"Come in, *Sebastian*," came a resonant voice from inside. "And your girlfriend too."

Vickery pulled the flimsy door open and held it for Castine, who muttered "Girlfriend!" scornfully as she stepped past him. Vickery followed her in and closed the door.

On a boxy old computer monitor in the far corner, a screen saver video of swimming fish threw a faint glow, and the room was only spottily lit by the many little windows in the west wall, but after a moment Vickery could make out the couch and table and overstuffed armchairs, and he saw that the east wall was still hung with a dozen paintings of dogs and cats. The air smelled not unpleasantly of fried onions and tarry latakia tobacco smoke.

"It's been a long time, Sebastian," said a man who was sitting deep in one of the armchairs. Again he slightly emphasized the name.

"You're wasting your snark," said Vickery irritably. "She knows about Herbert Woods."

The man sat up and set a briar pipe in an ashtray on the table, and now Vickery could see the familiar horn-rimmed glasses and narrow moustache. The man stared at Castine for a moment and then turned to Vickery with raised eyebrows.

"How does she know?"

"That's not important," snapped Castine.

The man in the chair nodded slowly and touched his perfectly combed dark hair. "She knows what's important and what's not! Enviable. And evidently what we have so far is not." He blinked through the lenses at Vickery. "You drove down to the mailbox, then back up to Mulholland, then down again. I think you should go away and come back if something should in fact prove to be important."

Vickery clicked his tongue impatiently. "She works for the agency that has wanted me dead these last four years. Today they contacted my wife's ghost, and used her or it to find my apartment, and this lady stopped me from going there and getting caught—oh, Jack Hipple, this is Miss Castine; Miss Castine, Jack Hipple."

Hipple and Castine nodded to each other, not warmly.

"It's, uh, Ingrid," said Castine.

Hipple looked back at Vickery. "Go on."

"No, don't," said Castine. "You at least used to have a Top Secret security clearance. Why are we here, anyway?" She glanced around the dim room with evident distaste.

"We're *here*," said Vickery to both Hipple and Castine, "because I, and possibly Miss Castine too, have connections to ghosts who can track us, and her agency wants to use them to find us and kill me, and probably kill her too, now. We need to know about camouflage." He looked squarely at Hipple. "I'm scheduled to drive for Lady Galvan tomorrow, and I can't afford to skip out on that."

"You'd be wise to stay in her good graces," Hipple agreed, "and at least her Unter cars are stealth-equipped." He held up his hand. To Castine, he said, "Until today you worked for the Transportation Utility Agency?"

"How do *you* know about it?" asked Vickery. He was ignored by the other two.

"Can you break our connections to deleted persons?" Castine countered.

Hipple laughed softly. "Deleted persons! No. But I can tell you measures to take which are likely to make it difficult for them to find you, and I can provide you with some helpful apparatus." He leaned back in his chair. "The TUA has been very busy these last few months—the retro waves on the freeways are happening more often, and some of them now form self-consistent solitons that move backward for miles. And they're always moving away from the omphalos—south on the 110, west on the 134, even east out the 60 toward Palm Springs."

"That's fine," said Castine. "We don't have anything to do with whatever you're talking about. Omphalos! Sultans!"

"Solitons," said Vickery. "Waves that hold their shape longer than they should."

Castine rolled her eyes. "We don't deal with *any* of this stuff."

"In that case," Hipple said with a sigh, waving at the wall away from the windows, "perhaps you have a cherished cat or dog you'd like to have a fine art portrait of. Guinea pig, parrot. I do acrylic paintings of pets, from photographs. Very reasonable rates."

Vickery explained to Castine, "You people are evidently causing weird freeway conditions lately by calling up so many ghosts out of the current."

"Well why didn't he say that?"

"Miss Castine," said Hipple, "did you see a man and woman climbing the hill, as you came down? The man probably still had a beard."

She blinked at him. "Yes."

"You need my help, not a pet portrait." He shook his head sternly, as if she had come to him asking for one. "Only someone compromised by a ghost could have seen those two."

Castine bust out, "Oh, give me a break! What, they were some of your *ghosts?* Easy to say, now that they're gone." She turned to Vickery. "I've got to get a phone. This man's a charlatan. Deleted persons have no visible substance. We researched that."

"He's a lot of things," said Vickery, "and probably a charlatan too, a lot of the time. But ghosts *are* visible to some people. And vice versa."

"And you're one of those people," said Hipple, apparently unoffended. "You are indeed trackable by them. Obviously you have been intimate with someone who died within the freeway current."

Vickery looked at Castine. "You were less than a hundred yards away from the freeway. These days that's in the current."

"I was never *intimate* with him!" she protested. "This is ridiculous."

"Did you kill him?" asked Hipple.

"What? What's that got to do with—"

"Answer him," said Vickery. "Or I will."

Castine bit her lip. "Yes. I—I killed him."

Hipple nodded. "Ending someone's earthly life from him is about as intimate as you can get. Was this recent?"

"An hour or so ago," said Vickery.

Hipple stood up and crossed to a television set beside the computer, and twisted a knob; the screen stayed dark. Then he stepped to a door in the south wall and pulled it open. Sudden bright daylight showed drifts of dust on the pattern of the rug underfoot, and a breeze tossed Castine's short hair and fluttered papers on the table. Fresh air blew away the tobacco and onion smells.

Vickery and Castine followed him and looked out over a view of descending green canyons to the distant spires along Sunset Boulevard.

Vickery looked straight down, then took a step back; the house sat flush on the edge of a sheer cliff, and he estimated the drop beyond the threshold to be a hundred feet.

"*That's* a door you don't have to lock," said Castine, stepping back herself.

"On the contrary," said Hipple, moving back to the television, "I get more visitors by way of that door than the one you came in through. The couple you saw climbing away up the hill, for example." The television screen now glowed gray. "Let's see how close your astral companions are. Stand closer to the door so everybody can see you."

"I don't want to be seen!" said Castine.

"I don't think I do either," said Vickery. "Just tell us how to hide ourselves from them!"

"I need to know how heavy a dose to prescribe." Hipple crouched beside the television, peering at the screen. "Analog TV broadcasts stopped eight years ago, so there's bandwidth free for a more fleeting sort of signal on this old set." He sat back on his heels. "Ah, Sebastian, do you recognize this face?"

Vickery peered warily at the screen, and saw a brighter oval against the gray, with dark spots that might have represented eyes and a mouth. The mouth spot was changing shape, as if the face were trying to speak.

It might have been an image of Amanda. "Switch it off, damn it!" Vickery said hoarsely.

Hipple shrugged and clicked the channel selector knob a few notches.

After a few seconds he said, "Miss Castine, does this seem to be your intimate friend?"

Castine glanced at the screen, where another pale oval was collecting.

"No," she snapped; then added, "Turn it *off*."

Hipple chuckled indulgently and clicked the set off. "The surprising thing, really, is not that their unwitting self-portraits on the cathode ray tube are good, but that ghosts can produce them at all. And your two *admirers* are in fact very local and wide awake."

Vickery glanced at the open doorway, and saw two vertical areas where the sky appeared to be rippling, as if seen through agitated water. He stepped forward and closed the door firmly.

"Oh," said Hipple, straightening up, "yes. You don't want *them* coming through here and scampering away up the hill as well."

Vickery suppressed a shiver, and Castine muttered under her breath.

"So how do we evade them?" Vickery asked, trying not to imagine his wife's ghost hovering insubstantially in mid-air outside the closed door.

"I charge fees for consultation, Sebastian."

"Sorry, what? Oh—I have money."

"I'm sure you do, and I'll be happy to take some of it for incidental extras, but for my expert consultation . . ." He squinted from one of his guests to the other. "You're both carrying guns. Miss Castine, is yours the one you killed—" he nodded toward the dark television, "—with?"

"Well . . . yes."

"I'll take that for your payment. A weapon that's participated in killing a person never loses a valuable connection with that event. Sebastian, how about yours? Was it ever used to kill a person?"

Vickery looked at Castine, and after a moment she nodded. "Terry shot one of your crazy freeway gypsies last year." She faced Hipple. "I'm not giving you my gun. It's registered in my name, I could get in big trouble. And until I can get in touch with a certain person, I think I need to have a gun."

"I'll provide you with replacements in exchange," Hipple assured her. "I've got a couple of unassociated .45 autos, 1911 model."

Castine shook her head. "How do we know they're not stolen? And in California you can't legally just—"

"For God's sake, Ingrid," interrupted Vickery, "you've got bigger problems."

Her face lost all expression, and Vickery wondered if she was about to cry.

She closed her eyes for a moment. At last, "I've always obeyed the law," she said quietly. "Even with Abbott, it was a justifiable shooting."

Vickery thought of reminding her that she had almost certainly broken the law by warning him of the imminent arrest this morning; but, remembering that again, he just said gruffly, "He can have the gun I picked up this morning, and you can keep yours."

"Miss Castine's has the greater value," interjected Hipple, "having done its spiritual work this very day. I want both."

For several seconds no one spoke.

"Very well," said Castine finally, "yes, I'll do it." She smiled at Vickery for the first time, though it was an uncertain smile, accompanied by a worried frown. "We've fallen outside the law, haven't we? Even," she added, waving toward the southern door, "outside natural law. I don't know what I'm doing out here." She coughed out two syllables of a laugh. "I watch myself walk and talk, but I don't know what I'm doing!"

Hipple folded himself back into his chair and tapped the table. "Bring out your dead."

Vickery pulled the gun from his belt and laid it on the table. Castine made an aimless gesture, then quickly reached around behind her back, drew her gun, and clunked it down beside the other. The two stainless steel semi-automatics gleamed in the light from the western windows.

"Okay," said Hipple. "There are several things you should do and not do. Time spent in the ghost currents *is* said to keep a person young, but of course you must try to stay out of them. Ghosts are—"

A gust of wind shook the abyss door, and Vickery thought it went on rattling for a moment or two after the gust had abated.

"Ghosts," Hipple went on more loudly, "are compatible with alkaline bloodstreams, so you should be acidic—drink lots of Cokes and coffee, eat roasted nuts, blueberries, prunes. Pickles, chocolate. Right? You probably don't want to go into stores with security cameras, but I have packets of these things that I can sell you for plain cash. But avoid hard liquor—a lot of ghosts miss it, and they're drawn to the smell. And you want to change the aspects of yourselves that ghosts can recognize, so get rid of your rings, get uncharacteristic used clothes and wear them inside out or backward, replace your shoes with used ones as often as you can, part your hair on the other side if not shave it all off, wear your watches on the other wrist and set to the wrong time. You're pretty untrackable while you're on that velocipede you rode here, but of course stay off freeways if you can; and if you're in a car, be ready with a portable radio to check your immediate surroundings. Hop on one foot as much as is convenient. I have pogo sticks for sale with durable pads made of human hair, and these have proven effective. When using a rest-room—"

"Spare me," interrupted Castine. She glared at Vickery. "For this lot of nonsense I'm giving up my SIG?—and getting a .45 with a seven-round magazine? Pickles? *Pogo sticks?* What kind of—"

"This is good, as far as it goes," interrupted Vickery, "some of it, anyway, but—"

"And I can provide ten-round magazines for the .45s," said Hipple. "With one in the pipe, you've got eleven shots."

"But," Vickery went on, turning to Hipple, "aren't there ways to *repel* ghosts?—besides just eating a lot of chocolate? I mean, this is all good-sounding advice for avoiding their notice, but if one catches us with our shoes off or no part in our hair at all—how can we drive it off?" He made himself not look at the closed southern door.

Hipple rocked his head judiciously. "I won't lie to you, there's nothing foolproof. I can sell you a couple of spirit-level stars and fixed compasses, those can disorient ghosts . . . and it might help to recite the multiplication tables in a loud voice; math is deterministic, and ghosts are an effect of possibility extended beyond reason. It might repel them—they wouldn't like 'to know that two and two are four, and neither five nor three,' as A.E. Housman wrote." He leaned back and shook his head. "Get used shoes and don't take them off."

Castine was rubbing her temples as if she had a headache. "What," she asked with labored patience, "are spirit stars and fixed compasses?"

Hipple got up and crossed to a bookcase, and when he returned to his chair he was carrying a wooden cigar box. He pulled out of it a pocket compass and held it out on his palm.

"The needle points north, you see; but—" He flipped it over to show a knurled knob on the underside. To Vickery the thing now looked like a speed-loader for a revolver. "By twisting this knob," Hipple went on, "you can fix the needle in one position. Swing the compass around in a circle then, and the apparent shifting of north might induce a terminal y-axis spin in a ghost."

"Unless he won't look at it," said Vickery.

"True," admitted Hipple. He now lifted from the box a plastic disk on which eight little glass tubes were glued like spokes on a wheel. Each tube was partially filled with clear lucite, with a motionless bubble in the center of it.

"They're levels, you see. But each one in the ring is defining a different line as level. Looking at this might induce a negating z-axis spin in an attentive ghost."

An attentive ghost, thought Vickery. I don't think they're ever very attentive.

Hipple produced another of each device and slid all four across the table. "You owe me eighty bucks. And you'll probably want some packets of dried prunes and blueberries, and some Hershey bars, and maybe a couple of—"

"No pogo sticks today," rasped Castine.

Vickery was squinting skeptically at the objects on the table. "The old gypsies talk about some brass thing that repelled ghosts like WD-40 repels water."

Hipple smiled. "Yes, it's supposed to have been a brass capital letter *L*, as big as a chair. Some fellow brought it through the omphalos, the story goes, in 1960, from the other side, from the desert-highway afterlife. They say it was a supremely effective ghost repeller, but people got cancer if they owned it for very long, and it disappeared about thirty years ago. The word is that the Vatican bought it, and keeps it in a lead box."

"Is this the same guy," asked Vickery, "who supposedly did some kind of phase-change on the freeway around then, and just disappeared, car and all?"

Hipple shrugged. "Could be. If it ever happened at all. Stick to the multiplication table."

"This is the second time," said Castine, "that you've mentioned this omphalos. It sounds like something a proctologist would look for."

"It's an exit on the Pasadena Freeway," said Vickery, "where the freeway current was first used to open a conduit to the, uh, *other side*. That was in the '40s, I think. It's the center, the main . . . ghost drain, or ghost fountain."

"The Pasadena was the first freeway," remarked Hipple, closing the cigar box, "and they didn't know how to build them yet. The exits are too tightly curled for freeway velocities." He stood up and stepped to the bookcase to put the cigar box back. "Of course," he remarked over his shoulder, "sometimes a ghost can be induced to subsume itself forever in some organic physical object." A pipe rack with a dozen pipes in it stood on a higher shelf, and he touched two briars and a corncob, as if picking out notes on a xylophone.

Vickery nodded and said to Castine, "The wooden or bone knobs on the metronomes, for instance. The ghosts in those are in there for good."

"But that's generally ghosts who are fairly exhausted," said Hipple, turning back to the room, "or who were never born."

"They died," said Castine, "but they were never born?"

Vickery too was looking questioningly at Hipple.

"They never lived or died," said Hipple. "Expanded possibilities. In the desert-highway afterlife, personalities can exist whose potential for birth, for life, never quite got realized, for one reason or another. Children Romeo and Juliet would have had, as it were."

The dim room had come to seem narrow and oppressive, and Vickery reached into his pocket for the loose twenty dollar bills.

"Fetch out those two .45s," he said, "and we'll take the compasses and the spirit-level rings. And a few packets of raisins or whatever. We've got to get moving."

Hipple sighed. "Very well . . . Herbert."

"It's been fun," Castine told him. "Sort of."

↓ CHAPTER FOUR ↓

The glow through the skylights indicated that it was not much later than midafternoon, but Emilio Terracotta felt as if he had been running from room to room nonstop for days. He had sent an agent out for kale salad and tofu-and-avocado wraps more than once, and somebody had brought in bottles of Chardonnay, but all three auxiliary rooms were in tense use, and he had spent all his time crouched over one radio speaker or another, trying to derive sense from the frail voices vibrating out of them.

The three men around each of the radios had asked their relay-worded questions endlessly, and several times they had got Amanda Woods, once for as long as twenty seconds; one of the agents in contact with her had stared at Google Earth on a laptop monitor and moved the view according to her breathless directions; and before the contact was lost, she had seemed to be indicating that Herbert Woods was somewhere along Mulholland Drive.

But the ether was even more crowded with vociferous deleted persons today than usual, and Terracotta was sick of their whining demands for beer and tow trucks and baptism.

He had stepped out of the third radio room, which had been the personnel break room until a few hours ago, and he blinked around in the wide, high-ceilinged warehouse space. To his tired eyes the blue-and-white checkerboard pattern on the walls seemed arranged to provoke some optical illusion, and he looked away from it and trudged down the row of doors to the administration office.

The door was open, and he walked in and pulled it closed behind him. Ollie was talking on his cell phone again, and Terracotta stepped around behind the desk and sat down in the padded office chair. Against the far wall was a big whiteboard with a grid of vertical and horizontal lines drawn in purple felt pen; the columns were labeled *time, identity, questions asked,* and *questions ans'd,* and most of the squares in the grid were blank.

Ollie tapped his phone and put it away. "Westwood got some information about Herbert Woods' marriage. He married Amanda Cantrell in '06, she was twenty-three, he was twenty-five and he had been an LA cop for a year and a half at the time. They had cats, three of them over the six years of their marriage: Toby, Cosmo, and Myshkin. No kids, though. They both liked hang-gliding—they belonged to the Sylmar Hang Gliding Association, and Woods liked to build his own gliders. They visited San Francisco several times, and often ate at Alioto's on Fisherman's Wharf. Amanda's mother's name was Ruth, and she died when Amanda was twelve."

Terracotta nodded. "That's good stuff, prime the radio boys with it. Mentioning the cats, for instance, might establish trust, keep her talking. And tell Westwood to try to find out what they ordered, at that restaurant. It wouldn't hurt to mention foods she particularly likes." He stood up and yawned. "I'm going to be outside."

Ollie nodded, and Terracotta walked out from behind the desk and left the office.

As he walked across the wide blue floor, Terracotta was mildly surprised to see that there was a pack of Camel cigarettes in his right hand. He must have picked it up from a table in one of the radio rooms. It shouldn't have been there, smoking was forbidden in the building . . . but a moment later he realized that he had a tactile memory of his hand pulling the pack out of his pants pocket.

I must have bought it myself, he thought. Perhaps I've started smoking again. He touched the pocket and felt the once-familiar shape of a Bic lighter.

Interesting, he thought.

He tapped his code into a panel on the wall and pushed open the west door and stepped out, blinking in the sunlight, onto the breezy sidewalk that fronted the parking lot. He had called in personnel from the Victorville and Oceanside field offices, and gray Chevrolet sedans filled all eight parking spaces now, even with Abbott's and Castine's cars missing, and others were parked outside the fence along Bandini Boulevard, which was technically a violation of protocol.

Past the parking lot, behind the tall fence and a row of pink-flowering oleander bushes, Terracotta could clearly see half a dozen figures idly shifting back and forth. One old fellow in a suit and tie waved at him, but Terracotta didn't look closely at him or wave back.

He had first noticed them a week ago, and when he had asked Brett what those people were doing there, it had been clear that Brett didn't see them. Terracotta had hastily claimed to have been referring to the owners of the neighboring building to the west; but over the next few days he had established that Ollie couldn't see them either, nor could one of the radio monitoring agents Terracotta had talked to out here.

He was sure they were ghosts, Brett's "deleted persons"—these specimens somehow inadvertently drawn out from their afterlife by all the summonings and interrogations going on in the Extension building. Something analogous to quantum tunneling, perhaps, or wild tobacco growing outside cultivated fields. At first Terracotta had forced himself to approach the swaying figures, not daring to speak to them, but hoping they might reveal something about themselves and their situation; but they made no sounds at all, just waved and beckoned.

He had been frightened by them, and had wondered: Did they think? Did they know things about life and death that he didn't know, terrible things?

Now he simply tried to ignore them; and he had not told his agents that deleted persons apparently could, after all, be visible.

His right hand shook a cigarette out of the pack of Camels—the pack had already been opened!—and deposited it on his lip, and his left hand raised the lighter and lit it.

The freeway a hundred-some yards behind him pulsed with a sound like hands quickly brushing silk, and out in front of him, beyond the fence, cars in the right lane were moving slowly, each waiting to enter the southbound freeway onramp. The traffic control light must be on at the top of the ramp, cycling through its timed red-to-green-to-red pattern.

Do any of those drivers know, Terracotta wondered as he drew the smoke into his lungs, that the air here is as full of ghosts as it is of radio waves? The TUA had field offices in Chicago and New York and D.C., but none of them found their currents as thickly populated as the ones in Los Angeles.

Terracotta squinted to see the light and dark dots that were the faces in the cars. No, he thought, they don't know. To them the world was often inconvenient but always logical; they knew nothing of a secret Cold War in which ghosts were the half-wit agents.

And something bigger, something Terracotta didn't want to think about; wasn't able to think about, in fact.

"Chief," came a call from behind him. Terracotta turned around and saw Brett in the open doorway. "We got Abbott, pretty lucid," Brett said. "In the break room."

Terracotta tossed the cigarette and hurried inside, and as Brett pulled the door closed he hurried across the wide floor to the little room at the north end of the warehouse.

When he pulled the door open he could hear Abbott's voice buzzing out of the speaker, recognizable in spite of being produced without benefit of real lungs or throat or tongue.

"I need backup," the voice was saying, "these people won't hold still, they jump around like grasshoppers . . . the guy's gone now, but he had wings! He was flying around over that factory on the hill—I'm halfway between it and the highway, it's still a couple of miles away but I can hear it thumping and clanking . . . smokestacks, and the smoke blows around in all directions like a second-hand . . ."

One of the men seated by the radio glanced at Terracotta and tapped the keyboard on his lap, and on the monitor over the radio appeared the words, *says C was at house on Mholland—doesn't know xact loc—"low-rent oz."*

Abbott was now producing a noise like a coughing fit, and Terracotta wondered how he could cough without a throat.

At last the voice resumed speaking: "My mom and dad were here a minute ago, I think—somebody's mom and dad, anyway—listen, this place—the terrain is the body, the map is the anatomy chart—the second coming, scarcely are those words out—surely some consummation is at hand—a low'ring bull's mistaken lust—"

A sound behind the voice had grown from a faint rhythmic pulse to a hard thudding, and one of the men by the radio looked up at Terracotta uncertainly.

Terracotta pushed him aside and switched off the radio speaker. "What did you think that was, static? Damn it, when you get anything like drumming in the background—"

"Sorry, Chief." The man sat back and rubbed his eyes. "I thought it might just be the speaker here vibrating."

Terracotta took several deep breaths, noticing for the first time that the room was hot, and smelled sharply of sweat. "You take no chances. It's a toxic malmeme that rides on that noise. You remember when it started up in the Suburban on Wilshire four years ago? Those TUA agents couldn't quickly turn off the radio, so what did they do?"

The man nodded dutifully. "They jumped right out into the street."

"Lucky for them that they did. And Secret Service Agent Herbert Woods did hear part of it, that day. To his misfortune."

He frowned to discourage any questions.

"Reboot it in a minute," he said, "and concentrate on Amanda Woods for now. You know the names of the cats she had, right? I think if we find her husband we'll find Castine too—they seem to be traveling together, both somewhere on Mulholland within the last hour—and *push* it, will you? If we don't get Castine back by the end of the day, the odds will be too great that she's been tainted by the association." He sighed and waved toward the door. "With luck she'll have the sense to come back here on her own before that."

"After killing Abbott?" objected another of the seated men. "Abbott still insists she did—shot him twice in the throat, he says."

Terracotta shook his head. "She knows we'll take her back if she comes back soon. She's more valuable, and valued, than Abbott was."

Terracotta left the room and walked past the next two doors back to the administration office. Brett followed him in and closed the door.

Ollie sat at the desk, for once not talking on his phone, and he looked up. "Vendler is in a coma at Kaiser Permanente on Sunset, skull fracture. And the police found no guns on or near the spot where he and Abbott were assaulted."

"Odd," said Terracotta. "Woods might well have grabbed one, but I don't see why Castine would have wanted a second gun."

Ollie shrugged. "Maybe some homeless guy found it before the cops showed up."

Brett asked impatiently, "What *is* this 'toxic malmeme'? Why is it so important that nobody hear it? Woods heard it four years ago, and it doesn't seem to have done him any harm." He spread his hands. "A lustful bull?"

"A lustful bull?" echoed the mystified Ollie.

Terracotta made a chopping gesture. "Forget about it. It's dangerous, all right—I can't say how."

Brett laughed uncertainly. "Uh-huh. If I knew it, you'd have to kill me."

Terracotta waved the subject away. *I scarcely know it myself,* he thought; *but these are pieces of something that mustn't be revealed yet; mustn't be . . . hindered.*

The terrain is the body, the map is the anatomy chart . . . surely some consummation is at hand.

His mouth opened and he began speaking. "Leave the team in the break room tracking Amanda Woods. I'll join the team in Room Two, and go fishing for Abbott again. He needs to get closer to that factory on the hill—I'm sure we need to know about that place—but he's got to get away from it again to report. We can't have him talking while he's so close to it that we hear the noise of it."

"Place?" Brett threw a doubtful sideways glance at Ollie. "All that stuff, the highway in the desert and the flying man, and the factory, that's just hallucinations of deleted persons. Isn't it? Sensory deprivation fantasies."

"And good luck getting anything specific out of Abbott now," added Ollie, "wherever he is."

"We need to make him obey orders and answer questions," said Terracotta. "Get a microphone and another speaker in there so we can hit him with feedback if necessary."

Ollie shifted in his chair. "Jeez, Chief, feedback is like electric shock to deleteds. I hate to do that to poor old Mike."

"It's not *him*," said Brett. "Deleted persons aren't the people they derived from."

"They think they are, though," said Ollie.

Terracotta took a deep breath and forced himself to look at the situation in a way these men would understand. "It's essential that we get on top of this *whole phenomenon*," he insisted. "You think China and Russia aren't aware of this area of research? Iran, North Korea? American agents, and even government clerks and contractors, die in apparent accidents on highways—who do you suppose interrogates them as deleted persons? Damn it, Abbott is our man in place . . ."

His voice trailed off, and he found that he was thinking of the ghosts outside the parking lot fence. One of them had been waving at him—could that one know something relevant to all this?

He muttered, "Tell the agents in Room Two I'll be with them shortly. I'm going to get some fresh air."

Ollie raised his eyebrows at this second break in ten minutes, but said nothing.

Terracotta left the office, hurried across the wide warehouse floor and tapped in the code to get the parking lot door open. Out in the afternoon sunshine again, he coughed in surprise when one of his hands shoved a cigarette into his mouth, but he puffed on it when his other hand waved the lit Bic lighter at it.

He exhaled smoke, then made himself look toward the south end of the parking lot.

The shifting figures were still there behind the fence and the oleander bushes, and now he stared at them. Several of them waved. The old man in the suit and tie was opening and closing his mouth . . . and all at once Terracotta recognized him.

The next thing he was consciously aware of was leaning against the blue-and-white checkerboard wall inside the warehouse, gripping his knees and panting. The cigarette was gone.

He fought to think rationally.

Guilt, he reminded himself, is an electro-chemical event in the physical brain. It's one of the useless side-effects of consciousness, which itself is irrelevant. The ideal is the lines in Tennyson's "Locksley Hall:" "Let the great world spin forever down the ringing grooves of change." The important thing was that all of it moved in determinate grooves.

He had been an orphan when he'd had his name legally changed from Benedetti to Terracotta, and he didn't want to be reminded of his father.

The statue killed him, not me.

Terracotta straightened up, dismissed the ghost of his father from his mind, and strode across the warehouse toward Room Two.

↓↓↓

Vickery rode down Cahuenga and turned left on Santa Monica Boulevard, and then he and Castine were passing new Japanese take-out restaurants and gray office buildings with weathered cornices on the upper stories and garish liquor stores on the ground floors; and as the motorcycle gunned past the stone tower at the entrance to the Hollywood Forever Cemetery, he nodded toward it and said over his shoulder, "That's where we'll be spending the night."

He heard Castine mutter behind him, "I wouldn't be surprised."

He pulled in to the curb in front of an old building divided by contrasting bright colors of paint into half a dozen narrow-fronted business establishments, and between a *Ropa de Bebe y Nino* shop and a market advertising *Cerveza Fria* was an open door below a sign that read *Universal Prepaid*.

"You wait here," he told Castine as he stepped away from the bike, and three minutes later he walked out of the shop and handed her a red Doro flip-phone.

"I've got the charger and a refill card in my pocket, and you owe me fifty bucks," he said as he swung a leg over the bike's gas tank and started the engine. "We can get it charged and anonymously activated at the lot tomorrow morning." He accelerated back into traffic.

East of the 101 Freeway he slowed, and then leaned the bike across the oncoming lanes into a driveway beside a boxy blue stuccoed building whose only sign was a faded FOR LEASE banner. He parked in a dirt lot behind the building, which now could be seen to be an old two-story Victorian house, onto the front of which the stucco structure had at some time been added. The dirt lot was ringed by the back ends of similar old houses, and Vickery knew that from the streets their house-fronts too would be hidden by gaudy, grafted-on shops that crowded right up to the sidewalks.

Castine got stiffly off the bike while Vickery unlooped a chain and padlock from around the handlebars and threaded it through the spokes of the back tire and around an iron lamp post.

"We can eat here," he said, straightening up and waving at the old house. He unstrapped his helmet and pulled it off. "It's sort of a restaurant, and there's minimal chance of surveillance."

"No cameras," Castine said, taking off her own helmet.

"Surveillance of any sort."

She shrugged and followed him to the house's back stairs, carrying the helmet and a bag of supplies they'd bought from Hipple. The bag was light; Castine's new gun was jammed into her holster, and Vickery's was tucked into the back of his pants.

The back door creaked open when Vickery pushed on it with his free hand, and Castine followed him into a wide, wood-floored room with thick mismatched pillars at irregular intervals. The upstairs floor had been largely taken out, surviving only as three wide platforms overhead, and high above them was no ceiling, just the exposed beams of the roof. Bare light bulbs dangling on wires of varying length threw a yellow glow over the scene, and a dozen or so figures were visible sitting at tables that had been set out across the floor and on the platforms. Several clothing store mannequins stood in corners, and framed pictures of faces seemed to cover all the vertical surfaces, the highest ones on the east wall glowing with apricot sunset light from a porthole-window near the roof in the opposite wall.

"Is this place structurally sound?" Castine asked, blinking around at the unexpectedly open space.

"The pillars are what's left of the load-bearing walls," Vickery said, leading her across the room to a recessed alcove with two unoccupied tables in it. He set his helmet down beside one of them. "They ought to hold for the next hour."

Against the alcove wall ran a white-painted railing, interrupted in the middle by a newer-looking metal door. Vickery and Castine got out of their leather jackets and draped them over a couple of chairs before sitting down, and Castine set her helmet and the bag from Hipple's on the floor beside her chair. The smell here was a weird mix of curry and onions and, faintly, chlorine.

"Are there waiters?" asked Castine.

"There's people that bring food," said Vickery. "You get what's on the stoves tonight."

She nodded dubiously, then looked at the lower ceiling immediately overhead and the wall behind her chair. "Why a railing?"

"This alcove used to be the porch of the house." Vickery leaned out of his chair to tap the wall between two framed pictures. "In 1930 or so, long before a pool supply store was built onto the front, we'd be looking out across a lawn at the boulevard from right here."

She shivered. "I imagine ghosts sitting at that other table, with a pitcher of lemonade, staring at the wall. Staring *through* the wall."

"Not in here," said Vickery. "They don't like the uncanny valley. Too bad the management doesn't let people sleep on the premises! Ah, here comes our dinner—God knows what it is."

A heavily tattooed gray-haired man in a T-shirt brought two plates and set them on the table, along with plastic tableware wrapped in paper napkins. As he walked away, Vickery looked at what he'd brought them—it appeared to be cold marinated onion and carrot slices beside ladlefuls of steaming curried stuff, possibly chicken. By accident or design, it all seemed to conform to the diet Hipple had recommended.

Castine had freed a fork and was already digging in. "Where's the uncanny valley?" she asked around a mouthful.

Vickery waved at the pictures and the nearest mannequin. "All around you. All the faces in the pictures are waxworks or Japanese robots or characters from new animated movies like *Polar Express*."

Castine shifted around in her chair, still chewing, to see the ones on the wall behind her. She swallowed and said, "Oh. Yes. I thought they were pictures of real people." She looked back at Vickery. "It's kind of creepy, all these realistic fakes."

Vickery nodded. "Exactly." He paused to take a mouthful of the steaming curried stuff; it was very spicy with cumin and peppers, but it did seem to be chicken. After a few moments he went on, "People don't mind most representations of faces—statues, animation—they like them better the more realistic they look. But there's a point when they look just a bit *too* realistic, and the approval curve drops; that's the uncanny valley, that dip on a graph. We find it creepy, but ghosts can't stand the apparent contradiction—it looks genuinely human, but you can sense that it's not."

Castine blew air out through her lips. "This stuff's not bad, but it's hot. Do they serve anything to drink?"

"Beer'll be along shortly."

More people had come in, and Castine looked out across the broad room at the diners at the other tables.

"I think I know who *we* are," she said. "Who's everybody else?"

A young woman on one of the open second-floor platforms was leaning out over the edge, looking down and exchanging sign-language gestures with a man in a motorized wheelchair who could surely have no hope of joining her up there, and Vickery wondered how the man had even got the wheelchair into the building; a battered upright piano stood in a far corner, and an old man was laboriously plinking out some unrecognizable tune on the keys; and a trio of teenage girls huddled giggling over a cell phone.

"Strangers," said Vickery. "We'll never know."

"Your man Hipple didn't seem happy that I knew about the Herbert Woods identity."

"It's leverage he's had on me. I guess he figures it's worth less if he has to share it."

Castine nodded and took another bite, chewing as she blinked around. After a few seconds she started to get out of her chair, then subsided, frowning. "That woman over there just lit up a cigarette! I guess I shouldn't make a scene."

"No," agreed Vickery. "And in places like this, nobody cares. That kid by the far wall with the beer probably isn't twenty-one, either."

"Are we safe here? What if the police raid the place?"

"They won't. When I was a cop, we knew about a lot of places like this in LA. We figured they were private and harmless—a lot of them have the ghost-repelling pictures on the walls, but in those days I didn't know about all that stuff. I knew there were crazy fortune-tellers in shacks beside the freeways, too, but it didn't seem like my job to roust them, and I thought their metronomes were just set dressing, like the skulls and candles in Mexican *botanicas*."

Castine nodded, still looking out at the other tables. "You're supposed to say Hispanic," she said absently. "*Mexican* isn't PC."

Vickery laughed. "To me PC still sounds like Probable Cause. And there never was any, to investigate the freeway gypsies and their ways."

The tattooed old man made his way back to their table, and now set down two 16-ounce cans of beer, one Budweiser and one Coors.

Castine shook her head and finally took the Budweiser. "How long were you a cop?" she asked, popping the tab and taking a quick swallow. "What did you do?"

"Six years." Vickery opened the Coors can and took a deep sip. "Mostly I was putting together forgery and money-laundering cases." He smiled. "Though for a while it looked like I'd be an LAPD ultralight pilot. You know, those little one-man airplanes?"

"LAPD uses those?"

"No. The Downey Police Department was using one in the '80s

because they're cheaper than helicopters, but they shut it down—insurance got too expensive, and people would shoot at it. But in 2010 the LAPD looked into the idea, and they tapped me for it because my wife and I did a lot of hang-gliding, and they figured the skills were similar. But eventually they decided they had enough helicopters and didn't need the insurance headache."

"And now you drive a taco truck. And . . . unter cars, that Hipple guy said?" She took another sip of the Budweiser and smiled—a bit scornfully, it seemed to Vickery. "Is that like underworld Uber?"

Vickery decided not to take offense. "I drive people who don't want to be tracked by anybody, dead or alive. *Unter* is German for under—" Castine rolled her eyes to indicate that she knew that; he went on, "—I stay under the radar."

"So you take surface streets and don't go near freeways. Don't get in the *current*." She shrugged. "You can tell a GPS to show you how to get someplace with no use of freeways. What's the big—"

"It's—not that simple. Listen, after we get your phone set up tomorrow morning, I'll drive you back to the storage unit and—" He sighed, then resolutely went on, "—you can borrow my Chevy Blazer, but sometimes you *have* to drive on freeways—evasion, speed—and even on surface streets there's precautions you have to take. I'll explain it all for you. You should get a portable radio—"

"Get it where?" she interrupted, frowning now, "a store with security cameras? The TUA has state-of-the-art facial recognition software, and they're sure to be casting a very fine net, locally, now. And they're onto your car, even with dealer plates on it. Are you cutting me loose?"

Vickery bared his teeth in a grimace. "I'll *get* you the radio—they probably don't have much of a referent for my face in any recognition database—and I'll give you some money, but yes, I'll be cutting you loose tomorrow. You'll be in touch with your fiancé—"

"Maybe."

She didn't speak for a while, occupying herself with the pickled onions and carrots on her plate. Vickery tried without success to think of anything more to say.

"Oh hell, you're right," she said finally. "You've done—you're doing—much more for me than I could have had any right to expect." She gave him a melancholy smile. "I just wish you *could* get hold of an ultralight plane! The TUA's got access to cameras all over the ground—stores and intersections and airports—but the air—it's free of their attention." She laughed softly. "A really big catapult and parachute would do."

Something she had just said had stirred a memory, but Vickery dismissed it for now. "No," he said, "I—I can't. And I can't leave you to hang out in the cemetery all day." He took several deep swallows of the beer and exhaled. "You've got to come with me tomorrow. Galvan's unter cars are masked and secure, and I can claim you're an apprentice driver. It just slipped my mind for a second!—that we're allies."

"Honestly, Herbert, no, you *don't* have to, I'm sure my fiancé will be able to—"

"As soon as he does, I *will* cut you loose. And call me Sebastian now. But—" He held up his hand to stop any further protests. "Give me a minute here."

Castine nodded and took a sip of her own beer.

Vickery looked up and said, carefully, "Something something *thy dominion be, we'll go through air, for sure the air is free.*"

She raised her eyebrows.

"That's what the ghost said to me," Vickery told her, "four years ago, when the motorcade stopped on Wilshire Boulevard and the TUA guys came jumping out of that Suburban like it was on fire or something. I leaned in to see if there was anybody injured inside, and the voice on the radio said that."

She started to laugh, then choked it off. "*That?* 'For sure the air is free'? *That* is what they wanted to kill you for hearing?"

"And 'thy dominion be.' Yes." Vickery looked away from her, the taste of the beer sour now in his mouth. "And as soon as attention was called to my—illicit *intrusion*—"

"Sorry!"

"—Right away a couple of your guys cuffed me and shoved me into another car. They drove me out to the desert by Palmdale, away from any freeway or even paved road, and marched me out into an arroyo with their guns drawn, and if a pickup truck hadn't hit their car parked on the side of the road and distracted them, I'd be dead now instead of them. I nearly was anyway."

Castine, sobered, said nothing.

Vickery recalled that it had been a gray day threatening rain, and there had been puddles in the low spots of the little gulley. When the screech of brakes and jangling crash had shaken the air, the agent on Vickery's left had turned his head in that direction, and Vickery, though handcuffed, had instantly hopped forward and kicked him hard in the groin; and as the man was folding but determinedly raising his gun, Vickery drove the top of his forehead into the man's face. Then with a jarring *bang* a hammer blow knocked Vickery's right leg out from under him and he spun and fell face-up on top of the man he'd kicked and head-butted, his cuffed hands clawing desperately behind him for the man's gun as another gunshot shook the arroyo and a second bullet punched Vickery in the ribs. But he had got hold of the fallen man's gun, and managed to stretch his left arm across his back and partly roll over and fire twice from beside his hip, as a bullet kicked up sand beside him and another jolted the fallen man's body—and then the other agent bowed his head and knelt on the sand, halfway raised his gun again, and finally pitched forward on his face.

Dizzy and shivering, forcing himself not to look yet at the widening stains of bright red blood on his pants and shirt, Vickery had felt the pockets of the dead man beside him and then dug out the handcuff key.

By the time the pickup driver—finally, hesitantly—stepped down into the gulley, Vickery had managed to unlock the cuffs and was tying his belt tightly around his right thigh.

The driver had had a cell phone, and had handed it over when Vickery pulled out his commission wallet and waved his badge and photo ID at him, and with that stranger's phone Vickery had called his onetime LAPD partner and asked for a last enormous favor. Then, after the pickup driver had helped him back up to the road and broken out a first aid kit and applied makeshift field dressings to Vickery's gunshot wounds, the two of them had sat for half an hour in the cab of the crumpled pickup truck. Vickery was holding the gun with which he had killed one of the two dead agents, and conversation was limited. The driver obediently waved away the couple of passing cars that slowed at the sight of the accident, and fortunately neither of them was a random police car. When Vickery's old partner called to say that he was ten minutes away, Vickery had convinced the pickup truck driver that he'd be wise to make a blindfold for himself.

The ex-partner had not wanted to know anything about the

empty car the pickup truck had hit, and reluctantly consented to drive Vickery to the clinic of a veterinarian in Simi Valley who was known to treat gunshot wounds in humans and not report them, and the veterinarian was induced to do it one more time. The ex-partner had given Vickery a hundred dollars and told him never to call him again.

The two bullets proved not to have hit any arteries or vital organs, but Vickery had stayed in the back room of the clinic for a nerve-wracking and monumentally inconvenient week before he could move.

Vickery thought now of the way the shooting this morning had activated his memory of that desperate fight four years ago, and then he shook the memories away and drank the rest of his beer. Castine was chewing another mouthful and staring at him curiously.

"Sorry," she said again.

He waved it off. "You done?" He laid a twenty-dollar bill on the table and bent to pick up his helmet. "We should move on. It's starting to get dark out, and it must be after five by now."

Castine nodded and pushed back her chair, pausing to touch the railing and peer at the wall that crowded right up to it, as if hoping to see through the added-on shop to the lawn that must once have been visible from this now-enclosed porch.

She picked up her helmet and lifted her leather jacket from the chair. "Is that," she asked hesitantly as she slid one arm and then the other into the sleeves, "why *you* could see those people climbing the hill this afternoon? Four years ago, that . . . *intimacy* with those two agents, as your friend Hipple would say?"

"No." Vickery shrugged into his own jacket. "Don't forget our purchases."

He led the way around the other tables to the back door, and when they stepped out into the dirt lot, it was in shadow, and clouds overhead were streaked with a pink glow. A diesel-scented breeze swayed the shaggy tops of palm trees visible over the rooftops.

He unchained the motorcycle, and when he had kicked the engine to life and Castine had got onto the seat, he leaned back and said to her, "Those two agents picked a good place to kill me—or for them to die, as it turned out—far away from any current. No, it's not because of them. I can see ghosts because my wife killed herself on a freeway shoulder, in an intense current, a year before that. Homicide isn't the

only qualifying intimacy." He tromped the gear shift lever into first. "And now we're off to spend the night in a cemetery."

He let out the clutch and bumped across the lot and turned right on Santa Monica Boulevard.

↓ CHAPTER FIVE ↓

Vickery rode past the cemetery entrance and turned left on Gower Street, and halfway down the block he swerved to the right into a narrow alley that faced the back ends of apartment buildings and small-business parking lots. The alley was littered with fast-food bags and fragments of furniture, and Vickery rode along slowly in first gear, passing tiny back gardens and barbed-wire-topped walls and stacks of old tires behind chain link fences, and even one old clapboard house with a green-painted upstairs balcony that must once have overlooked something besides this alley. Vickery thought of the enclosed porch in the For Lease place. They passed through pockets of smells—garbage, flowers, gasoline, teriyaki.

He was considering parking the bike in the gap between an apparently non-functioning panel truck and a fence, but before he reached the next street he saw something that might be better—a stained old mattress that was leaned up against a cinder block wall. He stopped the bike's engine and told Castine to get off, then quickly looked around; there was no one in the alley at the moment, and no faces at the few apartment bathroom windows overhead. He leaned the bike against the wall and dragged the mattress over to it, then dug a jackknife out of his pocket and cut away the fabric and padding on the wall-side of the mattress so that the bike's right handlebar would fit partly in among the springs. He set both helmets on the bike seat and leaned the mattress onto the bike and stepped back.

"There," he told Castine quietly, "nobody'd think there was anything behind that, would they?"

"Even if they did," she said, tucking the bag from Hipple's into her jacket pocket, "I don't think they'd touch that mattress. You should wash your hands."

"Later. Come on."

Vickery led her back down the alley and across Gower, and paused beside the six-foot high cemetery wall.

A row of close-set, outward-curving spikes ran along the top of the wall, hidden in patches by big clusters of bougainvillea dotted with red flowers that were contracting in the dusk, and across the street was a wholesale carpet warehouse, closed for the night. Even in the shadows, the ground floor of the otherwise-gray warehouse was vivid with sprawling graffiti.

Vickery reached in behind a lush curtain of bougainvillea and for several seconds tugged and twisted at something; finally he drew out a yard-long section of two-by-four with five holes drilled along one of the narrow sides. He quickly leaned it against the wall and stood in front of it while several cars drove past.

"Act casual," he said to Castine. "We're just a couple out for a walk."

"Why," asked Castine wearily, "a cemetery?" A cooler evening breeze was drifting up Gower from the south, and she took a deep breath and let it out. "I shouldn't have eaten all those pickled carrots."

"They're acidic. And wandering ghosts seem to be excluded by clusters of stationary ones. Or so the gypsies say, anyway."

At last no car was in sight, and Vickery picked up the board and said, "Give me a boost—make a stirrup."

Castine crouched and cupped her hands, and Vickery stepped up onto them and straightened, and, wobbling for balance, fitted the holes in the two-by-four over five of the wall-top spikes.

He hopped down and made a stirrup of his hands for her. "Up and over," he said, "quick. There's grass on the other side."

Castine muttered, "Shit," but put her right foot into Vickery's hands, and then as he heaved upward she sprang to the two-by-four, gripped it and vaulted over the wall. A few seconds later Vickery jumped, took hold of the length of wood, and pulled himself up; he swung one leg over the board, then crouched on the wall top with his shoes between the bases of the spikes. He tugged the board free, and jumped backward with it.

He landed lightly on the grass and straightened up, and he laid the two-by-four against the inner side of the wall. The cemetery was in dusky shade now, and Vickery and Castine stood in deeper shadow between two of a row of cypresses that paralleled the wall.

"Come on," Vickery whispered, "there's an empty tomb to the south."

"Why empty?" she whispered back. "A salesman's sample? With a *Your Name Here* sign on the front?"

"Somebody thinking ahead. Shut up."

Vickery led the way between standing headstones, glancing frequently across the marble-studded lawn to the north, where the security office was. The only sound was the remote rumble of traffic on Santa Monica Boulevard.

At one point Castine gasped and clutched his arm. "There are people here! A lot of them! I just noticed. All sitting on—or are there?"

Vickery could see them now too. Dim figures were perched motionless on many of the headstones, all simply staring into the dimming sky.

"Don't disturb them," he whispered.

Ahead stood a tomb like a miniature Greek temple no more than twelve feet wide and ten feet tall, and Vickery started toward it, but a burly man in overalls stepped out from behind it and blocked their way.

"Not so fast," he said.

Vickery had a story ready. "We were in the mausoleum," he said quickly, "praying. Did we stay too long? Has the cemetery closed? What time does it close?"

It was hard to see, but the man seemed to be blinking rapidly. "Take a powder, Buttercup," he said.

The man's clothing shifted—now it was a sweater and pale slacks, and there was a dark patch on his face like a moustache. Vickery looked away from the figure's eyes and involuntarily stepped back across the grass; this was a evidently a ghost, and he had never been this close to one before.

He tried to think. It was too dark now to use a spirit level or a fixed compass, and too breezy to hope that a lighter might illuminate the things.

Vickery heard Castine inhale sharply, and he guessed that she had only now understood what this creature was.

The ghost turned to her. "You can stick around, babe."

Vickery's heart was pounding and he groped for something to say. "How old are you?"

"Seven," said the figure standing in front of the tomb. "How old are you?"

Seven was probably the age its atrophied mind recalled most clearly.

"Seven times seven is forty nine," Vickery said. "Forty-nine times seven is—"

Castine cleared her throat and said, in a small voice, "Three-hundred and forty-three."

The ghost shook its head violently, as if to clear it. "Sez you," it muttered. "I can take you."

"This isn't your tomb," said Vickery. "You're a hermit crab, you're not fooling anyone. You have no place."

"Three-hundred and forty-three," repeated Castine, more strongly.

"*No,*" came a deep rumble. "I can *take* you." The figure seemed to swell, or move closer. For a moment its face was Castine's, then Vickery's own, and then the mouth opened impossibly wide, splitting the face back to the ears—and its long tongue sprang out and struck Vickery in the face.

It was icy cold, and it clung; Vickery gripped the squirming cylinder, and his hands froze onto it. His panicky breath was whistling rapidly in and out through his teeth.

"And minus itself," yelled, Castine, "it's nothing! Don't take my word for it—think, do the math yourself. *Nothing.*"

They were out in the open, but the word *Nothing* seemed to call up a ringing echo from the landscape.

The ghost wailed and then imploded with a jarring *whump,* and Vickery fell forward onto his hands and knees on the grass.

His left eye was watering above his stinging cheek, but he blinked around anxiously; the ghost was nowhere to be seen now.

Castine was crouching beside him. "Let's get *out* of here!"

It was easier not to stand up, so Vickery crawled to the steps of the tomb and groped with numb hands in the grass beside the bottom step.

"No," he said breathlessly, then paused to spit; "no good. There's more like him—outside, and I think we're—*conspicuous*—you, anyway. These," he added, waving around at the headstones still dimly visible in the middle distance, "are here because they—just want to sit on their graves." He sat back and shook his head. "There's a key here," he said, "wired to a rock. Find it, I—can't feel anything."

"Where *am* I?" whispered Castine, but she reached past him and patted the grass. "Here's wire—yes, I've got it."

Vickery waved over his head at the tomb's two brass doors. "So unlock it."

She stood up and fitted the key into the lock. Vickery heard the bolt snap back, and then Castine had tugged the left-side door open on silent hinges. A puff of Pine Sol-scented air dispersed on the breeze.

Vickery crawled up the steps and into the marble-floored darkness. "Come in," he said over his shoulder, "and shut the door, all that racket might have alerted security." He looked back and saw Castine hesitating. "The door opens from the inside," he assured her.

She hurried in and closed the door, and the lock clicked. The darkness was absolute. Vickery had sat up against a vertical marble surface, and he was flexing his hands. Enough feeling had returned to them that he was able to reach into his jacket pocket and fumble out a Bic lighter.

"I've got a lighter," he said quietly; "give me your hand and I'll pass it to you."

Her hand bumped his tingling cheek and then found his hand, and a moment later he heard the *thwip* of the flint-wheel, and by the bright brushstroke of flame he could see her sitting a yard away on a patterned marble floor. He was leaning on one of two four-foot tall marble blocks, evidently biers awaiting caskets. High up in the far wall was a window crisscrossed with raised lines, but the picture in the stained glass was indecipherable.

"I never believed they could be—*physical*," said Vickery with a residual shiver. "I knew you could *see* them sometimes, but I thought it was like holograms."

Castine let the flame go out. "You're not supposed to talk to them in complete sentences," she said in the total darkness. In a lower voice she went on, "That thing *might* have taken you if I hadn't split its attention—did you see how its face was mine for a second, then yours? At the TUA, even just with radio speakers, we break our sentences up and have three guys take turns to say each word separately, in sequence."

Vickery nodded, though of course she couldn't see it. "There's sleeping bags behind your bier," he said, "unless the last fugitive to use this place swiped them."

He heard her scuffle on the floor, and then she said, "Yes—yes, two sleeping bags. When do we get new clothes? And I'd pay a hundred dollars to be able to take a shower." Her words had been punctuated by the hitching sound of the zipper on her old leather jacket yielding to tugging.

Vickery wished he'd brought one of the half-pints of Jack Daniel's from his storage unit. He stretched his fingers and then closed his hands in fists; feeling was coming back, and he rubbed his cheek where the ghost's ectoplasmic tongue had struck him.

He managed to unlace his shoes and take them off, and he set them carefully at the end of the pedestal; and he got out of his own leather jacket with little difficulty. "We can hit a thrift store for clothes tomorrow morning, and there's rest-rooms at the car lot."

He hiked himself into the sleeping bag and heard Castine doing the same, and he balled up his jacket for a pillow. For a while neither of them spoke, and the only sounds were slowing breath and shiftings to more relaxed positions.

"I guess we'll be getting up early," came her quiet voice from the darkness. "It's hardly five hours since I . . . took Mike Abbott's life . . . and wrecked my own."

"I do know exactly how that is," said Vickery, not without sympathy.

For several seconds neither of them spoke.

Then he heard paper rustling. "We've got what feels like some bags of peanuts, and four probable Hershey bars," she said, "and little boxes that smell like raisins. You want some?"

"A bag of peanuts, please," he said. He stretched out his hand and moved it around until it bumped Castine's; she rolled her hand over and spread her fingers, pressing a cellophane packet into his palm.

He tore it open with his teeth and picked one object out and popped it into his mouth. "Roasted peanuts," he confirmed, chewing as he shook some more out into his hand. "Thanks."

"De nada." Now he smelled raisins, and guessed that she was eating those.

Again there were several seconds of silence. "There," she said finally, "I've taken off my engagement ring. Do I dare leave it here?"

"I imagine it's hidden enough in your pocket." He touched his wedding ring. *You want to change the aspects of yourselves that ghosts can recognize, so get rid of your rings,* Hipple had said. Will I still dream of Amanda, Vickery thought, if her ghost can't find me?

Not sure if he was saddened or guiltily relieved at the idea, he slowly twisted it off of his finger and tucked it into his pants pocket. It was the first time he'd had the ring off in eleven years.

"I keep wondering how on earth I ended up here," said Castine. "I double-majored in college, criminal law and physics, and the TUA recruited me even before I graduated. Terracotta in person! I was hoping it would be something like forensics, lab work—I've always hated guns."

Vickery contented himself with just saying, "Oh?"

"Yes, ever since I was a little girl. They . . . horrify me. One time my mom told me that my dad was off with his shotgun to shoot skeet, and I started crying because I thought skeets were some little animal, like maybe hamsters. My mom thought I was worried that my dad might get hurt, so she reassured me about how safe it was—she explained that he was on a boat, and there was a catapult that flung the skeets out over the water, so my dad could blast them in mid-air." She laughed softly. "That didn't help."

Vickery smiled in the darkness. "Cute story."

"Oh, I was cute once." After a moment she added, "Several times, probably." He heard her yawn. "And now I do a lot worse than shoot hamsters."

"You saved my life. And Santiago's."

She was quiet for so long then that he thought she'd fallen asleep; but eventually she said, "When we talked on the sidewalk, four years ago on Wilshire Boulevard, after the motorcade stopped to let Obama get his chicken and waffles . . . before the bad stuff happened . . . you told me about going to Latin Mass. Do you go to Confession too?"

Vickery sighed silently. "Sometimes. And you said you'd been raised Catholic."

"I'm impressed you remember. Right now I feel as if I should be saying my prayers, sleeping in a tomb after all this." He heard the fabric of her sleeping bag slide on the marble; perhaps she was braced up on one elbow. "Did you and your wife have any kids?"

"No," he said, a bit hoarsely. And it was my fault, he thought, and she killed herself. "No."

"Oh." He heard her shift again, and he guessed that she was thinking about his wife's suicide. It sounded as if she were speaking toward the ceiling when she went on, "Terracotta says people can't help what they do, any more than a rock rolling down a hill can. The rock might *think* it has a choice about rolling left or right, just like people think they choose what they do, but really it's all just physics."

"I guess he can't help but say that."

She laughed again, quietly. "Right, no choice. In one of his books he wrote, *free will is a fiction,* and he liked it when a misprint made it, *free will is affectation.* He says consciousness is pointless—what's the use of a *you,* when all you can do is watch what your body does and says? Sometimes he seems surprised by what he does—though he'd say surprise is useless too."

"*He* sounds useless."

"I wish. Sometimes I think somebody or something finds him very useful." She yawned audibly. "Good night."

"Good night."

Vickery closed his eyes. The numbness in his hands had worn off, but now his right palm flexed with the remembered texture and weight of the gun he had picked up from the alley pavement immediately after Castine shot the Mike Abbott fellow. Jack Hipple had that gun now, but it had been a .40 caliber SIG-Sauer P229, and at the Secret Service training course in Laurel, Maryland, Vickery had shot thousands of rounds through pistols just like it.

And he recalled the recoil of firing the fallen TUA agent's gun in the arroyo four years ago, with his wrists in handcuffs and his left arm twisted across his back—and the hammer-blow impacts of the other agent's bullets hitting him in the thigh and ribs. He remembered that the impacts had been disorienting and strength-sapping, but they hadn't actually *hurt* as much as the wax-filled plastic "Simunition" bullets used in the Secret Service training courses.

At last he fell asleep.

He didn't dream of Amanda; instead he dreamed that he was at a crowded table in a bar, and for a long time he couldn't make out the faces of the others at the table, nor remember where this place was. The conversation was lively and loud, and the words his companions spoke were in English, but Vickery wasn't able to fit them together into comprehensible sentences. Eventually he heard explosions and gunfire from the street outside—but none of his companions paused in their conversation, and he realized at last that this was the King Tiki Bar, one of the fake buildings in Hogan's Alley at the Rowley Training Center in Michigan. Hogan's Alley was a specially constructed tactical village, like a Hollywood set, in which Secret Service agents were confronted with various simulated attacks and trained in how to react; so of course the gun-battle outside was not real. But even though his tablemates went on talking as energetically as ever, Vickery now saw that their shirts and blouses were blotted with blood, and when one of the men turned to face him, the previously averted half of his face was just a gory crater. Vickery touched his own face just as the other man did the same, and he knew that he was looking into a mirror on the wall.

In the moments before he forced himself to open his eyes to the darkness of the tomb, all the people at the table fell silent, and then began to sing, very softly, an old song that he knew—and as he rolled over in his sleeping bag on the marble floor, he remembered what it was: "Where Have All The Flowers Gone?"

And though he was now awake, he was still hearing it.

The tomb was not completely dark; a faint glow of ambient city light made a narrow upright rectangle of the door, interrupted by the standing silhouette of Castine.

He saw her head turn in profile. "You're awake?" she whispered. "Check this out."

Vickery crawled out of the sleeping bag and stood up, and the floor was cold through his socks as he crossed to stand beside her.

The singing was more audible from the doorway, though still very faint. Vickery rubbed his eyes and peered out across the cemetery, and each of the tombstone-perching ghosts that he could make out was swaying gently, and the spots that were their mouths were wide; it was the ghosts that were singing. He thought some of the frail voices seemed to be those of children.

Standing in the doorway of a tomb under the infinite night sky, Vickery shivered as he listened to this secret chorus of the dead in the middle of the sleeping city, and he was glad that Castine was beside him.

She took his arm, as if for support. "The poor things," she whispered.

The two of them stood there, breathing quietly in the night air, and the voices faded and returned and faded again like the scent of jasmine on the breeze. The lyrics of the song made it natural for the last stanza to lead to the first again, and the slow, melancholy song seemed likely to continue until dawn.

Finally Castine stepped back and looked at Vickery. He nodded, and she closed the door.

Back in his sleeping bag he went to sleep quickly, and was aware of nothing until he was awakened by someone shaking his shoulder.

After the events and memories and dreams of the day before, he awoke—as he had awakened a hundred times in his years as a Secret Service agent—anxiously wondering what country he was in and when he was expected to report for duty.

"Sebastian," came Castine's whisper, and that brought him back to his current situation. "It's dawn through the keyhole."

"Right." He sat up and ran his fingers through his disordered hair. "Right. Let's stash the sleeping bags and get back to the bike. How does breakfast at the For Lease place sound?"

He heard her shuffling around. "What do they serve for breakfast?"

"Same as last night, I imagine. They never really close."

"I'll skip the carrots this time."

↓ CHAPTER SIX ↓

The Galvan lot just off Normandie at Eighth Street was a half-acre of asphalt bounded on three sides by a wide car-repair bay and two low office buildings with windows painted over white, and on the street side by a chain link fence masked with green netting. At 7 AM the gate was already rolled back, and Vickery rode his motorcycle up the driveway and between two rows of cars and stopped it in front of an old silver Airstream trailer. Castine swung a leg over the seat and stepped away from the bike, and Vickery switched off the engine. The chilly morning breeze smelled of coffee and gasoline.

He gave Castine his phone—"You'll need it to activate yours," he told her—and directed her toward the restroom in the nearest building, then stepped up into the trailer.

Shelves crowded with file boxes, a glowing electric heater, and clocks set to various times surrounded a metal desk in front of him; on the desk were a computer monitor and keyboard and several motionless metronomes, and behind it sat a bald man in a sweatshirt.

The man looked up, then put on a pair of reading glasses and peered at the monitor. "Vickery," he said, "looking even crappier than usual, car five. You've got Bradley Arnold, pickup at 8:30. You've had him before."

"Sure, the guy who's afraid ghosts will read his mind. Pick him up at his house in Encino, take him to LAX, right? Delta departure terminal."

"Right. See if you can't shave first."

Vickery nodded. "Oh, and Tom, I want to take a copilot along—a trainee, if she works out."

"A . . . copilot."

"Right."

"*Trainee.*" Tom said it as if he might have to look the word up in a dictionary. "Has Galvan interviewed her?"

"Not yet. This girl wants to see what the work's like before she applies."

"Huh. Girlfriend?"

"Well, yeah," said Vickery, since it implied that he was fairly well acquainted with her. "Galvan does hire people sometimes," he added mildly.

"I've seen it happen." Tom scratched his scalp and then nodded toward the metronomes. "I gather she can see. You vouch for her?"

"Yes. And she can see stuff as well as I can."

Tom shrugged. "Well, Arnold is a routine job. Be sure she knows not to talk during the ride." He pulled a slip of paper out of a drawer and scribbled on it. "Have her fill the rest of it out," he said, handing it across the desk, "and get it back to me when you return the car."

"Right." Vickery hopped down from the trailer and nodded to another driver who was just stepping in. The top floors of the building on the west side shone with slanting sunlight against a blue sky, but he could see the steam of his breath, and he walked across the yard to the open-fronted repair bay where several urns of coffee stood on a wheeled cart.

He was finishing his third cup when Castine walked up beside him and handed him back his phone.

He concluded from her expression that she'd seen better restrooms. "At least there's an electric outlet," she said. "I got my phone activated, and it's charging."

"I told the yard manager that you're a trainee. Oh, and I said you're my girlfriend."

She looked annoyed. "I suppose you had to."

"It means I know you well enough to vouch for you." He rocked his head thoughtfully. "And we did spend the night together."

"In a goddamn *tomb.*" She sighed and zipped up her jacket, with some difficulty. "And there was that dinner, and that *breakfast.* You sure lay on the style for a girl."

He smiled wryly. "Under other circumstances I could probably do better."

"Actually," she said, then hesitated and touched his arm; "actually you did very well. I—I'm grateful."

"*Actually*," he said, bemused to realize that it was true, "I am too, in a way."

She gave him a surprised look. "Grateful that I messed up your life here?"

"That you . . . *shook up* my life here. It was getting a bit stagnant."

"You said yesterday that we're allies, but not friends. *Allies* is conditional, situational." She shrugged. "*Friends* lasts better."

"Yes," he said; then, "Yes, it does."

She opened her mouth to say something more, but—

"Vickery!" came a yell from behind him. He looked over his shoulder and saw Tom leaning out of the trailer. "Priority assignment. Car number two. Right now." Tom nodded emphatically and disappeared back inside.

"Okay, don't say anything," Vickery told Castine, tossing his plastic cup into a trash can, "just walk beside me and look confident."

"Are we leaving? My phone's in the rest room."

Vickery exhaled impatiently. "We shouldn't separate at this point. I'll walk with you, but we gotta walk fast. And there's a USB port in the car." They hurried to the nearby building, and at the restroom door Vickery said, "Give me your gun—they'll take them, but I don't want these guys to think you've been carrying."

She passed it to him and he stuck it into his left jacket pocket as she opened the door and went in, and a moment later she was out again, carrying her phone and charger.

"And stash that stuff." Vickery took her elbow and led her at a trot back to the bay.

Out on the pavement, a bearded attendant in coveralls was holding a red tablet like an iPad, and he waved Vickery over.

"Rush job," the man said. "Specified our best driver available, which at the moment is you. If you're carrying, leave it with the mechanic."

"Okay. Who's going to take Arnold to the airport?"

"Tom'll find somebody." The tablet the man was holding was an old Etch-A-Sketch, and he held it out toward Vickery. On the gray screen, spelled out in fine, jittery black lines, were the words VALERO AT WESTERN + FRANKLIN.

Vickery read it and nodded, and the man turned the thing upside down and shook it.

Vickery walked with Castine across the pavement to the left side of the bay, where one of the mechanics was pulling a cloth cover off of a new Ford Taurus.

Castine audibly choked back a laugh and whispered to him, "That's, uh, car two?"

Even for Vickery it was hard to recognize the vehicle as a Ford Taurus—the vinyl decals that covered every inch of the car's body were no thicker than a coat of paint, but big full-color photorealistic faces printed on them made it look swollen. The darkly tinted windshield and windows were the only evident geometry on the car.

Vickery mouthed *Shut up,* then pulled the two .45s out of the side pockets of his jacket and laid them on a workbench.

"Note the hardware," he called to the mechanic.

The man raised his eyebrows at the pair of guns. "You carrying now, Vick?" he said, then shrugged. "Consider 'em tagged and stashed."

Vickery stepped around the car and opened the gaudy passenger door for Castine, and the attendant came hurrying up as she got in.

"Whoa. Who's she?"

Vickery showed him the piece of paper that the yard manager had signed. "Copilot. I guess this is an important fare."

The attendant peered at the paper, then just said, "Okay, fine." He waved the Etch-A-Sketch toward the driveway. "Git."

Vickery closed Castine's door and got in on the driver's side. The key was in the ignition, and ten seconds later he had driven across the lot and was turning right onto Eighth Street. A radio was attached to the dashboard above the car's radio, and both were on and tuned to K-Earth 101.

Castine fitted the USB plug from her charger into a port on the console, then turned to Vickery and touched her ear and raised an eyebrow.

"No," Vickery said, "part of what the customers pay for is the assurance that the cars are never bugged." He glanced at her phone. "If your man calls while the fare's in the car, tell him to call you back in half an hour and then let the fare see you power down the phone."

"I might just ask you to pull over and let me out."

"That'd be better, really. If you do, I'll come back for you after I drop him or her off."

"I've *got* to get in touch with Eliot as soon as possible. Can we turn the radios down?"

Vickery reached out and turned both volume knobs down slightly. The music was still clearly audible. "It's like a police radio," he said, "I need to be able to hear it."

"It's an old David Bowie song."

"Yes."

"O-kay." She tapped the screen of her phone and held it to her ear. "Are you going to get in trouble, pretending the yard manager okayed me coming along on this fare?"

"Maybe. Not much."

"I'm sorry."

Vickery turned north on Western Avenue. "I owe you. I couldn't just leave you there at the lot."

"Baltimore, Maryland," she said into the phone; and a few moments later, "Minerva's Flowers." She gave Vickery an empty look. He glanced at the traffic ahead, and then at the oil pressure and battery gauge needles and the little ivory-capped metronome on the dashboard. They were all reassuringly straight up and steady.

"Hi," said Castine, "on the third floor of your building is the office of Eliot Shaw—I said *Eliot Shaw*—and if you give him this message he'll pay you a hundred dollars, if you say I told him to. Have you got a pencil? Yes yes, it's David Bowie. What? 'Modern Love,' I think. Pencil? The message is, call Ingrid at 818-555-3933, urgent. Hm? *3933.* Yes, I'm Ingrid." For several seconds she didn't speak, then went on, "You're risking a trip up the elevator against the likelihood of a hundred bucks. Good, thanks."

She tapped the phone again and laid it on the console. "That wasn't easy. Why do you have to listen to two radios? Or even one?"

"One has batteries in it, the other works off the car's electrical system. If they get out of synch—usually on a freeway, in the current—you know you're in a strong amplified possibility field. Then you better stay in your lane, keep your speed the same as everybody else, and hope your car doesn't stall or start misfiring."

"I always hope that. Why especially?"

"Oh—a lot of things can go wrong in a strong field. The engine, the tires, other drivers. Dust devils, sudden sandstorms." He smiled briefly. "They say you and your car can even disappear right off the freeway, and you find yourself in the afterlife."

"You mentioned something like that yesterday."

"Right, some guy in the 1960s supposedly did it, and eventually came back through the omphalos on the Pasadena Freeway to tell about it. Without his car. He'd done a hit-and-run and he had a concussion, and his engine was screwed up and he was on the freeway shoulder, going a lot slower than the other cars, see, so he was generating a little field, and he was the same sort as you and me—he was one of the people who can see ghosts." He steered quickly around a Metro bus. "And so he took an offramp that wasn't exactly there, in terms of our reality, at least. And he and his car just vanished from this world."

"That's something to . . . *worry* about?"

"Well, no. There's stories of it happening a time or two since, but there's lots of urban myths around this stuff. I'll believe it when I see it."

She shifted in her seat and glanced impatiently at her phone. "I suppose the faces all over this car are supposed to be that weird valley."

"Uncanny valley, right. It's an ad for some shampoo, but Lady Galvan likes it because the faces all look just slightly fake." He tapped the steering wheel. "This is her main stealth car, not cheap to hire—the coolant is changed after every trip, though that's really just to impress the customers, and the tires are run-flats with support rings inside them and they're rotated and reversed every time, and filled with air that's brought from Nevada in scuba tanks . . . the air filter is full of dust from Oregon or somewhere . . . even the name *Taurus* is supposed to scare ghosts away. We're way more shielded from ghost attentions in this than we were last night in the cemetery."

"This must be like driving the presidential limousine. 'The Beast,' as they call it."

"Secret Service guys never called it that. We all just called it Limo One. And I was never PPD, Presidential Protective Division; I was always just standing post at the curb as they drove by, or manning a restroom along the route. The PPD were a very elite group—we used to say they each carried two holsters, one for their gun and one for their hair-dryer."

"Manning a restroom?"

"You bet. Several restrooms along the route have to have Secret Service guys in place, with entries and corridors cleared, in case the President stops the motorcade to go to the bathroom."

"Did he ever?"

"Not in any restroom I was in charge of. But I'd have been there if he had, ready to hand him a paper towel."

"I hope he'd have tipped you. Oh, *when* is Eliot going to call? Eventually we're going to have to get out of this clown car—we've ditched our rings, but when do we get old shoes and foolish clothes?"

"After we drop this fare we can find a thrift store."

"And remember to wear our watches on the other wrist," she said, "set to the wrong time." She raised her left hand and spread her now-bare fingers. "We'll probably wish we'd got those pogo sticks."

Vickery was looking at his own bare left hand on the steering wheel, and he remembered the dream he'd had two nights ago—the dream which had led the TUA to him.

In that dream he and Amanda had been hang-gliding over Sylmar in the San Fernando Valley, launching from the summit slope of Kagel Mountain and spiraling on thermal updrafts in the rotating sunlight; her orange-winged glider had stayed above and ahead of his own left wingtip as the green mountains and patchwork city slowly turned below them, and several times she had smiled across at him before finally banking out of the updraft and swooping away to the east to begin the loop down to the landing zone. He had banked his red-striped white wing to follow her, and in the dream he had known that lunch and beer and affectionate conversation awaited them down there on the grass.

Watching the traffic ahead of them on Western now, he wondered if another dream might pick up where that one had left off.

He was approaching the Franklin intersection, and the turquoise Valero gas station sign was visible on the right. He steered into the lot, and even as he braked he saw a tall, silver-haired man in a business suit hurrying across the asphalt toward them.

The man opened the rear passenger door and folded himself into the car; clearly he had been told what car to expect. "Church of the Blessed Sacrament," he said as he pulled the door shut, "on Sunset, but the parking lot is at the north end, off of Selma."

"I know where it is," said Vickery, driving across the lot to make a left turn onto Franklin. Peripherally he saw Castine give a slight nod.

"I'll stay on Franklin to avoid the traffic on Hollywood," said Vickery, "and then take Highland down to Selma." It was standard protocol to announce the route to a fare, like a pool player calling shots. "ETA is 8:45."

The man in the back seat simply stared out the side window at the elm trees and old apartment buildings. He didn't remark on the music.

When Vickery had turned south on Highland and was driving through the crowded Hollywood Boulevard intersection—wondering how crowded the sidewalks might appear to someone not able to see ghosts—a repeated buzzing sound that wasn't from the radios made him glance across at Castine with a frown.

She raised her eyebrows and spread her hands, and a moment later Vickery realized that the sound had come from the back seat.

"Yes," said their passenger; "I'm in a shielded car now, they always have music on. No, I'll get in touch. I don't want to go anywhere near the 710 yet, but I may check in at Hsaio later in the day."

Vickery was aware that Castine had stiffened in the seat beside his, but he didn't glance at her, and the passenger didn't speak again until Vickery had turned onto Selma and driven into the church parking lot and stopped. Ahead to the left were the arches of the parish school, to the right a white building with a red-tile roof, possibly the rectory, and between and beyond these stood the tan Renaissance-style church with its bell tower and tall stained-glass windows.

The man got out of the car and began walking toward the back entrance to the church. Castine unfastened her seat belt and knelt on the seat to reach back and pull the rear door closed.

"He's with TUA!" she said breathlessly when she had resumed her seat. "Hsaio is the building their offices are in, in Westwood, and the Extension is right off the 710."

Vickery's chest was suddenly cold. "You think he recognized you? We should take off."

"No, I've never seen him before, and I don't think he even looked at me. I didn't look at him, except through the tinted glass when he walked to the car. He's probably from the D.C. central office, and they don't come west much."

The man had disappeared around the corner of the church. "You're okay then," Vickery said.

But Castine opened her door and swung her legs out of the car. "I've got to see who he's meeting."

Vickery sat up straight and unfastened his own seatbelt. "No you don't! Are you crazy? What difference does it make who he's meeting?"

He opened his door and stepped out. The sun was over the tops of the apartment buildings to the east, and Vickery blinked in the sudden glare.

Castine was standing on the other side of the car now, and spoke quietly and urgently across the garish roof. "He's got to be from the D.C. office, and he hasn't checked in at Hsaio or the Extension! This is covert, off the record. If he's meeting one of the top men *here*, like Wheeler, or Ollie or Brett, it's got to be because Terracotta's been acting so screwy lately, ignoring espionage taskings to concentrate on the desert highway afterlife—getting all paranoid about your dumb 'air is free' poem—" She shook her head impatiently. "If they do catch me before Eliot can rescue me, knowing about this meeting could be a bargaining chip."

"They won't catch you, I—wait, dammit!"

But she was walking rapidly away, her shoes knocking on the asphalt, toward the church. He started after her, then stopped. It would be no use getting into a physical struggle with her here. And, belatedly, it occurred to him that either party at this meeting might have arranged for backup; depending on the location of any such, his face might very well have been scrutinized by now. With luck any watcher was behind him.

He walked backward to the car, keeping his face turned toward the church as if he were just staring after Castine, and when he bumped against the fender he opened the driver's door and got in. He shut the door and then peered around through the tinted windows at the other cars in the lot, and the nearby apartment buildings and the rectory and the parish school, calculating the best locations for watchers. The only person readily visible was a little girl in a straw hat and overalls, standing by a row of bushes in front of an apartment building a hundred feet away to his left; she had not been there when he drove in, and she seemed to be staring directly at him, but she could hardly be TUA.

He concluded that an open gallery over the arches on the ground floor of the school would be the best place from which to watch the whole parking lot and be close enough to act. Vickery stared at the gallery, and after a few long seconds he saw movement; and then a dark-haired head and a white T-shirt were briefly visible moving from one pillar to another.

Even at this distance through the tinted windshield he recognized the boy Santiago.

Vickery sat back and chewed a knuckle, frowning. Santiago was only slightly more likely to be working for the TUA than the little girl was, but the boy would hardly be here if he wasn't doing some watching or courier job for somebody. And his position meant that he must certainly have recognized Vickery.

The car's two radios were playing a Tom Petty song now, and were still synchronized, and the dashboard metronome was motionless—at least there was no supernatural field in the immediate locality. The song ended and a Culture Club song started—"Karma Chameleon," and Vickery wondered if it was ironic.

Castine was visible now, alone, walking in his direction from the church. She wasn't hurrying, and she spread her hands to the sides and shook her head.

Apparently the meeting was over and the principals had left, no doubt on Sunset at the south side of the church. Vickery got out of the car without glancing toward Santiago, and he walked diagonally across the lot toward Castine, on a line that would take him close to the ground floor arches of the school.

When he was still a few yards short of meeting Castine, and directly below the gallery where Santiago hid, he stopped.

"I think you could come down here, Santiago," he said.

After a pause he heard, "Okay. Since you still owe me ten dollars."

Castine glanced upward in surprise. "That kid?" Turning to Vickery, she said quietly, "The other party was nobody from TUA. Some old guy with a white beard, on crutches. They left by the front— the TUA guy got in a car that pulled over on Sunset as soon as they walked out, and the old guy headed for a bus stop."

Vickery could hear the boy's shoes scuffing on stairs, and a moment later Santiago stepped out from one of the arches into the sunlight.

Santiago's hand was extended, and Vickery tugged a bill free of the roll in his pocket; it was a twenty, and he gave it to the boy.

"The extra ten is for not telling anybody we were here," Vickery said.

Santiago grinned and shook his head. "I got fifty to watch."

Vickery pulled three more twenty dollar bills from his pocket and held them up.

"I dunno."

"She saved your life yesterday! That guy was going to shoot you as you rode away."

Santiago shrugged, then snatched the bills and stood on one foot for a moment while he tucked them into one of his worn tennis shoes. Vickery went on, "Who was the old guy with the beard and crutches?"

"*Yo no creo* you got enough for that."

Santiago glanced toward the apartment building on the east side of the parking lot and then cocked an eyebrow at Vickery.

Looking in that direction, Vickery saw that the little girl was still standing by the bushes. "Do you know who she is?" he asked.

Castine squinted quickly in that direction. "Who? Where?"

Santiago had stepped back to one of the arches, and now got onto his bicycle. "Maybe!" he called, and began pedaling away across the parking lot.

"Who?" repeated Castine. "We shouldn't be seen."

"That girl by the—well, she's gone now. Anyway, just a kid."

"Okay, just so—" Abruptly Castine began slapping at her clothes, and then she juggled her phone out of a pocket and flipped it open. "Yes, hello? Eliot! Thank God." She caught Vickery's eye and waved toward the car, and he nodded and walked away from her.

He had got in and started the engine by the time she returned to the car. When she was seated and had closed the door and fastened her seatbelt, he put the car into gear and steered around toward the Selma entrance.

"How'd it go?" he asked.

Castine was looking out the side window. "He'll meet me tomorrow."

"That's good. We can hit a thrift store for uncharacteristic clothes on the way back to Galvan's lot, and we should have a lot of . . . oh, pickles and chocolate in soy sauce for lunch, to keep our intimate ghosts from noticing us. And tonight I'd advise just—"

"Ugh," she interrupted. "I'll do without lunch."

"Well, I didn't mean literally. Anything acidic—spicy Thai take-out would probably do. Tell me about this white-bearded old guy who met your TUA agent."

"The two of them were talking up by the altar at first, and I came in through the front, and I hurried into one of the confessionals and pulled the door nearly shut. Then they walked back and sat down in a pew not far from me. They talked for just a minute or so, arguing, and then they left."

"Could you hear them talking?"

"A bit. A few phrases."

"Well?"

"I really can't tell you. I'm still a TUA agent, at the moment."

Vickery suppressed his irritation. Nothing to be gained by arguing, he told himself. "Okay."

He had stopped at Selma to let a couple of cars pass, and Castine leaned over and kissed him on the cheek.

"Thank you, uh, Sebastian," she said, sitting back. "For all the things you've done for me here. When I'm gone, I want you to know I do truly appreciate it. Most guys wouldn't have taken me under their wing the way you have."

My broken, melting-wax wing, Vickery thought. He steered onto the street, heading east. "I've mostly enjoyed it, actually," he admitted, "having someone I can talk to about everything." He refrained from emphasizing the last word, and impulsively added, "I'll miss you."

"I'll miss you too," she said, almost too quietly to hear. She took a deep breath and let it out in a low whistle. "Let's go get our dumb costumes."

↓ CHAPTER SEVEN ↓

Terracotta had stayed up all night, through three shifts of radio monitors, but Brett had gone home to his apartment at 2 AM, and when he stepped into the office promptly at eight this morning, freshly shaved and smelling of Paco Rabanne cologne, Terracotta put down the purple pen with which he'd been scrawling notes on the whiteboard.

"We haven't found Castine," he told Brett in a husky whisper. "I need you to confirm, verify, something with the Westwood office."

Through the long night hours Terracotta had been reminding himself that guilt—and love too—were meaningless spasms in the consciousness, which itself was a superfluous delusion.

He had been working with Ingrid Castine for seven years, ever since he had recruited her as a graduate student at UCLA, and there had always been a mental sensation of pleasure when she had entered a room he was in; he had often noticed that his attention was drawn to the grassy smell of her hair, the light range of her voice when she spoke, the little folds in her lower eyelids which always made her seem to be about to smile.

Terracotta shook his head to dismiss the useless and distracting thoughts, and felt a tap at the back of his neck; the elastic band that held his pony tail had broken. He went on "We need to . . . Abbott has been asking for backup, as much as he's asked for anything. We need to get another agent over to where he is." Terracotta could feel sweat on his forehead.

Brett raised his eyebrows and stepped back. "Oh yeah? Who?"

"Oh God," Terracotta burst out, "who do you think?" Even in his meaningless unhappiness it surprised him to hear himself refer to the imaginary deity.

"You wouldn't be this upset over Ollie or one of the radio monitors. Or me. Castine?"

"Yes, yes." Terracotta's damp gray hair had tumbled down around his shoulders, and he looked vaguely toward the desk for another elastic band. "She's been with Woods for too long now, the chances are too great that he has tainted her, told her what he heard in that motorcade four years ago."

"The lustful bull stuff, right." Brett shrugged. "Well, she did put Abbott there, so I guess it's only fair. Do you know where she is?"

"I know where she probably will be. I've told Westwood that I need a countermeasures team to . . . be there, and put her over. Today, this morning." Terracotta watched his hand pick up a couple of paper clips; was he going to try to hold his hair back with them? "But the mullahs at the Hsaio building, they say they need *confirmation* of the order from a senior agent here! When we've done this, I'm going to have to remind them of my authority. I'll brook no trout." He blinked. "Argument, I mean." His fingers were pulling one of the paper clips open, straightening one end of the short length of wire.

Brett stared at him. "A full team? Shooter and three backup cars?"

"Yes. Yes."

"Chief," said Brett slowly, "I think you should get some sleep first. Have the countermeasures team just grab and hold her. We can always—"

"No, damn it, don't you see? She might taint *them*. The toxic malmeme mustn't spread among our people." He blinked rapidly. "I can sleep and function at the same time." I seem to do it a lot, in fact, he thought. "*Call Westwood*, will you? They tell me they can assemble the team. There's not a lot of time."

Brett stared at him impassively, or speculatively, for several seconds; then he nodded. "Okay, sure. We could use Castine over there with Abbott—she's always been good at talking to deleted persons from this side, maybe she'll be as good at talking to *us* from *that* side." He looked away toward the much-scribbled whiteboard and said, "And I'll tell them they don't need me to ratify your orders."

Holding the still-curled end of the paper clip, Terracotta pressed the straight end into the tip of his right thumb until it punctured the skin. "It's all just physics," he said hollowly, "all of us."

Vickery steered the Taurus into the Galvan lot and parked it near the Airstream trailer, and when he had got out he opened the passenger door for Castine, whose arms were around a large paper bag. He took the bag from her and she climbed out and stretched, blinking in the sunlight.

"You can change first," she said. "I'll be over there having coffee."

Vickery closed her door and pressed the lock button on the key fob, then looked around at the several drivers and mechanics in the lot; he didn't see Tom the yard manager or the attendant who had directed him to the car an hour ago.

"Okay," he said. "I'll be quick—try not to talk much to anybody. You're my girlfriend and you're thinking of applying for a job here, that's all. If you speak Spanish, pretend you don't."

She nodded, and he started away toward the rest room, carrying the bag with their newly purchased used clothing and shoes. As he reached the door, Castine came hurrying up to him. "I left my phone under the seat," she said, "can I have the key for a minute?"

He braced the bag against his chest with one arm and reached into his pocket with his free hand. "Here you go. Lock it again after."

"Sure." She took two steps, then turned back and said quickly, "When I hid in the confessional? The phrase I heard one of them say was, 'exchange of force-carrying particles.' I think it was the old bearded man talking."

"Oh," said Vickery. "Okay, thanks."

"I—do hate keeping secrets from you." She blinked at him, then turned away.

"Uh, good," he said to her retreating back.

He opened the restroom door and set the bag on the closed toilet seat, then shut and bolted the door and began unbuttoning his shirt. He reckoned he could bathe, in a makeshift way, with soap and wet paper towels, if there were a lot of paper towels in the dispenser. He glanced wryly the bag of clothes; from among the random stock at a thrift store on Gower he had selected a pair of brown corduroy bell bottom trousers, a pair of Reebok tennis shoes that someone had once decided ought to be painted green, and a woman's flannel shirt because it buttoned right-over-left. He was looking forward to seeing Castine in the jeans and Hello Kitty T-shirt she had reluctantly settled on.

He had just started to unlace his boots when someone rattled the door and then pounded on it.

"Vickery!" came Tom's shout. *"Your girlfriend just drove away in car two!"*

Vickery's face was suddenly cold, and a couple of thoughts flickered through his mind: She lied to me about meeting her fiancé tomorrow—clearly she's meeting some trusted associate of his today; and she has now completely succeeded in wrecking the life I've made for myself during these last four years.

Luckily there's an iPhone under the dashboard of car two.

He quickly put his leather jacket back on, then unbolted the door and pulled it open. Tom's face was red and contorted with rage and a bit of fear, and his bald head was gleaming.

"She misunderstood me," Vickery said as he retied the laces of his boots. "I told her we need to top up the gas tank, but I meant she should wait for me. I'll give her a call and get her back here."

"Fuck that! I've got 'Turo tracking her. Trainee! I never even okayed her to go along on that fare!" Vickery had stepped past the furious yard manager and was buttoning his shirt as he strode across the asphalt toward the repair bay. Tom, puffing along right behind him, went on, "I want *you* off this lot *now!*"

Vickery nodded and waved without looking back, and a couple of the mechanics moved warily aside as he stepped in out of the sunlight.

"My guns," he said to one of them.

Tom was still following him, and now shook his head at the mechanic. "Not till that car's back here!"

Vickery could see the backstrap of one of the .45s on the usual holding shelf a few yards away, and he walked over to it and pulled it down and yanked the string tag off the trigger guard. He drew the slide back far enough to see that there was a round in the chamber, then let it snap back.

"Hold onto the other one as collateral," he told Tom as he tucked the gun into the side pocket of his jacket. He walked back out into the sunlight and headed for the trailer.

The trailer door was open, and Vickery hopped up the steps and ducked inside. 'Turo was at the desk, hunched over an iPad, and Vickery recognized the *Find My iPhone* app on the screen. Galvan didn't use the LoJack system because it brought the police into the situation.

Vickery leaned over the desk and picked up the iPad.

"I'll do it, 'Turo," he said as he turned toward the door. "It was my fuck-up."

Tom tried to block his way, but Vickery shouldered him aside and jumped down to the pavement. He shoved the iPad into his jacket and got onto the Husqvarna motorcycle, and he had the key in the ignition and had kicked the motor to roaring life before Tom could decide on a way to stop him. Vickery's foot hit the gear-shift pedal and the bike leaped forward.

He had hung his helmet with his sunglasses in it on the left handlebar grip, and it swung awkwardly and made working the clutch difficult, but he rode the bike out of the lot and a block down Eighth before he slowed and looked into one of the rear view mirrors. No cars had yet emerged from the Galvan lot, so he quickly leaned the bike into a right turn that took him across a 7-Eleven parking lot and around behind the store, where he braked to a halt beside a Dumpster.

He pulled the iPad out of his jacket and turned it on, and after he swiped aside the opening screen he saw a map of this area of Los Angeles, with a pulsing blue dot moving south on Western Avenue. He slid it back inside his jacket, and took a deep breath and let it out; then he put on his sunglasses and helmet, clicked the bike into gear and left the lot by a driveway onto a side street. He'd soon be able to loop around to Western, and on the motorcycle he would be able to catch up to her before long.

And ten minutes later he had found her.

He was now stopped halfway along a narrow jogging path on a slope below the Contreras High School football field; to his right the slope descended further, to a curve of a street called Emerald, and the gaudy Taurus was idling at the curb down there.

Vickery knew that a stairway led down from where she was parked to a narrow cul-de-sac off of 2nd Street. He guessed that she was supposed to meet her fiancé's associate down on the cul-de-sac, and, out of caution, had arrived early for the appointment and parked where she could watch the rendezvous point from above. He reflected that it wasn't the greatest neighborhood—the sidewalks on Emerald Street were scattered with broken couches and old TV sets, and he wasn't happy that the 110 freeway was only a quarter mile away to the east.

He pressed the Home button on the iPad, but before turning the thing off, he impulsively touched the Google icon and tapped in:

"thy dominion be" "air is free"

The results that came up all seemed to have to do with James Joyce's book, *A Portrait of the Artist as a Young Man,* and he tapped one of them and took several quick glances at the screen while keeping his main attention on the Taurus.

There was something in the online text about "Daedalus the artificer" doing violence to nature, which was no apparent help, and then he noticed that his remembered phrases were part of a passage from Ovid that was quoted in the text. In hasty, interrupted snatches he read the passage:

In tedious exile now too long detain'd
Daedalus languish'd for his native land:
The sea foreclos'd his flight; yet thus he said:
Tho' Earth and water in subjection laid,
O cruel Minos, thy dominion be,
We'll go tho' air; for sure the air is free.
Then to new arts his cunning thought applies,
And to improve the work of Nature tries.

He closed the Google window, turned the iPad off and tucked it back into his jacket; then he pulled his phone out of his shirt pocket and punched in the number of Castine's burner phone.

After a buzz, the line clicked and he heard her say, tensely, "Hello?" He could hear music in the background.

"Hi, Ingrid," he said. "Where are you?"

"I'm driving, I'm on . . . Hollywood Boulevard, I can't talk." She paused, then went on in a rush, "Oh, I'm sorry, Herbert! Sebastian! I lied to you, actually Eliot told me to rendezvous with a friend of his today, at ten. This guy can drive me fast to . . . out of the state, and Eliot will meet me. I'm sorry I'm leaving you in a jam, after we—after how kind you've been to me!—but I couldn't let anyone know, and

Terracotta probably has Abbott's ghost looking for me and I needed this stealth car; and I'll have Eliot get you out of trouble, I promise. I suppose your boss has reported it as stolen, but when I meet Eliot's friend I'll tell you where Galvan's car is."

I can *see* where it is, Vickery thought sourly, looking down the slope at it. No, you're not on Hollywood Boulevard, and in fact you're hardly more than a stone's throw from a freeway. "I think this is a trap," he said, "your man Terracotta knew about your fiancé, right? He probably—"

"It's not a trap. Or if it is, and I'm caught, don't worry, I won't betray you . . . any more than I have already! I've got to go. Goodbye."

She ended the call, and Vickery put his phone away and looked around at the visible buildings. The houses down there on Emerald Street showed no open windows, and the apartment buildings on the other side of Second Street were visible to him from his higher elevation but would have no view of her car on the street below him. To his left, though, was a seven or eight story apartment building with a lot of balconies, and open arches on the roof—if he'd been doing advance work for a motorcade, he'd have made sure that countersnipers were on that roof and that no facing windows were open; and if a previously checked window were to open, the motorcade would be rerouted.

He glanced at his left wrist, then swore under his breath, for he had switched wrists and changed the time by an hour; he calculated that it was now ten minutes to ten.

A shifting wave of about a hundred pigeons curled from east to west across his view of the farther buildings, their wings dazzlingly white in the morning sunlight; behind them, scraps of paper whirled in momentary updrafts.

Vickery snatched his phone out again and tapped her number.

A moment later she answered, speaking loudly over jangled music and a rapid clicking. "Yes?"

"They've extended the field where you are! It's a trap, get out of there fast, now!"

"It can't be a trap, you don't even know where I—"

"Damn it, that's the dashboard metronome I hear, isn't it? How about the radios?"

"They're—none of your business. Goodbye."

Looking down the slope, Vickery saw the car door open, and Castine stepped out.

The driver's side door of a gray Chevrolet sedan parked fifty feet behind her swung open, and a man got out and quickly raised a short rifle, aimed toward Castine.

Vickery dropped his phone and yanked the .45 out of his pocket, and in one stretched-out instant he calculated the distance and the downward angle and squeezed the trigger.

The loud, hard *pop* punched his eardrums and the Chevrolet's windshield turned white, and the man looked up the slope in surprise.

Vickery had corrected his aim to compensate for the slight error in the sights, and he fired again.

The man's head jerked back, and then he dropped the rifle and collapsed behind the open car door.

Two more gray Chevrolets raced into view now from around the curve to the right, and Vickery put a bullet through the left front tire of the one in front; it swerved abruptly, striking a parked car, and the front end of the car behind dipped as its driver hit the brakes.

Vickery screamed, *"Go!"* down the slope and Castine leaped back into the Taurus, quickly started it, and sped away to the left, out of Vickery's view. The second Chevrolet swerved around the stopped car and sped up after her, followed by still another that appeared from the right.

Vickery shoved the gun into his left pocket and tromped the bike into gear, and a moment later he was riding it down the slope; he bumped over the sidewalk and curb onto the street and swerved to the left, twisting the throttle back and forth as he clicked up through the gears and accelerated in pursuit. Peripherally he had glimpsed the passenger-side door of the stopped car swinging open, but Vickery was a moving target against the other cars, and no shots were fired after him.

The cars ahead roared around the leftward curve of the street to a north-south cross street, and Vickery glimpsed the colorful Taurus speeding away to the right, followed by the first of its two pursuers. Vickery jumped the bike onto the sidewalk and passed the rearmost Chevrolet, and then he had bounded back onto the asphalt and leaned around the right turn; he was now riding the off-rear corner of the car

behind Castine, trying to get close enough to disable it somehow, which would at least slow the one behind it.

Castine turned right on 2nd Street without slowing at all, and the Taurus would have spun out if its rear end had not slammed the side of a passing bus; the Taurus wobbled and then gunned away east, and the lead Chevrolet lost some ground in making a more controlled turn.

Vickery laid the bike so far over to the right that the footpeg briefly scraped the pavement, and when he righted it he downshifted and cranked the throttle, the bike kicked forward past both of the Chevrolets.

The next hundred yards was a straightaway with no traffic lights at the intersections, and Vickery was able to catch up to the Taurus. With his left hand he pulled the .45 out of his jacket pocket and started to twist around on the seat; but three gunshots from the closest Chevrolet were followed by a rightward swerve of the Taurus, and Vickery nearly dropped the gun as he yanked the bike to the right, one-handed, to keep from being sideswiped.

The Taurus had moved ahead of him in that moment, but not before Vickery had glimpsed blood on Castine's profiled face. The rear window of the Taurus was now frosted with cracks surrounding two small holes.

Twisting around again on the seat, Vickery fired a couple of fast shots at the sunglare of the lead Chevrolet's windshield; the car slowed, and the one behind it swerved into view. He tucked the gun in his pocket and got both hands back on the handlebar grips.

Castine was still driving, for the street bent slightly to the left and the Taurus stayed in its lane, and even sped up.

Vickery caught up with her again, then had to brake when she made a wild and squealing right turn across his lane onto Beaudry Avenue; but a moment later he leaned to the right himself and accelerated after her, hearing the roar of one of the Chevrolets close behind him.

Castine must have been alert, for she wove deftly around slower moving cars. Vickery was able to follow easily on his narrow and agile machine, and a quick glance in a rear view mirror showed him that the two pursuing cars were not gaining on them.

At Third Street she simply ran a red light to make a left turn; horns blared, brakes screeched, and a truck struck a glancing blow

the Taurus' driver side, but she straightened the car and sped away east, her rear bumper now dragging and bouncing on the pavement. Several cars had halted in the intersection, and Vickery steered his bike around them to follow her.

And half a block down Third Street she made a sliding left turn into an onramp to the 110 Freeway.

"You don't get on a freeway!" Vickery shouted, uselessly, and then he gritted his teeth and gunned the bike across the oncoming lanes and rode into the onramp himself.

Low bushes and trees swept past on either side, and he saw that the onramp split into two lanes ahead; the southbound lane was crowded with slow-moving traffic, so the Taurus took the right-hand lane, with Vickery now only a car length behind her and the pursuers a few car lengths behind him.

As the freeway lanes opened to their left, the Taurus swept carelessly out across them, raising a jarring cacophony of horns and wild swervings of the cars behind it; its rear bumper broke free and went cartwheeling into the median fence. Vickery swore and looked in a rear view mirror—the two gray Chevrolets were just emerging from the onramp and accelerating.

Then a gust of wind from the east made him wobble in his lane as he had to lean against it, and a moment later a veil of brown dust swept across the freeway. The battering wind was laced with stinging sand and the sharp smell of ozone. Immediately the wind broke up into a dozen spinning dust-devils, and the motorcycle shuddered under him as if the cylinder's spark plug were misfiring.

The Taurus was moving at sixty miles per hour or better now, and drawing further ahead of Vickery's bike, but he heard the roar of its engine interrupted by coughs and momentary haltings, and he guessed, with horror, that she was switching the engine off and on.

One of the gray cars swept ahead of Castine on the left, crowding the median fence, obviously only moments from being in position to cut her off; the other hung back, and Vickery saw its passenger side window going down, and a hand gripping a pistol rise ready to emerge.

Vickery's chugging motorcycle was falling behind, and he let go of the left handgrip to reach into his pocket for the .45—when through the columns of whirling dust ahead he briefly glimpsed an exit lane slanting away to the right, and his scalp tightened in disoriented shock

when he realized that the diverging lane was too long and straight, and the flat expanses of shoulder on either side of it too wide, for it to exist here in the middle of downtown Los Angeles.

And then he had to slap his hand back onto the handgrip and brake sharply, for Castine steered the Taurus back across all the lanes to the right and disappeared from his view in the direction of the briefly seen impossible offramp. He felt the iPad tumble out of his jacket.

He kept hard pressure on both the front and back brakes and steered the bike onto the narrow half-lane of freeway shoulder, and the dust devils were already dispersing in an ordinary breeze.

He spun the bike around and rode back along the shoulder, against the flow of traffic that now swept past in a windy stream to his right. Galvan's iPad was a scatter of plastic and broken glass in the middle lane.

He rode slowly all the way back to the Third Street onramp, without passing any diverging lane, before surrendering to the realization that the offramp down which Castine had disappeared was no longer there. And even if that had been a hallucination, he had passed no scarred or broken section of the waist-high retaining wall to show where a car might have driven off of the freeway.

She, and the Taurus, had simply disappeared out of this reality. Into . . . what?

I should have known, he thought bitterly, and convinced her, that the TUA would certainly have got to her fiancée, and that the proposed rendezvous *had* to be a trap.

And it was, and I shot a man.

He looked back, but neither of the pursuing cars had tried to pull over onto the narrow shoulder lane; they had been carried away north by the surrounding traffic. Vickery's motorcycle was running smoothly again, but he didn't ride away—instead he clicked the bike into neutral and flipped down the kickstand, for his face was suddenly sweaty and it seemed likely that he'd need to lean over the retaining wall and vomit.

He lifted his right hand from the throttle grip and stared at his trembling fingers. I aimed at the middle of his face, he thought, because my old training said that he might be wearing body armor. And I pulled the trigger, and he collapsed, out of sight behind the car door.

Vickery made a fist and pounded once, lightly, on the gas tank.

The man was about to kill Castine, he thought. That made it inevitable that I had to stop him with deadly force; really he killed *himself* by pointing that rifle at her!—and used me to do it.

Ending someone's earthly life from him is about as intimate as you can get, Hipple said.

He's the third man I've killed, but in each case it was to stop them from killing me . . . or someone I care about.

Vickery cut the thought short and tromped the bike into gear, raised the kickstand and turned the bike around. Traffic was clear again, and when a gap in the pattern of northbound cars appeared, he sped up along the half-lane and merged into the right-hand lane.

He nodded firmly, thinking again: *He killed himself.*

And where do I go now? he wondered as the mounting headwind cooled the sweat on his face. My apartment's gone, my job's gone . . . and my ally is gone.

Ally? He gunned the bike angrily around a slow-moving Volkswagen. She lied to me so she could steal Galvan's precious Taurus, and then she banged the shit out of it before finally tossing it right out of the world, and herself along with it! *Like a skeet out of a catapult . . .* And all because she was fool enough to trust her cowardly fiancé— just like I was fool enough to trust her.

Though whatever else she was, *she* certainly wasn't cowardly.

The 110 branched into a complex interchange ahead, and two big green freeway signs over the lanes offered several choices—the 5, north to Glendale or south to Orange County, Old Man 10 out toward San Bernardino, the 101 to Hollywood, or continue on the 110 to Pasadena—and Vickery found himself in the lane that would take him northwest to Hollywood.

So be it.

She did apologize, he told himself; on the phone, there, in the moments before that damned TUA guy with the rifle tried to kill her. And really, would *I* have done any different, in her situation? Wouldn't *I* have stolen a car to save my life and—

And he recalled what she had said to him then: *It's not a trap. Or if it is, and I'm caught, don't worry, I won't betray you . . .*

She *was* just about caught—the men in those two cars were within moments of catching her, and if they'd got her alive—

—There was blood on her face—

If they'd got her alive, and interrogated her, she might have had to tell them everything she knew about me. Perhaps she chose the nonexistent freeway exit to prevent that. *Don't worry, I won't betray you.*

Did she dive out of the world to save me? In fact she nearly knocked me off my bike to do it, but—is that, could that be part of, why she aimed herself into that exit-to-nowhere? She was never cowardly, and she knew what the out-of-synch radios and the clicking metronome meant.

He sped contemptuously around another slow-moving car and cut in sharply in front of it, and in a rear-view mirror he saw the car's windshield wiper sweep up and down, once. Vickery grinned sourly, realizing that the driver had flipped him off with his car.

He waved and rode on toward Hollywood.

↓ CHAPTER EIGHT ↓

Vickery walked along the Hollywood Boulevard sidewalk and looked around bewilderedly. He seldom drove down the always-crowded boulevard, and he had not been a pedestrian here for years.

Gold letters over the high concave pediment in front of him now spelled DOLBY THEATER instead of the KODAK THEATER he remembered, and he wondered what else might have changed since he had last stood on this wide, glossy black pavement with its inset pink stars. He was relieved to see that costumed characters still strode back and forth among the crowd, vying with curbside evangelists and food carts for the attention of the milling tourists in shorts and T-shirts and backward baseball caps.

He saw a Captain America, and a couple of Captain Jack Sparrows in tricorn hats and beaded beards, but he didn't see Wonder Woman. He edged and sidled through the crowd to the Chinese Theater forecourt, and he stood on tip-toe to scan the dozens of people peering at the handprints and footprints in the cement paving blocks. A portly man in a threadbare tuxedo and top hat was selling animals he made out of balloons, but no Wonder Woman was anywhere in sight. It was chilly in the shade, and the turbulent air smelled of chocolate from the Ghirardelli ice cream parlor across the boulevard and exhaust fumes from the roofless tour buses at the curb.

He asked a passing Spiderman if Wonder Woman was around, and got a garbled reply that seemed to be in the negative, and a tall yellow Transformer robot just ignored his question. He was about to give up when someone tugged at his sleeve and said, "Jeez, Woods, where you been?"

He turned and saw a Supergirl squinting up at him, trim and fit-looking in her red and blue Krypton suit and red cape. The blonde wig was new, but he remembered her voice.

"Hi, Rachel. Not Wonder Woman anymore?"

"Not for years," she said. "I'm really too short for that, but people like a short Supergirl."

"Does Supergirl drink? Wonder Woman used to, I recall."

She nodded solemnly. "Supergirl is always thirsty."

"Boardner's?"

"You're an evening type of guy, aren't you? Boardner's doesn't open till four. But we can get a couple of beers at the Snow White Café."

"East of here, right?"

"One block."

She took his arm as they joined the throng tangling in both directions on the broad sidewalk. She waved off several requests from Asian and German tourists to be photographed with her, claiming to be on a break. Men hawking guided tours recognized her as a regular citizen of the boulevard and let them pass unaccosted, though Vickery now felt like a foreigner himself as he blinked around at the tall new arches and glass walls and the towering Pepsi advertisement above The Gap clothing store.

They moved with the crowd across Highland Avenue, and managed to sidle out of the eddying flow of pedestrians when they reached the red awning over the entrance to the Snow White Café. Rachel led the way in.

The place was long and narrow, and dim after the morning sunshine out on the sidewalk. Below the high ceiling were murals of scenes from the Disney animated film *Snow White and the Seven Dwarves*. High up on the far wall, the Wicked Queen offered Snow White the poisoned apple, and Vickery and Rachel sat down at a small table beside a painting of the dwarf Doc.

After they'd ordered two Budweisers, he sat back and smiled at her. "So how's business?"

Rachel Voss, onetime Wonder Woman and now Supergirl, had been one of Vickery's off-the-books CRIs, confidential reliable informants, when he had been an LAPD officer. Though officers were supposed to register all informants in the Confidential Informants Tracking System database, Vickery had kept the knowledge of a few of them to himself, and Voss had been one of these. She had been very helpful in making a couple of ATM fraud cases—but now he was interested in an old case that hadn't panned out.

She took a long sip of the beer and sighed gratefully. "Oh, business isn't bad. I can make two hundred dollars a day having my picture taken with tourists, and I'm cool as long as I keep clear of street crazies and don't cross the other superheroes or argue with the customers. One of the Spidermans got arrested for beating up a tourist woman a year or so ago, and SpongeBob SquarePants always seems to be in some kind of trouble with the cops." She shrugged and looked across the table at him. "Are you still a cop? A couple of the guys selling pirated CDs are using cell-phone apps to process credit cards. I know one of 'em's selling the data afterward."

Vickery lifted his glass and took a swallow. "No," he said, exhaling, "I'm not a cop anymore, and I'm not after data thieves. I want to know about a guy you told me about in 2009 or 2010. He was—"

"Lord, that's ancient history! I'd have to really *bestir* my memory."

Vickery sighed and reached into his pocket and peeled off one more of the twenty dollar bills. When he laid it on the table, she grinned at him from under the blonde wig.

"And it's all the way up to 2017 now, honeybun," she said gently.

He dug out two more twenties and laid them on the first one, and raised his eyebrows.

"For old time's sake," she allowed, and tucked them into the neckline of her blue leotard, "since you never put me on the LAPD snitch list. Go on."

"Well, you told me about this old guy down in the Fairfax district who was charging suckers to get messages from their dead relatives; and I was working up a fraud case on him, but it fell apart when the ghost of some woman's uncle supposedly told her where he had hidden a lot of Krugerrands, and then there actually *were* a lot of Krugerrands where the ghost said. You remember that one?"

"Sure," she said, "that was a guy they called Ike Liquidatem, 'cause he later got arrested for murder, but they didn't pin that on him either."

"Right." Vickery thought back. "A couple of people saw him with a woman who was found strangled, but he was released when it turned out the body was found *before* the dates when he was seen with her."

"That's him." Voss gave him a quizzical look. "You didn't used to be interested in my occulty tips."

He could feel that his smile was strained. "I've got careless friends. Ike Liquidatem? Do you have any idea how to find him?"

"Oh gee, Woods, it's been years. Is it urgent?"

"A friend of mine is . . . in some trouble," he said, trying to speak casually, "and I'd like to be able to get her out of it. And it's the sort of thing I think this guy might know about."

"Well, he used to hang out at one of those kosher places down on Pico, where they're all in a row so a certifying rabbi can check them all in one visit and relight any stove pilot lights that've gone out. PKD, that was it—Pico Kosher Deli."

"Good, thanks, Rachel. Anything else you remember about him? What's he look like?"

"Big white beard; crippled up from a car accident."

Vickery made himself speak casually: "Crutches?"

"Sure. His main business is getting specific messages to and from people on the other side—people in the afterlife." She shrugged. "And maybe it's some Jewish kosher thing, but he wears his shirt and pants backward, with the buttons and zipper behind. And he sometimes wears two pairs of glasses at the same time, one pair over the other, though I suppose that's not a kosher thing."

"Unlikely," agreed Vickery. *Specific messages,* he thought.

He lowered his head so that Voss wouldn't see any fast pulse in his throat. This is definitely a guy I need to talk to, he thought—but he's also a guy the TUA thought was worth getting in contact with. And Rachel will likely try to sell the information that an ex-cop named Herbert Woods is looking for Ike Liquidatem, if she can find anybody who'd pay to know it. I'd better try to get to him soon; today.

Voss opened her mouth, closed it, then leaned forward. "Listen, Woods, you be careful with this stuff, right? You know about cops and robbers, but there's . . . *monsters* out there, if you go down the wrong sort of street."

"I've already got that idea," he said, getting to his feet. "Well, thanks, Rachel." He laid another of his diminishing roll of twenties on the table. "That's for the beers, and you can put the change on my account. I'll see you around, hm?"

Terracotta and Brett didn't speak until the Hsaio Tower was several blocks behind them on Wilshire Boulevard and they were passing the wide lawn of the National Cemetery on their right; Terracotta looked away from it, toward Brett, who was driving.

"Wheeler made me wait," he said, "and then told me nothing. He says when the report's ready they'll send it to the Extension. Did *you* get anything?"

Brett drove under the 405 overpass, and when they were out in the sunlight again he steered into the onramp to take the freeway back south.

He pursed his lips, then shrugged and nodded. "The counter-measures team . . . didn't get her," he said. "Yeah, I found one of the team, a guy I know, in the cafeteria, pretty shaky." He spread his fingers for a moment without letting go of the wheel. "Castine showed up, on a street overlooking the rendezvous point we had her fiancé give her, driving one of those cars with ads shrink-wrapped all over it—seventh floor is running the license plate now. Some guy on a motorcycle was—"

"This agent told you a lot."

Brett merged into the right lane and sped up. He opened his mouth, but it was a couple of seconds before he spoke. "Like I said, I know him. Anyway, Castine had backup. Some guy on a motorcycle killed the designated shooter—shot him in the head—and then impeded the pursuit. They figure it might have been Woods."

"Did your friend say how many cars we fielded?"

"Three, in addition to the solo shooter."

"Three cars, six countermeasures agents, and *one* guy on a motorcycle *impeded* them enough so that Castine got away?"

"Got away." Brett laughed briefly. "Well, Woods *was* Secret Service, and LAPD, if it was him. And whoever it was, he just delayed them long enough so that she was able to—uh, according to this agent—to disappear." Brett was staring straight ahead. "Here's the thing—she was on the 110 freeway and swerved straight toward the retaining wall, but didn't *hit* the wall. She . . . vanished." He looked over at Terracotta and raised an eyebrow. "Hm? Into thin air."

Terracotta sat up straight. "What do you mean? Where did she go?"

"She didn't go anywhere, is what I mean. What this guy meant. She just went *away*, in no direction. Out of existence."

Terracotta took a pack of Camels out of his jacket pocket and reached for the cigarette lighter on the console.

How will *that* affect the imminent consummation, he wondered. Does a car count as a force-carrying particle?

"Did he say if Abbott was any help?"

"Apparently he wasn't. They got him to extend the freeway field toward where they knew she was, but he didn't sense her. The agent said they suspect Castine's car was shielded or grounded somehow against spirit detection. That might have had something to do with her being able to vanish. We're on the frontiers of some truly weird shit, no getting around it."

"You think?" The cigarette lighter socket had a plastic lid and no heating-element plug. Terracotta frowned, and tried to get his hand into his pocket against the restriction of the seatbelt. "And they didn't get Woods either."

"If that's who it was. No."

Terracotta had got a lighter out of his pocket, and shook a cigarette out of the pack onto his lip. "At least she's not dead."

"Oh? You sure? Anyway, you *wanted* her dead."

Terracotta winced when he turned the flint-wheel with his punctured thumb, but he lit the cigarette and drew the smoke deep into his lungs. It was against protocol to smoke in agency cars, and he waited to see if Brett would object; it was exactly the sort of thing he *would* object to, strongly. "I wanted her *over there*," he said, each syllable a puff of smoke, "and now she clearly is. It's possible to be over there without dying. Look at . . . Orpheus. Dante. That radio evangelist from the '20s, Aimee Semple McPherson. They all went there and came back."

"Orpheus," said Brett, nodding. "Okay."

Terracotta exhaled a plume of smoke that curled against the windshield, and Brett had still not objected to the breach of protocol. Was it trivial, now, in light of some new fact? Terracotta had spoken to Wheeler, the Los Angeles TUA field office chief, and the man had glancingly referred to a visitor from the D.C. headquarters, and then pursed his lips and hastened to say that they merely anticipated such a visitor. Terracotta was sure now that an inspector was in town, covertly, and that Brett had spoken with *him* while Terracotta was uselessly questioning Wheeler; there was no way that one of the countermeasures team would have been idling around in the cafeteria so soon after a failed operation, and been so talkative.

Brett was the senior agent at the Extension, after Terracotta. Was Brett to be assigned to replace him, take over the Extension's activities?—pursue the political intelligence that headquarters was concerned with, at the expense of Terracotta's admittedly eccentric-seeming research?

Not *now*, not while the consummation was so close at hand!

But Brett must have known that Terracotta would doubt the story about the agent in the cafeteria. Perhaps he meant to implicitly warn him.

"Just in the last twenty-four hours," Brett went on, speaking more easily now, "less than that, actually, Castine meets Woods—who heard your *toxic malmeme* four years ago—gets hold of some kind of spirit-stealth car, wiggles out of our trap, and maybe crosses over alive into the afterworld hallucination state, however *that* works. And Woods backs her up and gets away. You think maybe she *intended* to meet Woods yesterday, and do all this? Maybe she's been a mole all along, like working for Putin or somebody."

"No, she's working for, always has been working for, her damned *conscience*. Woods probably provided the car, he's the contaminating influence." He pushed the button to lower the window and threw the cigarette out, then turned to face Brett. "Listen, whoever you talked to at Hsaio today, are *you* still working for *me*?"

"Uh," said Brett, reddening a little as he stared at the traffic ahead, "yes—till the end of the week."

"After that I'm working for you?"

"That's . . . oh hell, Terracotta, I don't know. No, I got the idea you're going to be extensively debriefed—after they figure out exactly what they want to ask you—and then you'll probably be sent back to D.C. Promoted sideways."

Terracotta nodded grimly. "*Something* sideways, anyway, I'm sure."

Then I've only got four and a half days, he thought—to accomplish the merger, the completion, the *consummation*, that I appear to be determined to accomplish; if the word *I* refers to any real purposeful entity, and is in any sense this body sitting beside Brett in this car.

"We need to get all three radio rooms working again," he found himself saying. "All scanners back on watch-and-watch. Interview any and all accessible deleted persons."

Brett frowned. "Any and all? Every dipshit deleted person who wants us to call his mom, or says he has a winning lottery ticket?"

"Yes yes, any and all. We need to . . . widen the conduit."

Traffic and idiot drivers will provide plenty of souls crossing to the desert highway afterlife from the LA freeways, he thought—we need to get as many ghosts as possible coming back the other way. *Exchange.*

"You're in charge," conceded Brett. He didn't have to actually say *for now.*

The Pico Kosher Deli was one of a row of narrow establishments on the south side of the street, and Vickery parked his motorcycle in a lot a few doors past it and walked back to the little restaurant. He shuffled in past a display case full of brownies and cakes and stood by the cash register, and very shortly a man in an apron stepped up and raised his eyebrows inquiringly.

"I'm looking for a guy I met in here a couple of times," Vickery said, "white beard, crutches? His name was Ike something." The name *Liquidatem,* if Rachel Voss had even remembered it correctly, was too melodramatic.

The man gave him a blank look. "Rings no bells, sorry." Then he sighed and said, "But why don't you sit down and have a sandwich."

". . . Okay."

Vickery walked on into the dining room and sat down at a green leather booth facing the street. Another man brought him a menu, and Vickery wasn't sure whether the man at the register had meant him to wait or just order something if he meant to hang around; but the spicy smells of pastrami and corned beef made up his mind for him, and he ordered a roast beef sandwich with horseradish on rye bread.

During the next twenty minutes a few people came in and sat down at other booths, but none were on crutches.

Vickery had finished the sandwich, and was considering ordering the kokosh cake for dessert, when he saw a familiar figure move past the window outside, and a few moments later the boy Santiago was standing by the cash register. He crossed to Vickery's table and sat down on the other side of the table.

"Now you getting in deep, hey?" the boy said cheerfully. "Your girl recognized the guy at the church?" He sniffed the air and stared at the crumbs on Vickery's plate, and Vickery noticed that the boy's wrists were thin in the loose leather bands.

"I want to see him, Santiago."

The boy rocked one hand in the air, palm down. *"Eso es nada,* but maybe he wants to see you. You know why the *fantasmas* spilled all over the city this morning?"

I'm not surprised, thought Vickery. "Yes, I guess I do know why. I want to talk to him about what happened there."

"Tell me something."

Anticipating a question, Vickery waited a few moments; then he realized that Santiago was asking for some fact that would confirm his claim to know something about the event.

"It happened on the 110," he said, "just north of the Third Street onramp, about an hour after we saw you at Holy Sacrament church . . . probably about exactly ten AM."

"Bingo. He wants to see you. You know Rambam? Place on Robertson?"

"Some kind of old folk's home. Sure."

"Tell 'em you want to see Isaac Laquedem—*Liquidatem* was just a name that got made up for a joke." The boy slid out of the booth and stood up, with a wary glance toward the waiter. "Did you ever pay me my ten bucks?"

"Yes, Santiago, and then some. This morning."

"Oh yeah. Well, see you."

The boy hurried outside, and Vickery got to his feet. He laid another of his twenty-dollar bills on the table and walked toward the door, but he paused just short of it and touched the bulk of the .45 in his pocket.

The old man met with a TUA official today, he thought; could he be a TUA ally? If Rachel Voss did contact him, she'd have said that it was Herbert Woods who wants to see him. The TUA would recognize that name.

Santiago might or might not know if there were snipers on a roof outside, and he might or might not have told me, even if he knew there were.

Vickery's palms were sweaty, and he could feel his heart beating.

I should leave this place by the back, and abandon the bike.

And abandon Castine—though realistically she's lost beyond any hope of recall anyway.

One guy came back, in 1960.

Sure, and the moon landing was faked and Tupac Shakur is still alive.

She saved your life yesterday, and today she sacrificed herself to avoid betraying you.

She'd never have had a chance to betray me, they clearly meant to kill her out of hand.

Still.

He took a deep breath and exhaled, then stepped out onto the sidewalk, his hand on the gun and his eyes rapidly scanning the rooftops and the few pedestrians and the parked and passing cars. He walked carefully to the bike, knees flexed and ready to dive in any direction, and he was strongly reminded of simulated attacks in Hogan's Alley at the Rowley Training Center in Michigan.

And, as in many of those simulations, nothing happened this time. He got on the bike, started the engine, and rode to the Robertson intersection.

RAMBAM was the name engraved in two-foot-tall letters in the stone lintel over the entry of a pre-war brick apartment building, and Vickery suspected that the current business had adopted the name just because it was so prominent there. He tapped up the steps and pushed open a heavy steel-and-glass door.

The lobby was narrow, with orange vinyl chairs around a table on the left side of an open hallway, and a sliding glass window in the wall on the right side, and the place smelled of floor polish and Ben-Gay. Little metal seagulls and palm trees were stuck onto the paneled wall behind the orange chairs.

The glass window slid aside, and a woman with rhinestone cat's-eye glasses stared out at him.

"Isaac Laquedem?" Vickery said. "He's expecting me."

"What's the boy's name?"

"The boy—oh. Santiago."

"Mr. Laquedem is in the dining room." She nodded toward the hall. "First doorway on your left."

The dining room was larger than the lobby, with long formica-topped tables running the length of it; faded advertising posters with French and Hebrew lettering were spaced along the paneled inner wall. The room was empty except for the white-bearded man sitting below one of the windows. A pair of crutches leaned against the wall beside him.

"The boy said your name is Vickery." The man's voice was low and grating. "I think it's not."

"Call me anything you like," said Vickery, crossing to take a chair near the old man. The front of Laquedem's white shirt was smooth, with no overlap or buttons, and two pairs of eyeglasses hung on string lanyards on his chest. One appeared to have no lenses. "I want to ask you about—"

"Tell me what happened this morning." The old man lifted the pair of glasses with lenses and slid them on. "Ghost voices pre-empted KFI on my radio, and even on the radios in the next rooms, and I got calls from freeway gypsies all the way out to Palmdale, talking about a huge surge."

"Okay. Well . . ." Feeling as if he were in a confessional himself now, Vickery leaned forward and clasped his hands together. "The current on the 110 was very powerful," he said quietly, "pigeons racing away to keep up with the expanding fringes, a dust storm in downtown LA, ozone smell, whirlwinds across the lanes—and a woman drove a car at the retaining wall and vanished up an offramp that was only there for a moment."

The old man's teeth seemed very white as his tanned and deeply lined face broke into a smile above the ivory beard. "Was it by any chance the car the boy described? With big faces printed all over it?" When Vickery nodded, he went on, "She must have had some inhabited item with her."

"One of the metronomes," Vickery said.

"And the caps on those pendulums are always a bit of bone or wood, with a ghost or never-born collapsed into it, I believe? It must have been shaking itself right off the metronome. And she must have killed someone on or near a freeway, to have a track to follow—probably pretty recently, judging by the scope and depth of the splash she made. And was she drunk? No? Then had she recently been severely struck in the head?"

Vickery thought of the holes in the Taurus' back window and the blood he had seen on Castine's face, and he nodded unhappily, hoping it had been a glancing impact.

Laquedem spread one hand. "It seems one must be at least partly dissociated from this world, mentally, to fit through." He sat back and crossed his arms. "What is it you want to know?"

"I want to know," said Vickery, "how to get her back."

Isaac Laquedem frowned and pushed his glasses up on his nose. "Why?"

"I . . . owe her."

"You can't owe *her* that much. You must have a lot of *yourself* invested in her."

Vickery considered that. I didn't have a lot to invest, he thought, and she's certainly not the most reliable or sensible investment, but—

"I suppose I have," he admitted. "She's . . . a friend, somehow, for better or worse. And I don't have a lot of those."

"Better or worse." Laquedem echoed. He turned to look out the window, though all he could see from his chair would be the top branches of an orange tree. "Getting her back would mean going there yourself."

Vickery had been forlornly hoping for a different answer. But, "So I had rather suspected," he admitted in a leaden tone.

"Had you indeed!" The old man turned to look at Vickery. "You were driving that car, earlier today—you brought an administrator of the Transportation Utility Agency to meet me. Are you an agent of theirs?"

"No, I work for a woman who provides stealth rides. The TUA fellow just booked a ride."

"Galvan? Yes, that seems logical, and I can check it. But you know about the TUA?"

"Are *you* an agent of theirs?"

"No." Laquedem smiled. "The man found me in much the same way as you traced me through Supergirl, Mr. Woods. My peculiar legal record is very evident to certain kinds of searches. He asked for advice about handling a dangerously unreliable section chief of theirs, which I gave him, and which I believe he will disregard. Which may be profoundly unfortunate." He reached to the side and took hold of both crutches in one big hand.

"Good old Supergirl," Vickery said shortly. "I hope you didn't have to promise her more than sixty bucks." He leaned back and ran the fingers of both hands through his hair. "The TUA wants to kill me because of something a ghost said to me once; and they apparently wanted to kill the woman who disappeared this morning, probably for helping me get away from them."

"And for killing one of them," guessed Laquedem, "unless she happened to kill someone else for some other reason, in the freeway current, recently. What did the ghost say to you?" The old man levered himself up out of his chair and fitted the pads of the crutches under his arms.

An answer for an answer, Vickery thought. "It's from Ovid, I discover. 'O cruel Minos, thy dominion be, We'll go through air, for sure the air is free.'"

"That's the Dryden translation." Laquedem's bushy eyebrows were raised. "Ooh, and they want to kill you for having heard it?" Laquedem stumped a few yards across the linoleum floor and shook his head, and Vickery saw that his shirt was buttoned down the back, and that he wore a black yarmulke. "They're more deliberate, more *aware*, than I had supposed!"

"What the hell *is* it?"

The old man looked sideways at him, his glasses catching the light from the window. "I'll tell you. And I can tell you how to come back again from the . . . afterworld."

"I truly hope you can, I'd hate to—" Vickery paused, staring at the old man wonderingly. "Are you the—you're not—how old are you? Uh, no offense."

"Yes." Isaac Laquedem's smile was mirthless. "And I was already an old man when I did it on the Pasadena Freeway in 1960."

The old man's gaze drifted toward the yellowed acoustic tile ceiling. "I took the name Isaac Laquedem in New York in the last century— sorry, the last but one—just because it's the traditional name for the Wandering Jew, and then more recently the papers thought *Liquidatem* was clever, after I was accused of murdering that woman. But my earliest memories are of . . . the opening of the Liverpool and Manchester Railway. . . the procession of motorcars from London to Brighton . . . always the moving charges, you see, the induced current."

Vickery understood that these must be events that happened a long time ago, evidently in the 19th century; and, at least for this dizzying moment, he believed the old man. *Time spent in the ghost currents is said to keep a person young,* Hipple had said.

"All this business," Laquedem went on, freeing one hand from a crutch to wave in a circle, "making use of the current generated when multiple free wills move at a constant speed past stationary free wills, in order to see little way into the future or past—it was harmless enough, back in the days when you could only work for the few seconds a train was passing, or by driving a wagon down a crowded street; though even from the first there were canny protests against railroads, and there was the law that an automobile must be preceded by a man on foot waving a red flag, which prevented any effects. That law pretty much ended with the convoy from London to Brighton in '96.

"But when the big roads came along, providing endless streams of steadily moving free wills, the supernatural current could be strong enough so that a man might open a conduit to a sort of—what you might call—*place,* that exists outside of *here.* A region, a . . . situation. Two times two might equal a million there, five times five might equal next Wednesday. It's a state in which irrationally expanded possibility prevails, and so ghosts gather there, and when a conduit is open they can come through to here." He pivoted on one crutch and scowled at Vickery. "Someone was bound to open it sooner or later!"

Vickery nodded. "You opened it."

An elderly woman pushing a walker appeared in the doorway to the hall.

"Get out!" roared Laquedem, and she muttered a rude word at him and retreated. Turning back toward Vickery, he said, "Yes, I opened it, God help me. I opened the . . . floodgates, and the Pasadena Freeway began to overlap with the Labyrinth. And as other LA freeways have spread out, and the gypsies and the TUA have made more and more use of the current, the overlap has become more extensive—the two worlds, as it were, have got closer to each other. Ghosts come right across now without even being summoned, even entities whose births never happened to occur, and all the souls who die in the freeway fields here go across the other way." He bared his teeth in a grimace. "Sometimes even living people go across the other way!"

"So I've seen," sighed Vickery, "so I've seen."

He looked up at the old man. "Last night I met a ghost who came across to this side. Do they . . . *stay* here?"

"No, poor creatures—not unless they subsume themselves into some organic thing like the knobs on those metronomes. There's a fellow out on Mulholland who paints Dorian Gray pictures of them, which is supposed to give them a sort of anchor here, in exchange for any secrets they may remember—but even so they slip back."

Vickery nodded and shifted in his chair. "Just as well. Now by *Labyrinth,* you mean—"

"I mean *the* Labyrinth, the contradiction that Daedalus the Artificer built to contain the, the *force* that's personified in mythology as the Minotaur!" Laquedem swung back to his chair, leaned the crutches against the wall and sat down. "It wasn't Poseidon in the form of a *lustful bull* from the sea that begot the Minotaur on Minos' wife, and she didn't climb into any damned artificial cow to consummate it, as the myth says—a vulgar bit of revisionist misdirection!—no, she got into what we'd now call a sensory deprivation chamber, and invited chaos to manifest itself there, though her. And it did, in ancient Crete. Daedalus managed to contain it in the insane world of the Labyrinth, which is arguably the Minotaur's own self folded back on itself, but that world is still out there, outside of our reality, and I connected it to ours—and then one day I fell into it myself!"

"What's it *like,* over there?" Vickery asked, a bit hoarsely. "In the Labyrinth, the freeway afterworld?"

What has Ingrid got herself into? he thought. What has she got *me* into?

"Oh, it's . . . confusing," said Laquedem softly. "It seems to be an endless loop of highway, as I recall, through a desert under a dark sky, but distances and directions aren't constant. And there's some kind of clanking, smoking factory, away from the highway . . . almost impossible to get to, you can't walk in a straight line, you can hardly walk at all, you can hardly *think* at all . . ." He shook his head, clearly reluctant to revisit the memory. "It's nonsensical. It has all the logic and coherence of a bad fever dream."

"How did you come back?"

"How?" Laquedem focused on him, and said, more strongly, "Do you know how Theseus found his way out of the Labyrinth that Daedalus built?"

"Who? Theseus? Oh—sure, that girl gave him a ball of string, and he unrolled it as he went in, so he could follow it back out."

"Yes, string. But all the earliest Greek representations of the Labyrinth show it as unicursal—that is, a continuous coiled path, with no forks or divisions. So why would he need a string?"

Vickery just spread his hands and widened his eyes.

"It *was* a string that Ariadne gave him," Laquedem said, "but it was a string with beads on it." Vickery was irrationally about to ask if it was a rosary, but the old man went on, "It was a string abacus."

"Okay." The idea reminded Vickery of something, but he just stared and waited for an explanation.

"Yeah. Natural math." Laquedem shifted in his chair. "The thing is, boy, free will is *super*natural; plain materialism has no room for it. A materialist would say that an atom *has* to go where Newtonian mechanics and quantum probability dictate, even if that atom is part of your hand—but if *you decide* to let a telephone just go on ringing, say, instead of reaching your hand out to answer it—or if you *decide* instead to pick it up—then *you choose* where that atom goes. Your decision *overrides* those physical dictates, you *violate* the default workings of the natural world. Every thinking human is a turbulent little pocket of supernatural freedom-from-causality, working against the constant resistance of an otherwise mathematically determinist world."

"I'm, uh, sure you're right. But what I—"

"Shut up. The Labyrinth is *not* a mathematically determinist world. With nothing rational to push against, the supernatural boils and sloshes everywhere, and individual free wills lose their boundaries, lose their places, and slip with no traction."

A cloud had moved across the sun, and the dining room dimmed.

"And," Vickery reminded him patiently, "I want to go there and get somebody out."

"Are you fit?" The old man squinted at him. "No use trying it if you've got a bad heart, or even bad eyes. And it requires some muscle to move around on that ground, in that air. And you'd better be solidly sane, at least to start with."

All in good functional order, thought Vickery, except for a vasectomy I got when I was twenty-three. And came to profoundly regret.

He shied away from thoughts of his wife's suicide and said, as lightly as he could, "Sound in mind and body."

"Okay." Laquedem sighed. "I'll tell you how, if you promise to bring something *real* back from there. It's important."

"Something real." Vickery forced himself to pay attention. *"Are there real things there? And can you bring them out?"*

"Yes, a few. *Hyper*-real things, in fact. The total chaotic randomness of that place has to generate patches of accidental order here and there, like if you keep shuffling a million decks of cards, one of them sometime will happen to come out in precise sequence. And when it happens there, it's a . . . degree of contrasting *preciseness* that's never generated here, in this world." The old man's mouth tightened and he seemed to suppress a shudder.

For several seconds then he was silent.

Vickery was about to speak, but the old man was talking again. "Parts of the highway there are real in that intense way, and that's easier than the other choice. And I did bring something back, in 1960, but I carried it away from the omphalos. It began to wreck my health," he said with a nod toward the crutches, "and I foolishly got rid of it."

Vickery nodded, remembering what Hipple had said yesterday about an object that supposedly repelled ghosts: *It's supposed to have been a brass capital letter L, as big as a chair—some fellow brought it through the omphalos, the story goes, in 1960, from the other side . . .*

"The highway is asphalt," Laquedem went on, "and it's crumbling at the edges, or was fifty-seven years ago, anyway. Pick up a piece of it and *bring it back with you,* and bury that piece in the dirt at the omphalos. That's where you'll come out, into this world again, the 43rd Street exit on the Pasadena freeway." He squinted at Vickery. "You understand? *Bury it there.*"

"What will that do?"

"What do you care? You'll be out by then."

"Okay," Vickery said, and took a deep breath. "How do I go there, and how do I come back?"

The old man sat back, collecting his thoughts for a moment, and then began speaking.

↓ CHAPTER NINE ↓

Vickery had lost his phone on the slope above Emerald Street when the TUA assassin had pointed a rifle at Castine, and he stood now in front of one of the few pay-phones left in Los Angeles, outside a liquor store on La Brea.

It's essential that you travel with some organic object that has a ghost subsumed into it, Laquedem had eventually told him. *It's the catalyst, the sourdough bread starter, the crystal in the saturate solution.* Vickery had gathered that the old man meant *the thing that directs the change.*

After the loss of Galvan's car, Vickery didn't want to risk going to the Galvan commissary kitchen to fetch one of the inhabited metronomes, so he tapped into the phone's keypad the number of the only other place he knew of where ghost-hosting objects could be found.

When Hipple's voice answered, Vickery said, "Hello, Jack. Sebastian Vickery here."

"My boy!" said Hipple. "I assume you're interested!"

Vickery blinked. "Uh—in what?"

"Didn't you get my text? Check your phone."

"I don't have it with me right now. Interested in what?"

"I thought of a good ghost-repeller you should have. I've got it right here."

"Oh? That's good, I'll want that, but right now I'd like to buy one of your inhabited pipes."

"Well, sure, your credit's good. Not for one of my Castellos, but I could let you have a solidly inhabited corncob. Are you in the area?"

"I can be, and a corncob's fine, I'm not going to smoke it. I—"

The back end of a big Corona Beer delivery truck stuck a few yards out from an alley to his right, and a little girl in overalls and a straw hat now stepped out from behind it into the sunlight. She appeared to be about ten years old, and, though he had not got a good look at her this morning, he was sure it was the same girl who had been standing in the parking lot at Blessed Sacrament church, only a few blocks away from here.

The girl was again staring straight at him, and now she solemnly shook her head. A moment later she had stepped back into the shadows behind the truck.

"—I'll come by, uh, soon, within the half hour," Vickery went on while he considered the girl's warning.

He thought of a test. Holding the phone away, he said, to no one, "What?" then into the phone he added, "Oh, right, and we'll want more raisins and peanuts—I'll be bringing Miss Castine again."

There was a pause, and then Hipple said, "Oh? Oh, yes indeed, by all means, lovely girl, yes. Raisins and peanuts, I've got you covered."

I bet you do, Vickery thought, with a shiver. The pause and then the too-hearty reply, along with the little girl's warning, had told him what he wanted to know.

He hung up the phone and glanced toward the beer truck. He strode to the corner of the truck, but there was no little girl to be seen in the alley; he sidled down the pavement between the truck and a brick wall, and peered around the truck's bumper, and then crouched to look under the truck, but the girl was gone. Vickery was certain that any nearby security camera would show that she had never been there at all.

His chest felt coldly hollow. A ghost, he thought.

A ghost who warned me that Hipple is aware of the day's big event and was pretending not to be.

He has sold me out at last, almost certainly to the TUA. I've got no choice now but to swipe a metronome from the commissary.

Vickery got back on the motorcycle and rode up to Sunset and turned right, toward Normandie.

As he rode past the tall Renaissance front face of the Blessed Sacrament church, he reflected that it was only about four hours since he had driven Galvan's stealth Taurus into the church's back parking lot, and first seen the little girl in overalls, and it seemed to him now that Los Angeles was closing in around him; and soon, if he went through with his plan, he would pop right out of it through a hole in reality.

He wished he hadn't lost Galvan's iPad—he'd have liked to look up the Dryden translation of Ovid's *Metamorphoses*. Somewhere in the Labyrinth, according to Laquedem, Ovid's epic poem must somehow be coherently remembered; and the TUA must know about the Labyrinth connection or they would not have wanted to kill Vickery just because he'd heard a couple of lines and might go on to investigate the source.

He slowed for a red light and looked to his right, at several people strolling up to a Rite Aid drugstore; and for a moment he fiercely envied them the ordinary worries of mundane life.

The light turned green, and he looked ahead.

Once he got hold of a metronome, he told himself, the rest of the endeavor should be manageable—string ten beads loosely along a cord knotted at both ends, fetch the Chevy Blazer from the storage unit, drink enough of the bourbon he stored there to be drunk, and then get on the 110 freeway. *It would be best,* Laquedem had told him, *to exit this world at the same point where your friend did. There should be ripples between the worlds there for hours, at least. And bring back something real!*

Manageable? he thought now, unhappily. I don't *want* to take all the risks of driving drunk—what becomes of me if I get arrested? What if, God forbid, I kill some other driver?—and then deliberately driving straight into a freeway retaining wall!—and *then,* if it even works, jumping straight out of this world into *some kind of antique Greek hell,* for God's sake.

What I *want* is—something I should admit is impossible. Ingrid Castine, back.

But maybe Laquedem's crazy proposal *would* work. Maybe I *would* find myself on that nonexistent offramp, and be able to find her; and maybe a pair of string abacuses really would hew a path for the two of us out of the Labyrinth, back to this real world. Laquedem did it, it seems. *Follow the math out,* the old man had told him; *make two and two tangibly be four, and nothing else, and then make three and three be empirically six.*

And yesterday Hipple had advised, *It might help to recite the multiplication tables in a loud voice; math is deterministic.*

Castine had driven away that ghost last night by loudly squaring its claimed age, and then subtracting that number from itself. *Don't take my word for it,* she had told the thing. *Think, do the math yourself. Nothing.*

And now she's lost in the afterworld that horrible thing came out of. And I'm planning—or considering at least—going there and rescuing her.

But she can't *expect* that of me, he thought suddenly as he gunned through a yellow traffic signal at Van Ness. Nobody could. No, I don't care what I told that crazy old man, I probably *won't* do it—oh, I may steal a metronome and go to the storage facility, and even get in the Blazer and start the engine—but then I'll surely reconsider, and face once and for all the fact, and it *is* a fact, that realistically there's nothing I can do—and switch the engine off. I can walk right up to the edge of doing it, dutifully and obviously prepared, and then be stymied by the fact that it's patently impossible.

The thought let him relax a little. At Normandie he turned south, toward the Galvan kitchen commissary.

He parked the bike under the same big old pepper tree where he had usually parked the Blazer, and he walked cautiously across the empty asphalt lot to the commissary door. *Yesterday you walked up to that door with Ingrid,* he though, and then suppressed the memory.

At least nobody's here except Galvan's old uncle Primo.

He pulled open the door and stepped inside, and as the door began to hiss closed behind him he heard a car entering the lot. He glanced back, and in the moment before the door shut he saw two cars rocking up the driveway. The lead one was Galvan's powder-blue 1972 Cadillac.

The door closed, with an echoing boom. Primo leaned out of his office, and the lights and air-conditioner came on. "Vick?" he said uncertainly. "I thought you—"

Galvan won't recognize the motorcycle, Vickery thought rapidly, but even if I snatch a metronome and dash out by the back door, Primo will surely tell Galvan that I was here a second earlier. And she's evidently got guys with her.

"I need to talk to Lady Galvan," Vickery said, trying to put confidence into his voice. "If she's not here I'll wait in your office."

"Sure, Vick, she said she'd come by this afternoon. Or I can call her."

Vickery had reached the door of Primo's office, and quickly sat down in one of the wicker chairs below the schedule chart. "Nah, I'll wait," he said.

"Okay. You want some coffee?"

"Yes, please," said Vickery, and he was slouched in the chair and holding a steaming cup when the door opened and Galvan and three men stepped into the commissary.

"Hey, boss," Primo called, "Sebastian Vickery's here to see you."

Vickery could see Galvan through the open office doorway. The woman was a head shorter than any of the three men behind her, but she drew his attention by seeming to be more sharply drawn than them—her broad, tanned face and short-cropped black hair, and her blocky figure in cargo pants and a khaki jacket, and most of all her protuberant brown eyes, combined to inspire wariness even at the best of times.

"Here?" she said, peering now in Vickery's direction. "That saves trouble, I want to talk to him." She strode past the ovens and refrigerators to the office doorway, followed by her three companions, no doubt cousins or siblings of hers, who were dressed in jeans and denim jackets. "Tio Primo, why don't you take your lunch break."

Primo nodded and hurried out of the office, and Galvan imposed herself through the office door and took the other chair, while the three men moved in and stood beside her, expressionless, blocking any exit from the office. The closing of the parking lot door echoed in the big empty kitchen beyond.

Galvan frowned and took a silver cigarette case from her shirt pocket, then looked up at Vickery. "Your girlfriend stole my best car," she said. "And maybe she disabled the iPhone—anyway, the car isn't showing up anywhere."

I daresay, thought Vickery. "You can take the cost of it out of my pay." If somehow I still work for you, he thought.

"You don't say 'I can get it back.'" observed Galvan.

Vickery rocked his head. "Okay, if I get it back, you can take any repairs out of my pay."

"But you know it's gone, don't you." Galvan opened the flat case and fingered up a cigarette. "My gypsies say they can't hear anything from the other side now except some old-school poem and a woman talking to *you*."

"To me?" Vickery made his tone light. "What does she say?"

"Well, it's steady the same thing, but sometimes she calls you Sebastian or Vickery, and other times she calls you Herbert. She says, 'Sebastian, friends we part.' Or Herbert."

Vickery could feel his face heating up, and he took a sip of hot coffee to cover it. "Ghosts are weird," he ventured.

As if in response to the word *ghosts,* the kitchen now echoed to the rattle of the little metronomes starting up.

Galvan was looking at the cigarette as she thoughtfully broke the filter off of it. "Well, that's an odd thing. My gypsies say it's not a ghost. They say this woman is alive, there." She looked up at Vickery. "Is my car there?"

"*There?* I don't see how. The woman who took it has a fiancé in Baltimore, maybe she—"

"Lying to me won't make me feel more kindly toward you." Galvan was looking down again, carefully cutting the cigarette paper from top to bottom with a thumbnail. "You took my iPad and went after her this morning, when the car was still trackable. You saw her disappear, didn't you?"

After a pause, Vickery exhaled. "Yes," he said. "And yes, your car's there."

"And my iPad?"

"It got run over."

"So we add another two weeks to the ten years I deduct from your pay?" It was evidently a rhetorical question, for she went on, "Or do I take the money that an independent party offers me?"

Vickery watched the three standing men out of the corner of his eye, and inhaled to expand his ribs and try to feel the alignment of the gun in his pocket. He wished it weren't in his left pocket. The metronomes were still making a rattlesnake background noise out in the kitchen.

He took another sip of coffee and then held the cup in his right hand. "What does the independent party want?" He was fairly sure that the independent party was Jack Hipple.

"You. Tied up. He says he has a buyer."

"The buyer wants to kill me. They've tried a couple of times already. Which do you want to do, dock my pay or take this party's money?"

"Tom at the yard tells me you don't work for me anymore, and this anonymous party will pay cash now. Is there some reason I'm not thinking of, that says I shouldn't sell you to him?"

"The, uh, *buyer* is a government agency." Vickery lifted his left hand to rub it over his face, and he had to contain a tense laugh at the craziness of this gambit—Ingrid, my friend, he thought dizzily, maybe I'll be seeing you soon after all. "The Transportation Utility Agency. I understand they've got offices in Westwood."

He let himself smile, a bit wildly. "There," he went on, "now you can leapfrog right over your independent party and deal with his buyer direct!" He was peripherally watching the hands of the three men beside Galvan. "But if they don't kill me first thing, they're likely to interrogate me, and I'd have to tell them about how you dealt with that Chinese guy who tried to muscle in on your occult rackets two years ago, or what became of the city councilman who got too curious about the freeway nests. Not to mention a plain old car service that hasn't paid taxes on its cash and barter income for years."

He was aware of a drop of sweat rolling down his chest under his shirt.

Galvan cocked her head. "I think your point," she said wonderingly, "is that I should just dispose of you." She turned to look at her men.

Vickery yanked the .45 out of his pocket just as the hands of at least two of them men darted into their jackets—but Vickery had instantly raised his gun and was pointing it at his own temple.

"Don't move," he snapped, "or the loonie gets it!"

They hesitated, wide-eyed, and he went on, "I should have mentioned that this Transportation Utility Agency monitors freeway ghost-chatter the way the NSA monitors phone traffic—the reason they want to kill me is that I heard something from a ghost that they didn't want me to hear."

Galvan had dropped her cigarette and case, and was staring at Vickery in, for once, open astonishment. Finally she cleared her throat and said, "Oh?"

"You hear those metronomes out there in the kitchen?" said Vickery, pressing the muzzle against his own temple. "We're in the current. If I die here, that agency will surely summon my ghost, and interrogate me that way. And I promise you I won't have anything to say except revelations of your crimes. I get the idea they could use some valid prosecutions lately."

For several seconds no one moved or spoke.

Then Galvan sat back and clapped her hands onto her thighs. She grinned, and then began laughing. "Good, good!" she said. She turned to the three men and made lifting gestures, and they began laughing too, bewilderedly. Vickery managed a smile.

Galvan's laughter stopped. "I'll tell the independent party—to go fuck himself," she said, getting to her feet. She looked down at Vickery with a baffled smile. "Don't move or the loonie gets it!" She shook her head. "You are one truly crazy *hombre*, Vick. I generally try not to kill truly crazy *hombres*. Go home. You owe me about forty thousand dollars. Oh, and a thousand for the iPad."

"And I want to take one of the metronomes."

One of Galvan's men raised his eyebrows, but Galvan flapped a hand. "I don't even know what those cost. Sure, take one. I think you still work for me."

"Thanks . . . boss."

Vickery slid the .45 into his right jacket pocket and walked carefully out of the office to the front door, stopping at a work-table to pick up one of the little twitching metronomes, half-anticipating at every step to be shot in the back; or in the leg, to facilitate transportation to some remote-from-freeways location for final execution. But he found himself out in the sunlight as the door closed behind him, and he forced himself not to hurry as he walked to his bike and started it up.

As he rode away down Normandie, he found that he was still tense—he was jerking the clutch lever unevenly when he shifted gears, and had to remind himself to breathe deeply.

Friends we part, he thought. *She* knows—to the extent that knowing anything may be possible in that place—that there's no way I can reasonably be expected to rescue her.

You are one crazy hombre, *Vick*. Yeah, Lady Galvan, crazy enough to point a loaded .45 at my own head, with my finger inside the trigger guard, but not crazy enough to jump into the place Ingrid voluntarily jumped into.

Damn it—I *can't!*

But at the storage facility he punched his code into the keypad beside the gate, and when the gate obligingly slid open he rode to the little garage that was his rental unit, flipped down the kickstand, and got off the bike. The padlock didn't refuse to open, and the segmented metal door rattled up on its track with mocking ease.

He went in and started up the Blazer, and then slowly backed it out and shifted it into park; and he wheeled the bike in. He opened a box and reluctantly lifted out a half-pint bottle of Jack Daniels bourbon and crossed to another box to fetch a carton of Marlboro cigarettes.

He walked out of the dim cubicle into the sunlight and dropped the carton and bottle onto the passenger seat of the Blazer, then went back and pulled down the cubicle door.

He paused to grin sourly at the padlock. I'll either be back here shortly to put all this stuff back, he thought, or I'll probably never be able to come back at all. Do I bother to lock it?

You don't have to decide *quite* yet, he told himself, and crouched and clicked the padlock shut. He straightened, took a deep breath, and walked to the idling Blazer, wondering where he might buy string and beads.

↓ CHAPTER TEN ↓

One cup to the dead already, Vickery thought dizzily, *hurrah for the next that dies!*

In the dimness of the parking garage under the Bank of America tower on Third Street, he screwed the cap back onto the flat Jack Daniel's bottle and sat back. He stared through the windshield at the EXIT sign on a far wall, and he had to keep snapping his gaze back to it, for his car seemed to be slowly rotating.

The metronome he had set on the dashboard was clicking back and forth, but the little black radio he'd bought at a Walmart had begun playing Blue Öyster Cult's "Don't Fear the Reaper," and it was still synchronized with the car radio. He felt in the pocket of his leather jacket to make sure both of the newly beaded strings were still there.

The last time he had been drunk had been in 2012, after he'd learned that his wife Amanda had killed herself, had parked on a freeway shoulder and put his .357 revolver in her mouth and pulled the trigger. She had hated all the times his Secret Service schedule took him away from her, but it wasn't until he confessed that he had got a vasectomy three years before their wedding that she had started drinking seriously. Reversal surgery had apparently not helped. On the night she wrote a bitter and largely incoherent goodbye note and got in the car, he had been on duty in Boca Raton, where President Obama had been debating Mitt Romney.

More lines from the old Bartholomew Dowling poem crept into his mind now:

. . . When the brightest have gone before us,
And the dullest are most behind—
Stand, stand to your glasses, steady!
'Tis all we have left to prize:
One cup to the dead already—
Hurrah for the next that dies!

The already overlapping vocals of "Don't Fear the Reaper" from the two radios were suddenly doubled, and the guitar was a jangling cacophony. The metronome had begun furiously rattling back and forth.

He dropped the bottle and made the sign of the cross with his right hand, then started the car and carefully backed out of the parking space, taking deep breaths.

Remember what you were taught about taking action while concussed, he told himself, this is probably similar—your executive functions are *dys*functional, so your flexible thinking and concentration are impaired, and you'll be bad at monitoring your own performance. Pay attention!

At the Flower Street exit from the garage he discovered that a validation or credit card was required to lift the bar; there was a button on the kiosk that would summon an attendant, but he simply drove ahead onto the street, and the snapped-off bar spun away to the side. If it made any noise, he couldn't hear it over the racket from the radios.

He managed to make a smooth left turn onto Third Street, squinting in the abrupt sunlight and blinking sweat out of his eyes, and when the big green freeway sign loomed overhead he swerved into the lane that would take him onto the northbound side of the 110.

A car honked behind him, possibly because he had unknowingly cut it off, but he gripped the wheel tightly and concentrated on staying in the middle of the lane that now bent away toward the freeway lanes.

On the freeway itself now, in the far right lane he quickly judged that the cars in the next lane to the left were moving too fast and close to one another for him to veer across that lane—but he needed to deviate sharply from his own lane while the current was still strong.

There was no shoulder he could drive on, just the half-lane marked with diagonal lines and then the retaining wall, but he swerved to the right, correcting when even over the radio noise he heard the passenger side abrading the wall. He was certainly generating his own field by moving much more slowly than the rest of the cars on the freeway—horns honked behind him and several drivers accelerated to pass him.

He freed one hand from the wheel to reach down and switch off the engine and then switch it on again. He glanced at the rear-view mirror but saw no flashing red and blue lights yet.

"Come on," he whispered through clenched teeth, "Ingrid!—Amanda, Minotaur!—*where are you?*"

The engine was running again but chugging unevenly now, and the yellow *Service Engine Soon* light was glowing on the dashboard; desperately he fluttered the gas pedal to keep the car from stalling.

Then the metronome thrashed to the floor and the wooden ball broke free of the pendulum and struck him on the cheek before ricocheting away into the back; and the whole car shook and the view through the windshield was obscured with a sudden dust cloud.

The dust funneled away in front of him, the radios went abruptly silent, and in the next moment he saw an offramp ahead that stretched straight for at least a couple of hundred feet; and the shoulder on both sides of it was flat dirt.

He swerved into it.

And even though the lane didn't shift in his view, he was weightless for a moment, and then the wheels slammed into pavement and the top of his head struck the headliner. He glimpsed a curved highway and flat desert, and then he was sprawled across the seat as the Blazer tipped over without a sound onto its right side.

He had forgotten to fasten his seat-belt, and his head and right shoulder were jammed painfully against the passenger side door and his legs were folded above him. The Marlboro carton lay across his face. The car had apparently stopped, all momentum somehow lost.

Grabbing a dangling seat-belt strap and then the steering wheel, he tugged himself up, and he was able to pull his legs down past the console—and then he was sprawled across the seat the other way, for the car was now upright on all four wheels. Had it actually tipped over at all?

He hiked himself up on his elbows and looked out through the window.

His attention was caught first by rapid motion in the curdled tan sky, twisting darker-brown shapes that seemed in one moment to be many-fingered hands, and in the next to be the eyes and snout of a vast, world-spanning beast; and in one corner of the sky a tornado appeared to be drawing distant dust motes up into it; but all these changing shapes seemed steady, not descending nearer, and he let his eyes drop to peer out at the landscape.

At first he saw only a broad highway, with flat desert extending away beyond it to a remote row of oddly identical mountains on the horizon; then, as if a focus had been adjusted, he saw dozens, hundreds, of human figures in the distance, all rushing in one direction and then in the other, like bubbles in a rocking pot, and, like bubbles, individuals among them seemed to wink in and out of existence from moment to moment.

He levered open the car door and crawled out on his hands and knees down onto the cold sand, wrinkling his nose at the sharp ozone smell on the gusty breeze, and his foot hooked the Marlboro carton out onto the sand after him.

When he got to his feet there were half a dozen indistinct people swaying and nodding on the sand only a few yards away.

Vickery found it difficult to see them clearly, but when he concentrated on one of them at a time he was able to see a young woman in a bathrobe with dark hair flying in all directions, an elderly man in a tuxedo . . . he met the gaze of a man standing further back—

—and in an instant, like a burst radio transmission, a compressed memory appeared in Vickery's mind; before it faded, he mentally touched it at several points, and sensed singing and orchestral music. It was some opera he didn't recognize, and a moment later it was gone.

The man clutched his head, and in an instant he was standing several yards further back. "What fell out?" he wailed, blinking down at the sand, where tiny lizards appeared and disappeared around his feet like fleas. Then he simply vanished, and Vickery thought a new and similar figure appeared in the shifting crowd out there.

Now he heard music on the wind, faint but possibly the same opera. Vickery was breathing shallowly in the stinging air, and aware of his rapid heartbeat, and he leaned back against his vehicle; but he felt an unfamiliar roughness at his back, and when he turned around clumsily he saw that his car had been replaced by a derelict wooden shack.

White paint had peeled in strips and patches off the planks, making it almost impossible to read HOT DOGS 25¢ in blue lettering over an open counter.

He took a quick step back, but the world moved back faster and his nose bumped against the planks. More carefully, thinking about it, he extended his right foot behind him, then followed it with his left, and straightened up—and he was relieved to see the shack recede. He turned to face the people who had appeared in front of him moments ago, but they were gone. Then he saw a group that might have been them, fifty yards away beside a white SUV, and he recognized it as his own car. On the far side of it the empty highway curved away into the distance. The nearly inaudible music had subsided to a faint, wavering bass tone.

Walking toward the vehicle was like driving a car in reverse—any errors in navigation led to wide swerves. When he had managed to plod up to the Blazer, the half-dozen ghosts were all on their knees—they had managed to open the carton of cigarettes and were scrabbling ineffectually at the spilled red-and-white packs.

The resonant air seemed to be fizzing like champagne. Bitter champagne.

"You got a light?" squeaked one of the ghosts. The others began chirping too: "These are mine!—high lead content is why they're so heavy—what else you got, you bring any Dunhills?—"

Vickery managed to step forward, and he crouched and stuffed the scattered packs back into the torn carton and stood up.

"Who wants one?" he asked. The astringent breeze hurt his teeth.

They all clamored for cigarettes, their arms momentarily appearing at several angles simultaneously as they waved and flailed.

Vickery stood up straight and looked at the figures close around him. "A woman came through here a few hours ago," he said, "and—and she doesn't like pickled carrots, you understand?" It seemed important that they understand this, if they were all to go to the For Lease place for dinner tonight. He lost his train of thought—what had he been saying, anyway? Not what he had meant to say—and he looked bewilderedly at the torn cigarette carton in his hands. His wedding ring was on his finger—hadn't he taken it off? Yes, he knew he had. Was this before he had taken it off?

One of the ghosts, a man in a threadbare suit and raddled tie, stepped forward and stuck his tongue out at Vickery. He retracted it and piped, "You're the guy! Up the hill, by the motorcycle!" His tongue emerged again, longer, but as it stretched it looked as insubstantial as smoke, and Vickery was forcibly reminded of the ghost he and Castine had encountered by the tomb at the Hollywood Forever cemetery—and he guessed that this ghost didn't have enough ectoplasmic substance here to hurt him. Still, he stepped back and fanned the tendril away.

What had it said? *Up the hill, by the motorcycle*—Vickery belatedly realized that this must be the ghost of the man he had shot in the head this morning.

"Take it back," said the ghost, and its wavering tongue flicked across Vickery's shoulder—

—And for a moment Vickery found himself standing beside a car on a curved street with old houses to his right, looking up a green slope to his left at a man sitting on a motorcycle. And then a stunning, mercilessly hard blow to the skull knocked him back and down, and in the moments before the vision blinked away he was on his knees on asphalt, peering blurrily and without comprehension at the bloody mess that had spilled out of himself onto the street, and trying to figure out what catastrophic thing had just happened to him.

Vickery reeled back, dropping the cigarette carton and bracing himself with one hand against the cold hood of the Blazer, and even though his own identity was rocking on its foundations he was able to once again recall Hipple's words: *Ending someone's earthly life from him is about as intimate as you can get.*

"I'm—sorry!" he gasped.

"Take it back!" the ghost repeated, more faintly.

It wavered and split into several figures, at least three, one of which was a young boy, and then they all vanished; Vickery didn't look out at the crazily running figures in the distance to see if their number appeared to be increased.

But you killed yourself, Vickery thought, as I recall—one of us killed somebody, anyway; possibly we killed each other. The thought fluttered away.

He straightened up and took a halting breath and looked at the remaining ghosts crouched and standing on the sand, and he struggled to remember what he had been saying. "A woman came through here in a car with faces all over it," he said, carefully considering each word before speaking it. He waved the Marlboro carton. "Who knows where she—"

He was interrupted by a deafening bellow that seemed to shiver the ground and the sky, a prolonged inorganic sound that expressed no comprehensible emotion but nevertheless drove Vickery to his knees in unreasoning panic. He turned to crawl under the Blazer, but it was now a rust-frailed shell sitting flat on the sand with no wheels. The terrible sound went on shaking the world, and the ghosts had all disappeared.

After some duration in which thought was impossible, the groaning bellow finally faded and rolled away past the distant mountains, and eventually a cramp in Vickery's right hand made him look down. Blinking tears or sweat out of his eyes, he saw that he had instinctively pulled the gun out of his jacket pocket—but it was a revolver now, and he couldn't focus his watering eyes well enough to tell what caliber it might be, just that it was something bigger than a .32.

He had apparently reached into his left pocket too, for his left hand was clutching the beaded strings he had made while sitting in the underground Bank of America parking lot.

He sat up and tried to take a deep breath.

A clear thought surfaced in his mind: *I can get back to the real world.* He opened his mouth and said, hoarsely, "Two and two are . . ." Well, an even number, anyway, he reasoned, since it'll be divisible or indivisible with liberty and justice for all, and—

That was no good.

He tucked the revolver back in his pocket and laid one of the strings across his left palm; and he carefully slid two beads to the knot at one end of the string, then pushed two more up to join them.

"Two and two are *four*," he said, seeing the fact. He raised his hand. "Don't take my word for it, look!"

And in the wake of that comprehension, he was able to think fairly clearly, at least for the moment. He got to his feet and looked over the lowered roof of his collapsed car, away from the highway. Hills mounted to another range of low, repetitive mountains, but on one of the nearer hills he now saw a structure—a high brick building with a row of smokestacks along the top. It appeared to be a factory. And he became aware that a nearly subsonic pulsing sound that he'd been feeling in his bones came from that direction.

The ghosts had fluttered back to him now that the worldwide bellowing sound had dissipated, and they were clucking about the cigarettes.

"That woman drove in here," piped one, "gimme a smoke I'll show you where."

Vickery shoved the beaded strings back into his pocket, then crouched and fetched up one of the spilled packs. He tore it open and pulled a cigarette free and held it out. The ghost's hands were only able to wobble it, though, so Vickery tucked the filter end into the ghost's insubstantial mouth, and it stayed there. When he dug a lighter out of his pocket and flicked the flint-wheel, the flame was a blue sphere rather than a vertical yellow feather, and it burned his hand, but in the moment before he dropped it the cigarette had caught fire and the ghost managed to draw several puffs of smoke out of it before the cigarette fell flaming to the ground.

The ghost was more opaque now, and its silhouette was that of a woman in baggy clothing. It raised an arm and pointed back, past where the hot dog stand had briefly stood. Looking in that direction, Vickery could now see the black hulk of a car with a figure sitting in the sand beside it.

"The faces all caught fire," said the ghost. "Stay away from her, Herbert, she's bad luck."

She's certainly that, Vickery thought. But I've got to get to her before this corrosive air kills us and we're here for good. For good. *For better or worse, she's a friend,* he had told that old man in the backward clothes. For bitter or verse, he thought now, and was my homework to memorize that poem? How the hell did it go? Sister Clementissima will give me an F if I can't remember it . . . *I think that I shall never see, O cruel Minos, thy dominion be, poems are made by fools like me, we'll go by air, for sure the air is free . . .*

The ghost in the baggy clothing stretched a hand toward him—

—*and suddenly Vickery was in bright daylight, precariously upright as he ran fast down a steep grassy slope, gripping the slanted down-tubes of the triangular control bar and dragging the wide glider through the air over his head. He was running downhill too fast for his legs to keep up with his body, beginning to fall forward but resolutely not looking down at his feet, and then his feet were just scuffing the receding grass as the harness straps gently, and then firmly, lifted him into the air.*

The summit slope of Kagel Mountain dropped away below him as he shifted his hands to the horizontal base tube of the control bar triangle just inboard of the wheels, and he folded one leg at a time and tucked them up into the cocoon harness. He swung his body to the right on the hang-strap and the glider banked to the west, away from the lee side of Trash Mountain, where rotor downdrafts could pull a flier down fast. He found an updraft over the reservoir lake at the bottom of Pacoima Canyon and pulled himself forward on the bar to get more speed as he soared over the suburbs of San Fernando.

But when he looked up, he saw that his glider wing was orange fabric; and off to his right and below him sailed a white wing with red stripes.

But that's my glider, he thought—the orange wing is—

Before he could complete the thought, the memory fell out of his mind.

He was looking up into the turbulent burnt-ochre sky of the Labyrinth, and he realized that he was somehow lying on his back in the cold sand. Had the ghost with the cigarette hit him? On one side of the sky, toward the hills, a small angular black object was moving against the shifting brown—he focused his eyes on it and saw that it was a man high up in the air, a man with wings, gliding, spiraling. The sight reminded him of something, but a gust had blown the memory away.

The ghost of the woman was gone. He rolled over, coughing in the bitter air, and for a moment lizards no bigger than matchsticks appeared and disappeared on his hands. He jerked his hands up and shook them, and the little creatures did not reappear.

Vickery struggled to his feet, squinting at the other vehicle, the blackened Taurus in the changing distance. He knew it was important that he make his way to it, and his left hand pulled one of the beaded strings out of his pocket and he began trying to walk in that direction. The air seemed both thick and effervescent—it took some work to drag his legs and torso through it, and he could feel it dragging through his damp hair like cold fingers.

Staring into the palm of his hand, he moved the beads and described the results aloud: "Two and two is four, look; plus two more is . . . six! Anybody can see that . . ."

He had worked all the way up to dividing the ten beads by five, sweating even in the chilly breeze but peering triumphantly at the palpable enactment of five pairs of beads, when he heard a voice call, "My God, Sebastian?"

He looked up, and saw that he was only a couple of yards from the charred-looking Ford Taurus, and Ingrid Castine was getting awkwardly to her feet beside it.

"Sebastian!" she said. Her face was streaked with dried blood and the front of her blouse was still wet and red. He stepped to one side to squint anxiously at her head; he saw a two-inch raw gash above her right ear, but it didn't seem to be deep, or still bleeding.

"What time is it?" she asked. "Are we still in the tomb?"

"In another one," he said, "but I know the way out. Here." He handed her one of the strings. "Look at it! At the string I just gave you! How many beads are on it?"

"A lot. My mom was just here, maybe she could—"

"Count them! You know, one, two, three . . ."

"Oh, four, five, six—ten. What's burning? It's something toxic, our lungs—"

"Now subtract two. Move two away from the others. What's left?"

"Why? There's so many!—uh, eight."

"Good. Look, I've got a string of my own, let's do it together as we walk. Can you walk?"

"Yes," she said, blinking around now at the desolate landscape. "Is that some kind of factory over there?"

"Who cares? Walk along the highway shoulder here with me. Let's push all the beads together and then slide three away. What have we got left?"

"Seven. I can do this!" She looked at him with what might have been a tentative smile behind all the crisscrossed lines of dried blood. "Now take two from that."

"Five," he said.

"I know what twenty times five is," she said in a confiding tone.

"Never mind that, just do ones we can physically perform here. Take one away and what's left?"

"Four." Staring at the string in her hand, she stumbled and nearly fell. "Can we rest? It's hard to walk through this air."

"No. Keep moving."

A regularly interrupted chiming sound started up somewhere nearby, and Vickery knew it was a familiar sound that was incongruous here; and he identified it as a telephone ringing in the same instant that he noticed a candlestick telephone standing upright on the sand a few yards away. He took a step toward it.

"No," gasped Castine, "don't answer it. It's got to be Terracotta's people."

Vickery reluctantly pushed his way through the air past the gleaming black thing, though he was irked that she wouldn't let him answer it. It might have been anyone.

The wind was at their backs for a while, then blowing in their faces, and the factory on the hill was sometimes ahead of them, sometimes off to their left, and sometimes nowhere to be seen. Vickery found that he could follow the highway if he kept it in his peripheral vision to the right, but didn't look directly at it.

At one point they passed a square hole in the sand, and as Vickery stepped around it he felt a metal surface dent and spring back under the sand, and guessed that the hole was the side window of a buried car.

He paused. I remember that *my* car fell over sideways, he thought; is this mine? Did I leave the keys in it? Why don't we clear away this sand and just *drive* everybody to the For Lease place?

He crouched and began sweeping the sand away. It was a relief to stop trying to walk.

Castine had plodded a few yards further, then halted and made her way back. "What," she panted, "are you doing?"

"My car," said Vickery. "Those kids took it, and now look."

"Sebastian," she said, "pick up that string. We have to keep moving, remember?"

"Galvan keeps an iPhone under the seat. *It's* not ringing, so we're okay. We can call Triple A."

She leaned down and slapped his face hard. "You must take the string and stand up." When he had grumblingly complied, she told him, "Push the beads on it together. Now move one away." She took a deep, wincing breath. "What's left?"

"Oh," said Vickery, "nine, if you must know."

"Get up. Walk."

"Right. Yes, I remember." Vickery picked up the string and got wearily to his feet, and they resumed their effortful trek along the highway border.

The highway pavement was asphalt, split and crumbling at the edges. It reminded him of something, but Castine interrupted the thought by asking what six from nine was.

"Sixty—wait, let me do it on the string—three," he said.

"Right. Keep walking."

After a while the air seemed a bit less oppressive, and Vickery no longer had the sensation of pushing himself through it.

Castine sniffed the breeze cautiously. "Do you suppose," she asked, "that we may be getting somewhere?"

"I think we are. Slide 'em all together again and tell me what you've got."

"Ten, boss."

Vickery kept his concentration on the simple math they were performing, while peripherally keeping the crumbled edge of the highway in sight a few yards to his right. And after a dozen more steps through the ever less-resisting air, he heard a new sound on the breeze—the rapid swish-swish of rushing cars—and for a moment he thought he caught a whiff of engine exhaust.

And he remembered what the highway had reminded him of. "I need to get a piece of the pavement," he said.

"No," said Castine, "two plus two."

"Four, I'm thinking clearly! I promised to bring a piece of it back to the omphalos. It's . . . important. Give me a second."

He looked toward the broad expanse of black pavement, but as soon as he did, the landscape rotated and the highway swung out of sight behind him.

He slowly turned his head, squinting, until he saw Castine a couple of yards away. "I'm going to shut my eyes," he told her, "and move toward the highway. Don't look right at me!—but tell me when I'm beside it."

"*Please* come along—!"

"Damn it, *pi* is 3.14159 et cetera, okay? I really do need to bring a piece of the pavement back to LA! My eyes are closed, talk."

He heard her anxious and impatient sigh, and then she said, "Oh— shuffle to your right. Now back up and turn around." With his eyes closed, Vickery followed her directions. "Crouch and reach out straight ahead of you," she added.

Vickery got down on one knee and stretched out his left hand—
and felt flat, hard roughness. He trailed his fingers across it toward
himself, and at the edge of the surface he felt loose pieces. He closed
his fist around a baseball-sized chunk and stood up.

"That's got it," he said, opening his eyes, "now let's—"

He stopped talking, for the piece of asphalt had abruptly become a
handful of cold black water.

"For God's sake," said Castine.

But now another voice, from ahead, said, "Herbert."

He looked up. One of the insubstantial figures blocked their way.
Squinting at it, he saw that it was the woman in baggy clothes who had
briefly puffed on a cigarette.

He peered at her shadowy, half-transparent face, but it wasn't until
the wedding ring twisted suddenly on his wet left ring finger and the
ghost said, "You took my wing," that he recognized her, and flinched
back.

He wondered what she meant. Her wing? In the old days when
they'd gone hang-gliding? Her wing was orange, he thought, and mine
was a red-striped white one. I never used hers.

"You took my memory of it," Amanda's ghost went on, "it's gone,
now the little lizards have it. And you took more, held back more. Stay.
Give it now." Her ghost frowned and its eyes closed or disappeared. "We
can," it said, apparently with some effort of unfamiliar concentration,
"have our children. Here. Anything is—p-possible, here."

Castine stepped to the side and stood up straight. "Three and three
is six," she said, "and nothing else."

The ghost of Vickery's wife flickered, and he said, quickly, "Wait a
minute, it's my wife. I think I should—"

"It's *not* her," said Castine, "We can't stop. Your wife is in Heaven or
Hell—this is a, an animate cast-off shell. Five and five is ten, ten, *ten*."

"Stop it!" cried Vickery, for his wife's ghost was now just a two-
dimensional sheet flapping in the breeze. "It *thinks* it's her, I can't
just—"

"Castine!" came a yell from some sort of distance.

Vickery looked behind, and saw a figure running this way across
the sand; it was a man, and he seemed to be wearing a white robe that
tautened with every upward jerk of his knees and flailed behind him
like a cloak. As his head rose and fell with the effort, his neck visibly

gleamed bright red. He appeared to be running very fast, though it was difficult to tell if he was getting closer, or even from exactly which direction he was coming. He seemed to be very tall.

"It's Abbott," gasped Castine, and then she was hurrying away down the highway shoulder.

Amanda's ghost had vanished, and Vickery cast one last glance at the approaching figure and then took off running as best he could after Castine. "One plus six!" he yelled.

He heard her hoarse "Seven!" and then—

A tuft of weeds tripped him and he sprawled onto patchy green grass at the foot of a tall, leafy eucalyptus tree, panting in air that seemed supremely fresh despite reeking of engine exhaust. He rolled over and squinted against a bright sun in a cloudless blue sky.

I'm in somebody's memory vision again, he though in alarm— where are Castine and Abbott while I'm hallucinating?

↓ CHAPTER ELEVEN ↓

Men's voices were exclaiming nearby, and he sat up. A tent made by draping a blue tarpaulin over several six-foot wooden stepladders stood between two more eucalyptus trees, and several men in jeans and ragged coats were huddled around a body in a leather jacket and gray trousers lying beside the tent. Three ball-topped metronomes were shaking furiously back and forth a few yards away, and the treetops shook in a whirlwind.

Vickery's heart thudded with sudden hope.

He got to his feet and hurried to the group. The body, as he had guessed, was Castine, and she was on her hands and knees now, bracing one hand against a tree trunk as she dragged one leg under her and, in stages, stood up.

Vickery exhaled, only then aware that he had been holding his breath. *We're back,* he told himself. *We both actually got out.* The breeze cooled the sweat on his face.

The freeway gypsies who hadn't got a clear look at her yet flinched at the sight of her bloody face and blouse. She waved off hands trying to steady her, and blinked around until she saw Vickery.

"Sebastian!" she said. She paused to cough, then said hoarsely, "You—went in and got me out!" She stumbled across the clearing to hug him tightly. "God bless you."

One of the metronomes threw its pendulum away into the trees. The others kept rattling back and forth.

"You're the one," quavered a gray-haired gypsy, staring at Castine, "who drove off into the desert world from the 110 this morning! We heard about it."

The others all took a step back in evident awe, and Castine moved away from Vickery and sat down in the grass. "I think we can rest now," she said, and lowered her face into her hands. "I won't cry. That would be . . . unprofessional."

Vickery's legs were aching from the effort of walking in the afterworld, and he was glad to sit down beside her. "Yes," he said. "How do you feel? It looks like a bullet just scraped your scalp. It's stopped bleeding."

She raised her head, touching her cheek now. "My face is all stiff. Blood?" When he nodded, she said, "I can't go anywhere like this."

"Did you bring anything back?" called another of the freeway gypsies.

Vickery grimaced, remembering the piece of asphalt that had turned to water in his hand. "No," he told them. "Just ourselves."

"They say you gave them cigarettes," the man went on. "That was a kindness."

Vickery nodded and turned back to Castine. "Let me look at your pupils."

She pushed back her sweaty hair and stared at him.

Her pupils were the same size. "Who's the President now?" he asked.

"Donald J. Trump."

"And the date?"

"Monday, uh, May eighth. 2017."

He nodded. "Okay, I guess. But I'll keep checking you. If your condition starts to deteriorate at all, I'll get you to a hospital, quick. But right now I don't think you're dying."

Castine flexed her fingers. "I feel . . . very alive, actually," she said, "by recent comparison." She gave him a haunted look. "But when I *do* die, I'll by God make sure it's very far away from any freeway."

"Don't want to be back there, ever," he agreed with a shiver.

We can have our children here, Amanda's ghost had said. *Anything is possible here.* He looked at his left hand and saw that his wedding ring was no longer on his finger. No, Amanda, he thought—I closed that door; on them and, as it turned out, on you.

Castine evidently saw the direction of his glance. "It wasn't her," she said quietly.

Vickery shook his head and lowered his hand. Remembering something, he patted his right jacket pocket, and he could feel the flat shape of the .45 semi-automatic, not the bulky cylinder of the revolver he'd had in the afterworld.

"I've still got my gun," he told her quietly.

"Mine's still at your car lot, I hope."

"We should get moving, if you feel up to walking."

"Sure."

Castine sighed and got to her feet. She turned to the men in front of the tent and gestured toward her face. "Do any of you have some water I could use?"

Vickery stood up himself, suppressing a wince.

"I do!" called one, shrugging out of a knapsack and digging in it. "Our lady of the freeways!" he said as he handed her a tall plastic Arrowhead water bottle. He dug further and came up with a white athletic sock and held it out to her.

Vickery admired her for not hesitating to accept the dubious offering, and when she had unscrewed the top of the water bottle she splashed some liberally onto the sock and then rubbed it over her face.

"Here," Vickery said, "let me help."

He took the sock from her and poured more water on it, and gently wiped dried blood from her forehead, nose, cheeks and chin, then turned the sock around and scrubbed at a few clinging spots.

He handed it back to her and said, "Once more over all and you'll be presentable. More nearly presentable, anyway."

She poured half of the remaining water onto the sock and mopped her face thoroughly, then shook her head and blinked at the man who had handed it to her. "Can I pay you for the water?" she asked.

"Just let me have the sock," he said, and when she gave it back to him he folded it carefully, even reverently, before sliding it back into the knapsack.

Castine and Vickery exchanged a brief, ironic glance, and he knew they were both thinking, *Like Saint Veronica's veil.*

"You need that wound cleaned up and bandaged," Vickery said. "I think we go back to the Galvan commissary."

Castine nodded, then said, "Oh!" and looked at him uncertainly. "You can still, uh, go back there?"

"Yes. I threatened to shoot myself, and she let me keep my job." He smiled, for the first time in many hours. "I'll tell you about it."

She glanced around, tugging up the zipper of her jacket. "Do you know where we are?"

"Sure," he said, taking her elbow and starting toward the surface street away from the freeway, "by the Avenue 43 exit from the Pasadena Freeway. The omphalos, the conduit between the worlds, where else?"

"Let's get *away* from it. Quickly."

"Good idea. Can you walk half a mile? There's a Metro station on Pasadena Avenue."

"Of course!" She took a deep breath and let it out in a cough. "That is—with a rest stop or two, maybe."

They walked carefully across the grassy freeway island and stepped onto the sidewalk.

"We've got to cross this bridge over the freeway," said Vickery. "I don't know how we'll interact with the current. Just walk as fast as you can and don't look at anything till we're well past it on the other side."

She nodded, tight-lipped. "At least you can breathe this air, and it lets you pass through it."

Vickery kept his eyes on his shoes as he took her hand and trotted along the bridge sidewalk, not looking over the low wall at the freeway lanes below, and though at several points there seemed to be many other people on the bridge, he and Castine got to the far side without interference.

"The bridges of Madness County," panted Castine when they slowed to a walk. She spread her hands and glanced down at herself and then at Vickery. "Good lord, look at us."

She had zipped her battered leather jacket all the way up to her neck to hide her bloodstained blouse, but her gray trousers were sooty and wrinkled and spotted with blood, and one cuff was torn nearly off, and her hair was darkly matted on one side. Vickery's jeans and leather jacket were dusty and scuffed, and when he touched his face he could feel whiskers. If we were indoors, he thought, I don't imagine we'd smell very good. His comb was still in his back pocket, and he dragged it cursorily through his tangled hair.

As if reading his thought, she said, "I *require* a shower and some clothes."

"And some food." She nodded, and he went on, "We can hit a thrift store again for clothes, and there's a shower at the commissary. And food, obviously."

For several minutes they trudged in silence past craftsman bungalows and fenced-in yards, and then they turned south at the wider lanes of Figueroa. Vickery's watch had stopped, but the distinct shadows of telephone poles on the sidewalk indicated that it was about four o'clock.

"Those beads," Castine said at last, "on the strings—we'd still be there, if you hadn't had those."

"Thank Ariadne," he said.

"Ah! Don't tell me. Let me think about that."

At the Heritage Square Metro station platform he bought two five-dollar TAP cards, and when a few minutes later a train came sweeping around a curve, its two headlights flashing alternately and then shining steadily as it slowed to a stop, Vickery led Castine across the brick pavement to the emptiest-looking car. He was reassured to see that the seats were upholstered in tough dark-blue fabric; he and Castine probably wouldn't leave any visible grime.

"We'll transfer to the Purple Line at Union Station," he said as the train surged forward, "and get off at the Wilshire/Western stop. From there it's only a half hour walk to my storage place. We can pick up the bike and ride from there."

"Your Chevy Blazer . . .?"

"Is in the same place as Galvan's Taurus."

"Oh. Sorry." She touched his hand. "I owe you. Again."

"We both owe everybody."

Looking out the window at empty lots and the back sides of factories sweeping past, she said, "Speaking of Taurus—did you hear—in that place—"

"It *was* like a bull, bellowing," agreed Vickery with a reminiscent shiver, "if God were a bull."

"You said Ariadne," she began, then jumped and unzipped her jacket to reach inside; when she pulled her hand out she was holding her phone.

"Your phone still works?" said Vickery. "My watch—"

She waved him to silence and flipped it open. After a moment she exclaimed, "Eliot? What the hell happened? Of course it's me! Yes, it's Ingrid, are you okay? Where are you? What happened?"

"They can triangulate this," whispered Vickery, wearily trying to remember what the next stop on this line was.

"Eliot, *what?*" She frowned for a few moments, then said softly, "Oh my God. Eliot, I'm so sorry." And she closed the phone.

"What?" asked Vickery.

Castine just waved at him and then bit her knuckle, blinking rapidly.

"He's dead," she said finally. "I got him killed, getting him involved."

"What, he was killed just now, while you were—?"

"No, I don't know when he died. He started reciting fucking ring a ring of roses, all fall down, and—and giggling—" There were tears in her eyes when she looked at Vickery. "They must have kidnapped him, tortured him!—to make him send me into a trap today."

Vickery could only nod in helpless sympathy.

For several seconds neither of them spoke, as trees and telephone poles rushed past outside the windows.

"Eliot's dead," she said then—quietly, as if trying to encompass the thought. "I don't even know where his body is." She sniffed, and took a deep breath and let it out.

The faint traces of blood still on her face were now transected by the tracks of tears, but the look she gave Vickery was resolutely calm. "He talked to me through a phone. And I spoke to him in complete sentences! But when we talked to—" she waved vaguely, "—it was always through special radios."

Vickery sighed. "The current is *much* more powerful now. Tomorrow you could probably talk to . . . uh, a departed person, with two Dixie cups on a string."

She was rocking back and forth on her seat, her arms crossed, gripping her elbows. "Do you still have your phone?"

"No, and I'm not going to go look for it. I left it with three ejected .45 shell casings on a bicycle path, above that street where you nearly got killed this morning. The police are likely to find it." He pursed his lips. "With luck it didn't have any distinct fingerprints on it."

"I'm sorry. I knew it must somehow have been you who shot that guy, on that street. I'm sorry I put you in that position. That's what I do, to the men in my life, wreck their lives—or end them." She leaned her head back and stared at the ceiling. "Don't worry about your prints—

the TUA will have taken preemptive jurisdiction of the event, and they already mean to kill you and delete all records of it."

"Good news."

Beside him, Castine shivered. "Let's get on your motorcycle and just ride east till either your money runs out or the motorcycle breaks down or we hit the Atlantic Ocean."

"Not on that bike," said Vickery absently, "especially with a passenger." He shifted in his seat to look directly at Castine. "Is the TUA likely to interrogate my wife again? She got pretty distinct, there." God help me, he thought. "Probably more accessible."

"What? Your wife? Oh, sorry, right. I don't know, *maybe*. Yes, probably. But it's not *her*."

"It's part of her, or was part of her. And it *thinks* it's her."

"So?" She spread her still-bloodstained hands. "Eliot's g-*ghost* thinks it's still Eliot! And lots of crazy people think they're Jesus or somebody."

There's a real grievance, though, thought Vickery, whoever has the right to hold it. "Well, we need a proper vehicle, if we're going to . . . flee. In the meantime—"

"If your motorcycle won't do, you must know how to hot-wire a car! Fill the tank and drive east!"

"And get located by our ghosts before we even get past San Bernardino. We've got to get a durable vehicle, and fix it up to avoid their attention, and calculate the safest route—lots of considerations. In the meantime, we can wear ghost-camouflage clothes and eat peanuts and chocolate. I think we could sleep tonight in one of the taco trucks—they're shielded almost as well as Galvan's cars."

"We can?" She sniffed and rubbed the back of her hand across her mouth. "Why didn't we sleep in one last night?"

"Because Galvan is very careful about drawing official attention. California Retail Food Code, Article Four: *an area used as sleeping quarters shall not be used for conducting food facility operations*. It's a firing offense, but we should be able to get away with it for a night or two, just till we can figure things out."

Castine leaned back and closed her eyes. "And tomorrow?"

Vickery shrugged. "We go out with the fleet. We'll already be right there at the commissary."

↓ CHAPTER TWELVE ↓

On a narrow overgrown island in the Los Angeles River, Santiago sat in the shade behind a curtain of willow branches, holding a fishing pole that stuck out over the water. Leaves hung limp in the warm morning air, and dragonflies paused frequently to hover in place over the slow-moving water, but he was wearing a zipped-up windbreaker, gloves, and a wire-mesh fencing mask.

The Long Beach Freeway was less than half a mile away to the east; and to the north, just past the train tracks at the top of the concrete embankment on that side of the river, was a building on Bandini Boulevard that Laquedem said was familiar to certain ghosts, and might attract them. Santiago had long ago learned that ghosts could often be found lingering on the many little islands in the LA River, generally in the freeway-side stretch from Dodger Stadium down to Bell Gardens; and if he were separated from the mainland on all sides by running water, he could speak to them in complete sentences without them following him afterward.

Santiago was perched on the west side of this island, with a thicket of sumac and willow and tall weeds behind him, and in front of him, through the willow branches, a view up the concrete slope of the western embankment to the back side of a furniture warehouse.

The hook on the end of the boy's line was a binder clip, and the bait was a parking sticker with TUA printed on it. He had broken the side-window of a car on Bandini Boulevard an hour ago to peel the sticker off the inner side of the windshield, a risk he would not have taken for anyone besides Isaac Laquedem. Two years ago the old man had found him hiding out in a packing crate behind a Home Depot on Figueroa, when Santiago had been ten years old and virtually starving, and Laquedem had given the boy food and money and directed him to various sorts of unofficial shelter, in exchange for agreeing to run errands that the old man couldn't do himself.

It had been the leather bands that Santiago wore on his wrists that had led Laquedem to him—the boy was in the habit of sleeping with his hands crossed and clasping the bands, and that frail connection of the ghosts in the two bands had been enough for Laquedem to sense and locate him.

The boy flexed his hands now on the cork grip of the fishing pole, and looked with melancholy affection at the sweat-stained strips of leather.

The bands held the subsumed ghosts of Santiago's mother and father, killed one midnight in 2015 while trying to cross the San Diego Freeway, south of the Border Patrol checkpoint at Camp Pendleton. The *coyote* who had smuggled the little family up from Rosarito in a truck camper had dropped them off on the freeway shoulder and told them to cross the freeway to the Buena Vista Lagoon, follow its banks down to the beach, and then walk north past the checkpoint; but Santiago's parents had never seen a freeway before, and had not known how quickly a distant pair of headlights could become a deadly immediate hammer, and though young Santiago had managed to whirl away from the rushing bumper, his mother and father had been struck and flung tumbling back onto the gravel of the eastern freeway shoulder. The car that had hit them had not paused in its northward course.

His dying mother had unhooked the bands from her wrist and muttered over them, and she had touched one with her tongue and whispered to Santiago that he must touch the other to his father's bloody lips; then she told her son to wear them on his own wrists so that his parents could always be with him; and then she shivered and was still. Santiago had taken all the papers and money from their pockets, then dragged their bodies down the slope away from the intermittent glare of the freeway lanes. He had tried for an hour to dig a hole with his bare hands before he finally despaired of burying them, and in the end he had just covered the bodies with palm fronds and tufts of flowering mustard.

Back up on the freeway shoulder, he waited for nearly half an hour until he could see no headlights at all in the northbound lanes, then sprinted across them to the median wall, climbed over it, and crouched by a cluster of sunflowers until the southbound lanes were empty. He ran to the west side of the freeway and scrambled down the slope to the marshy border of the lagoon, and the sky had faded to gunmetal gray and the sun had risen behind him by the time he had made his way to the beach. There he had eventually met a handful of other fugitives, and, tagging along with that shifting and changing group, he had within a couple of days found himself in Los Angeles.

The line on his fishing pole twitched, and he gripped the pole more tightly. It vibrated for several seconds, and then a figure stood beside him, swaying and mumbling. The image of a business suit with a white shirt and a tie hovered stiffly in front of it, like an oversized cutout for paper dolls.

Its words became more distinct: "Hey, kid, let me use your phone, government emergency, I need paramedics, a pair o' medics, parameciums . . ."

It was the silhouette of a man, its face a churning blur; but the fact that it spoke indicated that it probably still had a tongue, and Santiago was glad he was wearing the fencing mask.

He had conversed with ghosts several times in these past two years, but it was still profoundly disturbing to talk to a cast-off ectoplasmic shell that believed it was still part of a human.

Reminding himself of Laquedem's instructions, the boy took a deep breath and then in a fairly steady voice asked, "Have you caught Herbert Woods yet?"

An answer to this question, Laquedem had said, would indicate whether or not the ghost was indeed a onetime agent of the nearby TUA, and would also be a clue to how recent its death might have been.

"Woods!" said the thing. Its face was still an indistinct blob. "Was that him, who shot me? What are you wearing, Terracotta? I caught up with the Castine woman, in a circus car, and how can you drive with faces looking in all directions at once? That's what I want to know."

Santiago had no idea whether or not this was an answer Laquedem would find useful, but he pressed on. "How many ghosts have we been interrogating per day?" He substituted *we* for the prescribed *you* since the ghost seemed to believe it was speaking to another TUA employee.

A wet snuffling seemed to be the only answer to the question, and then Santiago jumped as the thing's tongue flicked out and slapped across the wire mesh of the fencing mask. The still air seemed to shake with subsonic drumming. "D-deleted persons, please!" the thing said when the tongue vanished. "Retrievable! Castine and her pal, they were here but they went back to the world *whole,* not all fucked up like this! Now talking fame, through every Grecian town, has spread, immortal Theseus, thy renown. Get *me* back!"

The subsonic booming seemed to be synchronized with Santiago's heartbeat now. "We need to know how many we've been calling up," he said, sweating behind the wire mesh, "for the—" he groped for an authoritative word, "—for the *settings.* On the *machine.*" Surely, the boy thought, some sort of machine must be involved.

"*You're* the one who's been talking to everyone in Hell, I see your dumb old telephones everywhere. Did you lean on that guy in the weird house out on Mulholland yet? When was it he called you? I didn't get any of the cigarettes, and the hot dog stand fell to pieces."

"A lot?" pressed Santiago desperately. "A lot of deleted persons?"

"You think you're so big. You say you got this, and you got that, and you got clothes that don't evaporate . . ."

The thing's tongue sprang out again, thudding against Santiago's chest, and its face had become clearer now; the boy could see wide, staring eyes below a bloody forehead.

Santiago hastily decided that the interview was over, and he fumbled a plastic disk out of his jacket pocket and held it up. It was one of Jack Hipple's spirit level stars, with short glass tubes glued on it like spokes on a wheel.

"Why are you tilting?" Santiago asked in a shaky voice.

"Wha—am I?" The ghost peered at the disk, presumably noting that each of the radiating tubes indicated a different line as level. "Damn, I—"

The figure rocked from side to side as if pivoting on a hub in its midsection, then turned upside down, and then began rotating clockwise like a big pinwheel. The rotation got faster, and when it was a spinning blur the thing winked out of existence with a thump that stirred the willow leaves.

Santiago let out his held breath and peered through the wire mesh at the river and the weeds and trees around him; but he saw no incongruous figure anywhere, and the faint thudding sensation had ceased too. He relaxed at last, and tucked the spirit level star back in his pocket.

Lifting the sweaty fencing mask off his head, he stood up on the muddy accumulated soil of the little island and hefted his fishing rod. He pulled in the line and noted that the black metal binder clip held nothing now; perhaps the ghost had taken the parking permit back with it to the afterworld.

Santiago stepped out into the flowing water; it was barely a foot deep, and the only risk was of slipping on the slimy cement and falling, which would leave his clothes smeared with green algae. But he made it to the embankment without even a wobble, and sat down on the slanted cement halfway up to street level.

Laquedem had said that the Herbert Woods whom the TUA was looking for was in fact Sebastian Vickery. Santiago had more-or-less introduced Vickery to the Castine woman beside the 10 Freeway two days ago, and yesterday the two of them had driven a TUA man to meet Laquedem at Holy Sacrament. Shortly after that Castine had driven the funny car right into the afterworld—and, according to this recent ghost, she had *returned* from there, with a guy who was apparently Vickery. Hm!

Laquedem had bought tickets for Santiago and himself on a bus to Barstow this evening, but the old man had told Santiago to try to find Vickery and bring him to him. *I'm afraid you won't find the poor devil,* Laquedem had told the boy, *but it's possible. If he succeeded in doing what I told him to do, we don't need to take that bus.*

Santiago had ridden his bicycle to the Galvan commissary kitchen, and had been told that Vickery was out on one of the trucks and was scheduled to be back sometime after five. Santiago would check back then. In the meantime . . .

This ghost had said, *Did you lean on that guy in the weird house out on Mulholland yet? When was it he called you?*

Santiago didn't trust Hipple, but he had done some business with him during the last year or so—the boy had bought ghost repellers from him, and had twice brought him ghosts that wanted to be subsumed into organic objects. It might be profitable to let Hipple know that the TUA apparently had plans to "lean on him."

Los Angeles buses all had bicycle racks on the front, and Santiago could be at Hipple's place in an hour.

Two days ago Santiago had ridden his bicycle back to the place where the Castine woman had shot a TUA man; two men had been lying inert on the pavement, one with a puddle of blood around his head, and Santiago had known that police would be arriving shortly, but before riding away again he had picked up the dead man's pistol, and later stashed it under a rock in a fenced-off lot near Western— probably he should retrieve that before going out to Hipple's place.

The boy stood up, tucked the fishing pole and the fencing mask under one arm, and walked up the embankment slope toward where he had left his bicycle.

Castine had proved to be competent at writing up orders and hanging them on the metal strip above the window and taking payments, so Vickery devoted his attention to spinning corn tortillas on the oiled grill and folding them and stuffing them with carne asada and shredded lettuce and cheese, while 'Turo was manning the deep fryers, shaking the baskets of churros and chicken and beef taquitos and dumping the browned contents onto big paper towels laid across a stainless steel tray. Vickery wiped his forehead with the sleeve of the white shirt he'd bought for five dollars at a thrift shop yesterday afternoon, and opened an oven door to check the progress of a rack of enchiladas. The air conditioner roared in the truck's low ceiling, but it must have been ninety degrees in the steamy interior.

The truck was stopped down the street from a high school, and even though it was presumably against the rules for students to leave campus, it seemed to Vickery that every one of them was spending the lunch hour waiting in line on the sidewalk out there.

Castine threw him a brief glance over her shoulder. "Who'd have thought teenagers all have credit cards?" She slid a card through the little black PayPal reader and handed it back across the open counter to a girl with blue hair. Castine's own auburn hair was disarranged by a bandage taped onto the side of her head, and today she was wearing black jeans and a sweatshirt with flowers embroidered on the back. The sweatshirt was dark with sweat under the arms, and she would surely have taken it off if she'd had a blouse on under it.

In addition to the long-sleeved white dress shirt, Vickery wore faded gray jeans and a pair of fairly new black wingtip shoes. They had kept the leather jackets, which hung now on the truck's back door.

Castine slid another credit card through the PayPal reader and hung the order slip on the strip above the window.

"By the time they're twenty they'll be in lifetime debt," Vickery grumbled, returning his attention to the tacos. He had an anonymous pre-paid Visa card himself, but was seldom able to load it with more than a hundred dollars.

After fetching his motorcycle and riding it to another thrift shop yesterday, they had proceeded to the commissary, where they'd been able to shower and change into the new lot of secondhand clothes. With the commissary's first aid kit and his memories of emergency medical aid training, Vickery had cleaned and disinfected Castine's head wound and put a bandage on it, and they had both agreed that a scar and the future necessity of brushing her hair over a bald patch was preferable to the risks involved in going to an emergency room with a gunshot wound. Galvan had not put in an appearance. Dinner had been microwaved burritos and frijoles filched from one of the refrigerators, and after everyone had gone home they had made themselves comfortable in the fully-reclined front seats of the truck.

"Ariadne, and strings," Castine had said then, her profile inter-mittently visible against the old cycling sodium vapor lights in the commissary parking lot. "Was that the Labyrinth, where we were?"

Vickery had already closed his eyes. "It was no part of the LA freeways, for sure."

"Didn't used to be, anyway," she had said, then said nothing more, and within a minute he had fallen asleep. At some point during the night he had awakened to hear her crying, very quietly, but he had pretended to go on sleeping, and after a minute her breathing became regular, with only an occasional hitch.

Headlight glare from cars pulling into the lot at 5 AM had awakened them, and they had pretended to have arrived only moments earlier.

Then they had spent a busy hour in the crowded kitchen, swiping heads of lettuce across an electric slicer, chopping tomatoes and onions and peppers and whirling them in food processors, and pre-cooking chili verde and carne asada for later reheating in the trucks. By six-thirty the trucks had been loaded, and Vickery had checked the oil and coolant levels and tire pressures of the one they'd slept in, and dawn had found the fleet of trucks trundling out of the lot, bound for curbside locations all over Los Angeles.

Vickery now slid two tacos toward Ramon, who was loading trays, and when he looked at the bar over the counter window there were no more order slips. He straightened up and peered out past Castine through the counter window, and saw only a couple of teenagers looking at their phones.

Ramon stepped from the kitchen area into the truck's cab, and called, "We're done here. On to the building site on Olympic?"

Vickery peeled off his polyethylene gloves and pushed them through the trash slot. "How's the metronome? That's only a couple of miles from Old Man Ten." He wiped his sweaty hands on his jeans.

"Quiet right now."

"Okay, but be ready to shut down and scoot."

When the last cardboard tray of tacos had been handed out through the counter window, Vickery closed the shutter and latched it, and he blinked around in the new dimness as Ramon started the truck and shifted it into gear.

Vickery unhooked a scraper from a rack and pushed it across the grill while 'Turo put a couple of small steel bins back in the refrigerator. Castine folded a seat down from the wall and perched on it, bracing her feet on the corrugated black vinyl deck.

"Can I help?"

"Today you just do sales," Vickery told her. "We'll work you up to cooking."

He caught her frown as he moved to the sink to wash the scraper.

We'll flee LA as soon as we can figure a secure way to do it, he thought irritably. Our first concern is to try to get you hired and find some sort of shielded lodging. Maybe a boat somewhere. We can't go on sleeping in trucks and tombs.

Ramon had been driving down Crenshaw, and Vickery braced his hand on the quilted metal wall over Castine's head as the truck made a left turn onto Olympic—and Castine yelped and leaped out of her seat in the same moment that Vickery heard the rattle of the dashboard metronome start up.

"Hot air from somewhere," Castine said, rubbing her left arm.

Vickery stepped past her and waved his hand through the space

where she had been sitting, and then yanked it back. The air was hot, but stationary there, not a draft.

"'Turo," he said, "feel around the refrigerator."

'Turo took one step toward the refrigerator and stopped, swaying as the truck straightened in an eastbound lane.

"The cold air is way over here," he said.

"Ramon!" called Vickery, "get us back north, fast!"

"You don't gotta tell me!" came the reply.

The air in the little enclosed kitchen had begun making a popping sound.

"Breathe shallow," Vickery told Castine. "I've heard of this— spontaneous vacuum bubbles. Give you nosebleeds."

'Turo grabbed a counter and Castine clutched Vickery's arm as Ramon made another left turn and accelerated. The popping continued for another minute, as the truck rocked through a couple of intersections, and then 'Turo waved his hand in the air.

"The cold air is back in the fridge, I think," he said.

Vickery gingerly extended his hand into the space over Castine's seat, and then exhaled. "The heat's back in the oven too." And a few moments later the rattle of the metronome slowed, and then stopped. The truck sped on northward.

"Amplified possibility field?" said Castine breathlessly, eyeing her seat.

"And then some," agreed Vickery. "I think the freeway current—" or the Labyrinth current, he added mentally, "—has become a big static charge."

"Can electricity do that?" asked Castine.

"I don't know. I think this stuff can."

She frowned. "What is there for it to arc to?"

"You get your finger too close to a cat in dry weather," said Vickery, "and a spark arcs to the cat. I think two worlds are getting too close together. Your old boss has made too many connections across the gap."

'Turo was staring at him uncomprehendingly.

Castine gave Vickery a look and sang a line from an old song about *"our mountain greenery home."*

"Soon," he told her, "soon."

"Up to the Koreatown Galleria?" called Ramon from the driver's seat.

"Yeah," said Vickery, "That should be well out of the current, and I'm not sure this lot of chili verde's good for another day."

Castine had carefully resumed her seat. "That . . . happens sometimes? The crazy air, not the chili verde."

"It used to be pretty rare," said Vickery. "Now maybe once a week." He smiled uncertainly and shook his head. "Galvan says if a truck gets stuck in it, we have to throw out all the bananas and ceramics—she says they contain Thorium 40, and its half-life might get lethally shorter in a field like that."

"Vick," said Ramon, "I called in the new location, and Galvan says we should just hang it up and drop you off at the car lot. They got a rush-order drive that needs an expert."

"Day like this, I'm not surprised," said Vickery.

"I'll just wait in the truck," said Castine. "She won't want to see me."

"No, you should come in. If we're going to get you a job with her, you two have to meet sometime."

"We still get paid for the full day, right?" called 'Turo.

"Sure," said Ramon.

"I don't *want* a job with her," said Castine, staring at Vickery.

He leaned down close to her and whispered, "You want to go to a bus station, buy a ticket? Ride a train for more than fifteen minutes? There were probably security cameras at Union Station yesterday. I'll *get* us a vehicle, and get it camouflaged."

But he had to admit to himself that he was thinking of their conversation yesterday: *Is the TUA likely to interrogate my wife again? Yes, probably.*

Can I just drive away from that? he asked himself. I can keep Ingrid safe, here, for now.

Ten minutes later Ramon steered the taco truck up the driveway into the Eighth Street car lot and parked beside the Airstream trailer.

"This . . . *interview* might take a while," Vickery told Ramon, "and I'm not sure how it'll work out, so don't leave yet."

Ramon nodded, switched off the engine and opened the door. Cooler air blew in through the steamy cab. "I'm gonna hit the head," he said. "I'll leave the keys in case they gotta move it."

Vickery pushed open the truck's back doors and stepped down to the sunlit pavement, then gave Castine his hand to brace herself on

as she followed. He reached up and unhooked his leather jacket and put it on as 'Turo climbed down from the truck too, tugging at his sweaty shirt.

Bald-headed Tom was standing in the open doorway of the trailer, and he glared at Castine and then raised his hand to stop Vickery.

"I got nothing," Tom said. "She says she'll give you the details of this one in her office." He nodded toward the building on the other side of the lot.

Vickery turned around and led Castine away from the trailer. In the maintenance bay sat another Ford Taurus, this one simply white, with no decals, and a stranger in a gray sweatsuit half-sat on the hood, holding a small valise in both hands. Vickery kept walking, making sure Castine stayed beside him.

"I doubt she wants to see *her!*" called Tom from behind him.

Vickery just waved without looking back, and then pulled open the glass door of the office building.

"Galvan's office is down at the end here," he said, leading the way along a hallway past the rest rooms. Framed pictures of sports cars and clowns were hung on the walls, and a pair of baby shoes dangled from a sprinkler in the flocked ceiling.

"When do I get my gun back?" Castine whispered.

"After we get back from this drive. Hush now."

He rapped on the metal door at the end of the hall and said, "Vickery," and from a speaker on the wall came Galvan's voice: "Get in here, Vick."

Vickery turned the knob and pulled the door open; he had only been in Galvan's office a couple of times previously, but he remembered not to blunder into the little plastic model cars hung on strings from the ceiling. Galvan stood at the far end of the room behind the lectern she used for a desk, and she frowned when Castine followed Vickery in through the door.

"Who's your—" she began, then shook her head. "No. Not the girl that flew my car to Hell?"

"The same," said Castine, sighing and stepping forward. "Sorry. It was kind of an emergency."

"Another truly crazy one. And you came back, huh? Move forward, into the light." When Castine had stepped closer to the lamp on a table by the wall, Galvan came out from behind the wooden lectern and peered closely at her, and at the bandage on her head. "I don't suppose you brought my car back."

"I'm sorry, no. It kind of burned up."

"She'd like a job with you," Vickery interjected.

Galvan reached up and batted one of the model cars. "Well! You must have some interesting sort of driving skills to get it there, anyway, right? You want to try out as one of my drivers, probationary? I could have two salaries to dock for the loss of that car."

Castine hesitated, and Vickery said, "Yes, she would."

"There's a guy out front," Galvan said, "who needs a ride right now, and the current is a damn hurricane today." She turned to Castine. "What's your name?"

"Betty Boop."

"Uh huh. Lucky I pay in cash, not with checks. You can go along, learn the routine—it ought to be a bumpier ride than usual, but you've seen worse."

Vickery took a firm hold of Castine's elbow then, and nodded emphatically toward Galvan—for the little girl in overalls and straw hat had just stepped out from behind the lectern.

"The *three* of us are *alone* here," he said quickly, speaking to Castine more than to Galvan; and, having thus tried to warn Castine not to acknowledge the girl, he was at a loss for what to say next; "uh, so I can tell you that the current is in fact *very* bad today," he finished lamely. "This fare can't wait till tomorrow?"

Castine nodded in what he took for acknowledgment—at least she wasn't looking toward the little girl—and Galvan cocked her head at Vickery.

"What's this," she said, "nerves? In fearless Vickery? Are you worried about Miss Boop's safety? The guy needs to travel today, and you'll drive him. Both of you. Now."

Peripherally, Vickery saw the little girl stare at him and slowly shake her head from side to side. Then she stepped back behind the lectern, and he was sure that she had disappeared. He wondered if Galvan would have been able to see her, if she had turned around.

"Okay," he said, in as level a voice as he could manage, "we're on our way. Come on, Betty."

As they stepped back out into the hall and Vickery closed the door, he put a finger to his lips. When they had got outside and were walking across the lot toward the maintenance bay where their fare waited by the white Taurus, he whispered, "Be ready to run back to the taco truck if I say 'commence.'"

Castine gave him a wide-eyed questioning glance, but nodded.

The same bearded attendant as yesterday came striding up as they stepped into the shade, carrying his Etch-A-Sketch like a tray. "She can't go," he said, nodding toward Castine. "I got in all kinds of trouble yesterday, letting her."

"Galvan said she goes along," said Vickery. "Go ask."

"Damn right I'll go ask." The attendant hurried away toward the office building, holding the Etch-A-Sketch level.

Vickery glanced at the stranger leaning on the white Taurus, and nodded. The man looked away, still holding the valise in both hands. Castine rubbed her palms down the sides of her sweatshirt.

Within a minute the attendant was hurrying back across the lot. "Okay," he panted when he had stepped up beside Vickery, "yeah, she can go too. Here."

He held out the Etch-A-Sketch. The letters on the screen were a bit blurred now, but Vickery could read BIG BEAR AIRPORT; and his heart was pounding as he slipped his right hand into his jacket pocket and glanced around at the lot and the fence and the street beyond, not looking directly now at the man leaning against the white car.

"Got it," he told the attendant. "I'll just move the taco truck out of the way first." He took Castine's arm and started back toward the truck.

"It's not in the way, Vick," the attendant said from behind him, "I'll have—"

"I—gotta get my phone out of it anyway," Vickery said, a little desperately.

"Vick," the man insisted, following, "I'll get it, Galvan said you're supposed to just—"

"Commence!" Vickery said to Castine, and she sprinted for the passenger side of the taco truck.

↓ CHAPTER THIRTEEN ↓

Vickery pulled the gun from his pocket and turned and fired two shots past the attendant into the grille of the Taurus; the man who'd been leaning against the car jumped clear, fumbling at his valise.

Castine was in the truck, and had reached across and pushed open the driver's side door, and Vickery ran to the truck and climbed in and started the engine. The dashboard metronome was rattling back and forth. He clanked the shift lever into reverse and backed the vehicle out into the street, then hopped down to the pavement and ran back to grab the end of the gate. Its wheels squeaked furiously as he dragged the gate fast across the driveway, and as he clicked the padlock shut he peered through the green netting wired to the chain link—the attendant had run away out of sight, and the man who was supposed to be Vickery's fare had pulled a pistol out of the valise and was running this way.

Back in the truck, Vickery gunned it in reverse along the right lane, facing hastily stopped traffic, then shifted to drive and drove it across the median line to force a merge into the eastbound lanes. He accelerated for a block, then turned right, into a narrower street lined with ivied fences and old apartment buildings. He drove down it too fast, honking the horn to keep any pedestrians on the sidewalk and discourage anyone from backing a car out. At the next street he turned left, driving at a legal speed now.

"The metronome . . ." said Castine, nodding toward the jiggling, rattling thing.

"That's why they were going to send us out to Big Bear," Vickery said, "far away from any freeway current. There's an iPhone under the dash below the radio, back against the firewall. Pitch it."

Castine bent over, groping under the dashboard, and straightened up with the phone and threw it out the window. She hesitated for a moment, then pulled out her own phone and threw that out too.

"You never know," she said. The windshield was tinted, so she swung the visor to the window and flipped it down, blocking any view of her face from outside.

"I'm afraid we've got to get on the freeway," Vickery told her. "The 110, in fact. They'll fan out and catch us if we stay on surface streets."

"Terrific." Castine turned toward him. "Who was that little girl?"

The truck swerved as Vickery jumped in surprise when a frail, high voice answered her from behind them.

"It was me."

Vickery looked quickly over his shoulder and saw that the girl in overalls was standing right there in the kitchen doorway. Seeing her up close for the first time, he was struck by how narrow and pale her face was, making her green eyes seem very big. Her expression was anxious.

After a moment of silence in which Vickery simply concentrated on staying in his lane, Castine exhaled and then asked, "Who are you?"

"I don't know," the girl said. "Sometimes I think I grew up in India, but my parents both died or something, and now I need to find my secret garden, with a wall around it, and a hidden door with a key a robin will show me. The flowers grow slowly there, and they don't change into other things."

Castine nodded and threw a helpless glance at Vickery, then looked back at the girl. "Is your name," she asked gently, "Mary Lennox?"

"I pretend it is," the girl whispered. "Where I am, things fall out of the people's heads, and I pick them up before the lizards can. I found Mary Lennox."

Vickery was glad that Castine seemed to know what the girl was talking about. "You warned us," he ventured, "about driving that man to Big Bear."

The girl nodded. "You know what would have happened."

The metronome's frantic pace was slowing down, and the girl leaned forward, her ragged straw hat nearly touching Vickery's face.

"Where I am is the opposite of the garden. One's dead and hard to get out of, the other's alive but hard to get into."

And then she was gone.

Castine slumped in her seat, and Vickery freed a hand from the steering wheel to brush damp hair back from his forehead.

"What was all that?" he asked hoarsely.

Castine was blinking. "A ghost, the ghost of a poor little girl! She's pretending she's the character in that book, *The Secret Garden,* by Frances Hodgson Burnett. An orphan named Mary Lennox, raised in India, who discovers a walled garden on a lonely British estate, and a robin shows her the hidden key and the doorway . . . Oh, I loved that book too, when I was a girl!"

Vickery swung the truck into a right turn, knowing that there was a freeway onramp ahead.

Castine was hugging herself and staring ahead. "I wonder who *she* was, behind the scavenged story."

"Well, God bless her, she's saved me twice. Yesterday she stopped me from going back to Hipple's place, and just now she saved us from being killed out in Big Bear by what must have been a TUA assassin. That guy with the valise, our would-be fare. I guess Galvan did decide to make a deal with the TUA after all, and cut Hipple out, as long as it was agreed that I—and you too, as it happened—got killed out where our ghosts wouldn't end up in the current, retrievable."

"I can't believe Terracotta would actually want to kill me," said Castine. She touched the bandage on the side of her head. "Well, not where my ghost wouldn't be retrievable, anyway. Maybe the assassin was supposed to kill us separately." She shook her head. "So are we fleeing, finally? This is a camouflaged vehicle."

"It looks like we are. Galvan's not likely to report this truck as stolen, she doesn't like involving the police in anything." An onramp to the 110 North loomed ahead. The dashboard metronome had resumed its rapid clicking, but the mariachi music from the radios was still synchronized, and he took a deep breath and steered the truck into the onramp. "I just want to make one stop on our way out of LA."

"No, why? The gas tank's full, you've still got money, and even if we throw out the chili verde there's easily a couple days' worth of food right here in the truck." She waved ahead. "Let's just go, follow the 10 straight east all the way to Florida."

Vickery had floored the gas pedal to get the truck up to merging speed; and when they were on the freeway and he had edged into a comfortable gap in the right-hand lane, he was careful to keep his speed steady and the wheels evenly spaced between the lane-markers, for the spot where he and Castine had exited the world yesterday was coming up.

"I've got to go see Jack Hipple one more time," he said, without looking away from his lane. "The treacherous bastard clearly sold me out. I'm sure there were TUA guys at his house yesterday, and he tried to get me to go there. But they won't be there now, since *Galvan* has stepped up to be the one to sell me to them." He nodded. "I'm going to make Hipple subsume a ghost, before we exit this picture."

"What, put it into one of these?" She waved at the rattling metronome.

"Or into some other piece of organic stuff. Right. Lay it permanently to rest."

"The Secret Garden girl? Why? She—"

"Not her." He thought again of two hang-glider wings spiraling over Sylmar. "My wife."

"Oh God, Sebastian. For her sake, or for yours?"

Vickery gripped the steering wheel tightly. "For hers, damn it! You don't—what was it you said on Sunday, you didn't use coercion when you interrogated her ghost, you didn't use feedback?" He spared her a glance. "What's feedback?"

"Oh, they—shit. You know what it is. What they do is, they set up a microphone connected to a second speaker, and they turn up the radio volume, so the microphone picks up the ghost's voice from the radio *and* from the second speaker. So you get a feedback sound-loop, that squeal. Ghosts—well, ghosts hate it, they—apparently when a ghost hears its own voice distorted to a screech, it feels as if it's losing its identity. Its already depleted identity."

"They hate it," said Vickery, now trying to puzzle out the oddly blurred letters on a green freeway sign over the lanes ahead. "It's . . . stressful. Traumatic."

Castine sighed deeply. "Yes."

"This is *legal*? The TUA is a government agency!"

"Ghosts have no civil rights! Sebastian, will you ever understand that it's *not her*? It's like—it's the equivalent of an old VHS tape of her. The image moves and talks, but—"

"And this Terracotta wants very badly to find you and me. Amanda can't track me while I'm in this truck, but Terracotta won't know that. He'll use feedback on her, won't he?"

Castine had leaned back and closed her eyes, and she nodded. "Yes." For several seconds neither of them spoke. "Yes," she said again, "okay, let's go to Hipple's place. I want to get my old SIG-Sauer back anyway."

But a familiar popping sound had started up in the kitchen behind them, and when Vickery was able to read the lettering on the freeway sign, his ribs went cold and a full two seconds later the backs of his hands tingled.

"That sign," he said unsteadily, "says 401 Beverly Hills Freeway west, in half a mile."

"Is that the one you want?"

"No. No, it's not. There *is* no 401 Freeway, no Beverly Hills Freeway."

The air around them had begun popping now, flipping cigarette butts out of the ashtray and fluffing Castine's hair.

Her hands were over her face. "Don't take that freeway," she advised in a muffled voice.

Vickery just held his breath and squinted against the distortions as the air warped and popped in front of him. He forced himself not to speed up out of this intense pocket, for the truck was now passing the spot where he and Castine had taken the phantom offramp yesterday, and any deviation from the surrounding traffic pattern might spill them into the Labyrinth again. In his peripheral vision the cars to his left seemed to swell and shrink in size, but he kept his eyes resolutely on the lane markers ahead of him.

The shadows of the car in front of him and the ones beside him were rotating, as if the sun were moving around in the sky, and then his view was entirely cut off by surging clouds of brown sand that swept in from the east. Sweating, Vickery kept his speed exactly at the previous sixty miles an hour, hoping the invisible other drivers would do the same—he didn't dare brake, in case a car behind him did not, and he hoped that the unseen car ahead of him would not. He couldn't see the lane markers, but the thump of his tires on the lane divider bumps let him know when he had strayed and needed to correct. He knew that the freeway curved to the left ahead, or had yesterday, anyway, and he prayed that the dust storm would abate before the lanes curled away from under all the blind cars.

But the sandstorm broke up into individual whirling dust-devils, and when he was able to see lane dividers and other cars again, Vickery swung the truck into the lane that would lead them to the 101 north, toward Hollywood and Mulholland Drive.

Castine's seat creaked as she slowly relaxed.

"Are we," she began hoarsely; then cleared her throat and started again, "Are we likely to run into more of that sort of thing?"

Vickery flexed his hands on the steering wheel and shrugged. "It's a long ten miles to Hipple's place, even as the pigeon flies."

Castine shook her head, and Vickery knew she wished they could just drive straight east, right out of LA.

Terracotta's thumb was swollen and had turned black, and he had pulled a glove over it to stop people advising him to go to a hospital. Now it was throbbing in time with the booming that shook out of the radio speaker in Room Two. When the sound had started up, one of the radio men had hastily tried to switch off the radio, but Terracotta had batted his hand away, and the three men had just hurried out of the room and closed the door.

It's no harm if *I* hear the malmeme, he thought, straining to catch Amanda Woods' voice over the background pounding—I already know what it is. It's all about me, if you subtract *Emilio Terracotta* from *me*.

Now that he was alone in the room, he had no choice but to speak to the ghost in complete sentences. "Amanda," he said, speaking loudly over the thumping noise in the background, "you told me your husband was there, where you are. And then he came back across the gap." The rapidly narrowing gap, he thought. "How did he do that?"

"None of your beeswax," came the frail voice from the radios speaker.

"He's got Toby and Cosmo and Myshkin," said Terracotta, remembering the names of the cats she and Woods had once had, "and we can bring them to you if we can find him. How did he get back across the gap?"

"Liar," came Amanda's voice. "They died, and I buried each of them with flowers. I keep looking for their graves here." The drumming from the speaker was louder. Her voice went on, "The clouds contort above, and if I speak, a dreadful deluge o'er our heads may break!"

Terracotta muttered, "To hell with this," and switched on the microphone, and even just the background drumming from the radio was enough to wring a jarring whistle of feedback out of the extra speaker. It wasn't a distortion of her voice, but it was a clear threat. He switched the microphone off.

"I can do that again," he said. "How did he get back across?"

"They had strings," wailed the ghost voice, "and that woman told me three and three is six and nothing else, five and five is ten, ten, ten miles as the pigeon flies."

Terracotta's heart seemed to stop—and then his individual mind fell away into a limitless void where things comparable to vast old memories moved and collided and receded: *imprisonment in one's own impossibly folded-back self, and another man who had had a string in his hand, and a duel of logic against chaos—Theseus—*

He was writhing on cold sand under a churning brown sky as a bone-jarring bellow shook the air and went on shaking it, intolerably not ceasing—any thought at all was impossible—

But the awful roaring did eventually recede, and someone was calling a vaguely familiar word—*Terracotta*—and faces hovered over him in warm air. He was lying on the vinyl warehouse floor, and the big turbulence, or alien entity, had withdrawn, leaving the Terracotta identity to gather the fragments of itself together.

"He chased us out," said a strained voice. "He stayed in there and listened to it by himself."

"It was that drumming sound he keeps warning us about," said another voice. "The big malmeme. And he stayed there with it."

Terracotta rolled over and slowly got to his feet. The five or six people around him stepped back warily, and he could see a dozen or so others standing further away, against the warehouse wall.

He patted his hair and cleared his throat. "Brett? Ah, there you are. I want to talk to you in the—the office. No, I don't need help, I can walk!"

In the administration office, Terracotta paused for Brett to catch up, then closed the door and sat down in the chair by the desk. A few personnel out on the warehouse floor hung back and peered toward the office window.

Brett spoke first. "I think you were Amanda Woods, there, for a few seconds," he said angrily. "You came bursting out of Room Two yelling."

Terracotta squeezed his eyes shut for a moment, then opened them wide. "Yelling what?"

"Nothing to reassure everybody who's been wondering about your sanity, that's for sure. At first you were shouting, 'Where is my husband? and then you said, 'Theseus, aided by the virgin's art, had traced the guiding thread through every part.'"

Again Terracotta's identity was shaken, but he lowered his head and breathed deeply for a few seconds, and he remained himself. She switched places with me, he thought; she *took* me. That's what I get for talking to her in complete sentences! She was in my place and I was in hers . . . and then it was the big *other*, eclipsing us both and breaking her hold.

Brett went on, "I assume that's part of your fucking malmeme, since it rhymes. *Everybody* here heard it, and I don't think it's feasible for you to kill everybody." Brett was scowling and shaking his head. "And the inspector from the D.C. office is due to come here at three."

"Inspector, here? Since when?"

"Westwood called a few minutes ago, while you were off in Dante's Inferno."

Ovid's inferno, thought Terracotta. He took a deep breath and let it out. "Okay." He stood up, bracing one hand on the desk. "The inspector. Okay, give everybody a half-hour break, then put three guys on the Room One radio, fishing for . . . oh, Mike Abbott. That's a legitimate tasking, since he's an agent of ours that got killed. I'll keep working, and at two-thirty I'll meet everybody else in the break room, and when the inspector arrives I'll be handing out some of those assignments Westwood sends over."

Brett had picked up the eraser from the tray below the whiteboard, and was quickly swiping it across the whole grid, notations and all. "You'll keep working till two-thirty. Working on what?"

"Amanda Woods."

She had said, *That woman told me three and three is six and nothing else.* The woman must be Castine, thought Terracotta. Has she come back across too? Yesterday I would have thought it was impossible for anybody to do that.

But Amanda Woods had said, *They had strings.*

I can't let Woods and Castine get in the way of the consummation.

Theseus, aided by the virgin's art, had traced the guiding thread through every part.

"Amanda Woods," he repeated. "We've got to find her husband, and Castine. And I don't trust that Galvan woman—she told me she *had* them, an hour ago, but they got away. I think it was one of her cars that Castine drove into nowhere."

Brett nodded impatiently. The license plate of the car in which Castine had fled the countermeasures team yesterday morning had turned out to be registered to a limited liability company in New Mexico; but the secretary of state office in New Mexico claimed it was not a New Mexico company. The TUA office in Washington D.C. was trying to track it further.

"And before the inspector gets here," Brett went on, "you'll begin doing the work the agency expects you to be doing?"

"I said so, didn't I?"

Brett pressed on, "You're sure you can *do* that? Act . . . normal? If you go poking paperclips into yourself and babbling about Theseus and lustful bulls, you're going to discredit *me too,* by regrettable association."

"The Terracotta Army will be in perfect order, no fear." He cocked an eyebrow at Brett. "Incidentally, you're angling for a bad performance evaluation."

"Which they won't even look at, man, if you don't pull yourself together before the inspector gets here." Brett crossed to the office door and opened it. "And we're not the damn Terracotta Army, for God's sake. Talk sense, *please!*" He stepped out and slammed the door behind him.

You are, though, thought Terracotta—just not in the sense you think I meant. If in fact there is a *you,* if there is an *I.*

He wished he had not thought of the Terracotta Army; the thought, so soon after seeing his father's ghost on Sunday, had roused unwelcome memories of his own.

He looked out of the office window at the far side of the warehouse. The ghosts who used to stand outside the fence were now in the building, clustered against the wall, swaying as if in an ethereal breeze. And, sure enough, the figure of Terracotta's father was again among them, smiling and waving.

Terracotta looked away, down at the floor. His heart was pounding. Why would his father's idiot ghost be *smiling* at him?

Terracotta had been seventeen years old in 1974, and his name had still been Emilio Benedetti, when his father had found the video cameras and 8-track stereo players the boy had stolen from neighboring houses; and his father had declared that he was going to call the police, and had gone so far as to pick up the telephone.

Young Emilio had snatched up a little statue from a nearby shelf— a foot-tall image of a woman, made of terracotta, unglazed fired clay—and swung it with all his strength at his father's head . . .

The statue had not taken fingerprints, and Emilio had claimed to have found his father's body, and in the end no charges had been filed.

But Emilio had loved his father, and had been left with no definition of himself that he could live with. He mentally repeated, and tried to believe, a reassuring mantra: *The* statue *killed him, not me.* But the phrase had soon shifted its emphasis to a plaintively insistent *The statue killed* him, *not* me.

And then one day he had read about the discovery, in the buried tomb of some Chinese emperor, of some 8,000 lifesize terracotta statues of warriors; and *National Geographic* magazine referred to them as the Terracotta Army. Each statue was a distinct individual— some with various sorts of beards, some clean-shaven, some heavy-set and some lean, and all with different facial expressions—and at first he had been struck by how much they were like living people. Later he had been struck by how much living people seemed to be no more than mobile members of the Terracotta Army.

Emilio had finally found peace in the conclusion that the statue had effectually killed both his father and himself; and, later, that he and his father had never been actual selves at all—nobody was—and whatever else the statue might had done, it had dispelled a particularly persistent illusion. Emilio had learned, with relief, that all motion or stasis, regardless of any deceptive appearances of willful purpose, was just physics.

Everybody was a member of the extended Terracotta Army.

He opened the door and walked down the row of doors to Room Two, ignoring the staff members who eyed him cautiously, and stepped in. The three chairs around the radio were empty, and he sat down in one. The radio was still on.

"Amanda," he said.

From the radio speaker came a querulous voice: "I ain't speaking to you."

He touched the microphone. "I think you will. I think you'll want to."

↓ CHAPTER FOURTEEN ↓

It wasn't until they had followed Mulholland Drive's twists and curves through the hills for several miles that they passed under a scattering of wheeling pigeons, and the distortions and alterations abated. The sun was at last steady in a blue sky, and shadows held still.

For the last hectic ten minutes, Vickery had steered the taco truck past exits to several other posted but nonexistent freeways, sped through clouds of fig beetles and monarch butterflies that exploded in puffs of white dust when they struck the windshield, and downshifted when his lane ascended or descended steep inclines that he knew weren't normally there. He had several times had to shift to neutral and gun the stuttering engine to keep it from stalling, and slowing down had often involved downshifting and pumping the brakes and engaging the emergency brake. The air vents had variously bathed the truck cab in scents of burning tobacco, broken stone, perfume, and decay. And through it all, he had had to struggle to keep his mind focused on driving, and not pursuing weird random trains of association.

When Mulholland subsided at last into the mundane road they had traversed on Vickery's motorcycle two days ago, Castine hummed for a moment as if to test her voice, then spoke, for the first time in ten minutes.

"Is it over? Finally?"

Vickery stretched and flexed his shoulders, and he noticed that his shirt was damp and clinging to the seat. "Till we get back on a freeway. Or near one."

"Get your kicks on Route 666," she said shakily. "This is what you do for a living?"

He nodded. "I've never seen it *near* this bad, though. This stuff is going to get noticed, get in the news. There were cars wrecked, maybe people killed—God knows what the papers will say it is. Earthquakes? Hurricanes? And if it keeps getting worse—"

"Much worse than this would be the Labyrinth itself," she said. Vickery started to say something, but she held up her hand. "Are the freeways *becoming* the Labyrinth?" She hiccupped. "I hope you've still got those strings with beads on them."

"String abacuses. Abaci. Yes, they're still in my jacket pocket."

"Good. We may need them again just to get out of LA." She peered at him narrowly. "Which I assume we're going to be doing pretty shortly here."

"With any luck. The truck took a beating in all that."

"You've got your gun. We can always hijack another lunch wagon."

"Oh, sure. LA's full of 'em. Start thinking about what sort of food you like."

He saw ahead the dirt track that led away from the road on the south side, and steered the truck onto it.

The boxy vehicle rocked down the sloping path to the clearing with the mailbox on the south side, and Vickery was glad the brakes still worked as he eased the vehicle to a halt. The engine was still running raggedly, and when he switched it off it clattered on for several seconds before subsiding. The ensuing silence, broken only by bird calls and the whisper of cars passing on Mulholland up the slope, was a relief.

Vickery got out of the truck and walked to the edge of the slope that stretched away for several miles down wooded canyons to Sunset Boulevard, though he couldn't see that far through the closer trees. The breeze from below smelled of pine, and he crouched and freed a golf-ball-sized pinecone from the dirt and put it in his shirt pocket.

He squinted at Castine and waved toward the bandage on her head. "You okay for a hike?"

She touched the bandage. "It's not bleeding. And no concussion."

"As good as it gets," he said, and stepped down onto the slope.

They picked their way down the hillside, kicking through drifts of leaves and occasionally slapping tree trunks to keep their balance. They passed the black robe that dangled on a coat hanger from a tree branch; the mirror which was its face was a web of cracks now. Vickery nodded when Castine pointed at it and raised her eyebrows.

Artificial Christmas trees and plastic flowers lined the banks of the trench he had ridden the motorcycle over two days ago, but there was no water in the damp cement channel now. A few yards further down the slope, they came across the other channel, in which water had flowed in the direction opposite to the first one; it too carried no water. The arms of the green metal statue just beyond it were still outstretched, though its arms ended at the wrists, its pinwheel hands gone.

Vickery pulled the .45 from his pocket and signaled to Castine to stop.

He lifted his head and opened his mouth, straining to hear anything above bird calls and the wind in the branches, but there was no other sound.

At last he whispered, "Somebody's dismantled his ghost distracters. Probably yesterday," he added, seeing Castine's alarmed look.

She spread her hands. "Let's just go," she whispered back.

Vickery considered that. Hike back up to the truck, find a cutout or fire road on Mulholland where they could just wait out this spectral earthquake, this supernatural hurricane; or maybe take Mulholland all the way west to the 405 Freeway—it was always clogged with slow traffic, so maybe it wouldn't be generating as intense a current as the 101 was doing at the moment. North on it to the San Fernando Valley . . . and Kagel Mountain, from the peak of which he and Amanda had so many times launched their hang-gliders . . .

You took my wing . . .

I need to lay her to final rest before we go, he thought. Try to, at least.

"You can wait in the truck."

She shook her head. "I wish I still had my gun, though," she whispered.

Vickery stepped over the second trench, careful not to place his foot on dry leaves or twigs, and Castine followed him silently as he led the way down the wooded slope toward Hipple's house.

When he could see the one-story clapboard house through the trees, he paused and waved Castine to a halt. The place looked exactly as it had two days ago—the dozens of tiny windows below the widely overhanging roof, the TV antennas with their dolls and false teeth dangling on strings—and the screen door was open, and Vickery saw Jack Hipple step out of the house and sit down on the front steps. The man didn't seem to be hurt.

Vickery was about to move out from behind the trees into the clearing when he heard thrashing in the underbrush among the trees behind him, up the hill. Castine didn't have to be told to step out of sight behind the trunk of an oak.

The noise halted, though Vickery could now faintly hear grindings of shoes on damp soil above him; it sounded like just one pair of shoes. Someone was descending the slope, trying not to be heard doing it. Perhaps the person had belatedly noted the empty channels and the handless statue, and likewise concluded that a silent approach was called for.

The sounds became fainter, and Vickery couldn't tell how far away among the trees the person might be; and then a voice spoke softly from only a few yards away:

"Don't shoot, *Señor* Vickery."

Vickery turned his head, and wasn't altogether surprised to see the boy Santiago peering at him from behind a carob trunk. The boy was holding a semi-automatic pistol that looked extra big in his small brown hand, but it was pointed at the ground and his finger was outside the trigger guard. Vickery saw that it was a SIG-Sauer P229, and he guessed that it was the gun he and Castine had left behind on that service road two days ago.

Santiago nodded to Castine, then asked Vickery, "You come to kill Hipple?"

"No. To collect on a debt."

"I believe I recognize that gun," said Castine sternly.

"Sure, lady."

Santiago pushed the gun into the waist of his jeans and pulled his shirt out over it. To Vickery he said, "I went looking for you at the Galvan kitchen this morning. Laquedem wants to see you."

Vickery shifted uncomfortably. *It's important,* the old man had told him. *Bring it back with you, and bury that piece in the dirt at the omphalos.* Well, Vickery thought now, the piece of asphalt melted. Nothing I could do about it.

"I talked to him yesterday," he said gruffly.

"Something else. Important."

Important. That word again. Vickery sighed and squinted at him. "Do you know what it is?"

"I don't ask him his business."

Vickery hesitated, then shook his head dismissively. "We talked enough already."

The boy gave him a quizzical look, then stepped past him into the clearing. Vickery and Castine followed him, looking warily around at the gaps between the trees. There didn't seem to be anyone else in the vicinity.

Hipple looked up as the three of them approached him. The sun was on his pale face, and his dark moustache and horn-rimmed glasses looked especially dark.

"Three blind mice," he said. "What purpose brings you all here?"

"I'm here because I believe you owe me a big favor," said Vickery. "Do I need to say why?"

"I don't know. And you, my dear? What did you do to your head?"

"I'm just along with him," said Castine. "I, uh, had a misadventure with a hair-dryer."

"And the Mexican boy," said Hipple. "You want more ghost repellers?"

"Maybe," said Santiago. "Credit for future stuff, anyway. For it, I trade you this: a ghost told me that the TUA people aim to lean on you."

"No doubt," said Hipple. "I tell you what, I'm not feeling well today, so why don't you all—"

"Let's talk in the house," said Vickery.

"Oh, very *well*." Hipple got to his feet and shuffled back into the dimness, and his three visitors followed. The tarry smell of latakia tobacco was strong on the stale air.

"I want you to summon a ghost," said Vickery, fishing the little pinecone out of his pocket, "and subsume her into this. If you do that, I'll write off your betrayal."

"Hmm, hmm, subsuming ghosts, are we?" said Hipple. "A good day for it." Castine had taken a step toward the door over the abyss, and he snapped, "Stay here by the table!"

Castine halted, then went back to stand beside Vickery.

Hipple peered at him through the manifying lenses of his glasses. "You were on the highway?"

Vickery nodded. "In one of the taco trucks. For a few miles."

"Overcooked?"

"Hm? Over everythinged, you might say."

Vickery peered past the couch, wondering what Hipple had not wanted Castine to see, and his eyes had adjusted to the dimness enough for him to make out a pair of men's shoes lying toes-up on the carpet between the back of the couch and the far door.

A suspicion dawned on him, and he sang, softly, "Three blind mice, three blind mice . . ."

Hipple began jiggling violently on the couch, and then his tongue shot out six feet toward Vickery; but Vickery had half-expected it, and sprang to the side so that the wiggling tendril fell on the carpet and was quickly retracted.

"Flee now the gun!" sang Hipple, "dum dum de dum! They epitaph the embalmer's life—"

"Two and two is—" began Castine quickly.

"No!" Vickery shouted at her, "he can still do it!" To what he now understood was Hipple's ghost, he said, "Stay where you are," and then he strode past the couch and pulled open the door over the cliff. Cool fresh air blew into the room, chilling the sudden sweat on his forehead, and in the wash of daylight Vickery saw Hipple's body lying face-up on the floor behind the couch. The eyes were open but not gleaming, and the shirt was blotted brown with dried blood. Vickery glanced behind him—Hipple's ghost was still on the couch, its head bobbing to the song it was now humming.

Vickery stepped back and switched on the old television set, then turned to face the sky beyond the open door.

He could hear Hipple's ghost still humming. Through the doorway the distant rooftops of Beverly Hills were confetti around the line of Sunset Boulevard. His heart was thudding in his chest.

The orange wing and the red-striped white one, he thought. We'll meet at the landing zone. He took a deep breath.

"Amanda!" he called out into the air. He dug a hand into a pocket of his jeans and pulled out his wedding ring and slipped it onto his finger. "Amanda!" he called again, holding his left hand up against the daylight.

He heard Castine gasp behind him, and when he turned he saw that she was staring at the television set. He followed her gaze and saw that a face had appeared in black and white on the screen.

This time it was recognizably Amanda's face. The mouth moved, and from the open doorway her voice shivered the air.

"Herbert."

A quick glance showed him that the doorway was still empty, and he looked back at the screen.

"Herbert," came her voice from the side again, "run, jump, quick get here where they can't find you, help me hide from them. Where are the children? I looked out in the yard, but it's just a big hole now. Were you going to put in a swimming pool? It's way too deep, I think it goes to China."

He held out the little pinecone in a trembling palm. "Amanda," he said unsteadily, "I want you to relax into this. The . . . person on the couch can tell you how. You've been too long out beside that desert highway—"

Castine emitted a squeak in the same moment that the light from the opened doorway dimmed slightly, and when Vickery looked up he saw a translucent silhouette framed there.

"I will not!" said Amanda's ghost. "*You* relax into it, if you want somebody to be a pinecone forever!" Her glassy arms rose, slow and disjointed, like kelp fronds in a slow tide. "*I* keep on looking for our *children,* when the bad man isn't asking me questions . . . but I keep coming back to the same place . . . the factory *moves . . .*"

"Jack," called Vickery desperately, "how do we do this?" He waved the pinecone toward the couch. "Like with your pipes, your Castellos."

"Dearly departed," said Hipple's ghost in an affected high, nasal tone, "we are gathered here to join this woman and this pinecone in holy oblivion—"

Castine and Santiago, wide-eyed, stepped back as Hipple's ghost rippled and blurred and then was visible standing up. It now appeared to be wearing pajamas.

"Amanda!" said Vickery. "Cooperate here, please!"

"But," said Hipple's ghost, "speak now and forever hold my peace." It faced Vickery, and again the tongue leaped out of its face, this time striking Vickery's outstretched hand.

Razory cold lanced through Vickery's hand, and the pinecone fell to the floor, jerkily, for the ghost's tongue was now attached to it—and the body of Hipple's ghost was shrinking, disappearing. Within moments the tongue was all that was left, and then it disappeared into the pinecone.

"No, damn it," gasped Vickery, "not *you*—"

His empty hand was numb and throbbing. He spun back to Amanda's ghost—and it was vibrating now, and when he glanced at the television screen he saw that her mouth was wide and her eyes had disappeared.

"I seen this," said Santiago softly. "They're shocking her."

"Feedback," said Castine. "I—"

"Amanda!" called Vickery, his voice cracking. "Stay here—damn it—"

The television screen showed only bristling gray now, but her voice came faintly from the clear doorway, *"Mulholland, please, Mulholland again . . ."*

The door over the cliff slammed shut with an impact that shook the whole house. The television screen went dark.

Vickery and Castine and Santiago looked at one another breathlessly for several seconds, and then Santiago walked around the couch and looked down at Hipple's corpse.

Castine exhaled as if she'd been holding her breath. "Is that his *body* back there?"

"What?" snapped Vickery, wincing as he massaged his hand. "Oh—yes, damn him. Looks like he's been shot, at least several hours ago." He looked at Santiago. "They already leaned on him."

"We've got to get out of here," said Castine. "She just told them where we are. And," she added, waving toward the body behind the couch, "they were here a while ago, they know where this place is. Where would he have put my gun, my registered SIG?"

"I don't know," said Vickery. "Look around."

She swept a quick glance over the shelves, then hurried past the television, down a hall.

Santiago had turned away and picked up the pinecone. He held it out toward Vickery. "You want it? Hipple's in it."

"I'd like to burn it," said Vickery. "But I suppose we can always use another inhabited piece of junk." He took it with his left hand and put it in his shirt pocket. This was a failure, he thought. Worse than a waste of time.

Santiago walked past him, toward the shelves. The boy dragged an ottoman over and stood on it, and pulled down the box that Vickery recalled held the spirit-level stars and fixed compasses. Santiago hopped down and opened the box.

"He still owes me," he said, taking several of the spirit-level stars.

"Fine, fine." Vickery looked around the dim room, but didn't see anything that seemed to him worth taking.

Castine reappeared from the hallway, panting. "I didn't see it. And we've got to get *away* from this, now!"

Santiago didn't look at her, and spoke to Vickery. "Laquedem needs to talk to you." Vickery started to tell the boy to forget it, but Santiago went on, "I think a lot of people are dying. Cars are crashing out there, a lot of 'em. This is your city." The boy tucked the spirit-level stars into the back pocket of his jeans.

Castine stamped her foot and waved toward the front door.

Vickery nodded to Castine, and told Santiago, "If he knows a way to fix it, let him do it."

The boy gave him an unfriendly look. "You maybe noticed he's old, and sick."

Vickery bared his teeth impatiently. Would it all have stopped, he wondered, if I had buried a piece of something real—hyper-real—at the omphalos? Might that have *closed* the omphalos, the conduit between the two worlds?

Cars are crashing out there.

Is there—by any chance—something I can still do?

This is your city.

"We can call him from *Nevada* or somewhere," said Castine, stepping to the door. "Sebastian! Will you come *on?*"

Vickery followed Castine. "The guy's just down by Pico," he said to her. "It's a quick drive."

"Not now," said Santiago, tossing the box onto the couch. "He's someplace else, not at Rambam now. I can take you to him, quick, in your truck. He's got tickets for me and him to take a bus to Barstow tonight. If the city can't be fixed, he wants to be away from freeways and north of the San Gabriel Mountains."

"We should go see him before we leave California," Vickery told Castine as they stepped down onto the astroturf in front of Hipple's house. The pine-scented breeze was chilly.

"This is the guy on crutches?" Castine asked angrily. "Who I saw at

Holy Sacrament yesterday? If he's so smart, why don't we do what he's doing? Away from the freeways, north of the mountains!"

Vickery started across the clearing toward the trees, squinting in the sunlight after the dimness inside Hipple's house. "Is he close by?" he asked Santiago. When the boy nodded, Vickery turned to Castine. "I should talk to him. I owe him—he told me how to rescue you, in return for me doing something for him, and I didn't manage to do it." He held up a hand to stop her further objections. "And if he knows a way"—another way, he thought—"to close the gate between the, the *Labyrinth* and this world . . ." He took a step up the slope. "People were certainly getting killed today on the crazy freeways. Still are, probably. Maybe we could help stop it, somehow."

"Would you still care about all that," said Castine, starting up the slope herself, "if your *Amanda* had climbed safely into the pinecone?"

Vickery opened his mouth to snap an angry reply, when it occurred to him that in fact he probably would be willing to leave everybody on the freeways to their perils, if Amanda had consented to take eternal refuge in the pinecone. Slowly he pulled the wedding ring off of his finger and pushed it back down into the pocket of his jeans.

"Maybe not," he conceded. "But if this guy Laquedem thinks he knows a way to save people from getting killed on these cranked-up freeways, don't you think we should delay our exit long enough to at least hear what he has to say?"

She was silent as the three of them clambered up the hillside, stumbling over roots and rocks. Vickery's right hand was recovering enough feeling and muscle control for him to use it to brace himself on tree trunks from time to time. When they reached the green metal figure, Santiago stepped aside and began tugging his bicycle out from behind a pyracantha bush, and Castine gave Vickery a doubtful frown and nodded toward the boy.

Clearly she meant, *Do you trust him?*

"I think he's honest, most of the time," said Vickery quietly. "Freelance, not loyal, but honest, to an extent."

"Huh. Like us all these days."

Santiago had freed the bicycle, and the three of them resumed climbing the slope, Santiago leaning on his bicycle to keep his balance, and Castine and Vickery sometimes proceeding awkwardly on all fours.

At the crest of the slope at last, Vickery walked a few steps across the clearing and sat down by the mailbox post to catch his breath. "We can put your bike," he said to Santiago after a few moments, "in the truck."

Castine flicked her fingers upward. "You can rest while you're driving."

"Ri-ight," said Vickery, getting to his feet. He trudged to the taco truck and opened the back doors. Santiago wheeled his bicycle over, and easily lifted it in and leaned it against the refrigerator.

"If everybody's tricky," the boy said, squinting up at Vickery, "you can't be loyal to more than one of them."

You can try, thought Vickery. He closed the doors and they walked to the front of the truck.

Santiago sat on the deck just behind Vickery and Castine, and Vickery gunned the engine experimentally, and pumped the brakes. Everything seemed to work well enough, and the dashboard metronome was motionless, so he shifted the truck into reverse and backed around in a half-circle, then shifted to low gear.

"But," said Castine, apparently continuing a line of thought she'd been pursuing, "*not* if it involves you going back into the Labyrinth!"

"No," agreed Vickery, with feeling. He could comfortably have carried Amanda's ghost, silent and safe and inert in the pinecone, for the rest of his life; but in the Labyrinth—even if a second trip didn't trap him forever in that insane hell—he might have to *face* her ghost again, hear what it would say to him.

He began driving up the path to Mulholland Drive. "No," he repeated; and just in case he might later change his mind, he reached to the side, took hold of the metronome's upright pendulum by the bone knob on top, then nodded, snapped it off and tossed it out the window.

Brett and Ollie, senior officers, waited in the administration office for the inspector, while in the break room Terracotta went through the motions of conducting the prescribed activities of the Operations Extension of the Transportation Utility Agency.

The assignment packets he had passed out to the dozen uneasy staff members were, in some cases, weeks old, and he knew that they were a waste of time in any case. The NSA wanted an interview with a Chinese embassy clerk who had been killed in a wreck on the 405, TUA headquarters was asking for interviews with anyone who had died on or near the 210/605 intersection between certain hours on a date a week ago, and there was even a request from an attorney having to do with a probate case; at least those would involve summoning ghosts. But there were also requests for analyses of highway deaths of American citizens in Moscow and Riyadh and Mumbai, which would be completely pointless. Terracotta knew these little goals were all just scattered artifacts, incidental noise at the periphery of a single entirely different, and transcendent, purpose.

Somebody had put a plate of broccoli and tofu in the microwave and then left it there after the bell pinged, and now the smell of it on the air-conditioned breeze made Terracotta wrinkle his nose. He wished the inspector would arrive and then leave, so that he could get back to the important work; before reluctantly leaving the radio in Room One to convene this sham meeting, he had briefly got Amanda Woods on the ghost frequency, and under feedback duress she had said that Woods was for some reason back on Mulholland Drive. The contact had lasted only a few seconds—Terracotta had switched on the microphone as she'd been babbling something about a pinecone, and when he switched it off, she had said, *Mulholland, please, Mulholland again.*

"Uh . . . is everyone clear on his or her assignment?" Terracotta asked now, pushing his chair back from the table and standing up.

They all gave him blank-faced nods, and he said, "Fine," and walked out of the room into the big warehouse space just as Ollie emerged from the office two doors down, pocketing his phone. Brett was already walking out away from the office. Terracotta didn't look toward the north end of the warehouse, where the ghosts still stood against that wall. He assumed his father's ghost was still among them, but he couldn't bring himself to make sure.

"Show time, boss," Ollie said, pointing across the broad floor. Terracotta took a deep breath and straightened his shoulders before turning to look toward the parking lot door.

Brett had opened the door, and a lean, silver-haired man in a business suit was for a moment silhouetted by the daylight outside, and then Brett was escorting him into the building. Four younger men in suits followed him in, and then the door was closed.

"Mr. Terracotta?" called the silver-haired stranger when he was still a dozen yards away across the blue floor.

Terracotta stepped forward—

But he rocked to a halt when the broad doors on the south side of the warehouse shuddered, shed clouds of rust, and, with a prolonged screech that echoed in the big warehouse space, began to move apart on their long-unused tracks. A billowing cloud of sand blew in through the widening gap, and the old truck tire that hung above it rocked and swung and then fell; the tire struck the floor and bounced high, and through the churning curtain of sand Terracotta could see that it was now hanging unsupported in mid-air. His nose stung with the smell of ozone. A roar like truck engines sounded from beyond the separating doors.

Terracotta glanced quickly around, and it was clear that this was not some private hallucination of his own. Several of the staff had hurried out of the break room, and at least a couple of them were now running away from the opening south wall.

"Turn off all communication devices!" shouted the inspector. The ghosts who had been standing by the north wall were now moving out across the floor, and the inspector sprinted right through several of them on his way to the office door.

Clearly he had not seen the ghosts, but the four men with him did; they stepped wide around the wobbling figures, eyeing them in alarm, and one man called, loudly over the engine noise, "Which one is Terracotta? We have to act *now*."

Smoky silhouettes of old trucks were moving through the big opening now, images from the days when this place had been a working warehouse.

Brett was holding a handkerchief across his nose, but he pointed toward Terracotta with his free hand. "Gray pony-tail," he called back. "*Not* here! Big Bear."

Et tu, Brett! thought Terracotta. But they don't dare kill me here in this current, in this *tsunami*. They aim to take me to where they *can* do it.

Promoted sideways!

He feinted to the right, toward the office, then dug the toes of his Birkenstock sandals into the vinyl floor and ran for the parking lot door, knowing even as he ran that they'd catch him before he could punch in the code.

But one of the ghosts had stepped between him and the four men, and one of the men yelled in surprise and fell over backward, and when Terracotta glanced that way he saw that a hose or cable connected the ghost's head to the fallen man; and when it retracted and struck another of them, Terracotta saw that it must be the ghost's tongue—and the ghost was his father's. A gunshot rang echoes around the walls, apparently hitting no one and possibly aimed at the ghost.

Out across the floor somewhere, the inspector was shouting, "Shut it all down right now, kill the momentum!"

Terracotta had reached the door, and his hand was tapping out the code. Looking back as he pushed the door open, he saw figures struggling in the whirling veils of sand, and Brett running out of the confusion toward him; but the tongue, if it was a tongue, sprang out of the cloud and hit Brett in the side of the head; he tumbled forward onto the floor, and Terracotta stepped outside, slammed the door behind him and hurried down the sidewalk to his own car.

Deleted persons are *not* the people they derive from, he reminded himself feverishly as he got in and started the engine. It was *not* my father, back there, who saved me from being driven to a place far from the freeway current and killed. In any case, love—and forgiveness!—are poisonous unwelcome illusions!

He rocked the car in reverse out of the parking space and then drove forward to the gate; for several anxious seconds he waited, wondering if Brett and the inspector could possibly have had time to delete his transponder code from the security system. But the gate rolled back at last, even as the rearview mirror showed him people staggering out of the warehouse door after him, and he sped through and turned right on Bandini to get onto the 110 north, to the Pasadena Freeway. He knew that he, or something inside him or something he was inside of, had to be at the omphalos now. There was no longer any hope of getting a TUA team together to find Woods, and it was apparently no longer necessary anyway.

Sounds and colors had become less distinct, and he knew that his superfluous personality was, finally, close to being entirely consumed by the perpetual chaotic ground-state remembered in mythology as the Minotaur. It was confined in the Labyrinth and it *was* the Labyrinth—*the terrain is the body, the map is the anatomy chart*—but Terracotta, or it through him, had done enough now to bring the freeways into the identity of the Labyrinth, allowing, no, *forcing*, a long-delayed, long-impeded consummation. And it surely was at hand.

↓ CHAPTER FIFTEEN ↓

"It's letting up," said Castine.

When they had turned south from Mulholland onto Cahuenga and driven for two tense but uneventful minutes, she turned on both of the radios. They were tuned to KOXR 910, and the mariachi music vibrating out of both sets of speakers was synchronized.

"I should get news," she added, reaching for the tuning knob on the dashboard radio.

"Leave it," Vickery told her, "you'd have to hunt and then get the same station on both of them, and things might change fast."

On the freeway lanes visible beyond the row of trees to their left, traffic was moving, though slowly, and in several quick glances Vickery had seen only a couple of instances of cars crumpled together, with other cars edging around the collisions in a fairly orderly way. Maybe it hasn't been too bad yet, he told himself.

"Oh, do let's make this *quick*," said Castine, her voice strained, "with this old crutches guy! We need to be going north, or east, *soon*, as fast as this damn truck will go. With luck we can be in Lancaster or Palm Springs before your horrible magic current starts up again."

Santiago was leaning forward between the seats. "He's at Griffith park. The observatory."

Vickery glanced at Castine. "That's not far, and no freeways." She shook her head impatiently.

Santiago shifted his sneakers on the vinyl kitchen deck. "This is a food truck," he added.

Vickery dismissed a sarcastic reply and said, "Yes, Santiago." Then he added, "Oh! Are you hungry? Go ahead and microwave something."

Castine muttered under her breath, then said, "I guess I wouldn't mind another burrito."

"Me either," said Vickery. Santiago had already shuffled back into the kitchen, and Vickery called, "Make it three!"

The freeway to their left was higher now, rising toward a bridge over an onramp, and to their right was a weedy slope and a row of seven cypress trees beyond the sidewalk—and in front of the first cypress stood a small figure with its right arm extended. Vickery was concentrating on staying in his lane and watching for deformations of the landscape, but Castine touched his arm and pointed.

The hitchhiker was the girl in overalls and straw hat.

After a moment's hesitation, Vickery slowed, then swung the truck close to the curb. He passed the girl, but as soon as her face had appeared outside the passenger side window, it remained there, motionless in the window frame, as he braked to a halt.

Castine opened the door—and Vickery gasped in surprise, for the image of the girl stayed in the window glass as the door swung away, and there was no one standing on the sidewalk. In the window glass, viewed nearly end-on, he saw the girl's face narrowed by perspective, and then it was gone.

Castine slowly closed the door.

Vickery looked ahead, and in the passenger side mirror, but there was no one at all on the sidewalk.

Several seconds later, after a couple of cars behind him honked, he lifted his foot from the brake; the idling engine rolled the truck forward slowly, and he moved his foot to the gas pedal and accelerated back up to thirty miles an hour, passing a median pedestal indicating the entrance to the Hollywood Bowl.

"Hollywood Bowl," Castine noted emptily. She cleared her throat and went on, "I won't roll the window down for a while."

Vickery nodded. The lost little ghost girl, who liked to imagine that she was the character in that book, might reappear in the glass.

At Franklin, Vickery turned left, and soon they were driving between old apartment buildings and cars parked fender-to-fender along the curb. He drove more slowly, careful not to clip the parked cars or drift into the next lane, and when Castine touched his arm again he didn't spare her a glance until he had stopped at a red light.

She nodded over her shoulder, back toward the dim kitchen, and when he turned around he saw two small silhouettes leaning over a counter. When the door of the microwave oven was briefly opened, he saw again the pale face he had seen moments earlier in the passenger side window.

He looked at Castine. She was frowning with evident concern, and mouthed, *Can they eat?*

"No," he whispered. "It's for us."

The light turned green and he drove forward, and a minute later he heard the microwave oven ping behind him. Vickery risked a quick look back toward the kitchen, and Santiago was now the only one back there.

The boy sidled up between the seats and handed him and Castine each a hot burrito wrapped in paper towels. Vickery reached forward and set his on the dashboard to cool off. Santiago was already eating one.

"You had . . . help, back there?" Vickery said.

"Yeah," said the boy around a mouthful. He swallowed, then added, "I didn't know how to work a microwave."

"I guess she picked that up sometime," said Castine softly.

"She looked at the food," Santiago went on, "like she would have liked some, but she didn't touch it."

Maybe she liked Mexican food when she was alive, Vickery thought.

At Western he turned north, and soon the avenue became Los Feliz Drive, with a tight turn northeastward, and now it was palatial houses above ascending green lawns on either side.

Castine had resignedly taken a bite of her own burrito. "I'd get tired of a steady diet of these," she remarked, "but right now they're damn good." She looked at Vickery. "Who *was* Hipple?"

Vickery dismissed the little girl from his thoughts. "Oh," he said, "small-time blackmailer, forger, ghostmonger. And painter—I always knew he did those pet portraits, by mail, with ads in the Pennysaver and all, but yesterday I found out he did portraits of ghosts, too, which were supposed to keep them anchored on this side, in exchange for . . . I don't know, useful information, blackmail stuff, I imagine. And for a while he was claiming he could get the ghosts of writers like Auden and Yeats to sign books posthumously—which some collectors value way more than books the poets signed when they were alive—but it turned out he was faking the signatures."

He steered the truck left on Vermont and followed the curving road up the hill between old trees and close-set houses.

"I knew about him from my days as a cop," Vickery went on, "and when I recovered from being shot by your TUA comrades four years ago, I went to him for help getting a fake identity, this Sebastian Vickery identity. I figured we had enough on each other to keep us mutually quiet, but after a while he wanted to make it blackmail, hinting that he might accidentally tell certain people about Herbert Woods if I didn't give him access to valuable ghosts that I came across in my work for Galvan." He smiled mirthlessly. "And then he did try to sell me out to the TUA, but our little Mary warned me away from him, and Galvan stepped in with a more reliable plan to get me, and at that point the TUA clearly had no more use for the . . . inconveniently informed Hipple."

"And Mary warned you off then too," said Castine.

Vickery nodded and quickly looked back again, but the little girl had not reappeared. "That's right. Anyway, that's how Hipple was— *somebody* was bound to kill him sooner or later."

"He always wanted to buy my wrist-bands," said Santiago from behind the seats. The boy held out one arm between Vickery and Castine, and the leather band swung loosely on his wrist as the truck rocked along. "My parents are *in* them," Santiago went on. "He said he just wants to give them a safe home, up on the shelf with his pipes and old teeth, but I know he would say he would burn them, if I didn't do stuff for him."

"I'm glad he's dead," said Castine with a shiver.

"I imagine a lot of people will be," said Vickery.

Castine shifted in her seat. "You know what he had in his bedroom? I looked in there, searching for my gun. Hung on the walls are about a dozen self-portraits."

Vickery thought of the pinecone in his pocket. "He decided to just hide out, instead. Insensibly, forever."

The curling road had narrowed to two lanes and climbed up into the hills, out of the clusters of houses, and now the truck was passing only occasional weather-twisted trees, with an ascending slope to the left and a precipice to the right.

"*Not far,*" said Castine.

"We're almost there," Vickery said, and he ignored a skeptical look from Santiago.

"You met this Laquedem guy yesterday," Castine said to Vickery. "Is he another . . . *ghostmonger,* like Hipple?"

"No," said Santiago sharply. "Whatever that means. He's nothing like Hipple."

"Sorry," said Castine. "Okay." She turned in her seat to face the boy. "Do *you* know what plan he might have, for closing off the—" She nodded back down the hill, "—the Labyrinth?"

"If I did, I would still let him tell you. Your people opened it up."

"Not my people anymore. You were there when I lost my job two days ago . . . and picked yourself up a gun."

Remembering that Santiago had extorted three hundred dollars from Castine for the return of her own gun, now lost, Vickery thought it was time to change the subject—but something twitched in his shirt pocket, and he jumped and slapped at it before remembering that he had put the Hipple pinecone there.

"What?" asked Castine in alarm. Santiago was staring at him.

"It's just the pinecone —" he began, but the battery-powered radio abruptly stopped playing music, and a man's hoarse voice came scratching out of its speakers.

"Hello-o—hello-o," it rasped. "Is this the Gulf of Mexico?" Then it began making a choppy sound that might have been an attempt at laughter, and it didn't stop. The radio mounted in the dashboard kept on playing mariachi music.

Castine reached for the knob, but Vickery waved her hand back. "Is that your man Eliot?" he whispered.

"Oh!" Castine winced, and shook her head. "I don't know . . ." She leaned forward and said, hoarsely, "Eliot?"

The laughter continued without a pause, and behind it a deep booming had started up.

"It's the malmeme!" said Castine. "We shouldn't listen!" She turned to Santiago and said, "Cover your ears!"

"It's not your *malmeme,*" said Vickery, "or not yet. Anyway, what Terracotta didn't want you to hear was just quotes from a poem,

Dryden's translation of Ovid's *Metamorphoses*—like my 'air is free' couplet." He glanced sideways at her. "I guess the quotes from the poem only happen when there's that drumming in the background?"

"It's when the ghosts are near that factory. It makes that noise. You remember—"

"I remember the factory."

Santiago shifted his position on the vinyl kitchen deck. "The factory moves, the ghosts say."

The voice on the radio had finally stopped its repetitive laughing noise. "The boy doesn't eat right," it said. "Get him to eat proper food— I would but cannot; my son's image stands before my sight." The booming was still going on in the background. "If nymphs were waiters and, with naked feet, in order served the courses of the meat, he'd still be a vegetarian." Vickery guessed that the odd phrases were more quotes from Ovid.

Castine waved, and when Vickery looked away from the road at her, she mouthed, *Terracotta is a vegetarian.*

Vickery nodded and gestured toward the radio, raising his eyebrows.

"In sequence," she whispered to him, "one word at a time." More loudly, she went on, "Terracotta . . ." and then nodded to Vickery.

He shrugged, frowning, but said, "Is."

"Your," said Castine.

Vickery guessed her intent. "Son?" he said.

"No, no!" said the voice from the radio. "Emilio *Benedetti* is my son! He wrote his name in wet cement when they put in the new post office. Is that stupid or what? I whupped him good for it too, don't worry." Again the ratcheting laughter started up, and it continued for so long that now Vickery reached for the knob.

"Wait," Castine whispered sharply; and she raised her palm toward Vickery.

Not knowing what she wanted to ask now, Vickery rolled his eyes and ventured, "Is."

Castine pursed her lips, then said, "his," and exaggeratedly mouthed the word *name.*

"Name," said Vickery obediently.

"Terracotta," said Castine.

Vickery had guessed where she was going. "Now?" he said, and Castine nodded.

"Terracotta is clay fired in a kiln," the voice said. "And it's *kiln* me, the clay statue, but the boy didn't mean to do it—the little scamp!—and now there he is, at the top of the tornado, I can see him up there in the sky, from beside the highway. Talk to him, make him stop, he's gonna break everything! What, what? This is a toll call, ask not for whom."

"Emilio," said Castine slowly, then nodded to Vickery.

"Killed," said Vickery with certainty.

"You?"

The drumming background noise was louder. "Ah!" said the voice, "the wretched father, father now no more, but stricken down lies prostrate on the floor!"

The booming and the voice both stopped, and now synchronized music was at last playing from both radios again.

When the music had continued for several seconds, and Vickery had concentrated only on steering the truck along the curving uphill lane, he heard Castine shift in her seat as she relaxed.

"He," she said, "wants us to get Terracotta to stop being a vegetarian."

"Make a note of it," said Vickery faintly.

"And get him down from the top of the tornado. I saw a tornado, when we were . . . *there*, in the Labyrinth."

"I did too," said Vickery, "way off in the distance on the other side of the highway. It looked like it was sucking up little bits of stuff into the sky."

"I watched it, while I was sitting by Galvan's burned-up car, before you found me with your strings. It was human figures being drawn up by the tornado. A lot of them."

"Ghosts," said Vickery.

"Well, obviously. Who else is there?"

The road straightened and leveled out at last, and cars were parked along the shoulders in both directions. Ahead Vickery could see the three black domes of the Griffith Park Observatory.

He guessed that there would be a few parking spaces available in the lot, despite the cars parked out here beside the road, and he pressed on. "In the church parking lot yesterday, you said that Terracotta's been acting screwy on the job, like ignoring his official duties to talk to ghosts about the Labyrinth—what is it he wants to find out, or accomplish?"

"I don't think *Terracotta* much *wants* anything, anymore," said Castine. "He'd say emotions, like *wanting*, are like insignificant vibrations in a machine. I think something else has stepped into the vacuum, the deprivation chamber, that he's made of himself." She smiled at him nervously. "I think *it* wants to combine that world with the freeways. Make itself bigger, more complete."

Vickery remembered the inhuman roaring in the Labyrinth and shivered, wondering if this detour was a waste of precious time after all. "We'll be on the road to Nevada right after we talk to this guy," he said, to himself as much as to Castine.

He drove up one aisle of the lot and down another, and did find a parking spot, and edged the truck into it; and after Castine and Santiago had climbed out, he pulled down the canvas covers on both sides of the truck.

Castine was pointing at a nearby kiosk. "You pay for parking there," she said.

"To hell with that," said Vickery. "Let Galvan get a ticket."

The three of them started walking between parked cars toward the wide, imposing white structure under the black domes a hundred yards away.

A broad green lawn lay between the parking lot and the observatory; three cement walkways extended across it, and Vickery led the way along the center one. The breeze across the hilltop was chilly. Late afternoon sun threw their shadows on the grass to his left, and to his right across the receding hills he could see the Hollywood sign and the distant towers of Westwood.

Halfway across the lawn they walked around a pedestal with tall marble statues of bearded old astronomers on it, and then a sundial. Looking ahead toward the Art Deco-style observatory with its three widely spaced domes, Vickery thought the place looked like a temple to gods of order.

"Uranus," said Santiago, who was walking behind Castine.

She turned to stare at him, but the boy was pointing at the pavement, where a brass plate was inset in a slightly curved groove that transected the sidewalk cement. Vickery peered at it and read ORBIT OF URANUS.

"Walk of stars," the boy said. He waved around at the broad view. "You can see pieces of their rings wherever there's cement. The marker for the sun is in the middle of all the rings, up there in the sidewalk by the doors."

"Planets," corrected Castine.

Santiago shrugged. "They're all higher than the moon, anyway." His tone seemed to imply that things under the moon were a mess.

Vickery was looking ahead at the tall bronze doors, and when he and Castine and Santiago tapped up the marble steps, a group of tourists pushed the doors open and came squinting out into the late afternoon sunlight. Vickery realized to his surprise that he had been hoping the place was closed, in spite of the crowded parking lot; and that he was ashamed at the prospect of meeting Laquedem again.

I promised to bring something real back from the Labyrinth, he thought, and I failed. He said parts of the highway there were real, and I grabbed a part that apparently wasn't—and then didn't try to find another.

Vickery caught one of the heavy doors and held it open for his companions and then stepped through after them.

The room beyond was under the middle dome, wide and octagonal, and high overhead the inner surface of the dome was a fresco of mythological figures from the zodiac. Through a hole in the center of the dome hung a long cable, and Vickery's gaze followed it down into a broad well that filled most of the floor. The well was ringed by a waist-high marble wall, and he shuffled across the tile floor to look down into it.

At the end of the cable six feet below, a big, highly polished brass ball swung ponderously from one side of the well to the other, and then all the way back, just above a reflective concave stone surface; a brass table only inches high had been set up at one end of the pendulum's long arc, and a couple of dozen black pegs were lined up on it. The six at the left side were lying flat, and as Vickery watched, the pendulum, which he now saw had a spike extending from the bottom of it, swept over one of the fallen pegs and then began its long retreat to the other side of the well.

"You didn't succeed," said a gravelly voice beside him, "or more likely you didn't even have the guts to try. *Some* poor devil crossed over yesterday at around 2 PM—could have been a plain accident, the way things are now. The ghost voices drowned out KFI again on my radio, and the freeway gypsies were all excited about it. But the conduit between the worlds remains open."

Vickery sighed and turned to face Isaac Laquedem. The old man was still wearing his shirt and pants backward, and along with one pair of glasses dangling on a lanyard around his neck he had a blue canvas bag slung over one shoulder.

Vickery was trying to frame a question, but the old man waved down at the pendulum and said, in a voice flat with evident control, "Ordinarily its arc shifts enough to knock over one peg every ten minutes, and if you waited twenty-four hours the arc would rotate clockwise all around the circle. But the pendulum itself doesn't shift—it just appears to, because the earth rotates counterclockwise under it."

"—Oh," said Vickery.

"But today," Laquedem went on, more harshly, " it's taking more like fifteen minutes for the pendulum to knock over each peg in the line. The Labyrinth's lack of rotation—or counter-rotation!—is imposing itself on Los Angeles; there'll be stretch-marks in the hills, riptides offshore, cesium clocks deviating from one another by whole seconds. Spiritually, the city and the Labyrinth are now very close to merging, becoming one. I've been watching the pendulum here for hours, to see if you might yet do what I said." He nodded toward the swinging brass ball. "It's clear you did not. And so the boy and I are getting on a bus to Barstow."

Laquedem pushed himself away from the wall, and Santiago held his crutches while he fitted them under his arms. "Let's go outside. I have some time before we need to be at the bus station, and I want to know what didn't happen."

"Look," said Vickery, "it's getting late—"

"Tell me about it. You can spare me a couple of minutes, though, right?"

Vickery spread his hands. I owe him that, he thought. "A couple."

Castine had been hanging back by the wall, but when Laquedem began making his way toward the door, she fell into step behind Vickery and Santiago.

Out in the coppery sunlight, Laquedem poled his way down the steps and then swiveled to the left and sat down on a knee-high concrete slab with a planter on it.

He looked up at Vickery, then at Castine, who was now standing between Vickery and Santiago.

"Who's this?" Laquedem asked.

"Uh," said Vickery, "this is Ingrid Castine. Ingrid, Isaac Laquedem. She's the friend," he added, "who I went into the Labyrinth to fetch out."

Laquedem cocked his head and frowned. "It *was* you who crossed over, yesterday? Deliberately?"

"*Yes*," said Vickery.

"That's what a ghost on the island told me," put in Santiago, almost too quietly to be heard.

Laquedem turned a stern look on Castine.

She nodded. "He did. And it's not an easy place to get out of."

Laquedem waved at her bandaged head. "You got injured?"

"Oh, no. Somebody shot me earlier in the day."

The old man raised his white eyebrows. "Must have been quite a day." He swung his gaze back to Vickery. "I apologize, sir. I had concluded that you were too cowardly to try. But—" and he made a snatching motion in front of his face with one hand, "—weren't you able to get to the highway? Or did you just forget what I told you, what you promised to do?"

"I don't think you remember what the Labyrinth is like," said Vickery, wishing his tone didn't sound defensive. "I did pick up a piece of asphalt from the highway edge, like you said—but it turned to water."

Laquedem shook his head, baring his teeth in a grimace. "I *told* you that only parts of the highway would be real. *Que balagan!* Why in literal hell didn't you try grabbing *another* piece of it?"

"A ghost was chasing us," protested Castine.

Laquedem was staring at Vickery now in open dismay. "Is that true? Is that why?"

Vickery wished Castine hadn't tried to help. "Partly," he admitted.

"*Klutz mit aoygn!* Idiot! You ran away! because—a *ghost* was *chasing* you?"

"We were—in that place, you—" Vickery let out the rest of his breath in a sigh. "The short version is, yes, that's why we ran away. But you *didn't tell* me—remember?—that planting a piece of something at the omphalos would stop the Labyrinth from crashing into LA.

I meant to do it, I *tried* to do it, but I thought it was just some private concern of your own." He slapped his pocket to make sure he had the truck keys. "And now, if you'll excuse us—"

"Wait, you're right, I was wrong not to tell you. I wasn't sure of you. You work for Galvan, and without ghost traffic most of her business enterprises would surely be gone. Many a career would surely evaporate. In contrast with those certainties, I didn't think you'd find my purpose entirely desirable, any more than the TUA man did yesterday." Laquedem had rocked back to look into the sky as he spoke, and now he lowered his head. "Do you know why the Minoan civilization fell to the Mycenaeans?"

"No I don't. And we only came here to drop the kid off." Vickery took Castine's arm.

"Wait, wait," the old man went on. "Listen to me, please! Daedalus built the physical part of the Labyrinth on Minoan Crete, at Knossos, but the Minoans later built a duplicate of it on the island of Thera, sixty-eight miles away. This was all four thousand years ago. On Crete they were careful to send only a limited number of slaves through the Labyrinth—just enough to get the field effect, see a ways into the future. But on Thera they pushed it. Wait, look."

Vickery caught Castine's eye and nodded toward the parking lot, but she shook her head and looked back at Laquedem.

The old man unzipped the blue canvas bag and pulled out a pair of glasses and a sheaf of papers. Vickery noticed a couple of blocks of Blue Ice in the bag, and saw frost on the glasses.

"You keep your glasses cold?" asked Castine.

"I have to, the lenses are ice. Shut up." Laquedem rubbed off some of the frost and unfolded the pages. The top sheet was a photocopy of sketchy squiggles arranged in a spiral, and he fitted the glasses on over his nose and peered closely at it.

"This script is Linear A," Laquedem muttered, "the written script of the old Minoan culture, and only a few very secretive people have figured out how to read it—and it helps if you read it through lenses that are frozen water from Lake Kournas, on Crete."

Santiago gave Vickery a stern look, as if daring him to laugh at the old man. Vickery shook his head.

"The two Labyrinths became *the same thing*, it says," said Laquedem, touching a pair of symbols on the paper, "same identity, you see. If two things become in some important sense identical, become the same entity—well, they can't go on being two separate things any longer, can they? They strive to become one. And the old Minoans had foolishly made this *second* Labyrinth, *another* living image of the thing they remembered as the Minotaur."

"What happened?" asked Castine, clearly interested in spite of herself.

"Thera tried to merge with Crete—and blew up," said Laquedem. "The whole island blew to smithereens, and so Thera was gone, and even Crete never recovered from the resulting tidal wave damage, and the Mycenaeans conquered the crippled Minoan civilization. It was a truly devastating explosion." He looked up, and his melting glasses made tracks like tears down his furrowed cheeks. "That's about to happen now, here."

Vickery had heard of the volcanic explosion of ancient Thera, and he tried to grasp the idea that Los Angeles was about to experience a similar, or identical, disaster.

Castine looked to her right, at the Hollywood sign visible on a hill a mile or so away. "Is there still a way to stop it?"

"There's still the same way," said Laquedem. "A piece of something real, from the Labyrinth, needs to be situated at the omphalos, to close the conduit."

"The conduit you opened in 1960," put in Vickery.

"Shall we discuss that?" asked Laquedem. "Or the present situation?"

"Get somebody from the TUA to do it this time," said Vickery, again slapping his pocket for the truck keys. "They're a government agency, and they know about this stuff."

"Until Sunday I worked for the TUA," said Castine. "I think the work we did was responsible for this. The work they're still doing."

"Yes," said Laquedem, "your section chief, Terracotta. He has had you shifting ghosts to this side, from the Labyrinth, and traffic accidents on the freeways provide ghosts going the other way." Laquedem squinted up at Vickery. "When two masses are drawn together by gravity, or a piece of iron is drawn to a magnet, how do they know to approach each other?"

"For God's sake," muttered Vickery, glancing uselessly at his stopped watch.

Laquedem answered his own question. "They exchange force-carrying particles. Gravitons or photons. The closer the things get to each other, the more force-carrying particles are exchanged, and the stronger the attracting force is. In this case—" He paused and shrugged.

Castine nodded. "Ghosts are the force-carrying particles, of course." She spread her hands. "The TUA hoped to interview them, learn what they knew."

Laquedem made a spitting sound. "Perhaps at first, lady, but that wasn't why they *kept* summoning the poor idiot revenants, poor fragments. Your boss just wanted *two-way traffic,* whatever he may have told you his purpose was."

Vickery was still smarting from the old man's scorn, and impatient with his know-it-all tone. "They're not all idiots," he objected, thinking of the girl in overalls. "Ghosts, I mean."

Laquedem opened his mouth, then closed it, and Vickery suspected he had been about to say something like, *One idiot can't recognize another.* "You've met good chess-players among them, have you?" the old man said finally.

"One ghost," said Vickery, "a little girl, has twice warned me when I was about to get killed." When Laquedem raised his eyebrows in mock interest, Vickery went on to describe his encounters with the phantom who called herself Mary, and at several points Castine and even Santiago nodded.

Laquedem's mocking expression had sagged. "You poor fool," he said when Vickery stopped talking. "That was your daughter."

"Wrong," snapped Vickery. "I—well, I happen to know that I have no daughter."

"Obviously."

"Damn it, I—"

"I wasn't contradicting you. You noted that she doesn't suffer from the dementia that ordinary ghosts exhibit. The never-born ones are . . . naïve, but they've never had the mind-fracturing experience of death, since they never quite got to live." He stared at Vickery. "Expanded possibility there. She's a daughter you might have had. That's the only reason she would follow you, look out for you, as she has."

Vickery's face was suddenly damp and cold, and he could hear his pulse thudding in his temples, and he lowered his head and stared at the cement. For several seconds his thoughts whirled in broken fragments, and then two came to the fore: *She did look like Amanda*, and, *I threw them both away*.

He remembered that the phantom girl hadn't eaten anything, after showing Santiago how to work the microwave in the truck; *She looked at the food*, Santiago had said, *like she would have liked some, but she didn't touch it*. And Vickery had supposed that she had liked Mexican food when she'd been alive.

No. She had never got to taste food at all.

Castine had asked, *Can they eat?* and Vickery had answered, *No, it's for us*. Like life.

"What," he asked, but he had to swallow before going on, "happens to . . . never-born . . .?"

"If you were to close the conduit," said Laquedem slowly, in a carefully level voice, "the ones who have come across stay here, and eventually fade to nothing. Painlessly. If the Labyrinth—which is to say the Minotaur—is imposed here and explosively strives to fully become the freeways, they'd be consumed by it, along with everything else."

For a long ten seconds while nobody spoke, Vickery looked away from the others, across the hills. Finally he asked, *"Can I still close it?"*

The breeze blew across the grass and tossed Castine's hair.

"If you go back into the Labyrinth now," said Laquedem, "and do what I told you yesterday, bring out something real and fix it at the omphalos. Yes. It'll be worse in the Labyrinth now; that state is getting more polarized and churned up by the hour—something like tidal forces as the worlds get closer together—and the highway might not be accessible anymore. But," he said, rubbing a hand across his eyes, "there's another real place there."

"The factory," said Castine with sudden certainty.

↓ CHAPTER SIXTEEN ↓

"Yes," said Laquedem, "the factory." He took hold of one of the crutches and poled himself up from the planter wall. "I've got a bus to catch. If you can drive me to the Greyhound station on 7th, I'll tell you more, on the way. If you're not interested in all this, I'll go inside and have them call me a cab."

"You *can't* go back there, Sebastian," said Castine. She looked around at the lengthening shadows, then added, "And how long will a detour to 7th Street take?"

"*You* go on the bus with him, for sure," Vickery told her. "If I . . . don't, I'll split the rest of the money with you. But—do you remember that noise, that roaring, in the Labyrinth? It knocked me flat, and I couldn't think at all till it stopped."

Santiago was helping Laquedem with his crutches. Castine stepped forward as if to help too, but the boy frowned at her and she moved back.

"Yes," she said bleakly, "I remember it."

Vickery choked out two syllables of a laugh. "She said she needed to find her secret garden, remember?—with a wall around it and a robin to show her where the key was. I can't—after everything else, I just don't see how I *can* let her be devoured by that thing that roared."

"I'll *take* the bus," she said, "I don't need to be driving around in a stolen taco truck—but you'll take the bus too. Damn it, Sebastian, *think!* You might be able to get back *into* the Labyrinth, but there's no way you could ever hope to get out again, by yourself. Do *you* remember how hard it was to hold a thought, how we had to keep reminding each other to work the math? Do you remember just trying to *walk*? And this guy says it's way worse now! That little girl . . . she doesn't *exist!*" She turned on Laquedem. "Does she?"

"No," said the old man. "She just might have."

"She's imaginary!"

"A daughter times the square root of minus one," said Vickery. "Right now it seems like all I can *do,* Ingrid—besides maybe kill myself on the freeway and join her. And her mother."

"And very shortly be consumed by the Labyrinth, the, the *Minotaur.*" She punched him hard in the shoulder. "Another great plan. What was it this guy called you? Something like klutz mit aygen? What does that mean?"

"*Aoygn,*" said Laquedem, correcting her pronunciation. "It's Yiddish for 'a plank with eyes.' Not a compliment." To Vickery he said, "You still have your string abacus?"

Vickery looked around, as if there might be some direction in which he could run away from all this, then reluctantly nodded. "We'll at least drive you to the bus station."

Vickery drove them all back down out of the hills to Hollywood Boulevard, and then straight east till the boulevard slanted south and became West Sunset. The truck was again showing a tendency to stall at stoplights, and several times he had to shift to neutral and gun the engine until a traffic light turned green.

Laquedem was sitting back in the kitchen area, on the folded-down seat by the oven, and for the first twenty minutes he didn't speak at all, and neither did anyone else in the rattling truck. From time to time Vickery glanced to the side at Castine, but her face in profile gave him no clue to what she was thinking. His own thoughts were in suspension, though *daughter you might have had* and *a truly devastating explosion* hovered at the fringes.

As he steered across the curved bridge over Glendale Boulevard, Vickery heard the microwave ping, and half-fearfully glanced over his shoulder; but there was no figure back there besides Laquedem and Santiago, who had apparently used his new skill to heat another couple of burritos.

A moment later he heard Laquedem say, "Thank you, boy," and

then the old man went on in a louder voice, apparently addressing Vickery, "That poem you heard a piece of, Ovid's *Metamorphoses*—ghosts often use lines from it to express their thoughts when they briefly drift near the factory, probably because it's constantly in the thoughts of . . . an actual dominant person there. And the poem is remembered in 18th century English, not the original Latin anymore, which implies that the person in the factory is slowly picking up some memories dropped by the ghosts, century by century."

"So how will—" began Vickery, but Castine interrupted.

"Wait a minute," she said, *"dominant person?* In that factory?" She had popped her seatbelt loose, and now turned around in her seat. "Who's that, Satan?"

"By now, maybe," came Laquedem's voice.

"Think about it, Ingrid," said Vickery. "He's imprisoned in the Labyrinth; he's in the factory, he's an artificer; and I saw him flying, there."

"His prison cell, if you want to call it that," said Laquedem, "the factory, is the only *enduring* pocket of randomly-generated precision in the Labyrinth. According to ghosts, the highway comes and goes but the factory has always been there."

"Are you two *serious?*" Castine looked from Laquedem to Vickery and back. "Are you crazy?"

"Definitely serious," said Vickery.

Castine exhaled and sat down again. "Good God," she said softly. She crossed her arms at was silent while Vickery drove two more blocks. Finally she said, "I thought he escaped. His son, Icarus, flew too close to the sun and it melted the wax of his wings, so he fell in the ocean—but I thought Daedalus *escaped* the Labyrinth."

"He did," said Laquedem, "but his son's ghost was still there, exerting a pull. And then King Minos caught him again by tricking him into re-enacting his entry into the Labyrinth, and it counted for real."

"I don't remember that part."

"Something about a snail shell," said Vickery.

"A spiral seashell," said Laquedem, possibly nodding, "like a whelk, or a conch. Minos made a big bet that nobody could thread a string through the shell, and Daedalus did it by gluing a thread to an ant, and then luring the ant through the shell's coils by putting honey at the exit. Apparently he thinned the glue for its tiny application by licking it."

"Ah," commented Santiago, "using his spit, in a little Labyrinth! Like knocking on the door—them and their tongues."

"And he had made the Labyrinth, remember," said Laquedem. "It was an entrapping funhouse-mirror image of the Minotaur, but, like any artist's work, it was also in some sense a self-portrait. Close enough, as it turned out; especially with the ghost of his beloved son already there, calling to him, as it were. It wasn't as big a step-across— as big a fall-into—for him as it would have been for anybody else."

He paused, apparently to take a bite of burrito. After a few moments he went on, "It would be best if you *could* avoid his factory. With luck the highway is still there, where you saw it, and you can break off a piece of its pavement; and if it turns to water, you *get another*. Even if a ghost is chasing you. Bring it back to this world, and then bury it in the center of the omphalos—right?—that freeway island by the Avenue 43 exit on the Pasadena Freeway. My mistake in 1960 was taking it away from there, taking it home with me."

"A big brass letter L," said Vickery.

"It doesn't matter what it was. The Vatican's got it now."

Vickery frowned, keeping his eyes on the traffic ahead. "So how does putting a piece of broken pavement on that freeway island prevent—" He waved around at the buildings they were driving past, at the whole city. "Is it radioactive? You said you got sick from hanging onto your brass L."

"It won't hurt you," said Laquedem, "if you leave it at the omphalos and then get away from it. It's not radioactive. It's the opposite of radioactive." The old man sighed and went on with strained patience, "Listen—when the endlessly expanded possibilities of the Labyrinth happen to generate something *real*, that thing is actually more solidly defined than anything *here*—more than these streets, this truck, this burrito. It excludes all randomness, it has zero possibility of variation. Its field *can*, eventually, interfere with things like natural nerve function."

Vickery heard him shift on the seat back there, knocking one of his crutches to the vinyl floor.

"But more to the point," Laquedem went on heavily, "it repels irrational possibility, which is to say ghosts. Placed at the omphalos, it should keep any more ghosts from coming through from the Labyrinth, and shoo away all the ghosts of freeway casualties from this side. It's a rectifier that blocks *both* directions, so there'll be no more exchange of force-carrying particles. The omphalos should close up, heal, and the imminent merger of the worlds should be prevented."

"*Should*," said Castine derisively. "We're all getting on that bus."

Vickery started to speak, then just pressed his lips together. For several minutes they drove on in silence.

Then Laquedem burst out, "Your metronome doesn't have a cap on it! You can't get across without one of those things!"

That's right, thought Vickery, I broke it off and threw it out the window.

"I can't go back to the Galvan commissary to get another," he said.

A tightness in his chest seemed to loosen. Maybe this has all been academic, he thought; maybe I have no decision to make, and we do all get on the Barstow bus after all.

"You've got Jack Hipple's ghost in a pinecone in your pocket," said Santiago.

Vickery had forgotten that; and he winced as the awful choice opened up before him again.

"Really?" said Laquedem. "Jack Hipple, subsumed in a pinecone?" He laughed briefly. "Yes, good, that'll do."

"Throw it out the window now," said Castine.

Vickery emptied his lungs in a sigh. "Maybe later," he told her. "Time yet for a hundred indecisions."

He could feel her stare as he slowed for a red light. The brakes squealed.

She nodded, grudgingly. "If it makes you feel better to wait."

"It doesn't make me feel better."

West Sunset crossed over the 110 Freeway, and Vickery realized that while they were on the bridge they were only a few hundred yards north of the spot where Castine, and then himself, had driven out of this world and into the Labyrinth yesterday; he held his breath for the ten seconds it took to cross the bridge, but there was no sandstorm, and the radios stayed synchronized.

"It was just down that freeway, wasn't it?" Castine said quietly. When Vickery nodded, she said, "The weird effects really do seem to have stopped."

Behind them Laquedem snorted. "When the ocean suddenly pulls way back away from the shore, does that mean you can relax about tsunami warnings? Hurry up to that bus station."

The clearing in the freeway island by the Avenue 43 exit from the Pasadena Freeway was quiet in the slanting, early evening sunlight, but the ground flickered with dozens of tiny lizards that darted from one place to another, apparently without crossing the distances between. Whenever Terracotta tried to focus on one of them, it wasn't there.

He had expected to find the usual band of freeway gypsies here, but in fact he was alone on the island. Even the lizards hardly counted as present, the way they behaved.

He sat under the blue tarpaulin hung from the stepladders, and he was dutifully divesting himself of himself, to make room for the big other. The outermost fringes of the Labyrinth must already have been seeping across through the omphalos, for every memory he called up immediately fell out of his head, never to be recovered. Perhaps the lizards were eating them and jumping back to the Labyrinth to regurgitate them onto the cold sand there.

He thought of Ingrid Castine, and her smile, and of the intentness and compassion she showed when interviewing deleted persons, and of one time when she had stood so close to him while giving him a report that her breast briefly pressed against his arm; and then there was a new gap in his memory where someone had been—a woman?— and the little lizards appeared and disappeared like bubbles in a simmering pot.

In 1973, the year before his father disappeared from his life, the old man had taken 16-year-old Emilio on a charter boat deep-sea fishing down the coast of Baja Mexico, and one morning when the sky was still only reddening in the east, his father had taken him up on deck and shown him a carpet of crabs on the sea, all linked claw-to-claw in a vast, rippling lattice. And then the memory was gone, leaving only the idea of some number of primitive creatures holding hands.

Terracotta blinked around at the lengthening shadows in the clearing. What had he been thinking of? Something about his father? The dirt at his feet seemed alive.

And he thought of the ten-year-old boy he had been, riding his bicycle to deliver newspapers in the rain, with the taste of Brylcreem hair tonic in his mouth as the water ran down his face from his hair, and how he had saved the money he made to buy a microscope—that was when he still believed in important choices and rewards, before he came inevitably to the realization that purpose and person were meaningless illusions; but the realization had had to happen sooner or later. The vacuous truth had been waiting out there all along. What had Neitzsche said? "If the abyss gazes at you long enough, you'll look back into the abyss."

He could still remember that his name was Emilio Terracotta—no, Emilio Benedetti, of course—not Terrafirma or whatever that was that had first occurred to him—but he knew he would shortly lose it, lose his entire self, and be replaced by an entity that could not ever have such a thing as a name.

At the back end of the Greyhound bus station was a cafeteria, and Laquedem and Castine were perched on stools at a long, low counter while Vickery and Santiago stood in front of them with their backs to a chest-high counter. Castine had kept her face averted as they walked in, and had immediately stopped at the counter and bought big sunglasses and a floppy hat that she pulled down around her face.

Vickery and Castine had ordered coffee, and Laquedem and Santiago had Cokes. The lenses of Laquedem's glasses had melted and left dark streaks down the buttonless front of his white shirt.

"The way it is now," said the old man to Vickery, "you should be able to get across even without a concussion, or being drunk. The same place you used before would be good—go up Alameda and then turn left—"

"I know how to get there," said Vickery. He was holding his paper cup of coffee with both hands to make sure they didn't tremble.

"You can't actually do it," Castine told him. "It's been, I don't know, *therapeutic* to consider the idea, but now it's time to face reality and—"

"I've decided," Vickery said. "I'm going to do it."

"Sebastian," she said, pushing aside her coffee and standing up, "*Herbert*, no, come with us, please! Don't go and die—or worse, be lost forever—uselessly!—in that—" She stopped talking and just bit her lip; then she held up two cards that looked like airline boarding passes. "I bought you a bus ticket, too."

Vickery remembered giving her three hundred dollars, two days ago. He pulled the battered envelope of twenty dollar bills from his pocket and held it out to her. "Try to get your money back on my ticket," he said. "Even with this, your getaway fund is damn slim."

Castine didn't look at the envelope. "I don't want," she began, then shook her head. "Half an hour ago you said you'd give me half the money—now you want to give it all to me? You don't expect to come back, do you?"

"I don't think there's a lot of time left," said Laquedem, gently.

"Stay with me!" said Castine suddenly, drawing startled glances from other people in the cafeteria. She snatched off her new sunglasses and stared at him, then looked away, visibly angry and embarrassed. "I—I can't lose you too, damn you."

Vickery reached out with his free hand and gripped her shoulder. "Ingrid. I have to. Think about it. It's all that's left that I *can* do. You'll be okay." He gave her a crooked smile. "Put the sunglasses back on, they've certainly got security cameras in here."

She nodded absently and fitted the sunglasses back onto her face.

A dark-haired man in a business suit had been blinking around at the brightly-lit menus on the wall behind the cashier, and he was now looking toward Vickery and his companions.

"There you are!" he said.

Castine turned toward the man; and Vickery caught her arm, for her face had gone suddenly pale.

"Eliot!" she said. "Oh God."

"Why would I give a stranger a hundred dollars?" said the figure facing her. "For all I knew, she was just g-going to go buy drugs with it. Did you see her eyes?"

Santiago had reached into his back pocket; Laquedem was watching the ghost warily. Vickery shifted his feet to be able to pull Castine away. "Six and six?" he whispered.

Castine shook her head, without looking away from the ghost. "The girl from the florist?" she asked the thing.

"Ring a ring of roses," the ghost chanted, "pocket full of posies, ashes, ashes—I can't think!—so I called your office to verify it, and agents with proper identification told me . . . audits! Income and taxes, all the way back, and fines and disbarment! So of course, meet me on Toluca Street at ten, like they said. You can see that."

Vickery was pretty sure Toluca Street was the cul-de-sac below Emerald Street, where the TUA agent had nearly shot Castine yesterday.

"I—thought they tortured you," said Castine, "to get you to tell me that; to send me into that trap."

"Traps, torture, pish!" The thing seemed to snap its fingers, though there was no sound of it. "I forgive you, my dear. I'm glad you at least had the sense to get us tickets on a bus—this place where they've got me waiting is *awful*—just a desert, and a bunch of retarded people, and my phone doesn't work—" The thing had been glancing around the cafeteria anxiously, and now it looked back at Castine, and licked its lips. "Let's you and me switch places, just to be on the safe side."

The ghost yawned, widely, and Vickery grabbed Castine and spun around as Laquedem boomed out, "Six and six is twelve, squared is a hundred-and-forty-four, squared is twenty-thousand-seven-hundred-and-thirty-six!" and Santiago had whipped a spirit-level star from behind his back and yelled, "Why are you tilting?"

Vickery was holding Castine against the counter he had been leaning against, facing away from the ghost, with his back toward the thing. Staring at the floor, Castine said, clearly, "I loved you, Eliot—but one from one is nothing. Don't take my word for it, do the math. *Nothing.*"

Vickery heard a hard *whump* from behind him, and then the rattle of a plastic cup hitting the linoleum floor; coffee spattered around his shoes and his dropped envelope.

He looked over his shoulder, and the ghost was gone, though people at other tables were again staring toward his party.

"I don't think that's right, Eliot," called an old man standing over a half-eaten cheeseburger a few yards further down the counter.

Vickery let go of Castine, who stepped around him and slumped back onto her stool.

Looking toward the man who had spoken, Vickery cleared his throat and said, unsteadily, "What?"

"Not what *she* told you, of course," the man went on, "one from one—I mean your friend's guess about the square of one-forty-four. I'm pretty sure that wasn't right."

Vickery realized that none of these onlookers had seen the Eliot ghost—evidently none of them had been intimate with a person who had died in a freeway current!—and that they must have supposed Castine had been talking to Vickery.

"I was," said Laquedem, rubbing his face with one hand, "using imaginary numbers."

The old man down the counter frowned, then shook his head and went back to eating his cheeseburger.

Vickery leaned back against the counter. Beside him, Santiago tucked the spirit-level star back into his pocket. Laquedem was frowning at Castine, who had lowered her head into her hands.

For a long moment none of them spoke. Around them, trays clattered and the other people had resumed their conversations. Then Castine raised her head and looked at the tickets she was still holding, and handed both of them to Santiago. "Here," she said, "get a refund on them if you can, and if I ever see you again you owe me seventy-one bucks."

"Okay, lady." The boy gave her a rueful smile. *"Vaya con Dios."*

Vickery understood what she intended, and he bent and picked up the envelope he had dropped. He brushed spattered coffee off of it and pressed it into her hand, closing her fingers over it.

"Ingrid," he said. "no, you can't come along. This isn't—"

Above the dark lenses her brows creased. "I *said* you couldn't get out of there by yourself. You know it's true. You'll need somebody to keep calling your attention to the math—and so will I."

"Castine," Vickery insisted. "No. He'll be *there*."

"You saw him, you heard him." Her mouth was bitter. "He's nothing."

Laquedem cleared his throat and began, "I don't think there's—"

Castine interrupted him. "I'll steal a car," she said to Vickery, "and follow you, if I have to. I think you know I will. I'm an adult—I can choose to do this. Allies. Friends."

Vickery stared at her. Then he turned to Laquedem and said, "Tell her she's crazy."

"She's right," said the old man, "you'll need help. Respect her choice."

Respect her choice. It was a big thought.

"O-*kay*," Vickery said finally. He tucked the wet envelope back in his jacket pocket and let his hands drop to his sides. "Ingrid. Thank you.

And he's right, there isn't a lot of time." He turned to Laquedem and Santiago. "And thanks for all your help, I think. Give our regards to the world."

"Yes, yes, and the world thanks you," said Laquedem, "now git, will you?"

Vickery nodded, and he and Castine hurried toward the 7th Street doors and the parking lot beyond.

Vickery had to grind the starter for a full thirty seconds before the taco truck's engine stuttered to life, and as he drove north he tried to catch green traffic signals so he wouldn't have to stop.

When he was driving west on Fifth Street with the low red sun in his eyes, the music from the radios fell into discordant noise; and after a minute of that, as they were driving past the wide lawn of Pershing Square, the music became clear again.

"Just an aftershock," ventured Castine. Her hands were clenched in her lap.

But Vickery could feel the pinecone thumping and twisting in his pocket. "I don't think so," he said in a tight voice. "Give it a minute." He had noticed that the ten-story purple bell tower in Pershing Square was wider than he remembered, and seemed to have more openings along its height, and the bushy heads of several palm trees hung in the sky with no trunks below them. And he could hear vacuum bubbles softly popping back in the kitchen.

The music blurred into cacophony.

"The waves are so out of synch," Vickery hazarded, "that they move over a whole cycle and synchronize there."

"Oh," said Castine. "I was hoping that it might all somehow be over."

Vickery had been breathing shallowly, and he had to take a deep breath to answer. "I think it soon will be, one way or another."

"How many blocks now, till we get on the freeway?"

"Just two."

She sighed and looked out her window at a fleeting parking lot. "Better than one. I hope they're long blocks."

Vickery wished they were.

"Eliot," she said slowly, "was just a venal fool, wasn't he? After all?"

Vickery shrugged. "Hard to argue."

"I'd like to be holding your hand," she said, almost in a whisper, "but you've got to drive."

He freed his right hand and for two seconds gripped her left, then returned his hand to the wheel. The freeway was coming up, and he would want to be over in the right lane.

"I don't think you're a klutz McMuffin," she said.

"Klutz mit aoygn," he corrected.

"Whatever." She shifted restlessly in her seat. "Three days ago I had a job and a fiancé. I discover I'm better off without either one. This has been a long day's journey into . . . what?" she said.

He didn't answer. All too soon he was driving the truck through the Figueroa intersection, and then the green freeway signs loomed overhead. His shirt clung to him and his hands were damp on the steering wheel as he stepped on the gas pedal and steered into the lane that would merge with the northbound 110.

The lane swept onto the freeway. The engine was stuttering, and cars behind him honked as he merged hastily into the right lane. Vacuum bubbles were popping in front of his face now, and he held his breath and narrowed his eyes. But there was no sandstorm yet.

He swerved to the right, slamming the side of the truck against the retaining wall, then swung the truck back into the lane.

"It's not working," he gasped.

Desperately he spun the wheel to the left, and tires screeched as he crossed the lane-divider bumps, and he heard a crash behind him.

He shrilly whispered, "Sorry, sorry!" and then saw piercing blue-and-red lights erupt in his side mirror, and heard a one-second whoop of siren.

A loud bang that he thought was a gunshot proved to be a tire blowing out when the right front end of the truck dipped and the vehicle slewed back into the right lane; over the racket from the radio he could hear the flapping flat tire and the wheel's steel rim abrading pavement.

He opened his mouth to say that they had failed, but before he could speak Castine grabbed the back of his head and slammed his forehead hard into the steering wheel. He rebounded back against the seat—a metallic taste filled his head, and his eyes were watering.

He was dizzily aware that she had taken hold of the steering wheel and that her foot was now pressed down on top of his own foot on the gas pedal, and that the pinecone was jumping and twisting furiously in his shirt pocket. Blood was rolling down his nose and cheek, and when he tried to focus his eyes, it took him a second to realize that the tan blur in his vision was outside the windshield.

The whipping clouds of sand cleared for a moment, and he glimpsed at last the straight offramp that should not have been there. Vickery blinked at the side mirror, but could see no red-and-blue lights now.

And then they were weightless—and a moment later he was thrown forward across the dashboard as the front of the truck crashed into deep water and the truck rolled all the way over. Vickery and Castine were upside-down in sudden darkness, hanging by their seatbelts. Icy water was spraying in at Vickery's left.

At the Rowley Training Center in Michigan he had many times practiced escaping from an inverted and submerged helicopter, and now he automatically braced one forearm against the headliner and unsnapped his seatbelt; he slid heavily onto the truck's ceiling, his shoulders taking his weight and his legs still braced against the dashboard above him, and a moment later he felt Castine splash down beside him.

"Open the window," he shouted, and he heard her gasp, "Right."

He had to reach up to grope for the window crank in the darkness, and when his fingers finally closed on it he couldn't get leverage to turn it. Cold water was heavily gushing in now from his right, indicating that Castine was having more luck with the window on her side. The cold was a physical shock, and he barely managed to take a breath before the churning water covered his head. Something pushed hard against his right shoulder and then quickly retracted, and he guessed that it had been the sole of one of her shoes. Perhaps she had got her window open and had thrust her way out.

It was too late to try to find an air pocket and renew his held breath. He pulled himself through the water to his right across the inverted seat backs, and he didn't collide with Castine—and as he groped for her door, a hand gripped his and tugged him forward; his legs slid free of the dashboard and his free hand found and gripped the edge of the doorframe, and then his knees bumped across the roof edge and he was out.

The black water surged as the truck sank away, and the water was too dark for him to see anything, so he had no idea which direction was up. But her hand still held his, and after a few seconds she tugged him firmly toward the side. He began trying to kick himself through the water in that direction.

But he could feel that the water was full of bubbles, and all his efforts didn't seem to move him at all. Her hand tugged harder, though, so he kept flailing his legs and his free hand in the oddly unresistant water. The bitter, penetrating cold leached strength from him, and his lungs were heaving against his resolutely closed throat.

When he was sure he must surrender and let his spasming lungs fatally exhale and then inhale water, his face broke the surface and he blew out the stale air and inhaled deeply—and it was the remembered astringent air of the Labyrinth. She let go of his hand and tucked something hard and angular in the back of his belt, and then she was gone.

He slid his hand into his left jacket pocket and pulled out the beaded strings and gripped them with his teeth, then quickly shrugged out of the leather jacket, but even after he had cast it away he could hardly stay afloat—he couldn't tread water normally, but had to thrash continuously with his arms and legs just to keep his head above water. The fizzing water still looked black, and the low sky was the color of scorched parchment.

"Sebastian!" came a call from his right, and when he managed a glance in that direction he saw Castine's head ten yards away across the agitated surface of the water. "This way—to shore!" she shouted.

He couldn't spare the effort to nod, but began to fight his way toward her, having to swim as if at racing speed to make any perceptible progress. The breath whistled through the strings between his clenched teeth. To the extent that he was able to think at all, he was bleakly sure he would lose consciousness from sheer exhaustion before he could get to any shore.

But after some interval of furious exertion, his hand brushed a slope of gritty stones, and he was able to crawl forward on his hands and knees, and he collapsed on rock-strewn wet sand and spat out the beaded strings. He rolled over onto his back, shivering and panting in the noxious air, while the water swirled around his waist and tugged at his legs.

Castine was already ashore, and crawled over to him. She picked up one of the strings and shoved the other into his pants pocket.

"I went back," she gasped, "but I couldn't—find you." She collapsed prone beside him, her face near his. The bandage over her right ear was gone.

"You didn't," he managed, "pull me out." He rolled over and gagged out some of the sulfur-tasting water that clogged his throat and nose. "By the hand." The darker clouds in the brown sky formed concentric arcs overhead, moving inward as if toward some center.

"No." She shivered in her wet clothes. "Did somebody?"

He sat up, shaking—with the cold, and with the thought of the hand that had grasped his, down in the black water. "Depends—" he paused to cough and spit—"on what you mean by—somebody."

He was certain it had been Amanda.

"You kept your," she began; she was clearly trying to remember a word, and finally just waved at his back.

He reached around, and his numb fingers brushed the grip of a handgun. He remembered Amanda's rescuing hand tucking it there when he'd been struggling in the water.

He drew up his knees and tried to rest his head on his crossed forearms, but the bruise on his forehead made him lift it again. "I wasn't drunk," he said, "or concussed—so you—shot me in the head?"

"That was me," she said, "who got shot in the head, remember? I shoved your face into the Ferris wheel . . . no, the, you know, the—damn it!" She took a deep breath, wincing, and then said carefully, "The steering wheel of your taco truck."

"That's right." He rubbed his face, trying to remember something very important. "The highway," he said finally, "we're supposed to break off a piece of pavement, and take it back to . . . out of this place." He squinted over his shoulder; there were a lot of low buildings standing at varying distances across the desert now, though when he focused his eyes on any one of them it disappeared. Farther away he could see the factory steady on its hill; and the tornado he had seen on his previous visit now stood sky-tall beside it, slowly flexing. The curved cloud-bands seemed to be converging there. "Quick," he added.

Castine had sat up. "That's the highway," she said, nodding in the other direction. "It doesn't have pieces anymore."

Vickery looked back at the expanse of black water, and he saw that it was a river, wider than the highway had been but curving away as the highway had done. Its rippling surface was hazed with mist. "Carbonated water," he said. "Aerated, that is. No buoyancy. A float wouldn't boat. I mean—"

"No use," interrupted Castine, "no highway. Let's go home."

"Yes." Vickery was pretty sure he didn't live in Barstow, but somehow that was the place he was thinking of.

The ground shook then, and the river surged up its bank, engulfing Vickery's waist and nearly pulling him back into its obsidian flow. Castine scrambled up the shallow slope and grabbed his upper right arm, and somebody else took hold of his left arm, and he dug his shoes into the rocky sand and thrust himself back, out of the current.

When they were several yards away from the water, he looked up to see who his second helper had been, bracing himself to face the ghost of Amanda.

But it was the little girl who called herself Mary, still in her overalls and straw hat, staring down at him with a concerned look on her narrow face.

"This is where I live," she said.

↓ CHAPTER SEVENTEEN ↓

He remembered who she was, and he flinched as the shock of it cleared his mind. My daughter times the square root of minus one, he thought. The daughter I might have had, should have had.

Castine straightened up and looked warily at the girl. "We're going back to the, the world," Castine said to her. "You should come along." She glanced worriedly at Vickery and said, "Ten minus three."

"Uh," said Vickery, "don't tell me. Seven."

Mary shook her head. "*There* is just *here,* soon." She glanced in the direction away from the river, toward the factory and the steady tornado. "I'll never find my secret garden." The wind was flapping her straw hat, and she tightened a drawstring under her chin.

A moment earlier Vickery's one vague thought had been to use the string abacuses to get out of the Labyrinth as quickly as possible, since the highway was gone. But now—

He made himself look at his never-born daughter, though it was hard to make his eyes focus.

But there's another real place there, Laquedem had said.

The factory. If it's possible to take something from there, and bring it back . . .

If you close the conduit, Laquedem had said, *the ones who have come across stay here, and eventually fade to nothing. Painlessly.*

It's what's left that I can do for her, Vickery thought. Let her fade to nothing in the real world, rather than be consumed by the thing that roars in this awful place. This so-called place.

He squinted at Castine, who was now holding her beaded string. "I've got to go on to that factory," he said carefully. "You should use your string to go back to . . . the world."

Beyond her he could see figures waving their arms overhead and rushing back and forth among the phantom buildings. The wind carried the sound of singing voices now, and smelled of fresh-sheared metal and curdled milk.

It'll be worse now, Laquedem had said; *that state is getting more polarized and churned up by the hour.*

Castine shook her head. Raising her voice over the monotonous chorus, she repeated what Mary had said: "There is here soon."

Vickery had no answer for that.

He got his aching legs under himself and stood up, blinking and swaying, and he pulled his string out of his jeans pocket and stared at it. There seemed to be a lot of beads on it, and for the moment he forgot about everything else.

"Ten," said Castine into the stinging breeze. "No more and no less."

He peered closely at the beads. "I think you're right." He slid two beads away from the rest. "Now it's eight," he said, fairly sure of that.

He took a step through the resistant air toward the buildings and the shifting crowds that lay between him and the distant hill on which stood the factory.

And he was facing the other way, toward the river.

He turned around, and was again looking directly at the surging black water.

"You'll never get to the artificer's castle," said Mary, "by *going* there." She ran toward the river, chanting words that were lost in the wind, and Vickery was startled to see her image fold away like a picture abruptly turned sideways.

He started after her, and the landscape whirled around and he was facing the buildings and the hill, and Mary was now walking away crossways, parallel to the river that was presumably behind them now.

Castine was beside him a moment later, gasping. "It was a number that you had," she said, "can I have it again? It doesn't seem to be in my phone." He mouth was working. "I don't feel so good."

"Look at your string," he told her. "Two from ten is eight."

Castine held up her string, and moved two beads. "Damn, you're

right. I see." She grimaced and spat, then peered in the direction that seemed to be ahead. "Where is she going?"

"One plus two. I don't know. Follow her." He was breathing shallowly. The harsh air was already giving him a headache, and his arms and legs still ached from the exertions in the river.

"Three."

Vickery took Castine's arm and hurried after Mary, keeping his eyes on the girl rather than on the shifting landscape. Both of them were shaking in their wet clothes; Vickery sneezed—then hurriedly spat several times after seeing half a dozen tiny flies come spinning out of his mouth. The girl seemed very far away at some moments and only a yard or two in front of them at others, but eventually he and Castine were plodding beside her through the sand, and now Vickery could hear what she was chanting.

"There was a man of double deed," Mary recited in a sing-song tone, "Who sowed his garden full of seed; when the seed began to grow, 'twas like a garden full of snow."

Vickery guessed that reciting this nursery rhyme was her way of holding coherent thought and purpose in this place, and he countered with, "Two plus two plus two—"

"Is six," said Castine, laboring along through the cold wind beside them, "and four is ten!"

Several of the flailing figures ahead were spinning toward them now, their mouths opening and closing rapidly.

"My garden is full of sand," said Mary sadly.

Vickery braced himself for some sort of irrational confrontation, but the approaching figures fell apart into cascades of tiny dark wiggling fragments, which he saw were little lizards as the things began hopping about on the sand. The air shook like jelly with a group of voices laughing, and when the voices paused and began laughing again, the sound of it was exactly the same, as if the laughter were on a rewound tape.

The river was no longer in sight anywhere, and the stumbling trio was moving now through a sparse cluster of low buildings. The buildings couldn't be seen by looking directly at them, but in peripheral vision they seemed to be mostly old bungalow houses with pulsing chimneys, and as Vickery and his companions passed between them, the houses could be glimpsed spinning ponderously in place while slow carnival music clanged in counterpoint to the endlessly repeated segment of crowd laughter. Several times they were approached by groups of the phantom figures, but though the things appeared to try to speak, they soon either unfolded into broad stained sheets and flew away on the wind or fell apart in wriggling torrents of lizards, like ruptured spider egg-sacs. The carnival music had faded to a thumping dirge, and the laughter in the air was loud, and shriller, like bird cries.

Vickery and Castine paused frequently to catch their breaths in the harsh air and hoarsely remind each other what various sums and subtractions were, sometimes desperately arguing about what the beads showed, and from time to time Mary would chant a line or two of her nursery rhyme.

The factory and the tornado slowly circled them as they walked in an apparently straight line.

Vickery peered at the distant hill, which at the moment appeared to be behind them on their left. He fought down nausea and made himself take a deep breath, and said, "I don't think we're getting closer."

"You don't get to it by getting closer to it," said Mary.

"Last time I was here," said Vickery, "I saw the, what I guess was the *artificer,* flying. Does he come from there? If we see him, maybe we could follow."

"You could try," said Mary, "if you see him. Sometimes he drops whistles with weird letters on them, but I don't have breath to blow them."

Vickery hadn't seen any sort of whistles lying around in the sand, and the winged man was not visible now.

The rippling sky was for a few seconds darkened by a riot of low-flying crows, and the eternal imbecilic laughter rang down from them; but Vickery looked away when he noticed that their heads were those of grimacing babies.

"I was one of those once," said Mary. "They fight the lizards for dropped memories."

Vickery's mouth opened, and he found himself saying, "Cute story."

Castine stared at him, wide-eyed, as she said, "Oh, I was cute once. Several times, probably. And now I do a lot worse than shoot hamsters."

"Several times, probably," said Mary.

The voices in the air were a choppy scream now, and suddenly they were eclipsed by a ground-shaking bass roar that shook the flickering houses into whirling dust and knocked Vickery to his hands and knees with an impact of compressed air. The huge inorganic bellow rocked the ground under his hands and seemed to echo from the throat of a miles-deep cavern, expressing an inorganic and incomprehensible passion, and the only thought in Vickery's shattered mind was to hide, to shut down, to stop presuming to exist.

The terrible roaring went on negating everything else for an unmeasured length of time, and awareness only came back to Vickery, cautiously, when he realized that the sound had at some point stopped.

His face was in the cold sand, and when he rolled over with some effort he saw that he had burrowed into it up to his shoulders. Castine was now propping herself up on her elbows and shaking sand from her hair; her eyes were empty, and her face was white even in the brassy light of this place.

Mary was still standing, though her eyes were shut, and over the ringing in his ears Vickery could hear what she was saying:

"When the sky began to roar, 'twas like a lion at my door; when my door began to crack, 'twas like a stick across my back . . ."

Vickery's face was cold with sweat and he was gagging, and Mary looked down at him. "Don't throw up," she said. "You won't like what you see."

He clenched his teeth and swallowed.

The girl looked from Vickery to Castine. "If it can know stuff," she said, "it knows you're here, inside it."

The earth shook under them, and Mary swayed to keep her balance. The brown sky looked crazed with cracks now, like an impacted windshield.

Castine tried to speak, then spat out sand and said, "I can't take that again, that—*noise*." She looked haggardly across at Vickery. "There'd be no *I* left. I want to go home."

"Four and four," croaked Vickery, hopelessly.

"Eight miles high." She looked at his hand. "You were what, going to—?"

Reminding himself that four and four were in fact eight, he looked down and saw that he had at some point during the auditory ordeal dropped his string abacus and pulled the gun from behind his belt.

He sat up. As in the last time he was here, the gun had changed from an semi-automatic to a revolver. For at least a few moments now he could see it clearly, and when he peered at it he saw not only that it was a .357 Magnum, but that it was one that he had once owned, with black rubber Pachmayr grips that he had cut away on the left side for easier application of a speed-loader.

But this gun shouldn't exist. The police had returned it to him after the inquest into Amanda's suicide five years ago, and he had beaten it to pieces with an eight-pound sledge and thrown the pieces into the ocean.

He flipped open the cylinder. Every chamber was filled with the bright brass of a Federal round, though the primer of one showed the dimple of a spent shell. The other five shells, he knew, would be loaded with Hydra-Shok hollow-points, and he shuddered as he remembered whose hand it must have been that had pulled him out of the submerged taco truck and tucked this gun into his belt.

Does she want me, too, to kill myself with it?—leave it on the sand here with *two* spent shells in the cylinder?

But in that case why rescue me from the sinking truck?

He stood up unsteadily and pushed the gun back behind his belt.

"Your string," said Castine.

"Right." He bent down, though it made him dizzy, and picked up the string abacus. The beads felt soft now, like miniature marshmallows.

Mary was walking away. Exchanging a rudimentary math problem and answer as if they were a password and a countersign, Vickery and Castine did their best to trudge after her. The river was once again on their right more than anywhere else.

Walking was exhausting work: moving through the air was like pushing between rubber curtains, and it was impossible not to stumble and sometimes fall when a level-looking patch of sand proved to be a steep upward or downward slope, and any careless off-course step would leave one of them heading directly toward the river, and the only way to get back was to deliberately try to approach the water. The air pressure changed from place to place, and several times Vickery had to yawn to make his ears pop.

Big raindrops began cratering the sand, and a new smell, like burnt plastic, steamed up from underfoot. Vickery took a step, and found himself alone—when he blinked around, he saw that Mary and Castine were twenty yards away; Castine started to walk toward him, and disappeared. A cry from behind him drew his raddled attention, and she was now farther away in another direction, hard to make out through the thickening veils of heavy, sour-tasting rain. His eyes were stinging. He had no idea where the river or the factory might be.

He looked down at his hand to see the string, but what he held was now a cigarette; when the rain hit it, it darkened and unfolded twig-like legs and began crawling up his wrist. He shook it off with a shudder.

He tried to remember what the string had been for; something like calculating mileage? Maybe it had been a makeshift pedometer. Probably it had clocked a million steps.

The sky had lowered and grown dark, and the rain was battering his bruised and aching head. He sat down cross-legged in the wet sand. When he rubbed his hand over his face it came away bloody; his nose was bleeding, apparently a lot.

The sand was coughing—gritty popping sounds simultaneous with wet clumps flying into the air; it baffled him until a moment when suddenly all the air blew out of his lungs, spraying blood across his ankles. Spontaneous vacuum bubbles, he thought as he reared back out of the bubble and inhaled deeply and then covered his face with both bloodied hands.

The popping was happening all around him, bursting up patches of wet sand and tossing raindrops in all directions; fearful that one of the bubbles might abruptly occur in his body, in his skull, he struggled to his feet and lurched a dozen yards and then sat down again.

The turbulent air seemed to rattle with fragments of music and laughter and weeping and droning voices—he knew they weren't real, just memories spilled from the leaky heads of the phantoms, quickened now by the rain—and then a clear voice intruded:

"Do you know any poems?"

He peered up through the stinging rain and saw Mary standing over him. Her curly hair was darkened and clinging in strands across her face and throat.

"Recite a poem," she said, speaking loudly over the wind, "if you know one that goes like a drum."

Vickery had played Prospero in a high school production of Shakespeare's *The Tempest,* and a couple of remembered lines from it suggested themselves: "Our revels now are ended," he croaked. "These our actors, as I foretold you, were all spirits and are melted into air, into thin air . . ."

"Get up," said Castine, who was now swaying beside Mary in the rain. "Like this insubstantial nightmare faded, leave not a rack behind."

That sounded to Vickery like more lines from . . . from that play, whatever it had been. He got his legs under himself and stood up.

And he had to count his companions—there was Ingrid, yes, and there was Mary, and he had apparently forgotten the name of the third person, the one standing in the rain behind Ingrid.

Castine twitched and shook her head, and Vickery glimpsed a tendril of mist or smoke quickly dissipate from around her shoulders. She stumbled forward, and Vickery caught her; and now he saw that the figure behind her was the ghost of Eliot.

"You took my memory of it!" the ghost wheezed. Its arms were hanging by its sides, but they disappeared and then were visible raised over its head. "Tell me what we had!"

Castine pulled free of Vickery and faced the thing. "Nothing beside remains," she said harshly, evidently quoting something else now. "Round the decay of that colossal wreck, boundless and bare the lone and level sands stretch far away."

Eliot's ghost was suddenly farther away, and it was peering down at the sand around its feet.

Castine reeled back against Vickery, clutching her head. "I know he was my fiancé," she said, "but what did we have?" Blinking in the rain, she looked up at Vickery. "What did we have?"

"I don't know," he said helplessly.

Now she too was looking down at the sand, scuffing it with the toe of her shoe. She looked up at Mary. "Did I drop something?"

The little girl shook her head. "Recite more of your poem."

"What was it, oh, it was 'Ozymandias,'" said Castine, "by P-Purse-Snatcher Shelley, right? But I think that was the end of it." She peered vaguely out across the sand, squinting through the downpour, then shook her head and stepped away from Vickery. "My abacus string turned into a Swiss Army knife," she said. "Rhyme and meter is all we've got to steer by now."

Vickery nodded. "Mine turned into a bug." He frowned. "Or a cigarette. Did I give it to you?"

Castine frowned and closed her eyes; then in a firm voice recited, "Other friends have flown before—on the morrow he will leave me, as my hopes have flown before."

The rhyme and trochaic meter cleared Vickery's head, and he recognized the lines from Poe's "The Raven."

He carefully pronounced the next line: "Then the bird said, 'Nevermore.'"

She was shivering. "Was *Eliot* just here? Oh God, I want to go *home.*"

Mary had walked on ahead, and Vickery took Castine's arm and hurried after her, setting each foot carefully in the loose sand and being careful not to let his eyes stray from the little girl, though the landscape tilted and spun in his peripheral vision. He and Castine took turns reciting lines from "The Raven," soon having to repeat themselves since neither of them could recall the whole poem.

At last Mary halted. A steady clanging and thumping was audible now on the wind.

"That place on the hill," Vickery panted, "things don't change there." Someone had told him that. He took a step forward, but his foot struck against something hard and he sprawled forward onto a set of wet wooden steps. A moment later Castine kicked the bottom step and halted.

"This *is* your home," came a new voice from above them.

Vickery was kneeling on the second step, and he squinted up through the cold drops battering his face; and quailed. The stairway extended upward farther than he could see, but Amanda stood above him on the fifth step, wrapped in a sodden sheet that flapped in the wind, and Mary now stood beside her. Mother and daughter, he thought, that should have been.

Amanda pointed down at Castine, who was standing behind Vickery. "I gave you the gun I killed myself with," Amanda said to him. "Kill her now, let her go join her man among the rushing phantoms, and you stay here, partway up, with your family."

Over the drumming of the rain on the steps Vickery could hear Castine retching. "Sebastian," she said, weakly. "Don't."

"I'm—sorry," said Vickery to the ghost of his wife. "I'm more sorry than I can say, for cheating you—both of you—but no, I won't kill her."

"Infirm of purpose," said Amanda's ghost, extending one skeletal arm, "give me the revolver. A crime I punish, and a crime commit; but blood for blood, and death for death is fit; Great crimes must be with greater crimes repaid, And second fun'rals on the former laid."

"That's the malmeme," said Castine. "You shouldn't listen."

But the meter and rhyme had gone some way toward clearing Vickery's head. It's more of Ovid's *Metamorphoses,* he thought. We must be close to the factory.

As if to confirm the thought, the rain shifted and the mechanical pounding was more insistent.

"Climb the stairs," he said, and pushed himself up to get his feet onto the bottom step. Standing up in the downpour made him dizzy, but he leaned forward and set a foot on the next step, and then the other foot on the one above that. He could hear Castine's shoes scuffing on the steps behind him.

When he passed Amanda's ghost she turned and stretched out her long-fingered white hands. "*Canst* thou throw off one," the ghost wailed, "Who has no refuge left but thee alone?"

"There *is* no refuge here," he told her, looking back as he climbed higher, "for anyone." Clenching his hands, he could feel that his wedding ring was no longer on his finger.

Amanda's ghost didn't seem to be able to ascend any higher than the fifth step; Castine passed her and Mary followed Vickery, and as they climbed higher, from one splashing step to the next, Mary gave Vickery a desperate look. "The neighborhood," she said, "shall justly perish for impiety: you two alone exempted; but obey, with speed, and follow where I lead the way: leave these accurs'd, and to the mountain's height ascend; nor once look backward in your flight."

The wooden stairway curled between outcroppings of rounded sandstone, and the pounding from above was steadily louder. Through the shifting veils of rain, Vickery could see bumps and hollows in the surrounding wet stone; their shapes suggested noses and chins and mouths, but he looked away from them and concentrated on the planks under his shoes after he noticed that the mouth-holes were opening and closing.

A wailing voice, and then a chorus, sounded from the plain below and behind them. "Don't look back," he said.

"Right," said Mary.

"As if," Castine gasped.

The rain eventually stopped, or else they left it behind and below them, and the coiling clouds thinned. Vickery could now see a black wooden arch up at the top of the stairs, silhouetted against the bulls-eye rings of clouds in the brown sky. The boom and thump of machinery shook the steps.

As he kept ascending, holding Castine's elbow to steady her, cranes and rows of smokestacks edged into view above them, and then high brick walls crisscrossed with pipes and fretted with rows of tall, narrow windows.

Mary halted and tilted her straw hat back to look up at Vickery. Her eyes were wide in her pale little face. "I stop here," she said.

"No," said Vickery, "come on, it's not much farther now."

She shook her head. "I can't *be*, there."

"But can't you—"

Castine took hold of his shoulder. "She's imaginary," she told him, "and the factory is real—hyper-real, according to that old guy. What we find up there might save her from. . ." She didn't finish the sentence, but Vickery knew she meant, *from being consumed by the Minotaur.*

"Mary," he said, "wait here, we'll—"

"Go," the girl told him. "Nor once look backward in your flight."

Vickery hesitantly reached down and touched her cold cheek, then turned away from her and resumed the upward climb. The blurring of his vision was only tears, for when he blinked them away he was able to see the grain of the wooden steps and the mud-caked laces of his wingtip shoes with eerie clarity.

It's more real now, he thought nervously. Hyper-real. What had Laquedem said? *Its field can eventually interfere with things like natural nerve function.*

Soon he and Castine were ascending the last steps up to the arch at the top, and as they passed through it they found themselves on a broad plateau. The wind was stronger up here, and they had to lean into it.

Across a rutted, gravel-paved lot stood, at last, the factory. Vickery tilted his head back to squint at the crenellations and smokestacks along the high roof; then he lowered his gaze. A banded iron gate was recessed into the wall directly ahead; to the left of the gate a dozen huge steel wheels connected by coupling-rods rotated counter-clockwise and then shuddered to a halt and turned the other way. To the right, three big exhaust fans spun in recessed circular openings in the wall, and beyond them a wing of the building projected onto a ridge that extended out past the end of the plateau, and a row of loading docks below high brick arches sat flush with a sheer drop.

Like Hipple's south-facing door, Vickery thought. He looked up.

Towering even above and beyond the highest smokestacks, the constant sandy tornado shifted slowly from side to side. Vickery could see tiny human figures being whirled upward in it, and at the top, where the funnel met the sky, a small black disk turned slowly.

Vickery's vision was acute—he could clearly see striations in every piece of gravel underfoot, and every curl or pit of roughness in the bricks of the wall ahead of him. He swung his head to the left—Castine was beside him, staring intently at the high closed gate.

He followed her gaze and noticed words in big brass letters over the black iron door: ASCIATE OGNE SCELTA VOI CH'ENTRATE.

Castine pointed at the words. "That's almost the inscription Dante had," she said, speaking loudly against the wind and the mechanical thumping, "over the entrance to Hell, in the *Inferno*."

"What does it say?" asked Vickery.

"The first three words are supposed to be '*Lasciate ogne speranza*,' which is 'abandon all hope.' But *scelta* is 'choice,' and *asciate* is . . . hew, chop. So altogether this says something like, 'Chop off all choice, ye who enter here.'"

"The original first word was *lasciate*? I gather that must be the verb 'abandon.'" He was pleased to note that his thinking was clear now, no longer battered by random diversions.

"Yes."

"Well, it was originally *lasciate* here, too." He remembered Hipple's description of the object Laquedem had brought back to the world in 1960. "Look, the inscription's not quite centered now."

"Yes," said Castine, "the first letter's missing." She looked at Vickery. "A big brass L. Laquedem took it, in 1960."

"That's right. It should be, *Abandon all choice, ye who enter here.*"

From the depths behind them sounded the bestial roar again, but it was tolerable up on the plateau, in the wind. Vickery only shivered at the memory of being immersed in it, dissolved in it.

"We could probably take the A now," he said, over the distant sound. "But . . . how can we get back to the world? Our abacus strings are gone."

Castine looked up at the immense clanking building. "Maybe we could make another pair of them here, out of something. If they were made of hyper-real stuff, they might not change away when we go back down into the . . . horribleness."

The distant inhuman bellow shivered to a halt, and it was followed by a closer crack and diminishing rumble. Looking back, Vickery saw the arch at the top of the stairway fold and fall away. Dust swirled up from the space below where it had stood.

He walked back to the head of the wooden stairway, and the top two steps were all that was left; that whole side of the hill had sheared off and dropped away into the clouds below, leaving a raw, nearly perpendicular cliff.

What had become of Mary? She had been only a little way down the stairs . . .

Castine had edged up beside him; she peered over the brink, and stepped back. "Maybe we can get back to the world from up here?"

Vickery stared down into the maelstrom. He thought he could see the river or highway, through the dust and the rain clouds. Mary doesn't exist, he reminded himself; a fall can't hurt her. I doubt if she even has the wherewithal to fall.

Still, his forehead was cold with sudden sweat. He recalled that Castine had spoken, and he turned to her. "What?"

"I said maybe we can get back to the world from up here."

He took a deep breath and let it out. "Two and two is four," he said. "The square root of sixteen is also four." He stretched out his hands, then shrugged and turned away from the abyss. "I don't think math gets you out of *this* place. It doesn't seem to be *contrary*, here."

He noticed something odd about the cracked-looking sky, and peered upward. Over the factory, the concentric rings of brown cloud broke apart as they converged toward the tornado, and the air above the factory was perceptibly clearer than the dusty haze everywhere else. After a few seconds he was able to make out the shape of the volume of air that broke up the moving clouds.

"There's a sort of cone," he began, but Castine interrupted.

"I see it. Perfectly clear air, like glass. It widens as it gets higher."

The pellucid cone over the hilltop was motionless, in contrast to the narrowing cloud rings and the dark, whirling, twisting tornado of ghosts just beyond it.

Vickery started walking across the gravel yard toward the factory gate, relieved that walking in a straight line was easy here, and Castine's footsteps were right behind him. When they were within a few yards of the gate, a section of gravel gave slightly under Vickery's step, and the tall iron door swung inward, revealing a cement-paved courtyard.

He took a last glance upward, and the edge of the clear cone, viewed nearly end-on, was clearly distinguishable; it enclosed the main building, though not the extension wing, and the open gate was inside it.

Castine looked down, evidently having seen the same thing. "We can't just stay out here," she said.

"We don't have to *abandon* all choice," he agreed. "It's been taken away already."

He stepped across the threshold.

And his thoughts blew away, leaving just a cold alertness. He had been aching with guilt about the apparitions of Mary and Amanda, but now all such illogical concerns were dismissed.

The simplification was a relief.

The courtyard smelled of motor oil and soap. The constant thudding of some immense unseen piston was now synchronized with his heartbeat.

His first concern was his gun; he quickly reached behind him, and his hand felt the straight grip and the flat frame of the .45 semi-automatic, no longer the revolver. At the same time his gaze swung around the hundred-foot-wide courtyard, noting every detail of the artifacts crowded against the black brick walls: a dozen bicycles with iron wheels and wooden frames, suits of armor made of panes of stained glass, rows of six-foot-tall telescopes that dwarfed the antique Martini-Enfield rifles attached to them, old-fashioned washing machines with big cranks on the fronts and rollers at the tops . . .

He was rapidly scanning each item to see if one would suggest a way of escaping from the Labyrinth, but none did. He stepped away from the woman who had come in behind him, Ingrid Castine, and he kept an unfocused wide-angle view of his surroundings as he reviewed his recent memories.

The memories were largely corrupted with confusion, but he recalled the ghost of the woman with whom he had long ago had sexual congress, and the animate image of a girl that had never existed. These memories had no relevance, and he began instead to make a mental inventory of this building's architecture, estimating likely locations of rooms and stairs.

The Castine woman moved forward across the pavement, and his eyes were instantly on her, alert for any action that would threaten or hinder him. She was watching him, too. Facial expressions could be clues to imminent behavior, but her face showed none.

Reasoning that this building probably contained many other manufactured objects, some of which might, on consideration, offer a means of returning to the world, he took a step forward, but halted when a five-second long series of musical sounds echoed around the courtyard in cadence with the unending mechanical pulse. The phrase was recognizably speech, but no more organic than words wrung out of a synthesizer. To Vickery the syllables sounded like Greek.

A wooden knocking sounded overhead then, and Vickery looked up to see a tall figure, consisting more of brass and polished wood than of flesh, step out onto a railed balcony on the third floor. Its height from this angle was difficult to estimate, but it was certainly more than six feet tall. A broad pair of wings, made of leather stretched across rigid frames, spread out for several yards to either side of it, secured by leather straps across its chest, and hand-grips dangled from pulleys on its shoulders.

The thing gripped the balcony rail with gloved hands and slowly inclined its face down toward Vickery and Castine. Its grotesquely oversized eyes were clocks with minute hands rotating rapidly counterclockwise behind the crystals.

A part of Vickery's mind had been expecting an encounter with the man or thing that Laquedem had called Daedalus the Artificer, and now he scanned the figure on the balcony with no emotion but cautious patience. In one corner of his mind he was aware that he would once have been uselessly awed at the sight of this millennia-old figure, prominent in classical mythology and still enduring here, in a perverse pocket of this non-world—but now Daedalus was just another factor in the situation.

Recalling that Daedalus was apparently familiar with 17th century

English, at least, Vickery called to it. "I have information you need. Come down here."

But the thing on the balcony was looking away now. It extended an arm made mostly of bamboo and wooden dowels, and then the musical tones of its voice started again, in a minor key, and this time the notes and stops and constrictions formed recognizable English words:

"The hour is come when my o'er-labored breast surcease its care, by final sleep possessed. All things now end."

"You need to hear what I can tell you," Vickery called again. Was the thing deaf?

The figure didn't move.

Vickery stepped back, clearly to increase the distance between himself and the Castine woman, and looked upward, past the balcony. Above the factory's highest catwalks and cranes he could see the surging top of the tornado, where the little black disk still rotated.

And in a moment when the tornado bent away like a drawn bow, before it swung back again, he glimpsed white pinpricks in the black spot. Stars, he thought—the earthly sky at night.

It's not a disk, it's a hole in this unnatural sky.

That must be the opening between the worlds, he thought. It was a miscalculation to think I could find a way to walk back to it now, but—he looked again at the unresponsive winged creature on the balcony, and his right hand slowly moved behind his back and closed around the grip of the .45—but I'll go by air, for sure the air is free.

↓ CHAPTER EIGHTEEN ↓

The construct that Daedalus the Artificer had made of himself over the centuries spread its wings.

In an instant Vickery had drawn his gun and pointed it up at the creature, estimating what spot on the segmented exoskeleton would be most vulnerable; but at the same time Castine had leaped aside, toward the eccentrically encumbered rifles, and was trying to yank one rifle free of the telescope it was attached to.

Vickery spun to aim the gun at her.

The rifle didn't detach from the barrel of the six-foot-tall telescope, and the whole contraption toppled to the pavement with a clang and a crash of breaking glass. Castine dove to the pavement behind it for its scanty cover as her hand leaped into her pocket—but what she pulled out no longer had the appearance of a Swiss Army knife.

It was again her original string with ten beads threaded on it.

The figure of Daedalus had paused, and the brief snatch of its voice that followed ended on a rising musical note.

Castine was staring in evident bewilderment at the string in her hand. "It's," she answered hoarsely, wonderingly, "I believe it's one decade."

The word 'decade,' which she pronounced '*deck*-ed,' coupled with the sight of the beads on the string, seemed to set off a depth charge below the automatic conscious level of Vickery's mind.

Spontaneous irrelevant memories bobbed to the surface: saying five decades of the rosary every morning in church with his eighth-grade class all in blue uniforms, the rosary said with his parents on the rainy night before the funeral of his grandmother ... there had been no rosary said before the funeral of Amanda. A year or so ago he had found a rhinestone-beaded rosary in one of the taco trucks, and he had meant to say the prayers for the repose of her soul, but it belonged to somebody, and he had returned it before he could carry out the intention.

Still sprawled on the cement pavement, Castine seemed to have momentarily forgotten the gun in Vickery's hand. "But that's all just spiritual," she said in weak protest, perhaps to herself. "The *knife* might have been *useful.*"

Vickery found himself suddenly wishing that his own string hadn't turned into a bug. If he could hold it again it would be a connection to something he'd nearly forgotten here—something that had once been precious to him.

But in spite of this delaying distraction, his conscious mind still intended to kill the Daedalus creature—and probably Castine too, depending on her reactions—and take the wings and somehow escape by means of them. Fly back to the world ...

The muscles of Vickery's arm contracted, lifting the gun, and his eyes focused on the center of mass of the Daedalus thing.

But the creature on the balcony made a sharp, chopping gesture, and the deep throbbing of some hidden engine stopped, and the high walls seemed to shudder as the whole building settled. The air was silent now, except for a faint sighing sound like distant freeway traffic.

And before Vickery could aim the gun, he thought of Mary, his square-root-of-minus-one daughter, somewhere in the chaos down on the plain. Imagining the imaginary now, he let himself consider other possibilities besides pulling the trigger, as many possibilities as he could quickly think of—

He could certainly shoot the winged figure; but he could instead preemptively shoot Castine, or shoot himself, or drop the gun, or run outside and leap off the cliff into the abyss—

A multiplying cascade of choices! And he found that, in the silence of the machinery, he could decide which action to take.

He opened his hand, letting the .45 fall and clank to the pavement.

There was a note of resigned fatalism in the song that skirled from Daedalus then: "Thus to prevent the loss of life and blood, and, in effect, the action must be good."

The Daedalus spread its wings to their full extent, then leaped to the balcony rail and swept the wings strongly down; and the ornate aggregate body lifted into the crystal-clear air.

Vickery automatically started to crouch toward the dropped gun, then reconsidered and straightened as the Daedalus thing flapped away upward, its multi-jointed legs swinging below the taut wings.

Castine gave Vickery a puzzled glance. "I don't know what I'm doing here," she said.

Vickery blinked around at the square, as if seeing it all for the first time. "Apparently," he said slowly, "we're *deciding* what to do."

"Oh, *deciding*." She rubbed one hand across her face. "It was easier when it was automatic."

Vickery nodded, already missing the clarity of purpose he had felt before Daedalus had stopped the relentless machinery.

"And we're allies," she said, and sighed. "I remember that now."

"Friends, even." For a fading moment the notion still seemed irrational.

"Yes, that too." She touched the spot above her ear where the bandage had been. "Why were you going to shoot it? I apparently meant to stop you."

"It's *not* irrational that we're friends," Vickery said, fully accepting the thought. He looked at Castine. "Why? I think I wanted its wings. Maybe you did too. But at best only one of us could have used them."

He looked up in time to see Daedalus disappear over the high roof, out of the now-rippling cone of clear air, in the direction away from the tornado.

Castine too had watched the thing fly away; now she shook her head as if to clear it, and frowned at Vickery. "Used his wings? To go where?"

He pointed at the feathery top of the tornado. "That round black hole up there? I'm pretty sure that's our own night sky—and right over the Pasadena Freeway, I bet. It may still be possible for us to . . . fly through it."

For ten long seconds neither of them spoke.

"Fly," she said at last, in a tone flat with disbelief. "Through it. To Pasadena."

"Well, LA."

She gave him a hesitant smile and touched his hand. "Let's find a way back down to the river, or highway, or whatever it is now. Come on. We can both look at my rosary—I mean my abacus—"

"Which would right away turn into something else, damn it. And leave us wandering around in, in *dementia*, till the whole place blows up. We have to go by air."

"For sure the air is free," she muttered; she went on more clearly, "It's crazy. He took the wings."

"His wings were made of thin leather, and I'll bet he had more of it here somewhere. And lengths of wood. Let's start searching." When she shook her head doubtfully, he said, "I can make a tandem hang-glider."

"You're serious? And sane?" When he nodded, she sighed shakily and held up the beaded string. "I'll say some prayers."

"If they can be heard from this place."

"Sure, they can go out through that hole in the sky."

Vickery gave her a grudging smile and walked across the paving stones to the only open arch in the courtyard wall. Beyond it, spiral stone steps descended out of sight, fitfully lit by electric arcs snapping in niches in the close brick walls. A cold draft welled up from the depths, carrying a subsonic vibration and the oily scent of ozone.

Castine looked at him and shrugged, then started down the steps. He followed her, several times glancing back up at the diminishing light from the courtyard arch.

The old stone risers were about a foot high, and Vickery counted forty of them before the floor leveled out in a wide, low-ceilinged basement, likewise lit by flaring electric arcs inset in niches in the otherwise shadowed walls.

There was nothing in the basement but a stout steel frame, bolted to the walls in four places, supporting and enclosing an enormous steel disk, easily a dozen yards in diameter, that spun horizontally on a vertical axle mounted in the low ceiling and the floor. A long pole with a car-tire-sized rubber wheel on the end of it hung over the rushing rim of the disk without touching it, and Vickery thought the whole thing looked like a Gargantuan platinum record on a turntable, complete with tone-arm.

Castine thought of the same thing, for she whispered, nervously, "Where are the speakers?"

But Vickery's chest had gone cold.

"It's a gyroscope," he said. He pointed at a loop of leather strap that hung slack from the hub of the rubber wheel. "I think the arm is supposed to be lowered, and that strap's supposed to spin the smaller wheel to keep the big gyroscope wheel turning."

She nodded. "Well, it is turning. Pretty fast."

"Coasting now," said Vickery, "with the arm lifted and the little wheel stopped." She gave him a blank look, and he went on, flatly, "The gyroscope is probably keeping this place level. With luck, that little wheel only disengaged a couple of minutes ago, when Daedalus turned off the . . . the determinism engine."

She took a step back, toward the stairs. "You think—what, the factory will tip over, if that wheel stops?"

"I don't know. Maybe this place will stop being the opposite of the rest of the Labyrinth." He shrugged. "Or maybe this was just a circular treadmill so the Daedalus thing could practice roller-skating in place. But I'd like to be out of here before that wheel finally slows to a stop."

Castine was hugging herself, gripping her elbows. "Out of here? How, again?"

Vickery was peering past the gyroscope's massive steel housing. "There's another door on the far side. We've got to find a lot of leather, or vinyl, or something like that."

He led the way around the huge humming wheel, stepping wide as he shuffled past the snapping arcs in their niches. The arch in the wall on the far side of the wheel was completely dark, but he could see far enough through it to make out steps leading upward.

The risers of this stairway were a good foot-and-a-half high, though the steps were no wider than before. He began groping his way in complete darkness up the stone stairs, brushing the close walls with his fingertips, sliding a shoe carefully up onto each step and then slowly letting his weight settle onto it before moving on to the next one, and listening to make sure Castine was coming up behind him.

This stairway was much longer than the one that had led them down to the basement—he counted sixty of these higher steps before he even began to see light above, and there were thirty more to be climbed before the stairs ended.

Neither of them called for a rest.

Vickery stumbled out at last through another arch into a wide octagonal chamber lit by tall windows overlooking the smog and remote hills of the Labyrinth.

He and Castine both leaned against the wall beside the arch and slid down to sit on the stone floor, panting. Vickery's legs throbbed with bone-deep fatigue; his muscles had already been aching from the swim in the unnatural river and the stressful hike across the sand, and the long, tense climb up these stairs had his heart pounding in his chest. Beside him, Castine had drawn up her knees and lowered her head onto them.

He rocked his head back. The ceiling far overhead was a dome, and the frescoes on the curving inner surface of it reminded him for a moment of the entry hall at the Griffith Park Observatory, though the frescoes here just seemed to be images of vague, curling, winged forms.

Castine had got her breathing under control, and raised her head. She looked around at the walls and windows and dome, and then at Vickery and herself. She exhaled, then said, "We're a mess. And whatever that river was, we smell awful."

"Stressful day," said Vickery, getting to his feet. Castine sighed and stood up beside him.

Half a dozen long wooden tables stood in two rows across the tile floor of the chamber, their surfaces crowded with various pieces of machinery—he saw an iron bar fixed on an axle inside a ring of fine coiled wire, a steel ball with curved spouts at opposite ends on a rotisserie over a charred tray, a rack festooned with strings and little pulleys, lenses and prisms arranged in rows, a couple of rapiers with helicopter-like vanes instead of bell guards . . .

"The artificer," he said. "These must be some of his inventions."

Castine made her way over to a cluster of stout poles, each three times the height of a man, that leaned against the wall between two of the windows.

"These are fishing rods!" she said. "With gunsights!"

Vickery stepped up beside her and looked the things up and down. They were clearly meant to be fishing rods, tapering toward the tops, with standing guide rings mounted at intervals along one side, but they seemed far too unwieldy to use, and he couldn't see the point of the telescopic sights that stood up on posts just forward of the giant reels, nor of the short, wing-like stabilizers a few inches further up. The line wound around the reels looked like fine woven steel.

"I bet he fished out of these windows," Castine said.

"I think he fished while he was flying," Vickery said, pointing at the stabilizers. He turned away and started toward another arched doorway. "Come on." In his mind was the image of the gyroscope wheel—it had still been spinning rapidly and smoothly, and it was massive, but it couldn't keep spinning forever, unassisted.

The next room was smaller, with fish skeletons and handsaws mounted on the tapestried walls; Castine paused to peer at the figures embroidered in the hanging fabric—a man leaning out from a castle turret, and a partridge flying away from him—but Vickery pulled her on into the next room, which was lit by a row of small square windows.

On one wall was a painting of a medieval-looking peasant guiding a plow behind a donkey, with an ocean bay and a square-rigged ship in the background. The stone floor of this room was wide, but the only object on it was a what appeared at first glance to be a tall stack of old pulp magazines.

At the far end of this chamber a yard-wide leather conveyor belt extended from an opening in the left-side wall, ran twenty feet along a shelf, and disappeared into a similar opening in the wall on the other side. The belt wasn't moving.

"Whistles," said Castine, who had walked over to the conveyor belt. She held up a little metal cylinder.

Vickery joined her by that wall. A dozen tin whistles lay evenly spaced along the belt; at the left end were three flat pieces of tin, similarly spaced, each a little bigger than a playing card. He picked up one of the tin pieces and one of the whistles and held them up next to each other.

"Before and after," he said. "These flat ones didn't get stamped into cylinders like the others."

"Well, the machinery is all stopped."

"Mary—" Vickery cleared his throat. "Mary said the winged man drops whistles, out in the Labyrinth."

"With letters stamped on them," she said. She peered more closely at the whistle she held, then nodded. "ΙΚΑΡΥΣ, all in capitals, with that squiggly Greek E at the end."

"Ick-a-poe," echoed Vickery. He shrugged. "Let's hit the next room."

But the stack of tan rectangles caught his eye, and after a moment's hesitation he walked over to look at it.

On the top sheet, solid and broken lines had been drawn in variously colored inks. He tried to flip it over, but only one corner lifted; it was just the top flap of a much bigger, many-times-folded sheet; and the resilient smoothness of it told him that it was not paper.

"Hey," he said, and the tautness in his voice made Castine put down the whistle and join him.

He slid the surprisingly heavy stack to a wall, then pulled the top end of it out across the floor, and it accordioned out as it unfolded. When he had stretched the thick sheet out in a line from one wall to the other, he saw an overlapping edge along the entire length of it— before it had been folded crosswise into a zig-zag stack, the sheet had been folded up lengthwise.

"You flip that end," Vickery told Castine as he walked to the opposite wall. When they had both knelt on the floor and turned over the top edge, and Vickery had shuffled on his knees to turn over the entire middle section of it, they flipped the whole heavy sheet, exposing more of the long edge. They did it again, and then again, and the still-folded remainder of the sheet didn't seem any thinner. Moving more quickly, they flipped the folded sheet out several more times, both of them scuttling back and forth on their knees to attend to the entire length.

Castine had been looking at the inked lines on it as their efforts revealed more and more of the sheet, and now she sat back and blew a stiff strand of hair from her forehead. "It's a map."

"Who cares," said Vickery. "Keep unrolling it—it's vellum."

Castine was still staring at the yards-wide strip of the map that they'd exposed. "I think it's a map of the Labyrinth—look, that black line would be the highway, or river."

Vickery wiped grimy sweat from his forehead. "Which line? There's six or eight of them just in what we've unfolded already."

"I'm sure when we unfold the whole thing we'll see it's all one line, looped around and around. The Labyrinth is way bigger than I imagined."

"Why would he have made a map of it? It would have taken him . . ." Vickery let his gaze travel from one end of the still-mostly-folded map to the other, "years. And gallons of ink."

She slid a finger across the surface of it. "I think these blue brushstrokes with arrows are wind currents. Look, they cross the black line in bigger curves."

"Well, he flies. Come on, we've got to get this thing spread out."

"Is this your hang-glider?"

"With luck. This stuff seems pretty durable." The unfolded map now covered more than half of the floor.

Castine looked up. "Vellum is what, sheepskin?"

"Or calfskin." Vickery flexed his hands and took a deep breath. "That gyroscope is slowing down," he reminded her.

They hurriedly unrolled a couple more yards of the huge vellum map. They were now kneeling close to the arch by which they'd entered, and they paused to catch their breaths.

"This seems to be all one piece," Castine said. "Where was there ever a sheep or a calf this big?"

Vickery thought about that. "Well, the Labyrinth is insanely expanded possibility, right?—and you noticed that the loading docks of this factory were outside the cone of clear air." He nodded back toward the other rooms. "That's probably how he got the raw material for all this junk. And it becomes real—hyper-real—when he gets it inside the cone, this pocket of counter-chaos."

Castine looked out across the extent of the map that they'd unfolded. "How much of this do you need?"

"This is enough," he said, getting to his feet. He stared at the expanse of vellum, recalling how he had built hang-gliders in years past. "I figure about a thirty-seven foot wingspan, roughly two hundred and thirty square feet altogether, plus a bit more for overlapping at the leading edges, and for harnesses and hang-straps. We can cut it up with the swords or the saws in the other rooms."

Castine sat against the wall, rubbing a fold of the vellum between finger and thumb. "It, your hang-glider, is going to need some kind of framework, isn't it?"

"There's those fishing poles in the first room," he said. He was picturing the frame of a tandem hang-glider, figuring lengths and stresses.

"Those even already have little wings on them," said Castine.

"Well, I'd have to break those off. We're going to make our own wing."

"Maybe he—" She stopped, and gave Vickery a startled look. "You said he probably carried one of the fishing rods with him when he was flying . . . and he has this map, and he drops whistles. I bet you anything he hovers, then, and listens for a signal in return. Ready to lower a line." Vickery opened his mouth to say something, but she waved him to silence. "I bet ΙΚΑΡΥΣ is the Greek spelling of Icarus! He's searching for his son. Still."

Vickery thought of Mary, his imaginary daughter, on her own somewhere out in that vast malignant delirium. The fact that she didn't exist, which was his fault, didn't make it any more tolerable.

"We can do some of the work in here," he said gruffly. "I'll fetch a sword and a saw so we can cut up his map."

↓CHAPTER NINETEEN↓

After walking around on the vellum sheet for a couple of tense minutes, Vickery used the point of one of the rapiers to lightly scratch lines in its surface, and then Castine gripped handfuls of it and pulled it taut; the saws quickly proved to be of little use, snagging and tearing rather than cutting, so he tugged the rapier's edge through the tough, thin leather. When he had cut out the shapes for the wing and a lot of extra strips of varying lengths and widths, he and Castine tied the lot together in a bundle and dragged it all back to the octagonal room.

The crazy flagpole-tall fishing rods would obviously not fit down the stairs, but one of the eight windows overlooked the courtyard, and Vickery tied lengths of the vellum to the rods and pitched them down. He tossed out both of the rapiers and several of the saws too.

The building shook then—and not as if machinery were working somewhere in it. When it subsided, Vickery was aware of a soft, nearby droning sound, and he saw several fat houseflies looping around over the tables.

"Out the way we came," Vickery said, starting toward the arch that led to the descending stairs. Castine waved him ahead, and he took two careful steps down into the darkness, bracing his hands against the rough stone walls on either side, and he extended his left foot for the next step—

And the building shook again, and he pitched forward, and the next step wasn't there. His arms flexed as he pressed his palms very hard against the stone walls. A sudden draft fluttered his hair, and, in a suddenly bigger volume in the darkness under his dangling foot, he heard echoes as the stones of the stairway knocked and clattered away far below.

He was tilted too far forward to push himself back; and after a tense moment his left hand slid an inch across the wall, though he was pressing so hard that he thought his bones must break through his flesh to abrade the stone.

And then Castine had grabbed the back of his belt, and was tugging him back—but he could hear fabric grinding against the stone, and he realized that she herself was braced precariously in the stairway, probably with a foot against one wall and her shoulder against the other, and slowly starting to slide. He got his left shoe back onto the second step, but to push against it would only tip him further down. Sweat ran into his eyes.

"Let," he said hoarsely, "go. You'll go too."

She didn't answer, but somehow forced her body to exert what must have been all her strength against the walls to hold herself steady, and pulled harder at his belt.

He was able to slide one hand up a few inches, and press; and then the other. He could hear the breath rasping through her teeth behind him.

Then, with a groan that became a short, strangled cry, she hauled him up with one last convulsive effort, and he was tilted back enough to shove his left foot strongly down, and they both pitched over backward onto the stone floor of the chamber. Vickery rolled off of her onto the cold stone, face down.

The floor was still shifting perceptibly, but for twenty seconds they both simply lay there and dragged breath in and out of their lungs. Finally Vickery rolled over and sat up, still panting, flexing his abraded hands.

"Thank you," he croaked; then he cleared his throat and said, "That was insane—but—thank you."

She had sat up too, and was rubbing her shoulder. "I don't—know how to make a hang-glider." She folded one leg under herself and then got to her feet, wincing. "I'm glad your belt didn't break."

Vickery stood up too, and ran his fingers through his sweaty hair. "I'd just as soon not think about it."

A swarm of flies now whirled up from the darkness where the stairs had been; they tapped against Vickery's hands and face.

"We gotta get out of here," he said, covering his mouth against them.

"Ugh," said Castine, batting at the things, "yes!"

Vickery looked at the window and then at the arch that led to the two rooms they'd seen, and he wished bitterly that he had not thrown both swords out the window—it would take several long, precious minutes, using just the remaining saws, to cut and knot a strip of the remaining vellum lengthy enough to reach from the window to a point not too far above the courtyard pavement. How quickly might they find another stairway?

"There'll be another way down," Vickery decided, taking her hand and loping across the floor and through the two rooms they'd already seen. Flies buzzed around their heads.

The arch at the far side of the map chamber opened on a wide corridor, lit by more of the electric arcs in recessed niches—and the snapping arcs had already lost some of their glaring brightness.

Vickery and Castine began running down the corridor. Through broad openings to the side, he glimpsed a library of suitcase-size books, racks of big Danish-freehand-style smoking pipes, an automobile like a 1930 Duesenberg Phaeton studded everywhere with shattered headlights . . .

The floor was perceptibly shifting back and forth under their feet, and they had to skip and shuffle to keep their balance.

"We should have made a rope out of what was left of the vellum," said Castine breathlessly, after glancing into a low chamber filled with aquariums.

Vickery glanced back at her. "Should have lots of things."

Suddenly Castine threw an arm across his chest to stop him. The flagstone floor ahead was rippling—and as they watched, it sagged, gratingly broke up, and fell away into darkness. The twenty feet of corridor ahead of them was now a ragged-edged hole.

"Back," Vickery said, waving flies away from his face, "make a rope."

"Wait." Castine got down on her hands and knees and crept to the edge of the hole, and, though one of the flagstones broke free when she touched it, she craned her neck to peer down past the uneven edge;

then she backed up six feet and sat down. "Take a look," she said. "There's water down there."

Vickery got down and crawled forward, and he took a quick look over the unsteady rim. Far below, oblique amber light glittered on a surface of liquid agitated by the fall of the hallway stones moments ago.

"Let's jump," said Castine.

Vickery pushed himself back across the flagstones and crouched beside her. "It might be only a couple of feet deep. And who says it's water? It could be sulfuric acid."

"We'd smell that."

A thundering crash echoed up the corridor from behind them, and a puff of air flicked at Vickery's hair and shirt. It was followed by another crash, louder and more jarring, as if a giant were stamping the place flat.

Vickery and Castine both hurried forward to the yawning gap in the floor, and jumped.

For two long seconds cold wind whipped up past Vickery's clothes and face, and then he crashed feet-first into icy water; he immediately kicked and spread his arms, and a moment later he was at the surface, blowing salt water out of his nose and swimming furiously toward a blurrily perceived light, confident that Castine would be doing the same. In a moment of catching a breath, he glimpsed the tan-colored sky of the Labyrinth between the blades of a big fan mounted in a circular opening in a wall. The fan didn't appear to be moving.

An instant later a loud multiple splash behind him was followed by a surging wave that threw him forward and sprawled him across one of the fan blades; the wave subsided and he slid down into the water, and he quickly splashed back to the surface and gripped the cement edge of the round opening.

The fan, like the rest of the machinery in the factory, was stalled and motionless. Castine was already crouched above him on the curved inner surface of the opening in the wall, bracing herself on one of the motionless blades. She nodded a breathless acknowledgment and then swung her legs outside and hiked herself out of the cement ring; Vickery heard her shoes hit gravel.

Vickery paused to take a few deep breaths and let his heart slow down before he jackknifed up and sprawled across the yard-wide inner surface of the opening, one shoulder braced against a downward-pointing blade of the stalled fan.

His head and shoulders were outside, in the open air, and he was looking across the gravel plateau toward the spot where the stairs up from the Labyrinth had been. The gravel was glisteningly wet now, with puddles in the low spots, and Castine stood shivering in her wet jeans and sweatshirt a few yards away.

"I," said Castine through chattering teeth, "would give up the whole rest of my life, if there is any, for five minutes in a hot bath. Are you going to come out?"

The gravel was only a few feet below him. Vickery considered rearranging his posture and stepping down, then just shoved himself forward out of the opening, landed on his palms and rolled. He had forgotten about the gun at the back of his belt, and the grip jabbed a rib painfully; he forced himself not to wince or groan as he got slowly to his feet. The breeze was witheringly cold, and he could again hear the textured background note that was like the muted roar from a distant crowded stadium.

He plodded out across the gravel and then looked back at the factory. Under the brass letters that spelled out ASCIATE OGNE SCELTA VOI CH'ENTRATE, the iron door in the courtyard gate was still open.

"Let's drag our stuff out here," he said, flexing his cold-numbed hands and dreading the effort. "And I'll give you a boost so you can pull another one of those letters down. We can take it back with us, like Laquedem did with the *L* in 1960."

"If I take the next one," she said wearily, "the A, it becomes complete nonsense. *Sciate* just means ski."

"'Ski all choice.' Oh well—the whole thing's likely to collapse soon. Let's get busy."

The sodium vapor radiance of a streetlight on Avenue 43 contended with the glow of a dust-fringed whirlpool that had now engulfed a twenty-foot patch of the triangular traffic island off the Pasadena Freeway.

Emilio Benedetti was standing back by the freeway-side boundary, under the blue tarpaulin draped over the pair of ladders, and he watched the tiny lizards glitter as they appeared and disappeared in the circular agitation; and in the amber glow he could also dimly see translucent human forms bursting up like spray from the middle of the vortex. And there were others, too, angling in from the direction of the nearby freeway, and these were disappearing into the edges of the broad round gap like curls of hair going down a drain. Aside from the perpetual pulse of traffic beyond the freeway fence behind him, the only sound was leaves shaking in the trees overhead.

Then he jumped in surprise, for he was not alone—someone was standing at the near edge of the rushing dust, only a couple of yards away, silhouetted by the streetlight on the far side of the gap—an old man in a tattered suit, with scanty white-lit hair blowing around his gleaming scalp.

Benedetti gasped, and choked—and even before he recognized the figure, his throat and mouth were forming words: "The key my father keeps; ah! there's my grief; 'tis he obstructs all hopes of my relief. Gods, that this hated sight I'd never seen! Or all my life without a father been!"

Dimly he knew that what he had found himself saying was part of the malmeme, the Dryden translation of Ovid's *Metamorphoses*—apparently he was already within the boundaries of the Labyrinth, and very close to the artificer's factory.

His father's ghost was shaking its head, and waving its arms as if to push him back, and it began shuffling toward him.

Benedetti knew there was enough left of himself to obey the old man one more time—to turn and walk away in the night, and remain at least somewhat a distinct person.

The ghost's face was visible now, and in spite of all of Benedetti's sins, it was smiling warmly. Benedetti found that he had taken a step toward it, but in that moment the ghost's expression changed—fond recognition became evident bafflement. The ghost's head shifted from left to right, as if Benedetti had disappeared; then the face of his father turned to look at him again, and this time the ectoplasmic eyes widened in alarm, and the ghost vanished.

Involuntarily, Benedetti's hand rose to touch his own face. What, he thought, I'm not recognizable anymore?

But the ghost had fled as if Benedetti was not even a human, just a deceiving simulacrum, and the falseness scared it.

Into his mind floated the thought he'd had moments ago—the idea that he might still be able to walk away from this imminent communion. But he had long ago surrendered to the insistent gaze of the abyss, and he couldn't now even imagine mustering the will to turn away.

His eyes swung toward the dusty, glowing whirlpool, and he saw that it was a hole—a hole out of the world.

He stepped across the dirt to the edge. The revolving wind plucked at his clothes and hair. Down in that other place, he knew, was the being that could entirely consume his abdicated identity.

"Hurry," he whispered. "Take me away from me."

And he crouched, and jumped.

Standing on Vickery's aching shoulders, Castine had managed to wrench the big brass A from the words over the gate, and now it lay on the gravel.

Vickery had sawn two long sections of the giant fishing rods for the leading edges of the wing, arranged them on the gravel in what looked like a proper delta angle, and cut another couple of lengths for the keel and crossbar. To attach the lengths of wood to one another, he had sawn notches into the poles and secured the joints with many turns of the woven-steel fishing line.

More rumblings and crashes echoed from the courtyard and shivered out between the motionless blades of the exhaust fans in the wall behind them. Vickery's wet clothes clung to him in the cold breeze, but his face was sweating as he made himself work fast but with careful calculation. Castine had her string in her hand, rolling the beads between thumb and forefinger.

"Do we," she ventured, "circle around the tornado?"

"Probably not," he said, cutting a length of the fishing line with the forte edge of the rapier. "It's all downdraft outside the funnel, if this is anything like a normal tornado. Likely we've got to go up *in* the spiral, with the ghosts."

She had no reply, and he was too busy to note any expression on her face.

With her help, he laid the biggest sheet of vellum over the wing frame, holding it all down against the wind with strategically placed piles of gravel, and he trimmed it to shape with one of the rapiers, leaving enough margin so that the vellum at the leading edges could be folded back on itself around the poles and sewn with more fishing line. The guide rings of the fishing poles were covered, but when holes were poked through the vellum on either side of each one and a short length of wire was knotted through them and the guide ring, the rings worked like mast hoops to keep the vellum firmly attached to the frame. The broad, billowing surface of the wing was featureless—the blue lines and black spirals were on the underside.

Vickery lashed together an extra-big triangular control frame and had Castine crouch under the wing and lift the whole thing slightly, with the windward trailing edge firmly weighted down with mounds of gravel, so that he could run strut wires from the bottom corners of the outsize triangle to the nose and the points where the leading edges were attached to the crossbar.

He had just finished wiring it up when the whole plateau shuddered and began rocking back and forth. Vickery looked up—several of the brass letters had now simply fallen off the wall; and as he watched, the top of the wall over the gate curled inward, then separated into dozens of pieces of masonry and disappeared, and with a roar a billow of dust burst out through the gate and was torn away by the wind.

Squinting upward, he saw that the cone of clear air was gone; and he guessed that the gyroscope wheel had slowed to a stop.

"We gotta go *now,*" he yelled to Castine. She started toward the brass A that lay on the gravel, but a crack split the plateau surface between her and the letter; and within seconds the crack was too wide to jump across.

"Now!" Vickery shouted.

She hurried back to where he crouched beside the wing. "Harnesses?"

"No time! I made the control frame big enough for us to stand in." He began dragging the nose around into the wind, digging in with his heels to keep the whole thing from blowing away. "You take the left side—hold it up, hang on tight, and run. When she lifts, step up onto the crossbar."

Vickery took hold of the right side of the frame, one hand on the diagonal bar of the triangle and the other on the horizontal control bar, and he began running across the unsteady gravel into the wind, toward the cliff edge where the stairway from the Labyrinth had been. Castine was pounding along right beside him, and the broad wing over their heads bellied taut.

In a moment their feet were just brushing the gravel, and then it had receded away below them and their weight was entirely on their gripping hands. Vickery heaved himself up and got his knees onto the horizontal bar, then pulled one foot onto it and stood up on it, clinging to the right-side diagonal bar as the wind whipped at his hair and the cliff edge swept past several yards below.

Then Castine had pulled herself up to stand beside him on the control bar, and they clasped their free arms around each other's waists. Vickery said, "Lean left," and the wing banked in that direction. He had to force himself to concentrate, and he added, "And give me some math! We're out in the Labyrinth!"

"Five and five!" she yelled into the wind.

Vickery found himself imagining a pair of dice, both showing fives. Ten was a hard point to make, in craps. "Two to one against," he said.

"What?" There was panic in her voice. "Five and five, dammit!"

"Sorry!" He shook his head and took a deep breath. "Ten! What's two and two?"

She didn't answer. An updraft mounting from below the cliff lifted them as the plateau and the factory turned and receded below; and the factory was imploding. The smokestacks bowed and broke up as they struck the roof, and sections tumbled away in a froth of cascading masonry. Erupting dust clouds dimmed the scene, and then the dust was pulled downward as the entire top of the hill abruptly sank into the plain, in turn throwing up a thousand-yard-wide ring of dust and sand. Several seconds later the gritty, blinding cloud whipped up past them, rocking the wing and tilting its nose up, threatening a stall. Vickery felt Castine's muscles flex, and guessed that she was getting a dislodged foot back onto the control bar.

"Tell him to slow down!" she gasped. "That was a red light!"

Vickery was trying to blink dust out of his eyes as he flexed his right arm to pull himself toward the nose, and he yelled, "Lean forward!"

Castine must have done as he said, for the nose came down and the wing picked up speed, now flying at a downward angle. Vickery wished he could free a hand to wipe across his eyes, but when he was able to squint ahead, he saw that the waist of the ghost tornado now stood squarely in front of them. The constant textured stadium sound was clearly coming from it, and was louder.

Doing math in their heads, with no physical referents, didn't seem to be working; so Vickery yelled, "What's the shape of our wing?"

Out of the corner of his eye he saw her glance up. "Delta," she said, "about forty degrees." The turbulent fringe of the tornado was only seconds away, but she gave him a quick approving nod.

"Hang on and brace your feet!" he yelled, and then the downdraft around the funnel tugged at the frame, and they were descending fast; Vickery had to push hard upward on the diagonal bar to keep his feet on the control bar.

The wing was tipping to the right, away from the whirling funnel that was so close, and Vickery's chest went cold—he couldn't brace himself to lean the other way, and the wing was about to slip into a sideways uncontrolled fall into the abyss of the Labyrinth—

But another wing was slanting in toward the tornado now, an orange one, on a rising and intersecting course. Vickery recognized it, and helplessly tensed himself for a collision and fall.

But when the other wing was ten feet below Vickery's control bar, it abruptly halted in the air, its orange fabric denting concave, as if it had come up against a repulsive force; and Vickery could feel that his own wing had been pushed upward—only a momentary jar, but it was enough to bring his right wingtip up and for him to be able to throw his weight to the left. The wing came back to level, and tilted past level to bank toward the funnel.

He glanced downward. The fabric of the orange wing had evaporated into fleeting streams of orange smoke, and Vickery could just make out a tiny figure spinning away below.

Amanda had saved them from the same fall—deliberately?

He tore his gaze away and looked ahead—and the rushing mottled substance of the tornado was directly in front of him.

All at once there was weight on his feet and the diagonal bar was nearly yanked out of his hand. The wing was *in* the whirling funnel now, and though he couldn't immediately make sense of the patches of light and dark that flickered around him, he could feel that the wing was rapidly spiraling upward. The wind battered his ears with a racket like tropical bird calls.

His voice was hoarse as he yelled to Castine, "Hold this angle!"

"*What* angle?" she called back desperately. Her right hand was clamped tightly around his ribs. She nodded upward. "What's our wingspan?"

After an instant's surprise, Vickery realized that she was keeping him grounded with natural math. "Thirty-seven feet!" he said, almost smiling.

And he forced his eyes to focus—to his right through a veil of turbulent distortion he could now see the Labyrinth's hills moving past in the distance, and to his left, over Castine's ruffling hair, flailing forms rushed downward in the funnel's core, which in a mundane tornado would be the condensation vortex.

"Just," he yelled, "let's don't fall in or out."

And in fact it was not possible to hold one angle without the risk of tipping into one of the downdrafts on either side; Vickery found himself constantly leaning to one side and then the other to keep the wing in the funnel's corkscrew upward current. There were no landmarks or visible horizon, and the spiral wasn't steady—several times he had to lean across Castine, or swing outside the diagonal bar on his side, to keep the craft from falling into the downrushing core or out of the capricious funnel altogether.

"Altitude?" called Castine at one point.

"Three thousand feet!" he panted; he was almost certainly wrong, but the question had at least made him consider an actual quantity.

He could see that the jiggling forms around the wing were ghosts. Below him, and in front of him beyond the delta angle of braced vellum, grimacing faces and long-fingered arms curled and stretched and snapped, and he could now discern the individual voices and wails and laughter that made up the roar of the tornado. He caught fragments of sentences: *don't let him—did you see—wait in the car—to go home, to go home . . .*

The light was dim and unsteady in the rushing spiral, but after a few squinting seconds Vickery was able to get some perspective. Farther away in the flock of flailing ghosts, ahead and below, he could see steady figures that held their humanoid forms for at least several seconds at a time, and he was briefly able to gauge his position by them; but the ones that spun closer to the wing blew apart in dissolving fragments.

He noticed one small figure that was constant, rushing along with the rest of them but maintaining a mid-air position perhaps six yards in front of the wing. He focused on it and saw that it was Mary, her straw hat fluttering behind her blonde curls, held on only by the drawstring.

Her open hands were held out in front of her, and she moved them toward the core; and a moment later Vickery had to lean hard in that direction to avoid being spilled right out of the funnel.

A thought flashed into his head: *She's giving me directions.*

He nodded emphatically, and when she moved her hands again, he corrected his angle accordingly without waiting to see one or the other edge of the spiral looming up at him.

He spared a sideways glance at Castine, who nodded; and a second later, when Mary indicated a shift to the right, Castine leaned with Vickery.

Watching the little girl closely now as she hovered steady in the turbulence, Vickery could see that she was frowning in concentration, and her lips were moving; and now he could hear what she was calling: "When the ship began to sail, 'twas like a bird without a tail; when the bird began to fly, 'twas like an eagle in the sky . . ." She was sustaining her form and position by reciting her nursery rhyme.

The spiral's angle was getting steeper—and just below the wired-together nose of the flexing wing, behind the diminutive figure of his daughter, he could now see the patch of blackness stippled with bright spots.

Stars! he thought. We're nearly there!

He glanced to his left at Castine; she too was peering up in that direction, but after a few rushing seconds she leaned toward him and said, loudly, "No—it's LA—from above!"

Mary moved her hands to the left, and he and Castine wrestled the wing back into line; and when he was again able to look beyond the little girl, he spent a full second making a mental snapshot of the lights in the blackness above.

And the headwind was cold on his suddenly sweating forehead. Yes, God help us, he thought as he returned his attention to Mary and the noisy, harrowing current. If the two patches of light next to each other were Hollywood and downtown, the one to the north would be Burbank, and the dimmer one to the northwest would be Sherman Oaks or Universal City. And this time he had even seen faint lines connecting the variously bright pinpoints of light—those would be the long diagonal of the 5 Freeway, with the 134 branching off west from Hollywood.

But the lights were *overhead.*

Were he and Castine going to emerge from the tornado *upside-down,* at an altitude of something like 30,000 feet? Even as he kept his eyes on the steady little figure of Mary, he was rapidly calculating how they might right the wing, and then quickly dive out of the freezing and oxygen-depleted air at that altitude.

But when he was next able to look up, the freeway lines were gone, and the view beyond the nose was definitely the deep night sky, across which were spread the distinct stars of one particular constellation.

He exhaled in relief through clenched teeth.

A moment later Castine's arm tightened around his ribs. "The bright one isn't Hollywood," she yelled in his ear. "It's Aldebaran."

Concentrating on leaning the wing back and forth according to Mary's signals, Vickery just nodded.

"It's the constellation Taurus," Castine added.

And as soon as Vickery thought, *Taurus—the bull,* the view began to change. Two wavy streaks appeared where he had moments earlier thought he'd seen freeways, and the star that Castine had identified as Aldebaran was growing brighter.

Then he had to tug at Castine to lean far to the right, for he had been looking at the sky and not at Mary, and the wing had tipped dangerously toward the falling ghosts in the funnel core.

When he looked up again he simply stared in horrified astonishment.

Aldebaran was now a huge eye, and the long streaks were wavy horns, and fully half of the sky was eclipsed by a vast bull's head staring directly down at the ascending wing. Vickery threw his weight forward, dislodging at least one of Castine's feet, to judge by the sudden tug of her arm locked around his waist; but the bull's face expanded and rushed closer.

Its enormous mouth dropped open, and then all sounds ceased and all light was extinguished. Vickery's right hand lost its grip on the diagonal bar, and he was no longer standing on the control bar.

He was falling.

In complete darkness, his shoes hit pavement, and as he tumbled forward across a rough, dry cement surface, he heard the knock and thud of Castine falling and sliding to a stop beside him. The ensuing silence seemed to press at his ears. They had lost the wing, and even after several seconds he didn't hear it hit anything. The surface he was now lying on was tilted slightly upward in the direction they were facing.

Over the pounding of his heart and his own harsh panting, he could hear Castine drawing ragged breaths nearby.

"I," she gasped, "hear you breathing. Are we dead?"

Vickery braced himself up on his elbows, peering around uselessly. He coughed and then managed to say, hoarsely, "I don't know."

"That thing—swallowed us! Didn't it?"

"I don't know." He flexed his hands. His palms stung from sliding on the concrete, but neither wrist was sprained. "Are you hurt?"

"Nothing broken, I think." He heard cloth slide on the rough surface of the floor, and guessed that she had sat up. "Do dead people feel pain?"

"Sshh." He was breathing as quietly as he could through his open mouth; a cold breeze smelling of alcohol and incense was in his face, and he tried to identify the faint sounds it carried. All he could think of was that they sounded like a massive person shifting constantly on a leather couch.

He got his feet under him and stood up carefully, stretching his hands to the sides for balance in the darkness, and his right hand brushed a vertical stone surface.

"You got a wall on your side?" he whispered. "I do."

He heard more sliding from his left, and a faint slap. "Yes," she whispered back.

He shuffled carefully in the downhill direction, brushing his palms along the flat stones of the wall, and after only a couple of feet he felt a corner: another stone wall extended out at right angles. He felt his way along it and came to a similar corner at the corridor's other wall.

He stepped back and spread his hands across the wall that blocked this end of the corridor, and crouched to feel it all the way to the floor.

"Uh," he said, "there's a solid wall back here."

"That's impossible," said Castine angrily. "We *came* from that direction." Her shoes slid on the cement, and then he could feel her breath on his ear as she slapped the crossways wall.

She stopped, and after a few seconds she said, "What the *hell* do we do? Now?"

Vickery took a deep breath and let it out. "Walk uphill, I guess." He reached around to his back and was reassured to feel the .45

semi-automatic still there, even though he was bleakly sure it would be of no use in whatever was happening here.

Further creakings sounded from the darkness in the other direction, with a measured, faint grinding that might have been something sliding at intervals across a floor, or might have been something big breathing. The sounds didn't seem to be getting any closer.

"But—I don't *want* to walk uphill," whispered Castine.

"Ingrid, We can't stay here. Not for long."

Her hand brushed his arm, then clutched it tightly. "When I was a little girl in San Clemente," she said, speaking quietly and rapidly, "one day all us kids had to get out of the surf because a shark was sighted, and we all came hollering up onto the sand."

Vickery was straining to see anything in the darkness. "I imagine—"

"Wait! I was in Catholic school, and our teachers were nuns, fresh from Ireland, and one of them told us, 'Girls, sharks are just as afraid of you as you are of them.'"

She let go of his arm, and he heard her step back toward the downhill wall. "But," she whispered, "we knew that some things aren't afraid of little girls at all."

"We can't run out of the surf," Vickery told her gently.

For several seconds she was silent; then he heard her take a deep breath. "Sorry," she said. "I know. I'm okay. Well, I'm *not*, but—" He heard her shuffle forward, and then her hand found his, and held it. "But dear God, where *are* we?" He felt her shiver. "Sorry, dumb question."

"God only knows."

"It swallowed us. I think we're dead."

"Maybe." Vickery shook his head. "Would that make a difference?"

↓ CHAPTER TWENTY ↓

The passageway uphill curved to the left, and soon Vickery could faintly see the stone walls by yellow light reflected from somewhere ahead of them, and he saw that Castine was limping.

A sound started up, making Vickery jump and Castine squeeze his hand; it was a long vocalized note, resonating as if in a big chamber; and when it wavered and stopped, it was followed by the same voice pronouncing a string of apparently nonsensical syllables.

If it can know stuff, Mary had said, *it knows you're here, inside it.*

Castine moaned softly, but stepped forward when Vickery tugged at her hand.

The light was stronger ahead, and when a tall arch came obliquely into view Vickery paused and looked at Castine. Her forehead was scraped, and the knees of her jeans were torn. Her hair was a matted thatch.

"Enter two scarecrows," she whispered tensely, then nodded toward the arch.

Still holding hands, they stepped to the arch. And they both flinched.

They were looking out across an aircraft-hangar-size chamber whose walls pulsed and foamed and shifted in streaks through shades of amber and gold, but their attention was fixed on the creature out there in the middle of the rippling floor, surrounded by a whirling ring of brightly glowing things that flapped through the cold air.

Vickery's first shocked impression was that it was a mastodon rolling, convulsing, on its back; then the tusks were long horns above a bestial snouted head, and a moment later the thing appeared to be a spiny black crab as big as a house, with an oversized human face at the front of it. The eyes were rolled back and the wide lips were opening and closing rapidly as the imbecilic syllables rolled out of it.

"Emilio?" cried Castine.

The crab-form shook and narrowed and grew taller, and then it was an enormous centaur, a man's outsize torso and crossed arms mounted above a furred barrel chest and four stout legs that ended in hooves. The floor of the chamber was now jigsaw-cracked asphalt. Looking up at the thing, Vickery saw that the broad face had not changed, though two thick, ridged horns now curved out from the forehead. The creature was silent except for the voluminous rumble of its breathing, staring down at the pair of humans in the arch.

The walls of the chamber had solidified into an infinity of golden honeycomb cells.

The creature out on the floor—it wasn't a centaur, Vickery realized; it had a bull's body, not a horse's—opened it mouth and spoke.

"Castine," it said, and its voice was deep now. "Woods. You don't—" The massive arms lifted and waved outward; "you don't . . . *prevent* . . . *consummation.* You die—did die—"

It was pointing at the honeycomb wall, and when Vickery and Castine helplessly looked in that direction, one of the cells expanded in Vickery's view and enveloped both of them.

And then he was in a desert under an overcast sky, able to see all around at once. To one side was a long dirt road with a gray car parked on the shoulder and a pickup truck approaching; away from the road, two men were pushing a third man ahead of them across the dirt and down a slope into an arroyo. The two men carried pistols, and the wrists of the man ahead of them were handcuffed behind him. The pickup truck nearly hit the parked car, but swerved around it and drove on past.

The pop of a single gunshot batted away across the desert, and then the two men were plodding back up out of the arroyo, holstering their guns.

Vickery recoiled out of the vision, but the monster's pointing arm moved, and he fell into another.

A car with decals of faces all over it slammed into the side of a bus, then righted itself and sped away down a sunlit avenue that Vickery recognized as Second Street in Los Angeles. Two gray Chevrolets rounded a corner and raced after what Vickery now knew was Galvan's Ford Taurus. Three gunshots could be heard over the roaring engines, and the Taurus swerved sharply, jumped a curb and tore through a chain-link fence and came to rest upside-down, tangled in the chain-link.

Vickery was forcibly pulled out of the vision, and he was standing beside Castine in the archway. Her jaw was clenched with effort and her face was pale.

"We," she said, "did—*not*—die."

"See," said the Minotaur, extending its arm again.

The desert highway vision exploded into Vickery's view again, and this time it was narrowed—he saw only the two men marching the third man down the slope; Vickery was able to recognize his own profile above the shoulders pulled back by the handcuffs.

Exerting all his will power, he pulled the view back, so that he heard the single gunshot but didn't see the result. The vision faded as the two men with guns were striding back up out of the gulley.

There was no pause between the visions now.

Again the sunlit expanse of Second Street filled his vision, and the inverted Taurus was closer, the wheels still spinning; the windshield was an opaque web, spotted with red—

And the imposed daylight dimmed and was just the radiance thrown by the flapping glowing things in the big chamber, and Castine was panting beside him.

"We *did not* die," whispered Castine, swaying with the effort of pulling out of the vision.

"See," repeated the Minotaur—

—And this time Vickery was looking straight down into the arroyo. The handcuffed man who was himself had been tripped and thrown to the ground, and the two armed men stepped back, one of them raising a gun—

But the scene warped, and seemed to bubble away like a stuck movie frame melting in the heat of the projection bulb. In its place was a view of a slim teenaged girl sitting in a recessed window, reading a book by lamplight. Vickery was able to see the title of the book—it was *The Secret Garden.*

The vision blinked away.

Emilio Terracotta's enormous head rocked back and its mouth

opened, and the remembered inorganic bellow shook Vickery's consciousness to fleeing fragments. The intolerable sound pulverized the sequence of time; while it continued, it was eternal.

When at last it had stopped, and he had begun breathing again, and his senses had trickled back into the mental crater that had been his attention, Vickery was staring uncomprehendingly at a gaudy car sitting upside-down in a mess of chain-link fencing. But before he could muster anything like curiosity, distorting bubbles broke up the imposed vision, and when they cleared he was seeing a dark-haired young woman laying a baby in a crib in a room with Winnie-the-Pooh wallpaper.

That vision too faded, and he found that he was sprawled on the cement floor of the archway. He rolled over, and felt the angular lump of the gun at the back of his belt; he reached around and tugged it out, and the feel of the grip in his hand roused a reflexive sense of urgency. A moment later he was up in a crouch, blinking around.

Castine was on her hands and knees a yard away, gasping, her eyes squeezed shut. Vickery raised the gun and looked toward the Minotaur, but someone was standing now a few yards in front of him, facing it.

He recognized the straw hat and the overalls.

Beyond the diminutive figure of Mary, the towering half-man half-bull creature extended an arm and pointed again at the honeycomb cells on the wall, and Vickery glimpsed the pickup truck passing the parked car on the desert highway—but almost at once it was eclipsed by a fleeting vision of a middle-aged woman in a greenhouse, holding a pair of clippers and leaning over a rose bush.

The visions, offensive and defensive, stopped altogether. The Minotaur's massive arm dropped to its side. Vickery realized that Mary had disrupted the Minotaur's lethal projections by interposing images of her own.

The little girl looked over her shoulder at Vickery. "It can't find a death for me," she called. "I never lived."

Keeping a wary eye on the monster beyond her, Vickery said, "Those were scenes from a life . . . yours?"

"Memories I picked up before the lizards could eat them. None of them—"

The Minotaur lowered Terracotta's huge horned head and shook the floor as it pawed up chunks of asphalt with its rear hooves. It lifted its massive front legs and brought them down hard as it began to lumber forward.

Vickery raised the .45. Mary didn't move, but he had long ago been trained to shoot precisely enough to miss close bystanders, and he fired twice past her, into the thing's outsize human chest. The hard pops of the gunshots battered his ears.

But the hollow-point 230-grain bullets had no effect, and Vickery spun with the recoil and threw his left arm around Castine, and both of them dove to the side, rolling out across the cracked asphalt floor.

Vickery looked up in time to see Mary, who had apparently spun away out of the Minotaur's path, lightly flick its tail.

And the giant beast faltered at the negligible touch, then spun around, its hooves ripping up arcs in the asphalt—but Mary had skipped back. She had her straw hat in her hand now, and she waved it.

"The other gun," she called.

Vickery opened his mouth to ask what she meant, when a bony white hand and forearm darted into his peripheral vision from behind him; the long fingers touched his wrist, cold as metal, and then the arm whipped back out of sight.

The gun he was holding was now the .357 revolver with the cut-away Pachmayr grip: the gun that should no longer exist, the gun with which his wife had killed herself.

And in the moment when the pale hand had been visible, he had seen the mate to his wedding ring on one thin finger.

The Minotaur had swung Terracotta's head back toward Vickery and Castine. Even as Mary darted in and touched the creature on the flank, Vickery raised the revolver and fired at the yard-tall face under the horns. The boom of the shot was louder than the previous two had been, and the glowing winged things scattered toward the walls.

A black dot had appeared beside the nose and rocked the big head back, and the leg Mary had touched folded, causing the beast to sit down heavily. Vickery fired twice more, another shot into the big face and one into the broad human chest.

The creature opened its mouth again, but it produced only the resonant note Vickery and Castine had first heard—and then the human parts of it, the face and arms and torso, gorily split and tore to pieces, leaving just the figure of a huge, raggedly beheaded bull.

The glows of the flying things abruptly dimmed out, and the chamber was in darkness.

"It can't die," came Mary's voice, "but a never-born touching it, and bullets from a gun a human erased herself with, take away everything but its own self." More loudly Mary said, "You're on your paper airplane! Open your eyes!"

Vickery closed his eyes in the darkness and then, with some unexpected effort, opened them again—and immediately had to squint against a battering headwind. His right hand was clutching the diagonal bar of the hang-glider wing instead of the gun, and his left arm was around Castine's waist and his feet were firmly set on the horizontal control bar over the whirling abyss. Overhead, beyond the point where the leading edge bars were wired to the keel, was the round patch of night sky, with a faint scattering of real stars visible in it. Translucent human forms were reeling bonelessly into sight at the edges of the earthly sky and tumbling away down the core of the funnel, even as ghosts spiraling upward were bursting away into the night up there.

Directly ahead of them, Mary gave one last wave for course-correction, and then disappeared over the top of the wing.

The wing's nose tilted up, threatening a stall, and Vickery flung his weight forward, pulling Castine with him—and the wing jolted to an abrupt stop as it snagged against something, and the two of them were flung forward, airborne for a moment, and they slammed to solid ground and rolled across shadowed dirt tufted with patchy grass.

Vickery came to rest lying on his side, gasping, and it was all he could do to lift his head. Nearby streetlights cast a fitful white glow, and with no surprise, but with profound relief, he recognized the trees and the freeway exit lane to his left; he and Castine were again in the triangular island beside the Pasadena Freeway at Avenue 34. The omphalos. Castine was lying one her back a yard away, and though her eyes were closed she was visibly breathing.

He looked back. From wingtip to wingtip the hang glider was jammed across a luminous hole in the clearing, ballooning up and dimly lit at its edges by the amber glow that radiated up from beneath it; the black and blue lines on the vellum weren't visible on the top side—the map was facing the other way, back down into the Labyrinth.

The Labyrinth is facing itself, he thought.

Castine had rolled over and hunched across the dirt to sit beside him, and now she too was staring toward the billowing underlit sheet of vellum. Their clothes were still damp, and she shivered in the breeze.

"We did bring something real, hyper-real, back with us," she said.

Vickery nodded. "The wing. The map."

Ghosts like big gelatinous moths were faintly visible circling the glowing hole now, but they were dispersing, losing even their provisional diaphanous shapes as one by one they retreated away to the highest branches and the night sky beyond.

The hyper-real wing, Vickery thought, is repelling them; just as the ghosts mounting the tornado from below are doubtless being repelled back downward. No more exchange of force-carrying particles.

"Were we in time, do you think?" asked Castine, exhaustion giving her voice a tone of indifference.

Vickery had sat up, but was postponing the effort of getting to his feet. He shrugged, feeling tension in his shoulders. "If we find ourselves suddenly in the Labyrinth—begging for cigarettes—we'll know we weren't."

Castine giggled for a moment, then choked it off. "Back in the Labyrinth, along with everybody who's within a couple of miles of us right now, probably."

The light below the wing was dimming rapidly, and by the white streetlight radiance Vickery saw the expanse of vellum settling and collapsing.

"I think we were in time," said Castine.

Vickery suppressed a groan as he got to his feet, and he limped across the clearing and paused a few feet away from what he could see of the vellum sheet. The glow beneath it had faded away completely. The ground appeared to be solid, and most of the structure of the wing was buried now. He stamped on the dirt, and it didn't yield at all, so he edged forward carefully and put the weight of one foot on the half-buried vellum; and it rested on firm ground.

He sighed deeply and felt the tense muscles in his shoulders begin to relax.

He walked back to Castine and sat down beside her. "We were in time."

She was leaning back, staring into the sky between the treetops. "I don't even *see* . . . that constellation now."

Vickery chuckled weakly. "Maybe we deleted it. Astronomers will remark."

For several minutes neither of them spoke. Then Castine said, "I need a bath, and decent clothes, like few people have ever need them before. Do you still have any money?"

Vickery thought of his envelope full of twenty dollar bills, sunk with his leather jacket in the bubbling river in the Labyrinth.

"A few twenties in my pocket, unless they've turned to mush."

"They probably have." Castine yawned. "Maybe a homeless shelter. We're homeless, aren't we?"

"I—"

"Vickery," came a voice from behind them, "and Betty Boop."

Vickery's gun was gone, and neither he nor Castine was in any shape to try to run, or fight.

He sighed and looked over his shoulder. A few yards away, the blocky figure of Lady Galvan stood with three taller silhouettes.

"Where's my taco truck?" she asked.

"Oh," said Vickery, "guess." He shifted around to face her.

She laughed merrily. "This here?" she said, slapping the shoulder of one of the men beside her. "This is one of my nephews, Carlos. I think you saved his life just now!"

Vickery licked his lips, then managed to raise his eyebrows politely. "Oh?"

"Sure. Your kite," she said, nodding toward the flap of limp, half-buried vellum barely visible in the shadows cast by the trees, "smothered the fuse, didn't it? Hah! The gypsies all said a big ghost bomb was gonna blow up LA if that hole didn't get closed, and Carlos volunteered to jump into it, and do his best to shut the whole thing down. He's got metronomes, holy water grenades, mirrors, a gun with silver bullets . . . but then you two came popping out, and the hole healed up." She turned said and said, "Carlos, say *thank you* to the people who saved you from jumping in there."

One of the men beside Galvan shuffled forward across the dirt. He had on a bulky jacket and cargo pants, and at first Vickery thought he was wearing a backpack; then he noticed that there were straps across the man's chest and between his legs. He was wearing a parachute.

Carlos extended his right hand to Castine and said, "Thank you . . . very much."

"You're welcome," she said bewilderedly as she shook his hand. "You were going to—parachute down the hole?"

Carlos didn't answer, but moved to where Vickery sat and held out his hand again. "Thank you . . . very much."

"No hay de que," replied Vickery, shaking the man's hand. Carlos stepped back and, after glancing anxiously at Galvan and getting a nod, began pulling the parachute straps off.

To Castine, Galvan said, "I promised to pay his debts and see that his wife and *niños* would be well taken care of, if he didn't come back." She shrugged. "Now it looks like they're all on their own again."

Vickery took a deep breath and stood up, and he thought of Laquedem and Santiago. "You didn't consider just . . . fleeing LA?"

"I've got family from Venice to Whittier," Galvan said. "I'd never have got them all out."

A movement on a tree branch behind Galvan caught Vickery's eye. He looked more closely, and shivered, then said to Galvan, "I don't think Carlos would have succeeded."

"Probably not," she admitted.

Vickery went on, rapidly, "We saved your family then. And you. That's worth a lot more than your Taurus and your taco truck, right? So you have to do us a favor, right away."

Galvan rocked back and peered at him. "You did what you say. What do you want?"

"What do we want?" echoed Castine as she too got to her feet.

"There's a Barnes and Noble on Colorado, five miles from here," Vickery said, "just east off the 710, on the left, on the north side. Do you have somebody you can call who's near there?"

"I got family everywhere," Galvan told him. She was smiling in puzzlement. "What, you want a book?"

"Yes—and can you get somebody here, quick, who knows how to subsume ghosts into—you know, organic objects?"

Galvan turned to another of the men behind her and spoke rapidly in Spanish. Turning back to Vickery, she said, "Yes, only ten minutes away. She charges fifty dollars."

"The favor includes you paying her," he said. "Get her here, and get somebody to go to that Barnes and Noble and get a copy of—"

Castine had noticed the motion on the tree branch too, and spoke in unison with Vickery when he said, *"The Secret Garden"*—and she added, "by Frances Hodgson Burnett."

Galvan apparently sensed Vickery's urgency. She had a cell phone in her hand and was tapping in a number. She gave somebody directions to get to the bookstore, then put the phone back in her pocket. "She'll call when she's there, and you can tell her the name of the book." One of the men behind her was talking on a cell phone now, and Galvan said, "He's getting the woman who can put a ghost in a thing." She shook her head and punched Vickery in the shoulder. "And I'll pay the fifty bucks."

"Thank you. Now—wait here, would you?" He hesitated, then said, "Ingrid, you come along."

Together he and Castine limped across the grass and dirt to the tree by the exit lane. Sitting on a branch just above Vickery's head, in the streetlight-shadows of the leaves, was the little girl, Mary, in her overalls and straw hat.

"I'm—so sorry—" Vickery began, but Mary interrupted him.

"I heard," she said. "Will you read the book sometimes?"

Vickery knew that it would always be an aching reproach to read the book that contained her, this imaginary girl, the daughter he should have had—but he nodded. "Every day."

"Thank you," said Castine, "for guiding us, back there."

"No hay de que," said Mary. "Don't talk now—I need to hold myself till they get here."

Vickery sat down in the dirt, blinking back tears as he stared up into the little girl's eyes, willing her not to disappear. After a while he heard Castine talking to someone, and then a car engine stopped on 43rd Street. A few minutes later he heard another car pull up, and then footsteps hurrying across the dirt.

"The robin, with the key," said Mary.

↓ EPILOGUE ↓

Westbound traffic on Old Man 10 was brisk on this late August morning, and chrome flashed under the cloudless blue sky as cars emerged from the shadows under the Crenshaw Boulevard overpass. The westbound onramp slanted down from Crenshaw to join the freeway, defining a wedge that widened as it extended back toward the overpass bridge.

The slope directly under the bridge was cleared dirt, all too visible to passing cars, but the broad eastern end of the wedge, right up against the bridge abutment, was thick with olive and pepper trees, and Sebastian Vickery sat in the dappled shade, screened by green branches from the view of motorists rushing past below. Beside him was a jar half-full of water with a popsicle stick laid across the top, and a string tied to the popsicle stick hung down almost to the water. The string was dry.

Vickery was wearing faded jeans, boots, and a black guayabera shirt with two gray stripes down the front, and a denim jacket lay nearby. In his hands was a trade paperback book with a red and green cover.

"The rain-storm had ended," he read aloud, "and the grey mist and clouds had been swept away in the night by the wind. The wind itself had ceased and a brilliant, deep blue sky arched high over the moorland. Never, never had Mary dreamed of a sky so blue. In India skies were hot and blazing; this was of a deep, cool blue, which almost seemed to sparkle like the waters of some lovely, bottomless lake, and *here and there, high, high in the arched blueness, floated small clouds of snow-white fleece. The far-reaching world of the moor itself looked softly blue . . ."*

Behind him shoes scuffed through the dirt; he looked over his shoulder, shook his head, then laid an olive leaf between the book's pages to mark his place, and closed it.

A few seconds later Santiago slid down and stopped in a crouch a yard away to his left. The boy was dressed, as always, in jeans and a white T-shirt, with the leather bands on his wrists, and his black hair was falling over his forehead.

Santiago grinned. "Lady looking for you. No gun now."

"Really!" Vickery looked back up the slope. "How did you find me?"

The boy shrugged. "First we checked the old nests at 10th and Arlington. One or two more and she would give up. Got a *plane* to catch."

Someone else was hitching down the wooded slope behind him now, and Vickery shifted around. A branch swung aside and Ingrid Castine slid down the last couple of feet and wound up sitting beside him, a gray skirt rucked up around her knees. Her auburn hair was longer now, and several oleander leaves were tangled in it.

"I go get my bike off the rack," said Santiago, straightening up.

"I can drive you back to Pico," Castine said.

"Nah," answered the boy, "I got business." He nodded and scrambled away back up the slope. After a few seconds Vickery couldn't hear him anymore.

"You'd think he wouldn't still charge me ten bucks," Castine said. "He says they wouldn't give him a refund on the bus tickets."

Vickery shrugged. "He was in Barstow. Missed the show."

Castine leaned back and looked through the foliage at the intermittently visible traffic below. After a while birds resumed chirping in the surrounding branches.

"You're not easy to find," she remarked.

Vickery carefully laid the book down on his denim jacket and looked at her. "Are you out on bail?"

She widened her eyes and shrugged. "There are no charges, actually."

Vickery cocked an eyebrow. "Very good."

"The TUA office in Washington doesn't want to poke into it very hard. Brett wrecked all the office hard drives and lawyered up, and the TUA closed down the whole western division and had a big organizational shake-up, and I think they hope Terracotta just stays disappeared."

"Safe bet."

A cool, diesel-scented breeze shook the branches over their heads.

"I'm on paid leave, for now." She reached out and tapped the book. "I'm glad you're reading it."

"I do an hour every day. I've already finished it once and started again. It's pretty good, really."

Castine sighed and nodded. "I loved it when I was a girl."

He hesitated, then waved down toward the freeway lanes. "When I read it in these old nests, I get the feeling that she's reading it along with me."

Castine started to say something, then fell silent. After a pause, she said, "They did try to give me a hard time about Mike Abbott, but I've retained Eliot's partner in Baltimore, and he showed them that they had nothing." She hesitated, then went on, "The police . . . found Eliot's body. A shallow grave alongside the 5 in East LA."

"Oh. I'm sorry."

She blinked and waved it off. "All done and gone." She pushed her disordered hair back with both hands. "My service gun turned up at Hipple's place, but ballistics showed it wasn't the gun that killed Hipple; and the two bullets that killed Abbott went right through his neck and away, so they couldn't do a comparison. And there weren't any witnesses, except for you, and they don't know that. Oh, and Abbott himself, but it would never occur to them to get testimony from a ghost."

"Sure, what do ghosts know."

She shifted and gave him an apprehensive glance. "I, uh, got my lawyer to check out your situation too."

Vickery raised one eyebrow. "Oh?"

"Listen, no charges were ever filed against you, okay?—he's established that. And you can't really sue the government, because of 'sovereign immunity' and the Federal Torts Claim Act, but the reorganized TUA would like to come to some kind of agreement, arrangement, settlement, with you—with a gag order and a heavy liquidated damage clause, to keep you quiet. And the lawyer would like to—all this would be on a contingency basis—he'd like to look into your old Secret Service pension and 401k funds, and even see how long they might have kept depositing payroll checks into your Herbert Woods bank account."

She had been talking rapidly, and now she paused and touched her purse. "You want his card? I gave one to Santiago to give you, in case we didn't find you."

Vickery stared down toward the freeway lanes. "This guy," he said after a few seconds, "this lawyer, he's . . ."

"He's smart, and careful. Way more careful than Eliot was."

He gave her a wry smile. "Okay, I'll probably call him sometime. Thanks." He leaned back on the leafy slope. "It's good to see you, Ingrid."

She had reached into the purse, dug out her wallet, and pulled out a business card. "Here. And I—I need to ask you about another thing—" She shook her head and tucked her wallet back into her purse. "Oh, it's good to see you too, Sebastian! I wanted to thank you, for everything—going into the Labyrinth to get me out, that first time, and then the second time, thinking of making a hang-glider . . . I could never have . . ."

"Well, I'd never have made it out, either time, without you. And—" He paused, and reached down to pick up a lump of soil, and he slowly crushed it in his fist as he went on: "And *Amanda* saved us, in that second trip, several times. Saved me, that is, and couldn't help saving you too."

"Your wife?" Castine shook her head. "She did?"

Vickery nodded. "She pulled me out of the truck when it was sinking in the river, and tucked that . . . *particular* . . . gun into my belt. And when our wing was about to fall away from the tornado, she steered her own wing right up under ours, so the repelling force would knock her down and nudge us up. And then when we were *inside* the Minotaur, she had got into it too, and gave me that particular gun again." He wiped his hand on his jeans and stared down at the occasional gleams of rushing chrome through the leaves.

Castine was silent for several seconds, then said, quietly, "I didn't know."

"Well, it wasn't her, was it? It was just something that thought it was her." He turned to Castine and managed a smile. "What did you want to ask me about?"

"Oh, right." She shook her head. "After all this—Well, I—I can trust you, if I can trust anybody, right?"

Vickery pursed his lips and nodded judiciously. "We already know a lot of each other's secrets."

"So anyway—so where are you living these days?"

Vickery knew she'd get around to asking him what she'd come to ask him, so he went along with the diversion. "Temporarily in a retired taco truck, painted over gray. Bunk, bathroom, obviously a kitchen. It's back there on Crenshaw right now, and I mostly spend the nights in Walmart parking lots. Galvan's taking the rent on it out of my pay. I keep meaning to get another apartment, but I discover I kind of like dislocation."

"Huh. I've been clinging to familiar things—landmarks, little routines—like I want every day to be a comforting duplicate of the one before." She looked around at the shrubbery on the slope. "You're driving for Galvan again?"

"Sometimes. There's not as much demand now," he said, gesturing down toward the cars rushing along the lanes, "since the freeways are kind of a dead battery, for a while. I do . . . sort of consultancy work now. For her, and people she refers to me."

Castine looked squarely at him, clearly excited. "I bet I know what sort of consultancy. You can find out what happened, in places, right? Sometimes?" She waved one hand. "I'm not going crazy?"

Vickery looked back up the slope, then gave her a sympathetic smile. "I wondered if it would happen to you too. It's not a lot of fun, really, is it? Even after you get where you can pretty well turn it on and off . . . most of the time."

She leaned toward him and gripped his arm. "Oh, Sebastian! For the first week I thought I was losing my mind—seeing people who weren't there, who couldn't hear me—walking into people who really *were* there—yes, I can do it or not, now, mostly. It was only a few days ago that I worked up the nerve, or negligence, to drive a car."

"Coffee helps. Drink lots of coffee before you get behind the wheel."

He shrugged and went on, "Even the casinos have corners the

security cameras don't cover, and an old friend of mine is putting out feelers to see if I could work with a very discreet LAPD detective."

"An old cop friend?"

"A superhero, actually. One of the costumed characters who hang around outside the Chinese Theater."

"You lead such a humdrum life. Uh . . . how far back can you see?"

"Oh—it seems to max out at about two hours. Three, maybe. Mostly it's a lot less. Minutes. How about you?"

"I guess it's about that. It's especially upsetting when I see *myself,* doing things I did a little while earlier." She shivered. "I still keep trying to talk to her, I can't help it. And then if there's anybody who's *actually* around, in the *present,* they think I'm crazy."

"It's like Scrooge with the Spirit of Christmas Past," Vickery agreed. "The worst part is that you can't *do* anything about what you see—you can't interfere, or help."

"I know! All you can do is watch! And the color's lousy." She shivered. "You're likely to see some terrible things if you work with a detective."

"I've thought about that. I just don't know if it's okay *not* to look, if it's there to be seen."

Castine frowned and looked away. "Obviously it's a consequence of us having been in the Labyrinth."

"Sure. I think it was our dip in the river. Our . . . baptism into insanely expanded possibility. We're not securely belted down in our car on the sequential time track anymore."

"And you can't undo baptism." She glanced at him and then away. "You still go to church?"

He nodded. "Latin mass, still."

"I should. I . . . bought a rosary. But I can't bear to look at it, after all the desperate math we did."

"It's a start."

Castine sighed and got to her feet. "I've got a flight back to Baltimore at three. It took a while for us to find you. I should probably get going."

Vickery looked at his new watch. "Set to the right time these days," he said. It was half past noon. "Yeah, they say you should be at the airport two hours early these days, and the 405 is always a mess." He glanced at the string hanging from the popsicle stick in the jar, but it was still dry.

"I'll probably be back one day. Can I find you through Galvan?"

"For a while. If I'm not doing work for her anymore, put an ad in the *LA Times* classifieds, run it for a week and I'll be sure to see it. Mention . . . skeet shooting, and give a date and a time, and I'll meet you then at Canter's deli on Fairfax. They're open twenty-four hours."

"Canter's deli, Fairfax. Skeet shooting. I'll remember." She smiled down at him. "We pretty much wrecked each other's lives, didn't we?"

He stood up and held out his right hand. "Got new ones. Can't tell yet if they're better or worse."

She shook his hand, then impulsively leaned forward and kissed him on the cheek. "Goodbye for now, Sebastian."

He smiled and nodded, and when she had disappeared behind the olive branches and climbed away up the embankment, he sat down, sighed, and opened the book to the page he had marked with a leaf.